N. C. SCRIMGEOUR

TIDES OF TORMENT

Contents

↑
NORTH, TO SKALLENAR AND BAININCH RISE
THE STRAIT OF SILVECKAN
← WEST, TO BREÇHON AND ILE DE DURGAVIE
EAST, TO SILVECKAN →
EILEANAN SELCH
(THE SELKIE ISLES)
CAIM
SOUTH, TO THE SOUTHERN REACHES
↓

SILVECKAN
The Drift
Cape Dromair
The Wilds
Kinraith
Carroncross
Blackwood Estate
Caolaig
Shielness
Tarmouth
The Teeth
Penchirn
Corran Narrows
Storwick
Isle of Corran
Arburgh
Mairburn
Corran Shipyards
Twaloch
Thiel

Aislingeach (noun): Dreamer, visionary. A selkie who holds the dreamwalker pelt.

Pronunciation Guide and Glossary

Persons of note

Isla Blackwood [EYE-lah]

Catriona Blackwood [kat-REE-nah]

Cormick Blackwood [CORR-mick]

Darce Galbraith [DARSS gahl-BRAYTHE]

Eimhir [AE-veer – 'ae' rhymes with 'stay']

Finlay [FINN-lay]

Hamish 'Jacques' Grier [HAY-mish 'ZHACK' GREER]

Lachlan Blackwood [LOCH-linn – soft 'ch' sound, known as a voiceless velar fricative]

Mhairi [VAH-ree]

Nathair Quinn [NAH-hir]

Nishi [NIH-shee]

Rhona [ROE-nah]

Ruairidh [ROO-err-ay – like 'brewery' without the 'b']

Sébastien [seh-BAHSS-tyan]

Locations of note

Adrenian Sea [add-REEN-ee-inn]

Arburgh [ARR-bruh]

Breçhon [BRAY-shon]

Caim [KAIM] – like 'eye'

Caolaig [cull-AEG] – 'ae' rhymes with 'stay'

Eileanan Selch [ill-ANN-inn SELCH – soft 'ch' sound]

Île de Durgavie [EEL day durr-GUY]

Kinraith [kin-RAYTHE]

Loch Mòr [LOCH MORE]

Silveckan [sill-VECK-an]

Storwick [STORR-ick]

Thiel [THEEL]

Vesnia [VEZ-nee-ah]

Animals and creatures

Brollachan [BROLLA-chan – soft 'ch'] – a shapeless, malevolent spirit that haunts the Wilds seeking unsuspecting bodies to possess

Cirein-cròin [KEE-rin CROW-inn] – a legendary sea monster once rumoured to roam the Silvish coast

Cù-sìth [coo-SHEE] – a dark, demonic hound found in the Wilds. Legend says those who hear its howl thrice will become paralysed with terror

Gun-anam [GOON-ann-AHM] – soulless spirits of slain selkies

Kelpie [KELL-pay] – an undead water horse made from salt and spray

Selkie [SELL-kay] – a seal shapeshifter which can shed its pelt and take the form of a human

Will-o'-the-wisp – a spirit taking the form of a ghostly light, associated with a warning of danger or death. Often rumoured to lead travellers astray

General terms

Aineol [ANN-yoll] – stranger, foreigner

Aislingeach [ASH-leen-gach – soft 'ch'] – dreamer

Anam-long [ANN-am-long] - soulship

Auld [AWL-d] – old

Bairn [bay-rne] – a young child

Blether [BLEH-thirr] – to prattle on, long-winded talk or chatter

Breçh [bresh] – language of Breçhon

Breeks [breeks] – trousers, breeches

Burr [burr] – common Silvish accent, with rolled 'r' sounds

Caraid [CARR-itch] – friend

Dachaigh [DACH-ee – soft 'ch'] – home

Dreich [DREE-ch – soft 'ch'] – dreary, grey weather

Du calme [doo CALM-e] – settle down [in the mixed Breçh/Silvish dialect of Île de Durgavie]

Feart [FEAR-t] – like 'feared': afraid or scared

Firth [firth] – an inlet or estuary leading to the sea

Gloaming [GLOW-ming] – dusk, twilight

Haar [harr] – a cold sea fog

Îleanach [EEL-ay-ann-ach – soft 'ch'] – islander [in the mixed Breçh/Silvish dialect of Île de Durgavie]

Ken [ken] - know

Laird [LAY-rd] – lord

Loch [soft 'ch'] – lake or sea inlet

Màthair [MAH-herr] – mother

Marées [MAH-ray] – tides [in Breçh]

M' ami [m' ah-MEE] – my friend [in the mixed Breçh/Silvish dialect of Île de Durgavie]

Nae [nay] - no

Shitehole [SHYT-hole] – Run-down, unpleasant place

Skerry – [SKERR-ee] – a small, rocky island

Sgian dubh [SKEE-an DOO] – a small ceremonial blade or knife

Wee [wee] – small

Wynd [wine-d] – a small alley or street

A message in a bottle

Read on for a recap of Mists of Memory...

Caraid,

Perhaps I shouldn't have started with that. Whatever ties us together now, it surely cannot be described as friendship. Still, I have no desire to scratch out the word and start over. After all, I doubt this letter will ever reach you.

They say humans used to slip parchment into bottles and send them out to sea, never knowing where they might wash up. The chance of these words finding their way to your shore is unlikely. But perhaps they are not meant for you, but for me—a way to make sense of all this pain.

I know how difficult it was for you to find peace here in Eileanan Selch, and I can't help but wonder if that was how I lost you. If the chieftains had only been more accepting, if Duncan had only been less suspicious...

But at first, everything seemed so hopeful. In claiming Mara's pelt, you inherited her ability to dreamwalk. You navigated through the memories of our ancestors and found something that should have been impossible—a sunken ship made of selkie bones. In visiting the memories of those who sailed on it, you discovered a truth lost to us all: we selkies once had ships of our own.

When the chieftains agreed to let you search for more wrecks, there was never a doubt that I'd go with you. I knew the danger you were in. The Grand Admiral was hunting you, scouring the waves for any sign of his daughter. He would have turned the sea red to get you back, and I played into his hands too gladly by bloodying those he sent after you.

It lingered between us, that violence. I felt it seep into my bones like a chill I couldn't rid myself of. But I pushed it aside and pretended it didn't exist, and when we finally happened across another wreck, what you discovered through your dreamwalking gifts changed everything.

Anam-long, they were called. Soulships, built from the bones of selkies whose pelts had been stolen from them. Instead of succumbing to despair and turning into wraiths, these ancient selkies spilled their lifeblood across their soulship's deck in sacrifice.

And thus, the haar was born.

It feels difficult to accept, even now. All I've ever known of the haar is its foul touch, its corruption and decay. Every time it brushed me, it took part of me with it. But for those ancient selkies, the haar carried no such rot. It answered the call of their magic, allowing their ships to cross into the soulless realm and hide from the dangers of this world.

You thought if we could bring back the soulships, our people would finally be safe from the Admiralty's violence. But fleeing an enemy doesn't mean they cease to exist. Our ancestors learned that all too painfully. The Admiralty hunted the soulships to extinction, leaving behind only wrecks. And without the soulships, selkies who lost their pelts had nothing to sacrifice themselves for. Instead, they became living wounds, wraiths of salt and spray.

They became gun-anam.

Finally, we knew the truth of how the haar came to be. The mists had been corrupted, infecting our people with despair and bloodlust.

Even as the warmth in my blood ebbed, you kept a spark in me alive. You convinced me that if we found an intact soulship, we could cross into the soulless realm and find a way to return the haar to what it once was.

But the chieftains' caution cut you deeper than I realised. You began to fear Duncan would take your pelt. In truth, he'd never have harmed you; you simply reminded him too much of Mara. He'd already lost his dearest friend to the Grand Admiral. He'd have done anything to avoid losing her daughter to him too.

I understand how restless you were, how desperate you were to do something. I urged you to wait for the chieftains' support. But in the end, the decision was taken out of my hands when the *Jade Dawn* arrived on our shores.

By rights, the Sea Kith ship should have been torn apart for daring to venture into selkie waters, but you got to Nishi before our raiders did. I stood by your side as she told us of her capture, the torture her crew had suffered at the hands of the Admiralty. There was a haunted look on her face when she spoke of her sentinel, Kerr, who still languished in the capital dungeons. But it was eclipsed by the look on your face when she told you about Darce.

It was brutally effective, even by Admiralty standards. The Grand Admiral only let Nishi go so she could deliver you a message. She came to Eileanan Selch bearing a gift—your sergeant's ear, bloodied in a box.

I knew then I had lost you. You were his. You always were.

After you left to rescue him, despair sank into me, and your betrayal—though I did not see it that way at the time—only carved room for the chill to burrow deeper. I'd felt the touch of the haar too many times, and the mist sickness began to infect me.

While I mourned what I had lost, you found your sergeant again, held prisoner in Arburgh after a bloody end to his commission on the *Vanguard of the Firth*. I still don't understand how he justified sailing with the Grand Admiral—the monster who stole Mara's pelt and kept her prisoner for years.

The monster who calls himself your father.

When I asked Darce about it later, he told me he had no choice, that he was trying to protect you. But I could never be at peace around him after that. He was a sentinel, after all. The Admiralty used people like him to hunt us. That wasn't something I could easily put aside, even if you could.

I suppose he did plunge a blade into the Grand Admiral's neck to help you escape. But even that wasn't enough to kill the bastard, not when his loyal sentinels were on hand to bring him back, turning on their own captains to pay the blood debt.

I told you I was wary of their gifts. Surely now, you must understand why. Their magic is twisted, as corrupted as the haar itself.

By the time I convinced Duncan and the other chieftains to rally to your aid, you had already fled Arburgh on the *Jade Dawn*. We arrived just in time to help you fend off the Admiralty's pursuit. But violence between human and selkie always summons the haar's cold, salt-sick mists, and it wasn't long before the gun-anam set upon us.

The mist seeped into my bones, deeper than ever before. I knew what it would cost me, but I pushed it away. You might have chosen Darce over me, over our people, but you were still my cousin, my caraid. I believed in you, even then.

In the end, it was Kerr who bought us our freedom. But for crippling the *Vanguard,* he and his guidebird paid a fatal price.

You tried your best to save him. I watched your hand tremble as you held a blade to Blair Cunningham's throat. You looked the Grand Admiral in the eye and offered to trade his nephew's life for Kerr's.

He refused.

Your blade was pressed against Blair's throat. You could have taken your vengeance for Kerr's death, for Shearwing's death, but instead, you let the lad go.

My troubled thoughts only became more clouded after that. Blair was your cousin by blood. Did you consider him family, now that you knew the truth? If you spared him, would you spare the Grand Admiral too? My doubts grew with the chill inside me, and piece by piece, I pulled myself away from you.

We finally found the last soulship, the only surviving vessel from the Admiralty's purge. You used the sgian dubh—the dreamwalker blade—to open a wound on your sergeant's hand. And as his blood dripped to the deck, the soulship quenched its thirst on his sacrifice, and the haar closed in around us.

That crossing was when I lost the last shred of warmth I was clinging to. The mists' icy touch sank too deep, smothering the last fragment of hope I had. The damp filled my lungs and settled there, almost drowning me. I felt like a ghost, and when we finally reached the soulless realm, there was nothing left of me.

I can't apologise for what I did. It's what you should have done. But you couldn't see it. You *still* can't see it. The gun-anam were never the problem. Humans were. Even if we cleansed the haar, even if we brought the soulships back, we would never be free.

There was only one thing we could do to save our people. I begged you to unleash the haar across Silveckan and let the gun-anam devour those who would destroy us.

Sometimes when I wake, I still see the shock on your face. The look in your eyes when you realised what I was, what I'd become. I'd denied it for so long, and admitting it came as a relief. The haar had infected me with its sickness, but my mind was clearer than it had been in months.

I knew what I had to do.

I took the sgian dubh and used its traitorous blade to carve open your arm. I smeared your blood across your pelt, then peeled it away from your skin and placed it around my shoulders. What was your birthright became my burden, and I don't know if I'll ever forgive you for that.

I don't expect you to forgive me, either. When I left you in that wretched place, I didn't believe I'd ever see you again. I grieved you as much as I grieved what I'd done. But I had a duty to fulfil, a duty to our people you refused to see through.

I gathered every selkie I could muster, and I struck at Arburgh.

There is no need for me to recount the horrors of that night. We've both seen that kind of violence too many times to forget what it looks like. But as the haar rolled in and the gun-anam began to feast on what I'd unleashed, I felt something change. This time, it *meant* something.

When I found you on the *Vanguard* hours later, I thought you were a ghost. But there you stood, wearing Mara's bones. They glistened white and clean, not blackened and rotting with the haar. I didn't understand how you'd survived. I didn't care. What was left of my heart broke when I saw you at the Grand Admiral's side. *This* was who you truly called family.

But as he readied his sword to kill me, you stepped in. You plunged a blade into his heart. You chose me.

When it was over, you told me how you'd freed Mara's spirit from torment, releasing her back to the sea. You told me you could give the gun-anam that peace too, if I returned your pelt.

For a moment, I glimpsed hope. All I had to do was grasp the truth in what you said. But I couldn't feel it. My heart was deadened to your words. I took your pelt—*my* pelt—and left you where you belonged.

You were never one of us. I should have seen that from the beginning.

I know only whispers of what happened after we parted. Word spread amongst the selkie scouts that another sentinel had made the twisted sacrifice to bring the Grand Admiral back from the dead. Your attempt at killing him failed.

It does not matter. We will find him. We will kill him as many times as it takes to set our people free.

And as for you... You took the soulship, didn't you? I imagine you're sailing north with your brother and uncle, with your soul-bound sergeant. That's the family you chose. The family I never was to you.

It doesn't matter anymore. I know what I must do. Arburgh has fallen, the Admiralty fleet has scattered, and Silveckan's coasts lie unprotected. I will lead my people against those who have wronged us. I will spread the mists across the island and its waters.

Then, finally, perhaps my people will be free of these tides of torment.

Still, every time I pull this pelt close, I can't help but dream of the way it might have been. This fur around my shoulders should be mine alone, but I feel you in it like a skin we share.

The last thing you said to me was how you would haunt me.

You were right, caraid.

CHAPTER ONE

ISLA

The damp soil soaked through the silk of Isla's dress as she sank to her knees and pressed her hand against the cold slab marking her mother's grave.

"It's done," she whispered. "They can rest now."

The granite gave no answer, just stood silent and solemn as the drizzle trickled down its long face, clinging to the carved edges of Lady Catriona's name like tears ready to fall. Isla pulled her hand away, digging out flecks of dirt she'd missed under her fingernails. If she looked closely enough, she could still see the soil staining her forearms, the raw skin on her palms from working the shovel.

She rose, a dull breath escaping as she stretched out the ache in her lower back. Beside the headstone lay a shallow mound of freshly dug soil—a twin grave to her mother's with no monument to mark it.

Tears thickened in her throat, and she forced herself to swallow them before grief took her to a place she couldn't come back from. She hadn't been able to visit Laird Cormick's quarters, knowing what waited for her there. Instead, Darce and Muir had brought her father's body out of the estate wrapped in a tartan shroud that did nothing to mask the stench of stale bones and rotten flesh.

They'd lowered him into the hole, and Isla had said her goodbyes with clenched fists and a tight throat, knowing she'd forever missed the chance to lay eyes on him one last time. He was gone. They all were.

She lifted her chin, trailing her gaze over the other patches of disturbed soil scattered across the grounds. Her family's attendants, the kitchen staff, the loyal guards of the Blackwood Watch. All that was left of them were bones buried in unmarked graves, their bodies long picked clean by the wolves that prowled ever closer around the estate. In the six months they'd been gone, the creeping edge of the Wilds had stolen into the abandoned grounds, springing over the walls in tendrils of ivy, pushing through her mother's flowers with spiteful thickets of bracken and gorse. Lachlan had worked himself to exhaustion clearing the worst away, but every time he hacked the sprawling roots, they crawled back with some unnatural kind of spite, burrowing deeper than before.

A guttural howl tore through the still night air. Isla's blood turned to ice, and she stepped back from the grave only to bump against something soft behind her.

Muir grunted. "That was my stomach you almost perforated with those bony elbows of yours."

"We both know your stomach is stronger than that." She turned, only to be met with the reek of whisky on his breath, smoky and thick with peat. "Tides, Muir. I thought you'd given up the drink."

He brought a tarnished brass flask to his lips, drawing a long, deliberate gulp. "Can't a man mourn his dead sister without a bloody sermon? Besides, there's little else for us to do in this shadow of a place. Better I drown myself in liquor than in grief."

An angry retort rose on Isla's tongue, but before she could voice it, another bloodcurdling howl echoed from the forest.

Her mouth ran dry. "We should go, before—"

"Before the demon hound roars thrice and paralyses us with fear?" Muir snorted. "The cù-sìth is nothing but a tale told by blethering fishwives and farmers who can't keep their ewes safe. We've got more to worry about than ghost stories. You should know that better than anyone."

The edge of his words was dulled with whisky, but Isla couldn't help but flinch. It was too much of a reminder of all that lay waiting for them outside the towering walls of Blackwood Estate, this place that had never felt like home until it was taken from her. Since coming back, she'd busied herself in helping bury the dead, grieving all she'd lost. But it was impossible to ignore the threat out on the waves, the danger tickling her neck like the chill of a bitter wind.

The haar was coming. If they didn't stop it, the entire island of Silveckan would drown in mist.

"Perhaps you're right," she said. "There are enough monsters in this world already."

Her words hung in the air, little more than a whisper. But louder were the parts she'd left unsaid, the echoes of pain filling the gaps.

Eimhir. Was she truly a monster? Had the mist sickness consumed so much of her cousin that there was nothing left of the woman she once knew, the friend she couldn't help but love, even after what she'd done?

Her hand drifted absent-mindedly to the rolled-up sleeve of her dress, and she traced her fingers along the salt scars trailing her forearm. The marks were faint and delicate, glinting like crystals under the stars. But that didn't soften the way they bit into her skin, reminding her of what Eimhir had taken from her.

Her pelt. Her *soul*.

"Does it hurt?"

She dropped her hand, letting her sleeve fall over the glistening scars. "I don't know what you—"

"Aye, you do." Muir gave her a sombre look, the moonlight casting a glow on his dark brown skin. "I've seen this before, remember. I saw what it did to Mara, what it drove her to."

"It's not the same. I'm not—" She swallowed. "I won't become one of the gun-anam. Not as long as Darce is alive. He bound his soul to mine. He stopped the tides from taking me."

"That wasn't what I asked, was it? I asked if it hurt."

Isla squeezed her hands into fists, turning from the quiet knowing in Muir's gaze before it broke her. It wasn't just the sting of salt on her skin, or the raw wound of Eimhir's betrayal. It was the hollowed-out ache behind her ribs, the feeling of having been found, made whole, only for it to be torn away by the same hand that once held hers.

You left me no choice, caraid.

"Aye," she whispered. "It hurts."

Muir didn't say anything else, and she was grateful for the silence, suffocating as it was. For a moment, she let herself pretend the estate's walls could keep out everything she feared, as if the stone that once held her prisoner was now her sanctuary. But the lie couldn't last. Not when she knew what was coming.

A faint glow fell over the headstone, and Isla noticed the familiar floating presence of the will-o'-the-wisp. It drifted towards them, lighting a path through the trodden-down grass. A shadow followed in its ghostly wake, rustling through dead leaves with the scrape of a rosewood crutch.

The wisp drifted higher, and Isla blinked away the soft glare of its light to find the hard-edged features of her brother.

"Lachlan," she said, his name aching from her throat. "I was just heading back inside. I'll give you some space to—"

He waved her words away, his tawny eyes falling across the headstone and the fresh mound of soil alongside it. The composure on his face cracked, and she saw a mirror to her own grief.

Of all the pain that had festered between them, how bittersweet it was that *this* should be the one thing they still shared.

"I sent word to the mason in Tarmouth," he said stiffly. "Our father deserves more than an unmarked grave. It might take a week or two, but I thought as long as we're here..."

Isla nodded, unable to speak. The wisp floated across the graves, its hazy light flickering as it danced back and forth. Then it sank towards the soil, its glow dimming until it disappeared entirely, leaving the three of them in darkness.

Beside her, Muir let out a heavy sigh. Lachlan shifted on his crutch, avoiding both their gazes. Nobody wanted to speak. The silence was a fragile thing, and Isla couldn't bring herself to break it.

In the end, it was Lachlan who cleared his throat, turning to her with a measured stare. "I suggest you stop off at the Auld Hall before retiring to your quarters."

Isla hesitated. She'd avoided the Auld Hall ever since they'd returned to Blackwood Estate. It was the last place she'd seen Laird Cormick alive, and the wound of that night still ran deep. "I'm tired, Lachlan. I hardly see the need for me to—"

"I suspect that will change when you get there." He drew his mouth into a tight smile. "That's why I came to fetch you. The captain is looking for you."

Stepping into the Auld Hall was like returning to a memory she'd tried to bury. The flagstone floor might have been thick with dust, cobwebs clinging to the wooden beams spanning the vaulted roof, but that didn't stop her imagining it the way it had been. Flames roaring from the hearth, carrying the earthy scent of burning pinecones. Tables set in uniform rows, laden with cuts of venison and wood pigeon, bottles of whisky and wine. The burr of chattering voices filling the hall with warmth.

Now, the chairs were empty. The fire sat cold. All she recognised was a single figure at the end of the room.

Nishi was sitting at the high table like she belonged there, waiting with an expectant gleam in her copper eyes. Her tricorne hat hung precariously on the arm of the chair, and as she leapt up, it toppled to the dusty floor.

"Blackwood," she said, a grimace twisting her mouth. "We need to talk."

"Aye, it seems we do." Isla folded her arms. "Perhaps you should start by telling me how you made it all the way up here alone when you should be recovering on the soulship."

Nishi scowled. "If the Admiralty lapdog over there can climb the trail on one leg, what makes you think a few burns would stop me?"

Isla glanced at Lachlan, waiting for his shoulders to tense, for his expression to darken at the insult, but he just rolled his eyes as he sat at the other end of the table. "As amiable as ever, Captain. Nice to see some things don't change."

"Don't talk to me like we're friends, lad. Not after what your lot did to my crew." Nishi's fingers jerked towards the pistol on her belt. "Push me again, and you'll see how *amiable* I can be."

"Nishi." Isla's voice rang across the room, sharper than she'd intended. She waited for the captain's eyes to flash, for her hackles to rise, but instead, Nishi sank down, slumping against the chair.

"Fuck," she said, dropping her head into her hands. Then she let out a hiss of pain and whipped her hands away like she'd been bitten. "*Fuck!*"

Isla winced at the raw agony in Nishi's voice. The salves they'd scavenged from the doctor's old stores down in the village had gone some way to soothing the infection from the burns, but there was no escaping the damage the flames had wrought. Nishi's brown skin was marred with patches of pink where her face had blistered, the scars weeping even after a fortnight. An awful cough had set in around her lungs, its remnants lingering in the thin rasp of her voice.

She'd lost everything, but she'd survived. She was the only one from the *Jade Dawn* who had.

Little wonder she wanted vengeance.

Muir broke the silence with a sigh, then took a seat along from Nishi and unscrewed his flask. "Here," he said, sliding it towards her. "I reckon you need it more than I do."

Nishi stared at it, eye twitching. Then she wrapped her fingers around the flask and brought it to her lips. The ochre swirl of her Sea Kith tattoos shifted across her collarbone as she drank, throat bobbing with each long gulp. Eventually, she set the empty flask on the table with a dull thump and wiped her mouth with her sleeve. "A Corran vintage, if I'm not mistaken? Not half bad."

"Cormick always did appreciate the good stuff." A smirk pulled at the corner of Muir's lips. "I like this one. For a Sea Kith, at any rate."

Nishi snorted. "You're not so bad yourself, for an Admiralty cur."

"*Former* Admiralty cur."

The tension strangling the hall loosened, if only a fraction, and Isla joined them at the table, trying not to wince as she slowly set herself down into the tall wooden chair. The last time she'd sat here, her father had been beside her, whisky on his breath and mourning in his voice. Thinking about it brought a fresh wave of grief to the surface. It had been too painful to bear the brunt of his sorrow. She'd made her excuses and left the hall for the respite of sea air and solitude. She couldn't remember if she'd said goodbye.

"Isla."

She looked up, blinking away hot tears. When the room swam back into vision, Darce was in front of her.

His brown eyes met hers across the table, soft and knowing. He'd cut the unruly lengths his hair had grown to while he was a prisoner of the Admiralty, and now the tousled locks hung neatly above his forehead. She noticed with a wrench that he'd found a new set of leathers from the Blackwood Watch, complete with a swathe of charcoal and grey tartan around his shoulder. He'd belonged here more than she ever had. It was he who'd been at her father's side at the end, something she'd never realised she was grateful for until now.

"I'm all right. I just..." She drew a breath. "I never thought I'd be back here. At least, not like this."

Across the table, Lachlan stiffened. Before Isla could say anything, he turned his attention to Nishi. "You said you dragged yourself up here because you needed to talk. If you're done with the whisky, perhaps you could tell us what this is all about."

Nishi's eyes carried a dangerous glint. "That's a matter for your sister to worry about, not you."

"We're family." Isla avoided Lachlan's gaze, afraid of what she might find there. "*All* of us here are family. What else do we have but each other? The Admiralty would kill us all on sight. Eimhir and the clans of Eileanan Selch won't stop until the haar swallows the entire island. If we're to survive this, we must leave behind whatever lies in our wake and move forward together."

A thick silence fell across the table, settling across tense shoulders. Isla's cheeks flushed. She shouldn't have said anything. Nobody needed a reminder of what they'd lost. The grief they carried was still raw; even the lightest touch would draw it out.

"You're right." The fire in Nishi's eyes faded, leaving behind a quiet acceptance. "My crew is dead. My ship is a burnt-out wreck at the bottom of the firth. I have lost—" Her voice cracked. "Well, you all know. But if we are kith, perhaps I have not lost everything. Not yet, at least."

She ran a hand through the charred ends of her black hair, then met Isla's gaze. "Before we left the Southern Reaches, I sent word to the other Sea Kith, calling a summit on the morning of the next new moon. That day is upon us, and I have no means of getting there."

Isla stilled. "You need a ship."

"I need more than that." Nishi glanced between them all. "We Sea Kith have always kept to ourselves. We don't engage the Admiralty or the selkies, not if we can help it. I see now that if we don't change, these waters will be lost to us. But convincing the other captains will take more than my voice alone."

"You think they'd listen to us?"

"They'd be fools not to. You're a selkie. Your sergeant has the auld blood." Nishi flicked her eyes towards Lachlan and Muir. "And you two wouldn't be the first Admiralty cast-offs to find themselves amongst our people. Together, we might have a chance of convincing them of what's at stake."

Lachlan folded his arms. "And then what?"

"Then we'll have allies," Isla said, her heartbeat quickening. "We can't stand against the Admiralty alone, and we'll never find Eimhir with just one ship. The Sea Kith could help us track her down. And when we do…"

The rest of her words dried on her tongue, turning her mouth stale. She knew what she had to do. The only way of stopping the haar was to give the gun-anam the peace they deserved instead of the violence Eimhir was feeding them with. But Isla couldn't take their pain away without her pelt, and Eimhir wouldn't give it up without a fight.

The thought turned the pit of her stomach to ice. She hadn't been able to stop Eimhir last time. If she failed again, if she couldn't bring herself to do what she needed to…

Muir gave her a sidelong look. "We won't be the only ones searching for her. The Admiralty may be licking its wounds, but it's only a matter of time before the fleet regroups. Alasdair will stop at nothing to get that pelt back. It's all he has left of Mara. All he has left of you."

"I buried a blade in his rotten heart," Isla said. "He should want me dead more than anyone."

"If you believe that, you don't know him at all." Muir shook his head, his white braids spilling across his shoulders. "He doesn't want to kill you. He wants to claim you, claim what he believes was unjustly stolen from him. And that is far more dangerous."

"That's not going to happen." Darce had been quiet, but now his voice cut through the air like steel. "Not as long as I draw breath."

"Aye, because you did such a permanent job of stopping him last time, as I recall." Muir snorted. "I say we take the Sea Kith's offer. We can't do this by ourselves, and the longer we wait, the more our enemies gather strength. If we're to survive, we need to strike quickly."

Darce stared at him across the table, a muscle twitching in his jaw.

Then he bent his head in a stiff nod. "Agreed. We need to put an end to him, whatever it takes."

"We need to stop Eimhir," Isla corrected. "The Admiralty might be a threat to us, but the haar threatens all of Silveckan. If we don't stop the mists from spreading, the soulless realm will bleed into our world. The gun-anam will roam wild, feasting on the blood spilled between human and selkie. *That* should be our priority, not Cunningham."

Darce flinched. "Isla, if he finds you—"

"She's right." Lachlan met her eyes fleetingly, then turned to Darce. "We all saw what happened in Arburgh. We can't let that happen again, not if there's a chance for us to stop it."

Darce's face was stony, but he said nothing. All around the table, the tension thickened until Isla thought it might suffocate her. The corners of the room rang with the echoes of everything they'd lost, everything they still stood to lose. It was a fear that would cripple her if she let it.

She pushed back from the table, the chair scraping across the flagstone floor as she rose. "If there's one thing we agree on, it's that we can't stay here. If we wait for the storm to break, it will be too late to stop it. Let's go to the summit. If we can make allies of the Sea Kith, we may have a chance of seeing the other side of this."

Across the table, Nishi straightened, her lip ring dancing in the light as she cracked a thin smile. "I told you once before I believed the tides brought us together for a reason, Blackwood. I think the time is upon us that we find out what that reason is."

She offered an outstretched hand, her forearm etched in intricate swirls of flesh-toned ink. The patterns were part of her brown skin, living and breathing across her muscles and tendons. They charted who she was, the victories she'd won and the losses she'd suffered.

Kerr. Shearwing. The *Jade Dawn*.

Nishi noticed her staring, and her expression grew sombre. "There's no changing what's already written. But what's to come? We can have our say on that."

Isla lifted her chin, meeting the captain's gaze with a steady resolve. A warmth spread behind her ribs like kindling catching the flame, rising until she thought it might burn right through her.

"Aye," she said, grasping Nishi's hand. "And it's time we made a start."

CHAPTER TWO

DARCE

Dawn brought with it a sense of relief, and Darce let go of the breath he'd been holding ever since they'd returned to Blackwood Estate.

He didn't like waiting. His legs grew restless, his palms yearning for the grip of a blade. He couldn't push away the sense that the longer they remained here, the closer their enemies would draw around them. Knowing they'd soon be moving on loosened some of the tension in his shoulders, eased the stiffness that had crept into his spine.

As he crossed the cobbled courtyard, the sky hung pale and grey, a thin veil of morning drizzle clinging to the air. Featherblade circled the lone sentry tower, the gannet's white wings blending into the clouds. No raucous caws rattled from its beak to disturb the morning quiet. For now at least, they were safe.

Darce knew that wouldn't remain true for long.

He trudged past the abandoned stables towards the stone steps leading to the armoury. Everywhere he turned, he found remnants of the raid that had upended their lives almost six months before. The blood had been washed clean, the bodies buried, but what lingered was the *absence*. The empty stalls that once held horses. A training yard with no clattering of whalebone swords. When the four of them left for the sea summit, only ghosts would remain.

The harsh scrape of wood across stone scratched at his remaining ear as he reached the bottom of the steps, and he rounded the corner to find Lachlan heaving a weapons rack upright from where it had fallen. His pale cheeks were flushed from exertion, his crutch tucked awkwardly in the crook of his armpit for balance as he tilted the heavy frame back into place.

Darce waited. He knew better than to offer help.

Eventually, Lachlan stepped away, wiping the damp strands of golden hair falling over his forehead. His eyes fell across the row of swords, no doubt seeing the same as Darce. Blades once oiled and gleaming now hung with rusted edges, their leather grips corroded from the salt-thick damp of the haar. Nobody had come back for them.

"A wee bit early for this kind of work, isn't it?" Darce asked, trying to keep his tone light. "The sun is barely over the horizon."

"I thought it best to stay out of Nishi's way this morning, lest she gut me while nobody is watching," Lachlan muttered. "Besides, the whole place is a bloody mess. I found a nest of adders in the cellar the other day. Not the usual kind either—big ones, from the Wilds. And part of the outer wall collapsed last night from those damn roots creeping in from the old yew."

"You can't fix it all, little laird."

"Then who will?" Lachlan's eyes flashed. "We buried my parents here, and your friends in the Watch. Would you be content to let this place fall to ruin around them?" He shook his head. "I shouldn't have stayed away so long. I should have come back sooner to right the wrongs that happened here."

Darce looked at the cold stone walls. Layers of dust and grime coated the armour stands. A beady-eyed starling peered down from the eaves, watching them like they were intruders. Remnants of loss clung to every corner, their shadows haunting Lachlan's expression.

"Blaming yourself won't change anything," Darce said gently. "No matter what we do here, it won't bring them back. We've done what we can for the ghosts of this place, but now we must focus on the living."

Lachlan scowled. "It's that simple for you, is it?"

"You know it's not." Heat rose in Darce's chest, and he struggled to keep his voice even. "This was my home too, damn you. Your father took me in as a lad. He was the first person to believe I had more to offer than the magic in my blood. He gave me a place to belong."

"Galbraith, I—"

"I *know* what you've lost, because I lost it too. Everything I've done since the day Cormick died has been to honour the last promise I made him." His voice tore, catching in his throat. "He entrusted you and your sister to me. I'll never forget that."

Lachlan's fingers tightened around the handle of his crutch as he stared at the floor. "I know what he meant to you. I shouldn't have—I'm sorry."

A heartbeat of silence echoed between them before a dry laugh escaped Darce's lips. "An apology? Tides, I never thought I'd hear such a thing from that proud mouth of yours. These are strange times indeed."

Lachlan cracked a smile, the tension loosening. "Aye, well, don't hold your breath waiting for it to happen again. One is about as much as I can stomach." His face fell, expression growing serious once more. "The captain...she's going to be a problem, isn't she? I think she might have killed me already, were it not for..." He trailed off, mouth twisting around the unspoken shape of his sister's name.

"Your old friend Nathair Quinn sent the Admiralty after her crew," Darce said. "They burned the *Jade Dawn* to ashes, and everyone on board with it. She won't forgive that."

"I didn't know anything about that. Nathair and I have been...estranged, of late. I had nothing to do with his schemes or the Admiralty's actions."

The way he chewed over the mention of Quinn gave Darce pause. "What happened with the two of you?"

"Nothing of any consequence. Just a parting of ways." Lachlan shrugged. "His interests lay in amassing his merchant fleet. My concerns were...different."

He didn't need to say Blair's name for it to ring in the empty space between them. The sting of regret clung to every word. Whatever ties Lachlan once had to the Admiralty, they'd been severed beyond repair the moment he turned against the Grand Admiral, against Blair's uncle. There was no going back. Not for him, not for any of them.

"You don't have to take any more part in this," Darce said. "Nishi tells me the sea summit is to be held in waters past the northern shores of Silveckan. We'll be passing Cape Dromair, and the Andersons were always on good terms with your family. If you wanted, I'm certain they'd offer you—"

Lachlan cut him off with a hollow laugh. "That's how things are to be, then? I'm a problem to hand over to someone else?"

"That's not what I—"

"You don't trust me." Lachlan threw the words at him like a blow. "Even after what it cost me to save your lives back in Arburgh."

"I'm well aware of what it cost you," Darce said. "And I wouldn't blame you if you regretted it, if you felt torn in your loyalties. I know how it feels to want to protect someone on the other side of a war."

"You don't know anything." Lachlan headed towards the steps, knuckles white around the handle of his crutch. "Believe what you like of me, Galbraith, but I have always put my family first. That will never change."

"And what of Isla?" Darce called after him. "Is *she* your family?"

Lachlan froze at the bottom of the steps, shoulders stiffening. The question hung in the air, growing sharper every passing second it went unanswered. Then Lachlan disappeared into the stairwell, leaving Darce with nothing but the faint echo of his crutch.

He stared after him, unable to swallow the sickly dread rising in his throat. The estate's empty hallways might have been a grim reminder of how much had changed, but the quiet resentment of Lachlan's wake was a strain he was all too familiar with.

Isla's quarters were empty when he pushed open the heavy oak doors. The hearth lay cold and bare, the bedsheets crumpled with the same mounds and troughs he'd left in them when he'd slipped away for the morning patrol.

It wasn't much of a surprise that she was gone. Ever since they'd returned to the estate, she'd flitted from one room to the next as if she were afraid to linger in the same place for too long. Sometimes when he glanced at her, he saw the same terror that had darkened her face that awful night all those months ago.

He wandered through the hallways on instinct, tracing steps he couldn't see. The ache of the blood oath binding them pulled tight in his chest, but he didn't need it to find her. He already knew where she would be.

The doors to Laird Cormick and Lady Catriona's room were ajar when he reached them. A sliver of pale morning light crept through the gap, spilling into the hallway. He took a moment to steady himself, then slowly pushed through.

At once, the memories hit him. The reek of salt and blood. The groan bubbling from Cormick's lips. The pool of red gushing from a wound that cleaved too deep and vicious to survive.

"I have one last order for you, Sergeant," Cormick had whispered, clasping his face with bloody hands. "Protect my children. Swear to me you'll keep them safe."

Darce had mumbled something he couldn't remember, words that burned in his throat. Then Cormick's cold hands had fallen limply to the floor, leaving Darce with nothing but the remnant of his touch and the echo of his final words.

"Darce?"

He jolted, the concern in Isla's voice pulling him from the dark grasp of his thoughts. She stood by the window, her sable hair catching the morning light. The emerald folds of her dress brought out a brightness in her sea-green eyes as she stared at him.

Swear to me you'll keep them safe.

He pushed away the ghost of Cormick's words as he crossed the room to join Isla at the window. Rain drummed against the glass, hushing the sound of his frantic heart.

This close, he could see the gooseflesh prickling her skin, the rise and fall of her chest with each breath. Spirals of salt glittered across her collarbone, a stark reminder of what Eimhir had stolen from her. He traced the lines, stopping when he reached the silk neckline of her dress.

His fingers brushed something cold underneath the fabric. The bone armour. Her selkie mother's last gift—a gift that allowed Isla to cross the haar without the need of a soulship.

Isla looked up, her hand finding his. "You seem troubled. More than usual."

He grimaced. "I saw Lachlan earlier. Tried to talk to him about seeking refuge at Cape Dromair, but—"

"It went about as well as I warned you it would?" A wry smile twisted the edges of her lips. "You had to know he'd baulk at the thought of being left behind."

"Perhaps. But I didn't think he'd be so bloody-minded as to not understand why." Darce pulled away, turning to the rain-streaked window. Past the trickling streams, he saw the grey-green waves chopping at the foot of the cliffs. Dozens of fishing boats bobbed in the swell, abandoned by their owners. And there in the middle of them all, its bone-hewn keel glistening through the drizzle, was a stranger.

The anam-long. The soulship.

A shiver crept up his neck, as if the haar's touch had already wrapped itself around him. "Only the tides know what we're sailing into, and this...this isn't Lachlan's fight. Is it so wrong to want to keep him from it?"

"He made it his fight when he turned against the Admiralty, when he freed you and saved Muir's life. That was his choice. You can't take it away from him." Isla pulled him around, holding him in the fierceness of her gaze. "There was a time not so long ago when you learned how to let me go. You need to do the same for him before it tears you apart."

Darce flicked his eyes towards the patch of pinewood floor at the end of the bed. He and Muir had scrubbed it clean, but he still saw the blood pooling there. He still saw Cormick's ashen face, the pain that had only eased with the promise Darce made him.

Swear to me you'll keep them safe.

Isla's cheeks were pale, as if she too could see the ghost lingering there. "You've honoured your word a dozen times over," she said quietly. "He'd tell you that himself if he were here."

Her hand slipped away from his arm as she crossed the room to kneel in front of a sturdy ironwood chest, its hinges glinting under a layer of dust. She wiped her hand across the lid, then worked the latches loose to lift it open.

Darce drew closer, half-afraid to look too closely. His eyes fell over the green and purple of Blackwood tartan lining the inside of the lid. Then Isla stood, drawing from the chest the long, gleaming blade of her father's claymore.

His heart seized. He'd seen that sword before. It was the elder brother of the blade Cormick had once presented him with—the blade Darce had lost to the gun-anam when he'd saved Isla's life. Its steel length stretched more than a metre, its hilt boasting enough grip for two hands to grasp it.

Cormick's hands. Not his.

"I can't." He stepped back, throat closing around the words. "That blade is not mine to wield."

Isla met him with a steady look. "My father once put a sword in your hands, and you carried it until it shattered in the haar. You saved my life with it. He'd want you to have it." She swallowed. "*I* want you to have it."

"Lachlan—"

"Already agreed. He knows he'll never wield a two-handed sword after what happened to him. He'd rather see it in your hands than abandon it to dust and cobwebs." She held it out to him. "Please."

Darce trailed his eyes over the blade. Its broad edges were keen and hungry, honed so sharp they seemed to disappear. The black handle glistened like onyx in the faint light, its crossguard boasting sloping quillons etched with intricate silver swirls. No gemstones were set in its pommel; it didn't need any such ornamentation. This was a simple blade, a blade with *purpose*.

Perhaps if he took it, he could fulfil his own.

He reached out, wrapping one hand around the hilt and using the other to balance the weight of the steel in his grip. The blade rested against his palm, its cool touch oddly reassuring. Despite his misgivings, it didn't feel wrong to hold it. It belonged in his hands.

A pained smile curled at the edge of Isla's lips. "I wish he knew all you'd done for us, all you sacrificed."

"The blood oath wasn't a sacrifice. None of this was." He lowered the blade to rest against the floor. "I won't deny the hold Cormick's words have over me. I would do anything to honour them. But you are more to me than the vow I made your father. You are everything I ever wanted, before I knew I wanted it."

"Darce." Her fingers found the edge of his jaw, tracing the rough stubble on his cheek. She wound her hand around the nape of his neck and pulled him towards her, rising on her toes to press her lips to his.

The taste of her was like a promise. Not to Cormick, not to the tides, but to *her*. He buried his hand in the tangle of her hair and drank in the softness of her mouth, casting a futile wish that this peace might last a wee while longer before it was torn from them once again. He just wanted to lose himself in her, drown himself in her fierce currents.

Too soon, it was over. Darce stepped back, cheeks flushed, a shared heartbeat in the sliver of space between them. He tightened one hand around the hilt of the claymore and reached for her fingers with the other. "Whatever is waiting for us out there, wherever the tides take us..."

"We'll face it together," Isla said. "No matter the storm."

She squeezed his shoulder and slipped past him to the grand oak doors, leaving him with an ache in his chest and the weight of her father's sword in his grip.

He stared down at the blade. Perhaps if it had been in Cormick's hands the night of the raid, things would have been different. But now it was his hands around the hilt, warm and certain against the sharkskin wrapping. It was up to him to wield it.

Outside, the rain was easing, its relentless patter fading through the window. Past the fog of the glass, Darce glimpsed a hint of blue fighting to break through the swathes of cloud hanging over the estate.

There would be worse storms than this on the horizon. All he could do was weather them, and pray the days brought clearer skies soon.

CHAPTER THREE

ISLA

Being back on the soulship brought Isla a sense of calm. Without her pelt, the depths remained agonisingly out of reach, but there was a comfort in the churning of the waves, the spray misting over the prow. The crisp bite of sea air burned the back of her throat, and she swallowed it hungrily as she set her eyes on the horizon.

"Ready when you are," she said.

Beside her, Darce spread his hands on the glistening white surface of the gunwale. His eyes closed as he took a deep breath and murmured something she couldn't hear. All at once, the wind whipped up, snarling and tugging with more spite than before. The waves rolled against the soulship's bone hull, answering the call in Darce's sentinel blood.

Then, the haar rolled in.

Though she knew it was at Darce's beckoning, she couldn't help but shudder as the dense sea fog closed in, smothering the ship with its stench. It carried the reek of rot and death, corrupted by the suffering of the gun-anam.

The suffering she alone could end.

Swirls of mist crept across the deck and climbed the bare masts. Their silvery tendrils wound around the yards, forming wisping sails. They caught a non-existent wind, pulling taut as the haar thickened.

On the quarterdeck, Nishi coughed, her lips blue. "I'm starting to feel grateful I was unconscious the last time you did this. I've never encountered anything so foul on the waves, and I've seen tempests that would sink even the *Vanguard*. It's like the chill of the fathoms themselves has risen to meet us."

"It may be foul, but it's keeping us hidden from the Admiralty patrols lurking in these waters," Isla said. "For all the horror it brought us in the past, it might be the one thing that saves us now."

As she spoke, the mists thinned, dispersing into a sky that was not the same as the one they'd left behind. It hung over them in an oily wash of red, as dark as a perpetual night. The black waves bruising the ship's hull settled into an unnatural silence, as still as glass.

This was what lay on the other side of the haar. A place where no ship could follow.

The soulless realm.

Isla flexed her numb fingers. The salt scars trailing around her wrists tingled unpleasantly. This was the place Eimhir had carved her arm open with the sgian dubh, the place she'd spilled her blood and ripped her soul from her.

It wasn't something Isla could easily forget. It would be even harder to forgive.

Lachlan joined her, his crutch scraping against the bone deck. His eyes gave nothing away as he stared out at the horizon, but there was a tension in his jaw she recognised well.

"This is what awaits us if we lose?" he asked. "If the mists swallow Silveckan, the horror of this world will crawl into our own?"

"We won't lose. We can't."

The corner of his mouth tightened, though whether in amusement or scorn, Isla couldn't be sure. "You really think you can stop her?"

Something in his voice caught like a barb. He hadn't been on the *Vanguard* that night. He hadn't seen her let Eimhir go. But he knew all the same. Sometimes, it seemed he knew her better than she did herself.

"I have no choice but to stop her," she said, her words hollow to her ears. "The gun-anam exist in the lingering memories of what was done to them, the echo of that violence and suffering. Until I can give those memories peace, the haar's corruption will spread. It will drive more selkies to mist sickness and bloodlust. Someone has to end it. *I* have to end it."

He shifted. "And to do that, you need your pelt back."

Isla's hand drifted to her chest. Instead of the fur that once hung around her shoulders, her fingers brushed the velvet lapel of her father's old dress coat. The wine-coloured tails were so long they reached her ankles, but the garment was loose enough to hide the cuirass of bone around her ribs and the seal-skull mask on her belt.

"Their pain had to go somewhere," she said. "It leached into the haar, twisting it into something it shouldn't be. I can take it away."

Lachlan frowned. "And what happens to you?"

You will bear it, for as long as you are able to. Mara's ghostly voice rippled in her head, rising from the depths. *Our people's pain is shared. It is remembered, like you will be.*

Isla pressed her lips together. "We have to find Eimhir first. That will be no simple task, even with the Sea Kith on our side." She hesitated. "I didn't expect you to agree with me so readily back at the estate. It felt nice to be on the same side again."

At once, she knew she'd pushed too far. Lachlan's shoulders turned to steel, and he stepped back, averting his gaze. "This isn't about you. The only thing I care about is stopping Eimhir. The blood she's spilled is on both our hands. I want to make that right, nothing more."

The sharpness of his words stung like a slap, but she swallowed it down, forcing her voice to remain steady. "I only meant...whatever your reasons, I'm glad you're here."

For a moment, Lachlan seemed on the cusp of saying something. His gaze fell across her, reluctant though it was, and something in the hard line of his mouth shifted. Then it was gone, and he traipsed across the deck without a backwards glance.

Isla released a breath, willing her aching heart to settle as she leaned over the gunwale. The soulless sea lay black and silent, mocking her with its unnatural calm. It knew as well as she did that some currents could not be fought.

The tides may have brought her brother back to her side, but she feared part of him remained as adrift as ever.

"Sails!"

Isla snapped her head up at the clear ringing of Nishi's voice and pocketed the sgian dubh she'd been flipping between her fingers. She clambered to her feet and ran to the quarterdeck, where the captain stood with her spyglass in hand.

As she approached, Nishi lowered the small bronze scope and passed it to her. "See for yourself."

Isla held the eyepiece to her cheek, peering through the lens. Under the tenebrous red sky, she caught a glimpse of something stark and white on the horizon. It was hazy, like a veil she couldn't peel back, but there was no mistaking the fluttering canvas.

Sails, like Nishi said. They'd found the Sea Kith.

When she lowered the spyglass, she found Nishi staring at her, a grin stretching the corners of her lips. "I was worried we might miss them. This tides-forsaken place has no dawn or dusk. Time doesn't seem to hold any meaning here."

"You're sure it's them?" Isla asked. "The soulship has no weapons. I don't like the idea of revealing ourselves only to meet an Admiralty patrol."

"Ask your sergeant to send Featherblade out, if it makes you feel better. But these waters are wilder than those where the Admiralty tend to venture. If they've strayed here, they won't last long." Nishi drummed her fingers on the wheel, copper eyes glinting in the low light. "It's been years since a sea summit was called. I forgot how rare it is for so many of us to share the same swell."

"How is this supposed to work, exactly?"

"Usually, the captain who calls the summit invites the others on board. But this is not my ship." She fixed Isla with a solemn stare. "That decision is up to you."

Isla shifted, casting her gaze over the deck. It didn't feel like her ship, either. It was built from the bones of her people, a floating monument to the sacrifice they'd made, the loss they'd suffered. The memories in her pelt—*Mara's* memories—had led her here, but that didn't mean she had any claim to the anam-long.

"You should bring them aboard." Lachlan hauled himself up the quarterdeck stairs. "We want them on our side, don't we? Showing respect for their customs would be a good place to start."

Nishi quirked an eyebrow. "Such magnanimity from someone who was licking the Admiralty's boots only a few short weeks ago. I didn't think you held the Sea Kith in such regard."

If Lachlan heard the bite in her words, he showed no sign of it. "Diplomacy can be as useful as any blade when it's wielded well. Call me a pawn of the Admiralty all you like, but don't mistake me for a fool."

"The lad is right," Muir said, joining them. "We have no allies, and we don't need any more enemies. If this is what the Sea Kith expect as a courtesy, we'd do well to play nice."

On the deck below, Darce met her eyes with a quiet resolve.

Isla nodded. "All right. Let's cross back and show this summit exactly who we are."

She braced for the haar to close in once more, returning them to the world of the living. The chill burned her throat and stung her eyes, but she refused to buckle under the mist's suffocating grasp. However it tried to drown her, it wouldn't be enough. Sooner or later, she'd purge it of its corruption and return it to what it once was.

Something lurched under her feet, and she staggered sideways, scrambling for balance as the deck rolled. She peered through the dissipating fog but was met only with a wall of rain.

"Hold on!" Nishi yelled, spinning the wheel through her hands. "Looks like we've caught the tail end of a tempest."

Isla gritted her teeth, ducking behind the gunwale as a wave crashed over the deck. It soaked the fabric of her coat, drenching the folds until they were sodden. The chill seized her lungs, and she forgot how to breathe.

A sharp pain wrenched at her heart. She'd never have felt like this if she had her pelt. The sea was meant to be her *home*, not her enemy. She'd forgotten how cruel it could be, how merciless it was.

She peered through the narrow gap in the railing. Nishi was right—a storm raged around them, whipping the waves into a ferocious swell. The tides had no presence in the soulless realm, but here, they showed their wrath. Spray misted in the air as the soulship crashed through another battering wall, its hull groaning.

Above, Featherblade let out a fearsome shriek and leapt from the mast, its wings a flurry as it flapped towards the ships on the horizon. Now that the haze of the soulless realm was behind them, Isla could see the shapes of their sails more clearly. There was more than a single ship waiting for them; she caught flashes of crimson, swathes of black. Perhaps two dozen in total, riding on the rise and fall of the waves.

She fought back to her feet, serpenthide boots biting into the slick deck. A low grumble of thunder rattled through her bones, but already it was distant, diminishing across the waves. Whatever storm they'd been caught in, it was passing quickly.

She only hoped their good fortune would hold.

"Everyone still with us?" Nishi called from the helm. Her tricorne hat had slipped askew, the soaking coils of her ink-black hair spilling across her shoulders, but there was a fervent gleam in her eyes as she wrestled with the wheel. A storm held no fear for the Sea Kith. They greeted it like an old friend.

Across the deck, Lachlan spat out a mouthful of seawater. Muir stood grim-faced and soaked to the bone as he loosened a length of rope from his wrist. "Never thought I'd miss the canals. Might've stunk like shite, but at least they didn't try to drown me."

Isla choked out a laugh, salt and bile burning her throat. Already, the swell was beginning to settle, the waves withdrawing their relentless assault. The wind raged, biting her cheeks raw, but there were no sails for it to catch, no canvas for it to pummel. Ahead, the horizon was dreich and grey, but it was steady. It beckoned them towards the Sea Kith ships waiting on the crests of the waves.

She moved to the bow, training her eyes on the ships as they drew closer. Some schooners, a few twin-masted brigantines, a monstrous galleon. They each cast a silhouette against the twilight sky, their painted hulls and billowing sails ranging from the inconspicuous to the macabre. For the moment, they hung back from one another, each holding to their own space.

A caw tore through the air, and Featherblade swooped around the masts, yammering from its long beak. Overhead, a score of other seabirds circled the soulship, filling the sky with their cacophony of cries.

Nishi glanced up at them, a satisfied smile tugging at her mouth. "Seems our invitation has been accepted. Welcome to your first sea summit, Blackwood."

It took less time than Isla expected for the Sea Kith crews to make their way aboard. They assembled gangways between the decks as they drifted past, their captains and sentinels crossing the wooden walkways with easy, practised strides. On the larger ships, they tossed thick lengths of rope and weather-worn ladders from their bulwarks, slipping down the sizeable drop in height to land on the soulship's deck.

For the first time, a prickle of unease crawled down Isla's spine. They were outnumbered. If the summit turned sour, they'd be no match for the Sea Kith's strength, their formidable cannons. Their only protection was the haar, and they'd left that behind.

A crease deepened in Muir's weathered brow as he surveyed the captains. "I hope we've not made a mistake."

"Wee bit late for that, uncle. You agreed to this, remember?"

"Aye, and I'm starting to wish I hadn't." He shook his head. "Maybe it's just my old Admiralty instincts rearing their head. The last time I was at sea, I was fighting these people. Pirates, we called them."

"It would be wise if you kept that to yourself." Isla glanced away, eyes flitting over the stony faces of the Sea Kith gathered on deck. They stood in long-tailed coats and serpenthide boots, waists laden with blades and pistols. Some of them wore tricorne hats like Nishi, others were adorned with tartan bonnets, or wove yellow-green strands of seaweed through their windswept hair. The only thing they had in common was the suspicion on their faces.

One of them knelt, pressing his palm against the soulship's bone deck. He frowned as he rose, muttering something to the captain next to him. The whispers spread like ripples, turning Isla cold.

"Kith. Friends." Nishi strode into the middle of the deck, her lip ring glinting as she smiled at the gathered crowd. "It pleases me to see so many of you answer my call. I wouldn't have sent it if I believed we could each weather the approaching storm alone. But I fear the squall coming will destroy us all if we don't meet it together."

The Sea Kith who'd touched the deck sent her a hard look from his single blue eye. "From what I can gather, that squall is entirely your own making. You provoked the Admiralty's wrath, bringing it down on all of us. Why should we pay the price for your foolishness?"

"There's more on the horizon to worry about than the Admiralty." Nishi dropped her voice, every syllable as sharp as steel. "And don't talk to me about prices paid. You can see as well as anyone here that I no longer have the *Jade Dawn*. It burned, along with my crew. And Kerr..." She swallowed, a muscle twitching in her neck. "Well, there's a reason the breaking of our blood oath didn't kill me. The Grand Admiral owes me a debt for my sentinel's death, and I intend to take it from his heart."

The Sea Kith said nothing. He stood close to seven feet tall, with a whaleskin coat covering his broad shoulders and sky-grey tattoos swirling in intricate patterns across his pale skin. Unlike Nishi, he wore the ink on his face, and it circled his one eye with sweeping strokes.

Tension thickened in the air, as suffocating as the haar itself. Isla sensed Darce shift closer behind her, the tip of his claymore biting into the bone underfoot. Her stomach twisted at the thought of this erupting into violence. The soulship's deck had gorged itself on blood before, but that had been spilled willingly. She had no desire to see more of it.

Before anyone else could speak, she stepped forward. The gathered Sea Kith turned their eyes on her, and she feared her words would dry up on her tongue. She pushed down the trepidation and met their fierce gazes with her own.

"Nishi is right," she said, keeping her voice steady. "The Admiralty threatens us all, but there is a far greater danger out there, one that could see Silveckan and its waters swallowed by the mists. Don't make the mistake of thinking you're safe from it out here on the waves. We've seen how quickly the haar can spread."

One of the other Sea Kith bristled. "Who are you to speak at our summit? You're not one of us, that's for certain."

Nishi stiffened. "She is—"

"The captain of this ship," Isla said coolly. Something swelled beneath her ribs, bringing fire to her blood. "The only ship capable of crossing the haar to the soulless realm that lies beyond. I may not be Sea Kith, but I know the waves better than any human."

The Sea Kith pursed her lips, eyes trailing over the salt scars marring Isla's collarbone. "Looks like you've lost your pelt, skinchanger. Why should we pay any mind to a captain whose days are numbered?"

Isla felt Darce stir behind her. This time, it wasn't his claymore he reached for; it was his sentinel magic. The deck heaved, waves crashing over the gunwale. A bitter wind nipped at her neck, its teeth bared. Her ears filled with a roar that trembled from the fathoms themselves, a roar filled with warning.

This was *her* ship. The tides were on her side, and by the look on the Sea Kith's face, she realised it too.

"My days are not as numbered as you might think." Isla smiled tightly. "Now, if you're ready, you'd do well to listen to what I have to say."

CHAPTER FOUR

DARCE

Darce shifted his hands around his claymore's hilt and willed the hum of magic in his blood to settle. The tension clinging to the air had dissipated, but he couldn't shake the sense of unease that lingered. While Isla and the Sea Kith talked, dusk fell across the water, shrouding the sky in a purple so deep it was nearly black. No moon hung above them tonight. The rest of the Sea Kith ships were little more than shadows on the waves, slipping in and out of sight as they drifted.

He cast his eyes to the soulship's mast, the towering bones holding a sheen in the darkness. Atop its yards were a dozen guidebirds, feathers shuffling and claws twitching as they peered down from their perches. Never had he seen so many in one place—guillemots and skuas, puffins and kittiwakes, each of them twice the size of any regular seabird.

A particularly raucous screech carried from the top of the mast, and he stifled a smile as Featherblade glared down, its blue-rimmed eyes fierce as it shifted its webbed feet on its perch.

One of the Sea Kith glanced up at it too—the hulking brute who'd challenged Nishi earlier. His single blue eye glinted as he observed, attention momentarily diverted from Isla's impassioned pleas.

Darce couldn't help but shudder. There was something about the man that put him on edge. It was clear he was no stranger to violence.

A scar carved down the right side of his face, bifurcated by the leather patch he wore. His head was shorn apart from a red braid twisting from his crown to his shoulders, and one of his huge hands rested on the hilt of a dirk with an iron blade the length of a common shortsword.

Nishi moved closer, lowering her voice as she spoke. "That's Ruairidh of the *Red Gale*. If we Sea Kith have a reputation as brigands and pirates, it's because of captains like him. As far as he's concerned, anything on the water that strays into his path is fair game to hunt. He stops short of attacking fellow Sea Kith, but even then…" She grimaced, lip curling in distaste. "We have little in common besides the waves we share."

Darce tightened his grip around the sword waiting patiently in his hands. His blood thrummed, but he couldn't rely on his magic alone. He was not the only sentinel on board, and the tides were capricious in who they favoured at any given time.

Across the deck, Ruairidh folded his arms across his broad chest, fixing Isla with an appraising stare.

"This Eimhir you speak of," he said, the rough burr of his voice drawing out each word. "You've talked a lot about what she means to do, but nothing about what she wants."

Isla's face turned stony. "I fear she is beyond anything so simple as wanting. The haar has taken hold of her, driving her to sickness. All that matters to her is giving the gun-anam the vengeance she believes they deserve. The more blood spilled in this conflict, the more the haar will spread, the more selkies will fall to bloodlust. Silveckan will be lost, and its waters will soon follow."

"And the pelt you claim she stole…" Ruairidh tilted his head. "How are we to help you hunt her if we don't know what it looks like?"

The hum of magic in Darce's veins grew to a roar, crashing through him like the churning of the waves. It felt like a storm was about to break, and Isla was in its path.

Isla narrowed her eyes, but she kept her voice steady. "You'll understand I'd rather wait until there's some measure of trust between us before I share that kind of information."

"But that's not the only information you're keeping to yourself, is it?" Ruairidh raised his brow. "When were you planning on admitting you're the Grand Admiral's bastard daughter?"

A hushed murmur broke out from the crowd. Darce readied his hands around his claymore, lifting the fearsome blade from where it rested on the deck. Beside him, Nishi's hand drifted to her belt. The restlessness stirred into something more, pulling the tension until it seemed ready to snap.

Featherblade shrieked, echoed a dozen times over by the other guide-birds perched on the mast. Isla glanced up at the clamour, then turned to Ruairidh, her expression cool. "I didn't realise the Admiralty's reach had spread as far as your ships. Nevertheless, your information is correct. I admit, Alasdair Cunningham is my father by blood." Her eyes hardened. "But that didn't stop me spilling his."

Ruairidh barked out a laugh, shoulders heaving under his whaleskin coat. His arms were folded, his stance loose and relaxed. That unsettled Darce more than anything else.

Another Sea Kith stepped forward, hand resting on the hilt of her cutlass as she shot Nishi an accusing glare. "You knew about this?"

Nishi stared back, face impassive. "Aye, I knew."

"And you decided to harbour the selkie bitch instead of handing her over?" The Sea Kith captain spat on the deck. "You could have got the Admiralty off our backs and earned yourself some coin in the process. I hear they're offering quite the reward."

"Everyone here knows I don't deal in living goods." Nishi drew her pistol, thumb brushing over the hammer. "And I'd caution you to watch your tongue, Aitken. Don't forget you're a guest on this ship."

"We only keep to the auld ways on Sea Kith ships." The woman called Aitken curled her lip. "I don't know what tides-damned manner of vessel it is we stand on, but it's not one of ours. This skinchanger is no captain, and after losing the *Jade Dawn*, it seems neither are you."

Nishi cocked the hammer, the click echoing through the air like a warning. Her pistol remained by her side, but Darce was close enough to see the twitch in her fingers.

A smile hardened across Nishi's face. "Go on. Keep talking."

Aitken seemed unperturbed by the edge in Nishi's voice. She spread her arms wide to the other Sea Kith. "The *Jade Dawn* and its captain brought the Admiralty down on all of us. If there's a way to get the fleet out of our wake, I say we take it. Not to mention the reward." She whirled back to Nishi. "There's no need to involve yourself any further in this. Let us take the selkie off your hands. You can keep her ship. Maybe if you look after this one better, you won't end up with a crew burned to ash and a sentinel at the bottom of the—"

The rest of her words were lost to the furious crack of Nishi's pistol. Aitken staggered, blood and bone splattering from her skull. She crumpled to the deck, a crimson hole in the middle of her forehead.

Smoke wisped from the end of Nishi's pistol. "Does anyone else care to test me today?"

Some of the Sea Kith drew back, exchanging knowing glances. But a group of six or seven advanced, expressions ugly as they looked between Nishi and the limp, lifeless body at her feet.

"You murdered a guest on your ship," one of them said. "The auld ways—"

"Don't apply here, according to Aitken." Nishi shrugged. "If you refuse to see this ship as a Sea Kith vessel, you forgo the protection that brings. I gave your captain more than one opportunity to stand down. Don't blame me if she was too foolish to take them."

The Sea Kith gestured to the others at his side. "Send her to the fathoms and take the skinchanger."

Before any of them could move, Nishi leapt, pocketing her spent pistol with one hand and drawing her rapier with the other. She slashed at the nearest Sea Kith, scoring a bloody line across his cheek before ducking out of the way as the crack of another pistol tore through the air.

The deck erupted into chaos. Darce could barely hear himself think through the roar of raised voices and the shrieking from the seabirds high on the mast. The noise rattled in his good ear, muffling everything but the thumping of his heart.

Isla. He needed to get to her.

He pushed through the bodies, dragging his sword by his side. There were too many people around to wield the claymore properly. It was as likely to cleave Lachlan or Muir as any of the attacking Sea Kith. He had to pull them away from the throng, somewhere he had the space to protect them.

A hot pain seared across his shoulder, and he snapped his head around to see a dark-haired Sea Kith glaring at him with murderous intent, cutlass bloody as he raised it for another blow. Before Darce could parry the strike, the blade slipped from the Sea Kith's fingers, falling to the deck with a dull rattle.

Darce sucked in a ragged breath as a bloom of red spread across the Sea Kith's tunic. He turned to see Lachlan standing behind him, hand curled around the mahogany stock of a pistol.

"Go," Lachlan said, jerking his head towards the far side of the deck. "I'll cover you."

A weight lifted from Darce's chest as he pushed through the crowd to where he'd last seen Isla. His eyes darted between the fallen bodies, the crimson blood pooling across the bone-white deck. None of them were her. They couldn't be her—if he'd lost her, he'd have felt it.

Then he caught a flash of burgundy: a familiar dress coat that had once belonged to Cormick, but now hung clumsily around Isla's shoulders. She was pinned into a corner, eyes flashing as she dodged the swipe of a needle-sharp rapier. The blade's thin point skimmed agonisingly close to her throat, millimetres away from drawing blood.

She fought back with a snarl, her cutlass flying, but the strike was ill-timed. The Sea Kith met it easily, dragging his rapier along the blade and knocking the sword from Isla's grip. Before she could gather herself, he followed with a vicious kick to her stomach, sending her sprawling to the deck.

Darce tightened his hands around his claymore, heart seizing. He'd never get to her in time.

He reached for the tides, begging every drop of auld blood running through his veins to rise to his call. He needed a jolt of the hull, a rogue wave to sweep the Sea Kith away. Something, *anything*.

But it wasn't the tides that answered his silent plea.

He hadn't seen Ruairidh cross the deck. Hadn't noticed him unsheathe the dirk on his belt, revealing a blade as long as Darce's forearm. All he saw was the dagger's serrated edge flying towards the Sea Kith's throat and the blood that poured out when the teeth found flesh.

Isla scrambled back, blood splattering across her face from the spouting wound in the Sea Kith's neck. She stared up at Ruairidh, stark with horror as he held the man aloft by his hair and watched the life drain out of him.

"What did you—what kind of..." Her voice caught, the rest of her words fading into the air.

Ruairidh's only answer was to throw the mutilated Sea Kith overboard, his lips curling at the splash.

Darce stormed forward, holding his claymore aloft as he set himself squarely in front of Isla. The dirk quivered in Ruairidh's huge hand, flesh and sinew clinging to its jagged teeth. It was a dagger that wanted to taste blood. A dagger made for someone who knew how to spill it.

He met Ruairidh's gaze. "You've overstayed your welcome. Take your crew and leave. I have no desire to do the Admiralty's job for them, but if that's what it takes to protect this ship, you'll receive no quarter from me."

The smile on Ruairidh's face didn't falter. He sheathed his dirk, eyeing the end of Darce's blade. "That's the thanks I get for saving your lass's life? Careful, auld blood. Next time, I might not bother."

Before Darce could bite back, Isla climbed to her feet, resting her hand on his arm. She turned to Ruairidh, fixing him with an even stare. "If you intend to explain yourself, now would be the best time. Otherwise, you'd do well to listen to my sentinel."

The sea surged in his blood at her words, begging to be unleashed. He could pull a wave from the fathoms, forcing salt water into Ruairidh's lungs, drowning him from the inside out. He could summon a swell to carry him to the crushing depths. The tides would give him whatever he needed to protect her.

Ruairidh hadn't moved. He cocked his head, his red braid slipping across his shoulders. "Take a wee look around you. What do you see?"

Something in the maddening calm of his voice gave Darce pause. He didn't lower his sword, but he allowed himself the barest of glances across the deck, eyes flitting as quickly as he dared.

The fighting had stopped. The Sea Kith separated from each other, weapons falling to their sides. Of the half-dozen that had turned on Nishi, only one still drew breath, kneeling wretchedly on the deck. All other eyes had fallen on Ruairidh. The moment he'd picked a side, the rest had followed.

An unwelcome chill prickled Darce's spine. If Ruairidh drew his knife again, he'd be dead. Isla, too. Lachlan, Muir, Nishi—all their lives would be forfeit to this mistake.

"You were right," Ruairidh said to Isla, the low lilt of his voice cutting through the air. "The Admiralty's reach *has* spread to the Sea Kith. I've suspected it for some time." He turned his eye to the last remaining aggressor from Aitken's crew. "I wanted to see how far it had buried itself so I could cut out the rot."

The kneeling Sea Kith paled. "You have no authority over anyone but your own crew. What arrangements Aitken entered into were our business, not yours. You can't..."

He trailed off at the cold amusement on Ruairidh's face. "You have no idea what I can and can't do, wee sprat. But you'll learn soon enough." He lifted his chin, sending a fearsome glare around the rest of the gathered Sea Kith. "If anyone else wants to bend over and offer their arse to the Admiralty, speak now. I'll offer you a cleaner death than those bastards will when they run out of use for you."

The deck was silent. No Sea Kith answered him. None dared breathe. All Darce heard over the whistling wind was the deep chuckle from Ruairidh's throat as he turned to Isla.

"You mentioned trust, selkie lass. Perhaps I have something to offer you on that account." His eye glinted as he gestured across the waves at a tall, square-rigged brigantine. "Why don't you and your crew come over to the *Red Gale?* I think there's something on board you'd like to see."

CHAPTER FIVE

ISLA

As Isla stepped off the gangway onto the ruby-stained wood of the *Red Gale's* deck, she couldn't suppress her shiver. The brigantine was larger than she'd realised, its two masts towering over the deck with blocky, carmine-coloured sails. Though only a few metres of water separated them from the soulship, it might as well have been a gulf. They were heavily outnumbered by Ruairidh's crew. If the Sea Kith decided to forgo the auld ways—their unwritten code of courtesy—none of them would leave alive.

She cast a surreptitious glance at Nishi alongside her. The captain was chewing on her lip ring, mouth tight. She clearly didn't like this any more than Isla, but whatever their misgivings, it was too late to turn back. Ruairidh had offered them bait—it had been their choice to take it.

The deck rolled beneath her feet, caught on the crest of a wave. Isla shifted her balance easily, not missing a step as she followed Ruairidh's long stride. The rest of the Sea Kith crews had returned to their own ships, but they remained close, drifting on the swell. Muir and Lachlan had stayed behind on the soulship, but that wasn't enough to loosen the knot of dread in her chest.

I think there's something on board you'd like to see, Ruairidh had said. Isla didn't want to think about what it might be.

At the stairs to the hold, Ruairidh whistled, and a young Sea Kith emerged. Their skin was a deep brown, and their amber eyes peered curiously from under the brim of a large cavalier hat as Ruairidh shoved forward the survivor from Aitken's crew.

"Take this worthless bilge rat to the brig, will you, Cam? But no drowning this time." Ruairidh grunted. "I need him to squeal, and he won't be able to do that if you fill his lungs with salt."

The young Sea Kith smiled. "You're nae fun."

Isla watched as they ushered the prisoner down the rickety wooden steps. "What will to happen to him?"

"I'd like to know exactly what the Admiralty wants with our people. What happens to him depends on how forthcoming he is with answers." Ruairidh paused. "And how I like those answers."

He didn't need to say anything more. The threat curled around every syllable; it dripped from his tongue like a morsel to be gobbled up. Isla was no stranger to bloodying her hands, but Ruairidh was the kind of man who enjoyed violence. The kind of man who hungered for it, and found himself starving when he went too long without.

"Is Cam your sentinel?" she asked, trying to steer her thoughts away from what she'd got into.

For the first time since she'd set eyes on him, Ruairidh stiffened. It wasn't much—a slight seizing of his broad shoulders—but it was enough for her to know her words had wounded, however unintentional it was.

"They're a sentinel," he said, the words careful and deliberate. "But not mine."

Isla knew better than to press the matter. She'd witnessed Nishi's anguish when the Grand Admiral had killed Kerr. The bond between captain and sentinel ran deeper than blood. If it broke, the death that often followed was a mercy. Surviving it, on the other hand...

She ran her fingers over one of the salt scars biting at her skin. She knew what it was like to live with that kind of loss.

The sound of a door creaking on rusting hinges tore her from her thoughts, and she followed Ruairidh into a large, dimly lit room, Darce and Nishi close behind. Each step was pulling her towards something she couldn't take back, but there was no stopping now. Ruairidh had brought them to the bowels of the *Red Gale* to show them something, and it was time to learn what it was.

He moved aside, red braid swinging over his shoulders as he gestured to the middle of the room.

Isla froze. Several dozen bodies huddled in filthy rags, bound to each other with thick knots of rope. Their eyes were stark and wide, their expressions ashen. Some sported ripe bruises and weeping cuts. Others were wounded more gravely, with makeshift bandages holding together mutilated limbs.

Rage flared in her chest, closing her throat as she struggled to find her voice. "What did you—what is the *fucking* meaning of this?"

"Ransom, no doubt," Nishi said flatly. "Back when I was a bosun, the *Red Gale* made a name for itself kidnapping high-profile captains from diplomatic vessels along the Bréchon coast and selling them back to their families. In pieces, if they took too long to pay up." She trailed her eyes over the quailing cluster of bodies. "Why are you showing us this, Ruairidh? Who are they?"

"They have tongues. They can tell you themselves." He shot a glance at the nearest man. "Go on. Tell these folk what happened in that shitehole of a village we found you in."

The man Ruairidh was addressing shrank back, a puddle of piss forming at the bottom of his ragged breeches. His cheeks were ruddy and etched with deep, weathered lines, his white hair thin across the crown of his head. As he looked at them, his cracked lips trembled, but no words came out.

"Enough of this," Isla said sharply. "I don't know what these people have suffered, but I'll not have you inflict any more terror on them, you tides-forsaken son-of-a—"

"The mists."

The words were so quiet, frayed with so much pain, that Isla thought she'd imagined them. But there was no doubt the old man had spoken. His jaw quivered, but his eyes were bright and feverish as he met her horror-struck gaze.

"The mists," he said again, his west coast accent soft around the words. "They came at night, when we were all in our beds. The air turned damp, suffocating us. I tasted salt on my tongue when I swallowed. And when I went outside..."

His eyes darted to the rest of the pale, stricken faces. Isla saw it now—the shadow they carried, the chill of what they'd seen. They were wounded and filthy, reeking of stale blood and piss and fear.

Darce tensed. "It's just like Caolaig. The haar, the raid. The flay—"

He bit down to stop himself, but it was too late. Even the ghost of the word was enough to turn the villager's eyes glassy. He mumbled something, then shuffled back, burying himself amongst the shaking bodies.

Isla shuddered. It was impossible to forget what she'd seen that night all those months ago in Caolaig. It was carved into her memory with a bloody hand, haunting her dreams. These poor bastards wouldn't forget what had happened to their home either.

She turned to Ruairidh. He wore a smile on his thin lips, but the edges were sharp, his humour not quite meeting his single, striking eye.

"Where did you find them?" she asked.

"I thought you might like to know that," he said. "This skinchanger you're hunting, Eimhir...she's the one responsible for this, isn't she? Do you think you can pick up her trail? Track her down through the blood and bodies she's left behind?"

"It's the only lead we have," Isla said curtly. "But you know that, don't you? What is it you want, Ruairidh?"

His teeth reminded her of a shark's, mouth stretched into a smile that would tear her to shreds if she got careless. Walking away wasn't an option, not now that she'd seen these wretched villagers. All she could do was let Ruairidh circle her and trust she had enough wits to keep out of reach.

"Our interests may be more aligned than you imagine," he said. "You want to find the slippery bitch who stole your pelt. I might be inclined to help you, as long as you understand I'll expect that favour to be repaid."

Isla narrowed her eyes. "What kind of favour are you talking about?"

The smile faded, and Ruairidh's features hardened, his scar shifting behind his eyepatch. "One of your people's chieftains owes me a debt. When you get your pelt back, you'll make sure I'm given the chance to settle it."

A sickening foreboding clenched in her stomach. "What chieftain? What debt?"

"You'll understand I'd rather wait until there's some measure of trust between us before I share that kind of information." His lip curled as he threw her own words back at her. "It goes both ways, you see. But the details don't matter. If you want my help, that's my price."

She felt Darce's eyes on her, dark and troubled. If she asked him, he'd tell her to walk away. He'd say there were other ways to track Eimhir down. But as she trailed her gaze over the broken, frightened faces in front of her, she realised she had no choice. She couldn't wait any longer, not if this was the kind of horror that would spread while they searched the waves for someone who didn't want to be found.

"What about them?" she asked, nodding towards the villagers.

Ruairidh shrugged. "That's up to you. I could keep the sorry bastards on board to force your hand, but I'd rather cut them loose at the next port and be spared the extra mouths to feed. So tell me, selkie lass, what's it to be?"

The threat fell flat to her ears. She'd already made her mind up.

Aineol, the echo of Duncan's voice whispered, quiet and accusing. He'd never accepted her on Eileanan Selch, never believed she belonged there. Part of her squirmed to think she was proving him right.

He chose to follow Eimhir, she thought to herself. All the chieftains had. What bloody choice did she have?

The only answer she found was the knowing glint in Ruairidh's eye.

"All right, Captain," she said, extending her salt-scarred arm. "It seems we have an accord."

The pressure around her ribs only loosened when she stepped back onto the soulship and drew a long breath into her lungs, relishing the sting of salt in the air. The *Red Gale* peeled away, but it remained on the horizon, its crimson sails like shadows under the cloak of night. Even if the haar closed in, shielding them in the soulless realm, there would be no escaping Ruairidh and the word she'd given him. It would follow her wherever she went, reminding her of what she'd done.

She found Darce's gaze. "We should talk. All of us."

They gathered down in the galley, sitting on a scrambled assortment of stools and chairs they'd scavenged from the abandoned dwellings in Caolaig. The soulship had been stark and bare when they'd found it marooned in the Southern Reaches, but they'd managed to outfit it with cobbled-together furnishings and the comforts they needed for the long weeks ahead at sea.

Human furnishings, Isla reminded herself. *Human comforts*. It was strange to see the oak chairs and velvet cushions set around the room, their colour vibrant against the pale bone floor and walls. This was a selkie ship, a ship she'd taken from her people. Part of her wondered if she'd made the right choice, if her actions were any less of a betrayal than Eimhir's. But though the guilt twisted her stomach, she couldn't allow herself to dwell on it. She knew how much was at stake.

She sank into one of the chairs, breathing in the scent of the fish stew Muir dished out in front of her. A hunk of crusty bread sat on a plate at her side, and she tore it apart between her fingers, dipping the crust into the steaming bowl before filling her mouth with the sweet, smoky taste.

The only sounds came from their smacking lips and ravenous gulps as they filled their bellies. After a while, the eating slowed, and the quiet clotted with tension.

Isla sipped slowly from her tankard. For all his claims of giving up the bottle, Muir had still managed to smuggle several crates of wine and whisky on board. But the Breçhon red she'd once savoured felt too rich on her tongue, and she had to force herself to swallow it down. "The *Red Gale* and several other Sea Kith ships agreed to help us search for Eimhir. Their guidebirds can cover more of the waves than we can alone, and if they find her, they'll send word to Featherblade. Then, it's up to us. It's up to me."

The echo of her voice rang in her ears. Nobody else spoke. The galley felt like it was closing in, suffocating the room.

Eventually, Darce lifted his head. "I know we need to find Eimhir. If we're to have any hope of stopping the haar, you need to reclaim your pelt. But, Isla, you won't be able to stop her if you're taken. The longer we leave the Admiralty unchecked, the tighter its nets will pull. We need to put an end to this—put an end to Cunningham."

She shook her head. "Cunningham can wait. We can't let Eimhir do any more damage than she's wreaked already."

"He can *wait?*" Darce repeated. "Did you forget he almost managed to get to you only a few short hours ago? Who's to say there aren't more amongst the Sea Kith who might be tempted to hand you over?"

"The sergeant is right." Nishi pursed her lips, as if the words brought a foul taste to her mouth. "It sickens me that any Sea Kith would lower themselves to do the Admiralty's bidding, especially after what happened to the *Jade Dawn*. But I can't deny what I saw today. We are not immune from the Admiralty's rot."

Across the table, Muir took a loud slurp from his tankard and set it down on the table with a thud. His eyes were glazed from the liquor, but that didn't dull the edge of the scowl he gave her. "I know Alasdair

Cunningham better than anyone. He might have failed this time, but he'll try again. This isn't a problem you can ignore."

"I'm not ignoring anything. But finding Eimhir has to take priority. I won't—I can't..." Isla curled her hands under the table, fighting to stop her legs from shaking. Every drop of blood Eimhir spilled was a stain on Isla's hands. She'd let her go. She'd sacrificed the one chance she'd had to take back her pelt, and instead she'd thrust her sgian dubh into Cunningham's heart. Now, Eimhir was out of reach, and the Grand Admiral had risen from the fathoms.

She couldn't make the same mistake again.

When she lifted her head, Lachlan's tawny eyes locked with hers, holding no bitterness, no resentment. For once, there was only a shared understanding.

"I'm with you," he said. "Attacking Arburgh was one thing, but picking off fishing villages, slaughtering people who would never have cause to hold a weapon... We can't let it happen. Eimhir must be stopped."

A strange relief fluttered through her. She hadn't expected that Lachlan, of all people, would be the one on her side. It was a truce too tentative to grasp at, but she couldn't stop herself reaching anyway.

She met his gaze. "Ruairidh can lead us to where he found those survivors. If I can pick up Eimhir's trail, I might be able to—"

"Isla, stop." Darce's voice was weary. "We can't fight a war on two fronts. And if I—if *we* lose you, we lose everything. The capital might have fallen, but the Admiralty's fleets are out there. They're hunting you."

"Let them come." The words leapt from her mouth as cold as if they carried the chill of the haar itself. "I won't let them get in the way of what I have to do. If I don't reclaim my pelt, Silveckan will be lost, and all the Admiralty will have to rule over will be ghosts."

The galley fell into silence once more. Darce stared at her, a vein pulsing in his temple beside his missing ear. Something in his expression sent a trickle of foreboding down her spine, as if her heart knew what was coming next, even as her head stubbornly refused to believe it.

"Then I'll go," he said, his words ringing off the stark bone walls. "I'll finish what I started and make sure Cunningham can't hurt you again, can't hurt *anyone* again. This time, when I kill him, he won't be coming back."

His gaze offered no apology, asked for no forgiveness. There was nothing she could say that would stop him. Just as there was nothing he could say that would ease the rage and grief clawing at her heart.

Promise you'll always find your way back to me, she'd said to him once. Her words rang in her ears as if she'd just spoken them, as if she'd known even then they'd return to haunt her. Was this how it was to be? Forever pulled apart by the will of the tides?

The tides have nothing to do with it, a voice in her head reminded her. This choice was Darce's to make.

It was hers, too.

She met his eyes steadily. She saw the disappointment there, the dashing of his hopes that she might change her mind. But she couldn't change the course she'd set herself on, even if it took her away from him. He couldn't change his, either.

"It's just another storm," he said. "I'll be waiting for you when it clears."

Isla hoped he was right.

CHAPTER SIX

DARCE

"I don't know why you expected anything different. As stubborn as gull shite on a ship's deck, my niece."

Darce gritted his teeth as Muir's throaty burr broke through the morning quiet, disturbing the peace he'd managed to find at the soulship's prow. He sat with his claymore across his knees, the sword loosened from its cloth wrappings as he oiled the blade by dawn's rosy light. The slow, careful task was a welcome distraction from the restlessness coursing through his body. Or it had been, until Muir decided to impose himself on his solitude.

"Keeping your distance?" Muir continued. "That's wise. She inherited Catriona's temper, that's for certain. My wee sister never was shy in letting someone know when she thought they were wrong."

"I'm not wro—" Darce snapped his mouth shut and busied himself with the cloth once more. He should have learned better by now than to rise to Muir's jibes.

Muir chuckled. "I forgot she isn't the only stubborn one around here. Ach, don't give me that look. Much as it may surprise you, I happen to be on your side in the matter."

Darce grunted. The blade glinted under the morning sun, and he gave it one last wipe with the oil-stained cloth before folding the wrappings around it. When he finally lifted his head, he found Muir staring at him, eyes dark and expectant.

"What do you want?" Darce asked tiredly. "I'm not in the mood for—"

"The same as you," Muir cut in, all traces of humour evaporating. "To put an end to Alasdair Cunningham."

His words hung in the air, as sharp as any blade, carrying the weight of what lay in front of them. Hearing it spoken aloud filled Darce with dread. He'd tried to kill Cunningham once before. If he failed again, the chances of him coming back alive...

He shook his head. "You should stay out of this, Muir. Isla needs all the help she can get."

"Whereas you're capable of taking on the Admiralty single-handedly, no doubt?" Muir snorted. "Don't tell me to stay out of my own business, lad. I should have dealt with Alasdair a long time ago. Everything he's done is on my hands as much as his. It's about time I started making up for that."

"You don't need to—"

"How do you plan to kill the most protected man in all of Silveckan?" Muir gave a maddening smile. "You won't be able to get the job done while he still has sentinels willing to sacrifice their own captains to bring him back. And if your friend Rhona was speaking the truth, those sentinels will never turn on him, not as long as he holds their families hostage."

Darce flinched. Hearing Rhona's name was like a blow. He couldn't forget the shadow that had darkened her eyes, the cold resolve steeling her features as she'd drawn her sword and plunged it through Mhairi's heart. The sacred bond between captain and sentinel, shattered in an instant. Corrupted by a rot one of them hadn't known was there.

There's nae going back after what I've done, Rhona had said. *But there's nae living with it, either.*

So much violence. So much death. All for the wretched life of a man who should have been condemned to the fathoms a dozen times over.

Muir must have seen the pall that had fallen across his face, for his voice softened when he spoke again. "If you're to have any hope of turning those sentinels, you need to find out where Alasdair is keeping his hostages. And to do that, you need my help."

"I thought you didn't know anything about the hostages."

"But I might have a way to find someone who does." Muir pursed his lips. "It's a thread I've been wary of pulling. Not many sentinels walk away from the Admiralty and live, and those who do...well, there's no returning to who we were before. But if it could lead us to where Alasdair is keeping those people, I can't let that chance slip. I have to do something, even if it means..."

His voice drifted into the wind gusting around the deck, but Darce understood. He knew the lengths they would have to go to, what might be asked of them.

If it keeps Isla safe, he thought. She might never forgive them for it, but at least she'd be alive.

He fixed Muir with a discerning look. "I'd be foolish to turn away your help. But if you want to come with me, you need to get your bloody act together. We can't do this if you lose yourself at the bottom of a bottle."

A ruddy flush spread across Muir's dark skin. "You're a self-righteous wee prick, you know that?"

"I'm trying to keep you alive, old man. For Isla's sake, if no one else's."

Muir glared at him, a muscle twitching in his neck. It seemed as though he was about to say something else, but he turned away, spitting over the gunwale as he stalked to the stairs leading down to the hold.

To the stores where he stashed the whisky, no doubt, Darce thought wearily. Part of him wanted to follow, to shake some sense into the prickly old bastard, but the heaviness in his chest told him it was no use. This was a battle not meant for him. It was Muir's fight, and Muir's alone. Nothing he could do would change that.

"Darce?"

Isla stood at the edge of the deck, the rose-gold light of morning breaking over her pale skin. All he wanted to do was close the distance between them, the distance he'd put there the moment he'd told her he was leaving.

He'd promised they'd face what was coming together. He'd meant it, too, even if the words tasted like a lie now.

"What was that about?" she asked, gesturing to the stairs Muir had disappeared down.

Darce shook his head, unable to answer.

She stared at him, her sea-green eyes calm and appraising. Then something crumbled, and he saw the pain underneath.

"Can we talk?" she asked softly.

He followed her to the cabin they shared, the cabin he hadn't returned to last night out of fear of the promises he might break. Being this close to her was agony, knowing that they'd soon be separated once more. It was his fault, and hers, and there was nothing either of them could do about it but be the one to yield. And he *couldn't* yield, not if it meant—

She pressed her lips against his in an aching, desperate kiss, silencing the frantic thoughts rushing through his mind. He could almost pretend that nothing was happening outside the confines of these bone-white walls. All that mattered was the two of them in this place, sharing the same gasping breaths. His hands found the loose lengths of her hair, and he buried them in it, holding her so close he felt her blood pulsing against his skin. This was all he wanted. *She* was all he wanted. If he had to leave her, even if it was to make sure she was safe...

The soft brush of her mouth lifted from his as she drew back, looking at him as though she'd heard his thoughts. "I never wanted this bond to become a chain," she said. "Neither of us would be able to live like that. But the thought of letting you go so soon after I got you back—"

"I know." He brushed her hair away, taking in her furrowed brow, her imploring eyes. "If I could see any other way... But, Isla, he'll never stop. He'll keep coming, no matter who he has to bribe or kill or torture to get to you. If I don't leave you, I fear I'll lose you instead. Don't ask me to accept that. Don't ask me to—"

"You should take the soulship."

He stilled. "What?"

"If you're going after the Admiralty, you'll be outnumbered and outmatched. You'll need a way to slip past their defences, and this is the only ship capable of doing that."

"This is your ship. A *selkie* ship. I couldn't—"

"You already have." She met his eyes. "It knows you, Darce. Its deck drank your blood. You alone can summon the haar to its empty masts. Its bones will carry you to where you need to go. And I trust they'll bring you back to me." She leaned into him again, cheek resting against the crook of his collarbone. "Finish this, once and for all. And then come back. Come *home*."

He tightened his arms around her. "What about you?"

"I already spoke to Ruairidh. He's agreed that Lachlan and I can sail with him on the *Red Gale* while we hunt for Eimhir." She grimaced. "He may be a brute, but he is no friend to the Admiralty, and he has a personal stake in keeping me alive."

"If you're wrong, if he betrays you—"

"I am no stranger to betrayal. I know exactly what it looks like." She rolled up her sleeve, exposing the long red scar where Eimhir had dragged the sgian dubh across her skin. A hard look settled across her face, turning her expression to stone. "I won't let my guard down again. Not with Ruairidh, not with Eimhir. I know what I must do."

The weight of her words echoed like a promise. Holding her felt like the still breath of air before the sky blackened and the storm rolled in. There was nothing Darce could do to stop it coming. All he had left was this chance, however fleeting, to treasure the calm.

He laced his fingers through hers and brought her hand to his mouth, lips brushing her knuckles. "My soul is yours, Isla Blackwood. As is my heart. When this is over, I'll remain at your side for as long as you'll have me."

Something in her features softened, and a rush of colour darkened her cheeks. "I…" Her lips trembled as she looked up at him, then averted her eyes. "It feels too much to hope for such things. As if daring to think about that kind of happiness might be enough to scatter it to the winds."

Darce gently brought her head towards him. "That's not going to happen. If tides be kind, we'll—"

"*No,*" she said fiercely. "It's not up to the fucking tides. *Tell* me, Darce. I need you to tell me this isn't the last time we'll see each other. Tell me—"

His mouth was on hers again, his hands wrapped in her hair as he obeyed her command. He told her with the urgency of each kiss. He told her with each shallow breath he gulped down, thick with the taste of her. He told her with the desperate need he met her with as they fell into the linen sheets and tangled together.

"I promise," he said, the words little more than a whisper as she quivered beneath him. "I *promise*, Isla."

He didn't need to say anything else. They spoke the rest without words, pronounced instead in the blood rushing beneath their skin, the fervent twisting of their bodies, the breathless sighs from their parting lips. He trailed his gaze over the tears trickling from the corners of her eyes, the ache of worry in her brow. He committed every part of her to memory for the sake of the promise he'd made, and reminded himself what it was he would shatter if he broke it.

INTERLUDE

She awakens in a cold sweat, as she so often does these days. Her hair clings to her clammy skin and her cheeks are warm and feverish. Not so long ago, she'd have held herself upright and sucked in steady breaths of crisp, cool air until the fog lifted. But the haze doesn't shift as easily anymore. It lingers, thick with salt, pressing on the cracks and seams inside her head until she fears her skull might shatter.

Her lungs strain, fighting against the damp cough that has made its home in them. It hurts, but not as much as the other ache. The one she doesn't allow herself to think about.

The small skerry is quiet under the stars. The only sound comes from the waves lapping against the rocky shore. Several of her people lie nearby in selkie form, their bodies rising and falling with each heavy breath.

For her, sleep is no longer a respite. Her dreams take her to places she doesn't want to tread. They show her things she doesn't want to see.

The flash of a blade in her palm. A splattering of red across grey fur. And, through eyes that don't belong to her, she sees her own face, as unforgiving as stone.

It will haunt you, a voice whispers from her memory. *What you've taken from me...what you've done.*

She presses her hands over her ears, but it's no use. The voice is in her head, in her *soul*. The grey pelt around her shoulders shines in the starlight, rippling with tones of subtle blue and gentle lavender. It's hers now, it belongs to *her*, but something in the fur lingers. Something she carries wherever she goes, something she can't dig out, no matter how hard she tries.

An icy touch brushes her bare shoulder, and she stiffens as a gun-anam drifts through her, filling her throat with salt. The wraiths follow her like a shadow. They know the promise she's made to them. When they feed, she feels their ravenous hunger like it's her own. She gorges herself alongside them, taking her fill of the blood and violence. It's the only thing that keeps her going.

And then what? the voice asks. *When Silveckan falls to the mists, when the soulless realm leaches into this world and all that remains around you are the ghosts of those you killed, what will you do? This can't be the future you imagined for our people, Eimhir.*

It's the name, more than anything else, that makes her snap. "*My* people," she hisses to the air. "Not yours. They were never yours."

The voice falls silent. All she can hear is the rasp of her own breathing. In, out, ragged at the edges.

Her lips sting from the venom in her voice. There's a part of her, locked in memory, that recoils at the words she uttered. But that part drifts further away each day, slipping out of reach beyond a veil she can no longer pierce.

Caraid, she once called her. *Cousin.*

Aineol, another part of her whispers, and the cold touch of the haar inside her agrees.

She's broken from her thoughts by a splash, and she lifts her chin to see Duncan and Angus emerge from the water. Their pelts hang from their bare shoulders, dripping salt water down their skin as they approach. It stokes a bitter pang of jealousy inside her, but she has to be careful. She carries the dreamwalker pelt, and with it, the hopes of her people.

She can't risk losing it. Not after all she did to make it hers.

Angus pushes his soaking red hair from his forehead, catching his breath before he speaks. "The surrounding waters are clear for us to move on, if that's your intention, aislingeach."

He addresses her with an old selkie word, one that hasn't been uttered since Mara was alive. *Dreamer*, he's calling her. She pulls the fur closer, feeling it pulse against her skin like a heartbeat. Its memories are hers. She drowns herself in them every night, bearing witness to decades of violence, centuries of loss. She sees pelts stripped from friends and lovers, throats slit and bodies tossed to the fathoms.

There could never have been peace. She knows that now.

"Eimhir?" Angus stares at her, freckles pinching together as he furrows his brow. "Did you hear me? The scouts are ready to move on your order."

"Aye," she croaks. Her voice is dry and rasping; she has little use for it these days. The gun-anam follow her wordless command, hungry for the vengeance she dishes them each time they strike the coast. She licks her lips, tastes salt and dried blood, then tries again. "Aye, I heard you. What of the Admiralty? Do you have a report on the fleet's movements?"

"They're scattered, but word from our patrols says they're heading to regroup somewhere on the northwest coast. Kinraith, most likely."

She nods. She knows that harbour well. If the Admiralty gathers its forces there... Something in her blood sings at the thought of it. It's a chance to finish what she started at Arburgh. A chance to unleash the gun-anam on the sentinels and rid the seas of the bastards and their magic.

Before she can say anything else, Duncan steps forward. His golden-brown skin is dark under the night sky, and he fixes her with an umber gaze so deep it looks black.

"Moving on Kinraith would be a mistake," he says. "We no longer have a soulship to shield us. They'll be waiting for an attack, and I'm not willing to send what's left of our people to slaughter. Not when we have nothing to gain from it."

He doesn't see it, not like she does. The blood spilled, the thickening of the haar...it's what will save them. When Silveckan drowns in the mist it created, consumed by the monsters it birthed, the sea will belong to the selkies again. There will be nothing left in the world to fear.

But she says nothing. She may be their aislingeach, but Duncan is their chieftain. She won't turn on her people, not while she can still save them.

The wind's bitter teeth bite her neck as she raises her chin to hold his solemn stare. "There are more ports on the northwest coast than Kinraith. Any one of them might provide the gun-anam with the chance to enact the justice they deserve."

"Carroncross," Angus replies. "Tavish's sister was taken off its shore a year ago. He never found any trace of her, or her pelt. If the tides had any mercy, I'd say she might have been killed. But more likely she's one with the salt and spray."

Something inside her stirs. It's as if the darkest reaches of the fathoms are rising in her chest, bringing with them salty rage and frothing spite. She allows them into her lungs, drowning in their grasp.

She might have feared this, once. Not anymore. Now, she can make them pay.

"Carroncross," she agrees, the word burning her tongue until all she can taste is ash.

CHAPTER SEVEN

ISLA

The soulship faded until it was a speck in the distance, then disappeared beyond the faint line of the horizon, taking with it the part of Isla's soul she shared with Darce.

She ought to have been used to the straining behind her ribs, the dull ache around her heart. But the loss ripped through her like a reopened wound, forcing her to suffer the pain anew. It would settle, if she buried it like she had before. She'd survived being separated from him once already. But part of her didn't want the pain to stop. If she felt it, it meant he was still out there, and she could allow herself to believe he'd come back to her.

The *Red Gale's* sails billowed, painting the dreich sky with a splatter of scarlet. The wind harried them across the waves, whipping the swell into a frenzy as they crashed through crests of seafoam. It *wanted* them to move faster.

Isla wasn't sure whether to take comfort from that.

At least Ruairidh had made good on his word and released the survivors at the last port they'd passed. Now, he steered the *Red Gale* down Silveckan's west coast to the massacred village he'd rescued them from.

Storwick. It wasn't a place she was familiar with, but from Ruairidh's account, it was a small fishing village with little in the way of passing trade and no ships to defend it, much like Caolaig. Eimhir would have found it an easy target.

The thought made her stomach churn. She wanted to find Eimhir—*needed* to find her. But that didn't stop the pinch of dread she felt when she imagined their paths crossing again. Would there be any trace of her cousin left? Or would all that remained be the dead eyes of a stranger?

"Are you prepared for what might be waiting for us here?"

Lachlan appeared behind her, leaning on his crutch as he scoured the horizon. The Admiralty dress uniform he once wore was long gone, replaced with sea leathers and a thick ermine cloak that covered the stump of his leg. His golden hair was longer than she ever remembered, tied in a simple sailor's braid. If she didn't know better, she'd think he belonged here.

"I don't believe it's possible to be prepared," she answered quietly. "From what the survivors said, it sounded like Caolaig all over again."

"I wasn't talking about the village." His jaw tightened. "Are you truly willing to do what it takes to stop her?"

He didn't need to say Eimhir's name. It hovered over them like an axe waiting to fall, ready to sever whatever fragile truce they'd cobbled together from what had broken between them.

She tried to bite back her anger as she replied, "If you don't know the answer to that, you should have stayed behind."

"It wouldn't be the first time you chose them, chose *her*." He turned to her. "Even after everything she's done, there's a part of you that loves her, that wants to save her. Whether you believe it or not, I know exactly what that's like."

His voice caught, and Isla couldn't help but wonder what it was he saw when he looked at her. Sister or selkie? Protector or traitor? Had she slipped beyond his grasp, or was he reaching for her even now?

"I won't give up on Eimhir," she said, the truth the only answer she could give him. "But that won't stop me from doing what needs to be done."

He nodded slowly, casting his gaze back to the sea. It was impossible to tell if he believed her. Part of her wasn't sure if she believed herself. Speaking the words was simple enough here on the deck of the *Red Gale*, separated from Eimhir by the rolling waves. But when she saw her again, when it came time to repay her betrayal and take back what had been stolen from her...how simple would it be then?

Lachlan shifted, reaching into his belt to draw a gleaming pistol from its holster. It took Isla a moment to place it, but when she did, her heart lurched. It was the same gun her old bosun had given her when she'd first returned to Silveckan all those months ago. Its mahogany stock shone in the sunlight, the mother-of-pearl casing glinting as Lachlan held it in his palm.

"Galbraith had me hold on to it," he said. "But it's better in your hands than mine. You...you always were a better shot."

The wry humour was so faint she might have imagined it. She looked up at him, careful. She knew how delicate this peace was, how easily it could crack under the slightest pressure. "Thank you. I wasn't sure I'd see it again."

"It would be nice to think you won't need it, but I doubt the tides will be so kind to us," Lachlan said. "The Sea Kith said they found Storwick slaughtered, but it's not far off the capital road, and abandoned settlements make for easy pickings when it comes to bandits. We'll need to be on our guard."

Isla wrapped her fingers around the pistol's polished stock, levelling it at the distant horizon. The engraved swirls along the silver barrel danced before her eyes as she held her hand steady, imagining the spark of flint, the cloud of burnt black powder.

Its weight in her grasp should have been a comfort. But the foreboding shiver prickling the hair on her arms was a reminder that bandits were far from the only thing she had to fear when they reached the shore.

"I don't like the look of this." Ruairidh stood on the forecastle, his huge arms folded as he surveyed the narrow mouth of the inlet where Storwick lay. His grey-white Sea Kith tattoos twitched as he furrowed his brow. "Tides be my witness, it was not like this when we left."

"I believe you," Isla said.

There was no sign of the fishing village. All she could see along the shore was the mist clinging to the waves.

The haar hadn't just swallowed Storwick. It was already spreading.

Lachlan sent her a stricken look. They both knew what lay in the thick of those mists. They'd picked through the bodies that had bloodied the beach at Caolaig. They'd seen Arburgh's cobbled streets run red through the gutters. There was only one thing that brought the haar to shore like this.

Isla swallowed. If she'd harboured any lingering doubts as to whether Eimhir was responsible, they disappeared now, drifting into the air. "I need to see what happened here."

"The word of those poor bastards wasn't enough for you?" Ruairidh snorted. "You can track your skinchanger friend from the ship. There's nothing to be gained by going ashore."

"That's not how this works," Isla said. "Eimhir's pelt—*my* pelt—is tied to our selkie ancestors through memory. If I'm to pick up her trail, I need to walk in the same places she walked. I need to see what she saw and hope the part of my soul she carries has left enough of a trace to follow."

Ruairidh remained silent, his blue eye cold as he stared into the mist. The haar hung from the sky, so dense it smothered everything. Even from here, Isla felt its salty breath on her skin, its unnatural chill dampening her clothes. The last thing she wanted to do was venture into it. But she had no choice, not if she wanted to find Eimhir.

"I'll take them, Cap'n."

The young Sea Kith sentinel sauntered across the deck, their amber eyes keen and sharp as they approached. Cam, Ruairidh had called them. They wore the same oversized cavalier hat as they had on the day of the summit, along with a tattered linen waistcoat and a dress shirt that clung tight around their wiry arms.

Ruairidh shot them a pointed look. "You know bloody well that's a bad idea."

"It'll do me nae harm for a couple of hours." Cam stared from under the brim of their hat, chin jutting in defiance. "I've got as much a stake in this as anyone. I want to go."

A growl rumbled from Ruairidh's throat. "On your own head be it. Damned if I care if you get yourself killed, so long as I get the tender back in one piece."

"Understood, Cap'n. Your lack of concern is duly noted." Cam quirked their lips into a grin, then nodded at Isla. "Tender's portside. I'll meet ye there in a few minutes."

Before Isla could say anything, they'd turned on their heel, ambling across the deck in the same light-stepped manner they'd arrived in. She glanced at Ruairidh, but she only received a steely glare.

"Go," he said. "And if you don't bring Cam back with you, it will be on *your* head."

The waves lapped against the tender as Cam rowed them into the mist. The sound echoed in Isla's ears, mingling with the thump of her own heartbeat. Everything else seemed deathly silent. Even the wind had settled, leaving an unnatural stillness in the air.

She should have been used to it. She'd learned to suffer the chill seeping into her skin and the salt burning her lungs every time Darce summoned the haar to the soulship's mast, carrying them across the waves with sails of spray. But this time, they hadn't called the mist. This time, it was waiting for them, ready to swallow them in its icy gullet.

One of the scars on her neck tingled painfully, and she brought her fingers to her skin, running them gingerly across the crystals biting into her flesh. She might not have become one of the soulless, but the loss of her pelt left its mark more and more each day.

Cam sent her a sidelong look as they rowed, muscles flexing beneath their shirt. "I hear that's a death sentence for your kind."

"For most of us, it is," Isla replied. "If I didn't have Darce to anchor me, I'd have been lost. I'd be one of the wraiths haunting these shores."

Lachlan shifted on the wooden bench, his lips pressed together. Part of her wanted to search the furrow of his brow for a trace of emotion, a sliver of relief that she was still here, still his sister. The other part of her feared to look too closely, in case she found something she didn't want to see.

They continued, the only sound the slap of oars against the waves. It was late afternoon, but already the sky had darkened, the sun hidden behind mist so thick it seemed to have no end. The gloom closed in, the threat of a world with no dawn.

"Tides protect us." Cam flicked their eyes upwards. "What's happening?"

Isla followed their gaze as the mists thinned to reveal a sky streaked with red so dark it seemed almost black. The sun disappeared entirely, leaving nothing but an oily wash of flickering shadow.

The soulless realm had begun to leach into their world.

Lachlan stiffened. "This is what's going to happen, isn't it? The haar will swallow more and more of Silveckan until all that's left is this tides-forsaken place."

"Aye," Isla said. "Unless we stop it."

The tender crunched on the gravelly shore, and she climbed out of the boat, boots splashing in the surf as she trudged towards the abandoned village. The haar lingered, but it was thin enough that she could see along the stone and shingle to a lone wooden jetty and the smattering of colourful buildings that lay behind it.

"This way," she said. "Let's see what happened to these poor folk."

The skies must have been clear the last few days, with no rain to wash away what had happened. As they drew closer to the village, the reek of death and decay hit Isla's nostrils.

The first bodies they found were half snatched by the sea, lodged face down amongst the kelp and crabs scuttling in the rockpools. Their skin had already turned blue and waxy, their chests bloated and full. But that wasn't the worst part. The worst part was what the selkies had done to them.

Hot bile burned the back of her throat. No matter how many times she saw it, the horror always hit her anew.

Flaying. The brutal vengeance the selkies, *her people*, carried out as a message to those who would steal their pelts.

The first corpse didn't look human. The tissue of their back was splayed wide, hacked into quarters and spread out to resemble some kind of grotesque, bloody insect. Underneath, all that remained was a ragged mess of flesh and sinew, stripped away until the chalk-white sheen of bone was visible underneath.

Lachlan stilled. "Isla—"

"I know," she said, gritting her teeth. Tides, she knew. She'd seen this before. But this time, the pain burrowed deeper. This time, she knew exactly who was responsible for it.

"I'm not talking about the bodies." Lachlan's breath clouded in the air, the vapour turning to ice. "I'm talking about *that.*"

Something in his tone turned her blood cold. She tore her eyes from the corpse at her feet and instead followed his gaze to the cluster of painted houses lining the shoreline ahead.

A shapeless shadow hovered over the blood-soaked cobbles, drifting through the dead air like a will-o'-the-wisp. But it carried no light as it shifted, held no ethereal glow. Staring into the swirling darkness was like looking into a void, utterly empty apart from two red pinpricks the same colour as the oily sky.

Eyes. Tides, they were *eyes*.

"A brollachan." Lachlan's voice was hoarse. "You used to frighten me with tales about them when we were bairns. I didn't think they were…"

"Neither did I." She stared at the formless spirit, mouth dry. Legends told of the creatures seeking out hosts, spilling their darkness into living flesh and warm blood so they might possess them. Human or beast, it didn't matter to a brollachan. They would take it anyway, turning their eyes red, forcing their shadows through flesh or fur.

We've got more to worry about than ghost stories, Muir had told her back at the estate.

He was wrong. This was what would happen as the haar spread. Wandering spirits slipping through the mists, crossing from the soulless realm into this world. Bringing with them their darkness, their horror. Feasting on the remnants of violence, leaving no trace behind.

Cam shifted uneasily. "I don't know if my sentinel magic will have any effect on that thing, and I doubt lead or steel will fare any better."

"Let's keep our distance," Isla said. "It doesn't seem to be doing anything, and I'd rather not provoke it if we can help it."

She picked her way towards the jetty, serpenthide boots biting for grip against the slick stones and seaweed underfoot. The coloured houses along the shore looked like something out of a painting as they drew near. They were too still, too quiet. Their once-bright facades of salmon pink and daffodil yellow were dull through the damp haze that had fallen over them. Some of their doors lay open, creaking on their hinges despite there being no breath of wind to disturb the air.

"There's no one left," Lachlan said, his voice little more than a whisper. "This place is abandoned."

"Not entirely." Isla cast a furtive glance at the brollachan. It continued to hover, seemingly oblivious to their presence. "We don't know what other manner of spirits might have been drawn here from the soulless realm. Keep your guard up."

Lachlan moved beside her, crutch slipping awkwardly on the gravelly shore as they climbed towards the boardwalk. "If the selkies keep striking at the coastal villages, they'll eventually reach the northeast. Caolaig may have fallen, but I thought we'd at least managed to give it some measure of peace. If the haar swallows the graves there, if it brings forth these foul spirits and other creatures..." He grimaced. "Our parents deserve to rest. I dread to think what these mists might do to them."

"We won't let that happen."

"You expect me to believe that?" He gestured around them. "Look at this place. Look at what Eimhir did to it. These people aren't Admiralty officers or sentinels. They're just...villagers. They were innocent, and Eimhir slaughtered them anyway. You *trusted* her. How can you see this and think you ever knew her?"

"This wasn't her," Isla snapped. "It's the mist sickness. Eimhir isn't—she'd never have..." She turned away, the denial bitter on her tongue. No matter what she said, no matter how much she wanted to push away the truth, she couldn't unsee what was in front of her. All this violence...it could have been stopped. *She* could have stopped it.

"We should keep moving," she said, her voice cracking. "The mists seem thicker this way. Let's see what they're trying to hide."

She didn't dare look at him; his expression was something she could imagine only too well. Instead, she edged deeper into the haar, bracing herself as the salty air forced itself into her lungs and sank its teeth into her skin. Somewhere behind her, she heard a wracking cough. Everything seemed muffled to her ears, lost to the dense shroud surrounding her.

Her boots crunched in the layer of frost covering the cobbles, and she looked down to find a deep semi-circle embedded in the ice.

She stilled. It was a hoofprint. Not just any hoofprint, but that of a kelpie.

The gun-anam were here—or at least, they had been. She felt it in the deathless chill permeating her bones, the air freezing inside her lungs. This was no ordinary cold. The soulless had swept through here with their dread mounts, feasting on the blood spilled.

"Fuck." Lachlan jolted to a halt, his crutch knocking against something with a dull clunk. When Isla followed his gaze to the cobbles, her blood turned cold.

It was another body. This one hadn't been hacked apart and flayed by the selkies, but that didn't mean the poor bastard hadn't suffered. The gun-anam's rotten touch was plain to see across every inch of the bloated corpse, from its black lips to its frostbitten skin.

Isla's salt scars burned ice cold. Beside her, Lachlan pressed a hand to his shoulder, clamping down on the wound the gun-anam had left almost six months ago.

"It was a mistake coming here," he said. "We should head back to the *Red Gale* before it's too late. Tell Cam..." He trailed off. "Shite, where *are* they?"

The haar was so dense that Isla could barely see a foot in front of her. There was no sign of the young Sea Kith sentinel.

"Cam?" she called out, their name echoing through the mist. "Don't stray too far. You'll only—"

"Keep your voice down," Lachlan hissed. "We have no idea what else is out there."

"We have to find Cam. If we return to the *Red Gale* without them, Ruairidh will kill us both." She started forward again, ignoring Lachlan's exasperated sigh as she climbed the cobbled steps leading further into the village. The haar was suffocating now. Each breath she took clawed at her lungs, scratching her throat raw.

At the top of the steps, she paused. A tall building stood nearby, its orange façade stark against the mist. Above its doorway was a wooden sign, hanging silent and still in the air. It was an inn of some sorts, but no glow of warmth lit the frost-coated windows. No hum of bustle and chatter spilled from the doorway.

Something in her chest tightened. Eimhir had been here—she was certain of it. If she closed her eyes, she could hear the screams rattling across the cobbles. Dreamwalking might have been beyond her now she no longer had her pelt, but the shadows of what had happened here lingered in memories just out of reach. If she could only grasp them...

"What are you doing?" Lachlan's voice cut through the air, low and urgent.

She hadn't realised she'd walked up to the inn's oak doors. Something was calling her, drawing her close. Part of her wanted to recoil from it, to turn around and leave this horror behind. But she couldn't. Whatever was waiting for her, she had to see it.

Her fingers were white as she brushed the frost off the handle and pushed through the door.

The first thing that hit her was the stench of rot and blood. She pressed her mouth shut and buried her nose in the lapel of her jacket, but that wasn't enough to keep out the reek. It clogged her throat, brought hot tears to the corners of her eyes.

All the oil lamps had burned out, but the fading daylight streamed through the filth-stained windows, its murky glow falling across the wooden floor and the bodies strewn there.

Flayed. Every single one of them had been flayed.

This time, she couldn't hold it back. She bent double, stomach seizing as she retched over the floor. The sweet, sickly stench of her vomit mingled with the foulness of stale blood and loosed bowels, and she struggled for breath as she heaved again.

"Shite." Lachlan hurried to her side. "We need to get out of here, Isla. There's nothing we can do for this place."

"Eimhir." She coughed her name, throat burning as she spluttered it out. "I need to find out where she's going next so we can stop this happening again. She was *here*. I can feel it. I need to..."

The rest of her words caught in her throat as she trailed her eyes over the bar. The innkeeper lay sprawled across the tabletop, shirt ripped open to expose his ragged back. But it wasn't his flayed flesh that Isla couldn't look away from. It was the rippling folds of silver fur hanging proudly behind him.

A pelt. A selkie pelt, held fast to the wall with four long, rusted nails.

She swallowed. By the looks of it, the pelt had hung there for a long time. Its fur had lost its lustrous sheen and become dull and dry. The iron nails left orange stains around the holes they'd torn in the hide. It wasn't part of the recent violence that had spilled over Storwick. It had been here far longer than that, displayed for all to see like a trophy.

They were innocent, Lachlan had said.

A shiver crawled down her spine. Not so innocent after all, it seemed.

She moved towards the pelt. Eimhir had seen this too. She imagined the rage coursing through her as if it were her own. The echo of that pain lingered here still. If she reached for it, she might find a frayed thread she could follow.

A scream tore through the air, and she froze.

Lachlan moved before she did, hurrying to the doorway. All she could see in his silhouette was the stiffness in his shoulders, the bracing of his hand around his crutch.

"They're here." He turned to her, eyes dark with horror, lips blue from the chill in the air. "The gun-anam have us surrounded."

CHAPTER EIGHT

DARCE

For the third time in as many days since leaving the Sea Kith fleet, Darce reached for the magic thrumming in his veins and called on the haar to shroud the soulship in its damp cloak.

Another Admiralty patrol had appeared on the horizon, this one smaller than the last but no less of a threat for it. The soulship carried no cannons; it had no defence against the fleet's arsenal of iron and black powder. If they were spotted, they'd be boarded or blasted into pieces.

It was Darce's job to make sure that didn't happen.

Featherblade landed on the gunwale, shuffling its feathers. Its beady eyes surveyed the waves as they turned still and black once more under the soulless realm's flickering red sky.

"This again?" Muir joined them, a grey pallor across his weathered skin. "Is it too much to ask that we go a bloody day without having to slink back into this wretched place like bilge rats scurrying from a leak in the hull?"

"Would you prefer to take your chances with the Admiralty?" Darce glanced across the waves. Even with the haze of the haar between them and the patrol, he could make out the tall, proud masts of a man-o'-war alongside a pair of formidable frigates. "I'd have thought you of all people would understand the need to stay hidden."

"Doesn't mean I have to like it." Muir pulled a familiar flask from his coat pocket and took a swig, grimacing. "I never understood how the selkies lost all their soulships when they had the haar to hide them. But I feel it now. The weight of this place drains something out of you. They couldn't have stayed here for long, not without drowning. Sooner or later, they had to come up for air."

"And more often than not, the Admiralty was waiting for them." Darce held his breath as they slipped past the patrol, the swirling mists around the soulship turning them into ghosts. It seemed impossible that they should be able to drift by without being seen. But Muir was right—there was a price to be paid every time he summoned the haar. He felt it in his bones like a chill he couldn't shake, a damp that sank so deep it would never leave.

He wasn't a selkie. He couldn't be infected by mist sickness. But that didn't mean the haar would continue to let him pass through unscathed.

"That's the last we'll see of those bastards for a wee while, at least." Nishi trudged down from the helm, shaking her wet coils of hair from her tricorne hat. "Île de Durgavie is too close to Bréchon for the Admiralty to maintain any more than a token presence out here. We might be sailing to the arse end of nowhere, but at least we'll be able to breathe easier."

Muir snorted. "You've clearly not spent much time amongst the locals, if that's what you think. The Îleanach are fiercely independent and see themselves neither as Silvish nor Bréch. They don't usually take kindly to outsiders showing up uninvited, no matter which side of the sea they're from."

"Clearly they make some allowances, if your information is sound." Darce folded his arms. "*Is* your information sound, Muir? If we've come all this way only to find—"

"You think I'd risk leaving my niece and nephew behind to chase after something I thought was a dead end?" Muir glared at him, screwing the lid onto his flask. "One of my best informants died during the fall of

Arburgh to get me this lead. I trust it as much as I can trust anything these days. If you want a shot at taking down Alasdair, this is our best chance of clearing a path through those sentinels willing to kill for him."

"I was only—"

"Fuck off." Muir dismissed him with a crude gesture and stormed towards the hold, muttering something as he trudged down the steps.

Nishi sent him a sidelong look. "He always this pleasant?"

"Muir is a...complicated man." Darce leaned over the gunwale, staring into the water. The depths were so opaque he couldn't see anything below the surface. "Sometimes I think he would do anything to atone for the mistakes he's made. Other times, I fear he's just waiting for the guilt to kill him."

Nishi quirked an eyebrow. "Is it true he has the auld blood, like you?"

"He is—he *was*—Cunningham's sentinel," Darce said. "I don't understand how he found the strength to turn on him. I know how deep the blood oath runs. But Muir...he cut himself off from the tides. The sea spirits no longer answer his call. All he has left are the echoes of the wrongs he feels he must right."

"I imagine that makes for pretty poor company." A shadow fell over Nishi's face, haunting the circles around her eyes. Her burns from the *Jade Dawn* weren't the only scars she bore. That kind of loss, that kind of grief, carved deep.

"The Admiralty has taken something from us all," Darce said. "Each of us has reason to want to put an end to Cunningham."

Nishi barked out a laugh. "I don't want to put an end to him. After what he's done, I want him to *burn*. Him and his entire fucking fleet. I want him to feel everything my crew suffered, and then I want to bring him back and make him suffer it all again."

Her words hung between them like a blade. Darce almost felt the edge of it on his skin. He couldn't blame Nishi, not after seeing the blackened wreckage of the *Jade Dawn*, the charred corpses strung up on its masts. Some wounds ran too deep to be satisfied with blood.

Yet we spill it anyway, a voice in his head reminded him. *Over and over again, until we forget where the first cut came from.*

A shiver crept over his skin. This was a course he'd sailed before. He only had the desperate hope that this time, things would be different. This time, the violence they were chasing might be the thing that brought change, brought peace.

Featherblade rustled its feathers and leapt from the bow, throat rattling with a low trill that sounded like a mournful laugh.

Île de Durgavie rose from the swell like a beacon, imbuing the dusky sky with an orange glow from the hundreds of lanterns strung around its steep stone streets. Most of the port was built into the huge cliff face that dominated the island, rising in uneven layers from the harbour to the summit.

Darce was grateful for the cover of darkness as they drifted into the docks. The sheen of the soulship's bone hull was less noticeable under a cloudy sky, and the less attention they drew to it, the more chance they'd have of making it back to open waters without any trouble.

Muir shot him a look as they traipsed down the gangway. "You still think it's a good idea to leave the Sea Kith behind?"

"She's saved our lives more than once," Darce said. "I trust her."

"You trusted her back in Arburgh. That didn't stop her running."

"She ran because the *Jade Dawn* was burning, in case you've forgotten," Darce shot back. "Nishi is on our side. She wants the same thing we want. Besides, I don't know how you expect her to run anywhere on a ship with no sails. The soulship needs me to carry it across the waves."

Muir grunted. "It needs a sentinel. Doesn't have to be you."

"Do you always have to be so bloody—" Darce suppressed a sigh and turned to the jetty. "Never mind. Let's get on with this. Featherblade will find us if there's any trouble. We should seek out this contact of yours and see if they know anything that will lead us to where Cunningham is keeping his sentinels' families."

He let Muir lead him through the narrow streets, keeping one hand on the hilt of the rapier. Bringing his claymore on shore would have been an invitation for trouble, Muir had warned him, and Darce had enough sense not to argue the matter. The rapier's blade was long and thin, but it knew the way to a man's organs. If trouble found them, he'd be ready to answer.

They climbed the port's sprawling levels, trudging up smooth marble steps and twisting through alleys and wynds. As night fell and the purple-washed sky darkened to a deep black, the streets remained bathed in a glow from the oil lamps in the windows and lanterns strung from building to building.

It didn't feel like anywhere in Silveckan. Darce caught snippets of conversation as he walked—a strange mixture of Breçh and Silvish, low and lilting all at once. There was a fervour in the air he couldn't place, a giddy tension in the bustle spilling out onto the street. Part of him felt swept away by it.

Muir chuckled. "Makes you wonder, doesn't it?"

"Makes you wonder what?"

"How it might feel to live in a world without the Admiralty." He jerked his head towards a young woman in a garish yellow skirt who was selling shortbread from a heather-woven basket tucked in the crook of her arm. "You think she needs a vendor's permit? You think the tavern in the corner there has a curfew? Cunningham's tariffs and taxes mean nothing here. These islanders don't live under his yoke, and you can smell it on them."

Darce snorted. "I hardly think tariffs and taxes compare to the other horrors that bastard has inflicted on Silveckan."

"Then you need to pay closer attention." Muir's eyes hardened. "All that time you spent at his side, and you still haven't got the measure of the man. Everything Alasdair does, everything he's ever done, can be traced back to one thing: his greed. His abject, insatiable desire to possess that which he does not have, that which he *cannot* have. The ever-expanding trade routes, the reaping of port coffers, the accumulation of sentinels at his side...it's all hiding the poison underneath—a thirst that cannot be slaked."

A cold trickle of understanding seeped into Darce's chest. "And Mara... *Isla*..."

"Aye, now you're getting it." Muir's mouth twitched into a grim smile. "He cannot simply *have* something without the urge to utterly own it, consume it. And then he wonders why he is left with nothing at the end of it all. He won't stop, not when he believes he was robbed of something that should have been his."

He tossed a coin to the woman with the basket, plucking a couple of squares of shortbread in return. Darce took the piece he was offered, savouring the sweet, buttery flavour as the biscuit dissolved on his tongue.

"Tastes good, doesn't it?" Muir wiped the crumbs from his mouth with the back of his sleeve. "Freedom does that to a person. I couldn't give Mara hers until it was too late, and I'll never forgive myself for that. But there's still a chance for Isla. Whatever it costs to buy that freedom, it's a price I'm willing to pay." He fixed Darce with a forceful, unblinking stare. "Do you understand?"

Something in the steel of his voice made Darce shiver. It was easy to forget the mettle of the man who lay underneath the liquor-fuelled guilt, a man fearsome enough to carve a place at the Grand Admiral's side.

He nodded. "I understand."

Muir held his gaze, brow furrowed as if he were about to say something else. Then he turned to the polished marble steps leading to the upper echelons of the port, where grand villas and lofty watchtowers loomed atop the cliffside.

"Let's go," he said. "We have an exiled sentinel to meet."

By the time they reached the brasserie where Muir's contact was rumoured to be found, Darce's legs were aching. The climb was steep and relentless, the steps too numerous to count. Far below, the harbour was a shadow, the docks too distant to pick out the soulship. Under different circumstances, he might have allowed himself a moment to admire the view: the muted orange warmth from the lanterns bedecking the buildings, the sheer steepness of the cliffs, the snaking streets and marble steps leading down to the sea. Instead, he focused on the pounding of his heart—not just from exertion, but anticipation of what might come next.

Muir was breathing sharply, a sheen of sweat pearling across his forehead. But there was a fervent glint in his eye Darce hadn't seen since Arburgh.

"This is the place," he said, gesturing to the brasserie. "Don't have much to go on but a name. Hamish."

Darce trailed his gaze over the building. Half a dozen archways were cut into whitewashed stone, leading into a cosy, bustling hall. Even from the courtyard, he could smell the scent of grilled squid and rich wine wafting out from the kitchens. It didn't seem like the kind of place Muir's smuggler contacts would frequent, but he'd learned by now not to leave anything to chance.

"I suppose there's nothing for it but to head inside and start asking around," Darce said. "Let's do it carefully, though. If these folk don't take kindly to outsiders, the last thing they'll want is us sticking our noses where they don't belong."

They ducked through one of the archways and headed to the bar. A gleaming quartz countertop stretched along the length of the room, surrounded by tall stools boasting plump cushions of lilac and mauve.

Darce climbed onto one, eyes flitting around the room as Muir leaned in to talk to the barkeep in hushed tones. There was nothing he could do but wait, but it was difficult with the restless energy coursing through him. It suddenly struck him how far they were from Silvish shores, how vast the distance was between him and Isla. If Muir was wrong about this, if they were chasing nothing but a dead end...

He bounced his leg and tried to ignore the low hum of chatter echoing through his remaining ear. The barkeep set down a carafe of wine, but Darce's stomach was wound too tightly for a drink. It wasn't just nerves—something was *off* about this place. He sensed it racing through his veins, almost like...

He stilled. "Do you feel that?"

Muir took a long sip of wine, the ruby-coloured liquid disappearing quickly from his glass. "Feel what?"

There was no mistaking it; his blood was singing with the call of magic. The restlessness he'd felt was the pull of the tides as they surged through his veins.

Another sentinel was nearby. And if Darce sensed their presence, it could only mean one thing—auld blood had been spilled.

"We should go," he muttered. "Before we overstay our welcome."

A low, throaty chuckle rumbled behind him. "You're a wee bit late for that, *m'ami*."

Darce turned, his hand drifting to the rapier tucked under his coat. A tall, flaxen-haired man stood before him, observing him with folded arms and a thin smile. There was nothing imposing about his lean stature, but one look at the twin stiletto daggers peeking from his belt told Darce all he needed to know about how much trouble they were in.

Muir, on the other hand, seemed unperturbed. "About time someone showed up. Was beginning to think I'd walked into the wrong bar."

"Oh, you are quite correct on that account." The man's smile grew sharper. "An unfortunate *erreur* on your part, coming here and asking all the wrong questions."

"On the contrary; it seems I was asking exactly the right questions. They drew you out, did they not?" Muir matched the man's smile with a maddening grin of his own. "Now, is Hamish willing to come and have a wee chat, or are we going to be stuck relaying messages through a lackey?"

"There will be no *chat*." The man's hands dropped to the leather-wrapped handles of his daggers. "You will leave, or we will return you to your precious Admiralty in pieces."

"Admiralty? But we're not..." Darce trailed off at the amusement on Muir's lips. "What manner of shite have you been saying?"

"Only that Hamish and I once shared a certain vocation, even if our paths never crossed." Muir tilted his head, regarding the flaxen-haired man with interest. "I didn't specifically mention the Admiralty. The Îleanach are notoriously distrustful at the best of times, let alone when the fleet is involved. So it seems strange that this charming fellow has made that connection. I didn't expect Hamish would be so open about who he once worked for."

There was no humour on the man's face now, just a stony glare. "This is your last chance to leave."

Darce eyed the daggers at his waist. The man might have been lean-built, but he was lithe. He'd strike fast and hard, looking to end things quickly with a slash to the throat. But Darce had more than steel at his disposal. The tides surged in his blood. With a flick of his fingers, he could summon a gust of sea wind to shatter the windows. The distraction wouldn't last long, but it might buy them enough time to escape with their lives.

Then he felt it again—the presence of the other sentinel's magic brushing against his own. He couldn't tell where it was coming from, only that it surrounded him, smothering his own connection to the tides. A lump lodged in his throat, and when he coughed, he tasted salt on his tongue.

"*Du calme,*" another voice said, soft and quiet. "I like this place, and I'd rather not have to find another establishment to drink in."

Darce turned slowly. Standing before him was a man a few years his elder, with dark hair greying at the temples and a calm, measured air in his green eyes. His goatee was trimmed in Breçh fashion, but when he spoke, his accent was thick with the rolling lilt of Silveckan's highlands.

"Hamish, I presume?" Darce asked guardedly.

"I was, once. In another life, when I was a different man." A strained smile stretched his lips. "These days, I go by Jacques."

Muir rolled his eyes. "Inspired. Well, *Jacques*, now that you've shown your face, you might as well join us for a drink. We've got a lot to talk about."

"Indeed." Jacques' smile tightened. "Like why a sea serpent presumed dead in the canals of Arburgh might show up in a simple brasserie halfway across the sea."

All the air felt like it had been sucked out of the room. Darce's mouth turned dry, his chest seizing. Muir had taken on an ashen hue, his fingers twitching around the neck of the carafe.

Jacques took the decanter from him and poured a glass, the ruby wine sloshing as he raised his hand in a sardonic toast.

"Now," he said, "let's find out what I've done to merit a visit from the Cirein-cròin himself."

CHAPTER NINE

ISLA

Isla stood on the tavern step, rooted in place by the cold grip of terror. Drifting across the cobbles were the wisping shadows of a dozen gun-anam.

She tried to breathe, but the wraiths had turned the haar thicker than before. It clung to every corner of the street, damp and freezing and saturated with salt.

"The scream," she rasped. "Cam—"

"Over there." Lachlan jerked his head towards the corner of the street, where a solitary figure had taken refuge in one of the doorways. Spirals of frost coated their dark skin as they shirked back from the approaching gun-anam, but there was no escaping the wraiths' frigid touch. Isla could already see tendrils of salt and spray forming, wrapping around Cam's exposed throat.

"Stop," she said, moving down the steps. "Let go."

The last time she'd commanded the gun-anam, the wraiths had bowed to her will. But she no longer had her pelt. The memories binding her to them were no longer hers. Without a way to reach them...

She drew the sgian dubh from her jacket. The diminutive blade glinted in her hand, its sharp edges waiting to be sated.

"I am trying to give you peace," she snarled. "If you would rather have blood, let it be mine."

A sting tore across her palm as she drew the blade across her flesh. Bright red droplets welled between her fingers, splattering onto the cobbles with a steady *tip-tip*.

"What are you doing?" Lachlan hissed.

She curled her hand and squeezed through the pain. "They follow Eimhir. Her blood runs in my veins. If I can use it to control them, I might be able to find her."

"You'll get yourself killed." He seized her elbow, pulling her back to the steps. "We need to grab Cam and return to the *Red Gale* before these mists drown us."

"They won't drown us if I—"

A guttural snarl tore through the quiet, and Isla froze, the rest of her words lost to the fear constricting her throat. She waited, heart pounding, as through the depths of the haar came a prowling shadow.

It was a deerhound. A worn leather collar hung around its gaunt neck, and its shaggy coat was matted with filth. But it wasn't until Isla saw its eyes that she understood.

They were red. Dark, glowing red.

"I suppose we know where the brollachan got to." Lachlan's hand drifted to the cutlass on his belt, but she stilled him with an urgent gesture. "Don't move. Don't do anything that might—"

The deerhound leapt.

She tightened her fingers around the bloodied handle of the sgian dubh, but Lachlan was quicker. He pushed her out of the way, lifting his crutch to fend off the snarling jaws of the possessed hound as it lunged for them. She felt its warm, rotting breath, the foaming spittle flying from its teeth. Its red eyes were deranged from the brollachan inhabiting its body, its mind lost somewhere under the spirit's hold.

Lachlan freed his cutlass from its sheath and swung it around, opening a gash along the deerhound's back. The dog gave a piteous whine, but it didn't flee like Isla expected. The brollachan wouldn't let it.

"Go, hurry." Lachlan glanced across the street to the mist-shrouded doorway. "Cam needs help. I'll be right behind you."

Not so long ago, she might have hesitated. The thought of leaving him to fend for himself... But Lachlan was not the same man she once knew. He'd changed—they both had. Pretending otherwise would only deepen the rift between them.

She nodded tersely, then hurried towards the other side of the street. The haar closed in, squeezing her lungs. Fluid filled her chest, and she coughed up a mouthful of bile and briny seawater. She was drowning, and this time, she had no pelt to save her, no sealskin in which she could retreat to safety.

The gun-anam hovering over Cam wavered as she approached. A fish-rot stench seeped from the decayed bones it wore in place of armour, each blackened rib dripping with silt and slimy fronds of seaweed.

Isla touched a hand to her own cuirass hidden under the woollen layers of her tunic. Mara's bones had once looked the same, rotting with the haar's corruption. Now they encased her chest in armour of glistening white, free of the rot that had infected them.

Take their suffering into your pelt, make their pain part of you, Mara had told her. *Without it, they'll be able to return to the sea. They'll be able to rest.*

But she no longer had her pelt. She had no way to take away this anguish, this agony.

The gun-anam released a low, rattling moan that shuddered through Isla's bones. She could *feel* the pain of it. Her fingers were numb around the handle of the sgian dubh as the wraith reached towards Cam, its tendrils squeezing the young Sea Kith's throat.

"No," Isla whispered, tasting blood on her cracked lips. "No more of this."

She lunged, sinking the sgian dubh into the gun-anam. The dagger met no resistance, and she stumbled, choking down a mouthful of seawater. Her ears filled with the rush of pattering droplets as the silver vapour of the wraith's remains dashed across the cobbles.

The haar swirled around her and the droplets rose, trickling back into the mists they'd emerged from. The gun-anam couldn't be killed. No matter how many wraiths she dispersed, it would never be enough, not until she had her pelt back. But at least she might have bought them some time.

Cam's neck was mottled with bruising and frostbite as they clambered to their feet. Each breath came faint and rasping, but when Isla met their eyes, she saw no terror there, only bewilderment.

"I didn't know," they muttered, head shaking. "How could I have known? That cold ..."

"It won't leave you, not entirely. But next time, you'll be ready for it." Isla stooped down to retrieve their cavalier hat from the cobbles, frost clinging to the wilting grouse feather tucked into the band. "Are you able to call on your magic?"

Cam took the hat, pulling the oversized brim low over their eyes. "The tides keep slipping from my grasp. I'll do what I can."

More gun-anam drifted towards them, their hollow breaths mingling with the roar of the sea. None bore any trace of the selkies they once were. All of that had been stripped away, leaving only the pain that had been inflicted on them.

One of the wraiths reached out with a wisping tendril, freezing the moisture on Isla's cheeks. She'd forgotten how cold their touch was, how deep it burrowed.

Her hand closed around the hilt of her sgian dubh, but Cam moved quicker, twisting their hands into a ward. A stream of filthy rainwater leapt from a half-frozen puddle at their feet in a glittering ribbon of water and ice.

"Stay back!" they snarled, thrusting their hands towards the wraith.

The stream of water arced like a whip, flying through the air to lash at the gun-anam. More silvery droplets splattered across the cobbles, showering Isla's face.

It wasn't enough. As the first gun-anam fell, more crept forward, billowing with the mist.

There were too many. The haar grew thicker, forcing seawater into Isla's bruised lungs.

She turned to the tavern steps. Lachlan was trying to fend off the brollachan, knocking the possessed deerhound aside with the end of his crutch as it lunged at him. He seemed loath to kill the creature, but the brollachan wouldn't give up control of its host as long as it remained alive.

Isla drew her pistol. It had been some time since the polished mahogany stock last rested in her palm, and it pulsed against her skin like the grip of an old friend.

Her finger curled around the trigger as she lined up the shot. At this range, the hound was an easy target. There was no wind, no rain to soak the powder and leave the pistol sputtering. All she had to do was squeeze.

The brollachan sprang again, its long, yellow teeth snapping mindlessly. It sank its jaws into the rosewood foot of Lachlan's crutch, almost tugging it free. There was no trace of the gentle, loyal deerhound behind those red eyes.

It was a pitiful, tormented thing. Putting it out of its misery would be a kindness. Yet her hand stayed.

She couldn't do it. It wasn't itself.

"Get moving!" Lachlan wrestled his crutch back and slashed at one of the deerhound's legs with his cutlass. A bloody gash opened across the fur, and the dog scrambled back with a yelp. "To the tender!"

He hauled himself across the cobbles, face pale and shining from exertion. Isla's fingers twitched around the pistol, almost slipping on the trigger. Then she lowered her hand, releasing a trembling breath. Something tugged in the pit of her stomach, though whether it was relief or shame or some twisted knot of the two, she couldn't be sure.

They stumbled through the streets, fighting through the blanket of fog shrouding the cobbled lanes and painted buildings. Isla could barely see a stride ahead. There was no way of knowing how much further it was to the shoreline where the tender lay waiting. She had to keep running, and pray the haar creeping at her heels didn't catch her.

"Almost...there," Cam spluttered. "Can feel...the tides again."

The mist was too thick to make out anything past the stretch of cobbles in front of her, but Isla could hear the lapping of waves against the shore.

Her heart leapt. The sea was near, promising to carry them from this horrid place. They just had to reach it.

Above, the mists thinned, revealing a dark sky. The oily red wash of colour was fading, leaving an eerie glow as the soulless realm bled away. Isla felt the change on her skin. The hairs on her forearms still stood rigid, but the bite came from the bitter coastal wind, not the haar's deathless touch.

It was a cold she welcomed, a cold she could live with.

She leapt from the boardwalk onto the shore, pebbles sliding beneath her boots. The waves broke against the stones in a comforting sigh, leaving trails of seafoam behind. Ahead, the tender rocked gently, waiting for them.

They were going to make it.

Cam reached the boat first, holding it steady as Lachlan hauled himself over the edge. "Those wraiths are still coming. I can call on the tides to carry us more swiftly, but if that mist catches us..."

Isla glanced over her shoulder. The gun-anam had followed them to the shore, their shadows rippling in the haar as they drifted closer. A fetid stench trailed through the air, carried by their brackish, rotten bones.

Cam was right. If they stayed any longer, the haar would smother them.

She hurried to the tender, boots splashing in the waves. Blood oozed from the gash on her hand, crimson droplets falling into the water. Her blood, *Eimhir's* blood.

She halted, staring at her palm. Why hadn't it worked? Why couldn't she control them like she had in the soulless realm?

"What are you *doing?*" Lachlan shot her a furious glare. "Get your arse in here before it's too late."

"I..." She couldn't explain it. If she left, part of her would linger here with the gun-anam. Part of her *was* gun-anam. "It's the only chance we have of finding her. The only chance *I* have. I'm sorry, brother."

She turned, steeling herself with an icy breath. There was no room for the guilt clawing at her chest, no place for the outrage that flashed across Lachlan's face. This was the only way. If the haar wanted to drown her, she would let it. She'd drown a hundred times over if that was what it took to find Eimhir. All she had to do was—

Something strong wrapped around her neck, and before she had time to struggle, she was falling backwards. A jolt of pain shot up her spine as she hit the floor of the tender, landing with a dull thud against the damp wood.

"Go, get us out of here!" Lachlan's voice rang out as he tossed his crutch to the side to grab an oar.

The next thing Isla felt was the heaving swell dragging the tender from shore with a gravelly crunch. Her stomach lurched as the small boat crested over the waves faster than the oars could carry them. Cam's magic at work, no doubt.

She eased herself onto her elbows, wincing at the dull twinge in her back. Lachlan's jaw was tight and unapologetic as he worked the oars. He'd done this. He'd dragged her away from the only hope she'd had.

"I thought you were with me," she said, anguish tearing at her throat. "You agreed Eimhir had to be stopped."

"I did. But that will never happen if you throw your life away trying to find her." His eyes darkened as he cast his gaze over the gash on her palm. "Tides, I thought you might have changed in these last few months, but you're as bloody-minded as ever. You never learn to let go, even when what you're clinging to is beyond your reach."

"She's not beyond my reach. The gun-anam would have led me to her."

"You don't know that. But you were desperate enough to gamble the lives of everyone on this entire island on it." He shook his head. "It isn't enough to find her, not if we lose you in the process. If we lose you, we lose *everything*."

Something in his voice splintered, and for a fleeting moment, she caught a glimpse of the brother she hadn't seen in months. One who was still reaching for her, though he'd never admit it.

She wasn't the only one who'd never learned to let go.

Before she could say anything, it was over. Lachlan's face settled back into the same rigid wall that had become so familiar to her, and he pulled away once more, leaving her with a dull ache in the hollow of her ribs.

Cam glanced between them uneasily. "Ye made it out alive. We all did. That's the only thing that matters. The *Red Gale* isn't far, and the tides seem to be on our side. It won't be long until we're back on board."

As they finished speaking, a wretched howl echoed across the waves, turning the hairs on Isla's arm rigid. The deerhound stood on the shore, its crazed eyes glowing red with the brollachan's infernal hold. It watched them as they slipped out of reach, saliva dripping from its rabid jaws. Then it retreated and disappeared into the mist.

Isla dug her nails into her palms in a fruitless effort to stop her hands from shaking. *You never learn to let go, even when what you're clinging to is beyond your reach.*

Was it any fucking wonder, when this was the sorrow it brought?

A sickening grief curled in her chest as she turned away and let the tears spill.

CHAPTER TEN

DARCE

Jacques led them outside to a private terrace at the corner of the brasserie, away from the bustle of the main establishment. The tension may have loosened a sliver, but Darce couldn't bring himself to relax. As far as he was concerned, the show of hospitality didn't prove anything apart from making it easier for the Îleanach to kill them without causing a scene.

As if to prove the point, Jacques' enforcer made a great display of drawing his stiletto daggers from his belt and laying them carefully on the table, where they glinted under the muted orange glow from the lanterns. He flashed Darce a smile that seemed more like he was baring his teeth. "Just so you don't fall under the illusion that this is a friendly chat."

"Peace, Sébastien." Jacques shot him a reproachful look. "None of us want this descending into bloodshed. We've all seen enough of it already."

Muir bristled. "Reckon you know me so well, do you, lad?"

"I know enough," Jacques said. "I don't blame you for not recognising me. You were an officer in the Admiralty last time we met, and I was a bairn barely up to my mother's waist. But I remembered you. Not many six-year-olds would forget meeting the legendary Cirein-cròin."

The weight of his words hung patiently in the air, as if waiting for Muir to catch up. There didn't seem to be any threat lacing their edges, but Darce had spent enough time around nobility to know better than to trust in pleasantries. It was too easy to get caught on the barbs under the surface.

Muir furrowed his brow. "Hamish, you said your name was?"

"It used to be, aye. Hamish Grier."

"Grier..." Realisation dawned on Muir's face. "Not Maggie Grier's wee laddie? Tides, I haven't seen your mother in over thirty years. That woman was the finest shipwright the capital had ever seen. She built—"

"The *Vanguard of the Firth*. I'm aware." Jacques' smile tightened. "She constructed the most fearsome ship Silveckan's shores have ever known. And then she died for the privilege."

Muir winced. "I heard rumours of an accident at the shipyards, but—"

"You heard wrong." An edge crept into Jacques' voice. "My mother did not have an *accident*. The Grand Admiral did what he always does with those whose gifts threaten his power. He removes them like pawns from the board."

The tension returned, making Darce's neck prickle in the cool night air. It was like his body knew something he didn't. Every muscle was on edge, waiting to strike.

On the other side of the table, Sébastien slouched in his chair, flaxen hair falling loosely. The way he regarded them seemed almost lazy, but Darce had seen enough to know those daggers weren't for show. If he needed them, they'd be in his palms in an instant.

Jacques fixed Muir with a weary look. "Why did you come here? You might have been the Cirein-cròin once, but the last I'd heard, that man lost himself in a bottle and wound up at the bottom of Arburgh's canals."

"Seems news takes a wee while to reach these parts," Muir said pleasantly. "I may have hit the bottle, but I also spent the best part of thirty years doing all I could to sabotage the Admiralty right under Alasdair's nose until I got caught a few weeks ago. Would have hanged for it, if it weren't for this one."

He jerked his thumb towards Darce, and Jacques' gaze followed, keen and appraising. "I felt your magic when you reached for the tides earlier," he said. "This place, and others like it in the port, are under my protection. The wards I set up here alert me to the presence of other sentinels. If the Grand Admiral thought to catch me off guard by sending you, he failed."

Darce bristled, heat rising under his collar. "Did you not listen to anything Muir told you? Neither of us is with the Admiralty. If you knew half the things—"

"This is a waste of time," Sébastien interrupted, leaning to retrieve one of his daggers from the table. He twirled the blade deftly, regarding them with hostility. "If Cunningham has sent his dogs, we should put them down."

Muir chuckled. "That won't be as easy as you think, lad. Better men than you have tried."

A strangled silence fell, ready to shatter at the slightest provocation. Darce was of half a mind to break it himself to be rid of the waiting. Whatever Muir had hoped to achieve by bringing them here, he wasn't going to get it. The way this was heading, they'd be lucky to get back to the soulship with their lives.

Jacques pursed his lips, turning to Muir. "You were his right hand, his sentinel. You earned a reputation as a seafarer with no equal but the serpent you shared your name with. The Cirein-cròin doesn't slink away like a common sea snake. And a man of your standing doesn't leave the Admiralty for no reason. I need to know why."

Muir scowled. "What does it bloody matter?"

"Because you're the reason he leashed the rest of us!" Jacques' voice rose, the edge of his words sharp and wounded. "Whatever manner of betrayal you inflicted on him, it was enough to condemn every sentinel who came after. He needed to be certain of his control. He needed a way to ensure we would do whatever was asked of us, because *you didn't*. You walked away, and he made sure nobody could follow in your footsteps."

"If that were true, you'd still be by his side."

Jacques gave a hollow laugh. "You think I didn't pay the price for my treason? It cost me *everything*."

"We know," Darce said. "That's why we're here. We know what Cunningham asks of his sentinels, what he takes from them to ensure their loyalty."

"You know, do you?" Bitterness curled at the corners of Jacques' mouth. "You understand how it feels to hold the weight of those you love in your hands, knowing you can only choose one of them? He took my mother. He held her life over my head like an axe waiting to fall. And when I told my captain the truth and we ran from the fleet, I knew what I'd forfeited by choosing to save him instead of her."

The echo of his words rang through the night air. Even out here, there was no escaping Cunningham's shadow. It stretched across the waves, poisoning everything it touched.

"We came here to start a new life away from the Admiralty, away from Cunningham's hold over us," Jacques continued, voice thin and distant. "It wasn't until a few months later that I heard word from home. News of the *accident*, as you called it. My father received a box, and in it, my mother's hands. He only knew it was her from the shipwright's guild tattoos on her wrists. Cunningham followed through on his promise."

"And your captain?" Muir asked. "Where is he now?"

"Gone," Jacques said stiffly. "I couldn't let go of my resentment, though it was my choice, and mine alone. I pushed him away. Our blood oath remains intact, but whatever else we were...that died when my mother did."

Darce's heart twisted. Jacques had made an impossible choice. For a fleeting, terrifying moment, he understood what had caused Rhona to drive a blade into her own captain's chest.

There's nae going back after what I've done. But there's nae living with it, either.

This was what Cunningham had driven them to. This was what they had to stop, no matter what it cost.

"Do you…" Darce swallowed, mouth dry around the words. "Do you have any idea where he's keeping the hostages?"

Jacques shook his head. "There's only one person I know capable of finding that place, and until an hour ago, I thought he was dead."

The air turned still. Not a breath of wind stirred. All Darce could hear over his own heartbeat was the muted conversation from the brasserie, muffled in his remaining ear.

Muir frowned. "None of this was happening while I was in the Admiralty. Alasdair had no need of prisoners or hostages back then—he had me. I have no idea where he's keeping those poor bastards."

"I didn't say you knew where it was. I said you knew how to find it." Jacques flicked his eyes towards Darce. "I told you before, this place is guarded by blood wards. As it happens, I got the idea from Cunningham himself. He's fond of using them to protect what's his." He turned to Muir. "He learned that from you, did he not?"

Muir's dark skin took on a pallor. Darce recognised the shadow behind his eyes; the weight of guilt measured in years.

"Your compass," Darce said slowly. "It led us to Mara's pelt. But it only started working after Isla held it in her bloodied hand. And the tomb where he kept her pelt…Isla said it was sealed. It only opened when her blood touched it…when *Cunningham's* blood touched it. You warded it."

"I was his sentinel," Muir said tersely. "There was a time I'd have done anything he asked of me. So aye, I set up those wards. I swallowed the lie, told myself I believed him when he said it was to keep Mara safe. But those were the only ones I cast for him. If he's got others, he's using another sentinel."

"Another sentinel, perhaps, but still his blood." A fervent gleam lit up

Jacques' eyes. "We both know how deep the oath runs between captain and sentinel. I've been separated from Ben for over a decade, and still I feel his presence like an ache. If I followed it, I'd find him. You could do the same."

The promise in his words crystallised in the air, and Darce's stomach lurched with a painful, desperate hope. If Jacques was right, if Cunningham had protected his prison with blood wards...Muir would be able to track them through his sentinel bond.

Muir's expression was like stone. "The wards you set up around this place...you say they alerted you to the sergeant, here. Tell me, lad, did they warn you of *my* presence?"

Jacques faltered, a small crease appearing in the middle of his brow. "I assumed—I didn't think you'd—"

"That'll be a no, then." Muir gave a hard smile. "There's a reason for that. The sea spirits haven't sung in my blood for twenty-five years. I suppressed my bond with Alasdair as much as I could without severing it entirely and risking killing us both. Whatever was anchoring me to him, it's long buried. And it's going to remain buried."

There was a cold edge to his voice Darce had never heard before. "Muir, think about what this means. You said you were willing to do whatever it takes. If we can use your bond with Cunningham to find that prison—"

"Not even the wrath of the tides themselves could compel me to open that bond again." Muir thumped his wine glass down on the table, splattering the cloth with ruby droplets. "We'll find another way to that forsaken place, or we'll crawl back to Silveckan empty-handed. But I won't go back to the man I was when I was his sentinel."

"Muir, wait."

It was no use. Muir was already rising, chair scraping across the terracotta stone as he pushed back from the table. His expression was impossible to decipher, so marred it was by the emotions etched in every line of his brow. Some of the pain, Darce recognised. The rest, he was glad he didn't.

Jacques watched him go, face pensive. "Who does he have?"

Darce frowned. "What are you talking about?"

"The Grand Admiral. There must be a reason you're set on finding his prison. A reason you sailed halfway to Breçhon chasing little more than a whisper. So tell me, who does he have?"

"It's not about who he has," Darce said. "It's about who he *doesn't* have. The woman I'm trying to protect, the one I made my blood oath to...she's his—she's a selkie." He closed his mouth around the rest of the truth. "Cunningham is hunting her. He won't stop until he finds her. I can't let that happen."

Sébastien flipped his dagger in his palm. "So it's not about freeing the hostages at all. It's about freeing his sentinels from the duty he's bound them to. You mean to take away all that protects him. You mean to kill him."

"I've killed him before," Darce said. "I mean to *end* him."

The words tasted like steel on his tongue. There could be no mistakes next time, no doubts about what he had to do. As long as Cunningham survived, Isla would never have peace. None of them would.

He pushed his chair out from the table, standing as abruptly as Muir had. "I have to go. Thank you for your hospitality, and your help. Whether you intended it or not, you've given us everything we need."

Jacques tilted his head. "You think you can change his mind? That didn't look like a man who could be talked down."

"He doesn't need to be." Darce glanced in the direction Muir had left. "Isla and I may be bound by blood, but she and Muir are family. That stubborn old bastard already knows what he's going to do, even if he isn't willing to admit it to himself yet."

Darce had almost made it back down to the harbourside by the time Featherblade found him. The huge white gannet was a strange sight in the night sky, wings stark against the darkness. It let out a customary shriek when it saw him, then banked sharply, leading him away from the docks towards an endless row of taverns lining the marina.

"No bloody surprise there," Darce muttered to himself, changing course. There was only one direction Muir turned in when the weight of guilt became too much to bear, and Darce couldn't let him drown in it. Not tonight, not with everything they'd lose if they failed.

He walked past the sheltered terraces with their hanging oil lamps and weaved through the stools and tables spilling across the boardwalk. There was no sign of Muir at any of them, but Featherblade glided overhead, a hushed yammering spilling from its beak as it led him further along the pier.

After a while, the tavern lights grew fainter and the bustle and chatter muted, leaving little noise but the gentle wash of waves against the cliffs. There was nothing ahead but a lone wooden jetty looking out to sea, and at the end of it, a solitary figure sitting in the glow of the moonlight.

Muir.

Darce approached slowly and sat beside him, taking in the stench of wine and sweat and salty air. Muir didn't say a word, just kept his dark eyes on the waves and drew a familiar flask from his coat pocket.

"Do you really think you should—" Darce reached for his arm, but Muir knocked it away.

Then he unscrewed the lid and toppled the flask on its side, dumping the amber-coloured whisky into the sea.

Darce sat silently, unable to find any words. A rich, peaty aroma wafted on the wind, then disappeared, carried off into the spray. For the first time in a long time, a measure of peace settled over him, loosening the ever-present knot in his chest.

"Sorry," Muir said, "about whatever speech you had planned to pull my head from my arse. I'm sure it was very compelling."

Darce chuckled. "You're an insufferable bastard, you know that?"

"Hardly the worst thing I've been called." He gave a tight smile, but the shadow hadn't lifted from behind his eyes. Darce could almost see Cunningham in their reflection, haunting Muir like a ghost.

"If I do this…" Muir grimaced. "I don't know if I *can* do this. But if it works, if I let the tides and their magic back into me, there's no escaping what comes next. Aye, I might be able to trace the wards Alasdair set around his prison. But it works both ways. The moment I reopen that connection, he'll feel it. He'll come for us."

"So be it," Darce said. "Better us than Isla and Lachlan."

"I didn't expect you to say something so reckless. From what I understand, your soul is the only thing keeping Isla from becoming one of those wraiths." Muir gave him a pointed look. "Have you considered the fate that would befall her should you get yourself killed?"

Darce stilled, fear turning his blood to ice. Muir was right. It wasn't just his life, his soul, he stood to lose. He'd bound himself to Isla.

There was part of me Eimhir couldn't take, she'd told him. *The part of your soul you gave me.*

All his darkest thoughts were consumed with the fear of losing her. But if he should be the one to fall, if she were to lose him…

There were some fates worse than death. The gun-anam were proof of that.

"If there is a price to be paid for what we're about to do, it's me who'll pay it," Muir said. "Whatever happens, you have to live. For her."

"You can't expect me to—"

"Those are my terms." There was no humour in Muir's voice now, only steel. "If you want me to get us to that prison, you'll bloody well accept them."

He climbed to his feet, tucking the empty flask into his coat pocket and offering an outstretched hand.

Darce took it. It was a bargain he wanted no part of, but one he couldn't refuse. Not with what was at stake for both of them.

They walked back to the soulship in silence. The sight of the mast rising into the sky, bone gleaming in the dim light of the moon, brought a swell of emotion to Darce's chest—hope and fear and dread all tangled together, impossible to unpick. As soon as Muir opened his bond to Cunningham again, they'd be summoning a storm they couldn't outrun.

A storm Darce didn't *want* to outrun.

"You two have some explaining to do." Nishi was waiting at the soulship's prow as they trudged up the gangway. Featherblade gave a cheerful cry and swooped over her head, almost taking her tricorne hat off. She glared up at it, then turned back to them, drumming her fingers on the gunwale. "I thought you went ashore to find information, not pick up strays."

"Strays?" Darce paused. "What do you mean by..."

Nishi stepped aside, revealing two familiar figures standing on deck.

"It wasn't difficult to track you down," Jacques said with an apologetic shrug. "We don't get many outsiders coming to Île de Durgavie, and your ship stands out."

Darce held his hands steady. This time, when he reached for the tides, they answered at once, filling him with their icy swell. He felt the salt in his veins, the currents rushing through him as the waves surrounding the soulship started to churn. Whatever wards Jacques had set up to protect the brasserie, they had no effect here.

Sébastien seemed to have come to the same conclusion and reached for the stiletto daggers on his belt. Jacques stilled him with a sharp gesture, then fixed Darce with a solemn look. "We're not here for trouble."

"Then what *are* you here for?"

"You came to us for help," Jacques said. "Are you so eager to leave without it?"

Darce loosened his grasp on the waves. The swirling eddies lingered around the ship, promising to rise if he called on them again. "We already have what we came here for. Muir can get us where we need to go."

"Getting there is one thing. But do you truly believe you can take that prison alone?" Jacques glanced at Muir. "You know the Grand Admiral better than I do, but I know him well enough to fear what waits in that place. The blood wards he's set up to protect it will be the least of its dangers."

Muir grunted. "If the thought of it is enough to make you piss your breeks like a bairn, why would you want to come? What's in it for you?"

"My mother died in that place." Jacques' voice pitched low, his throat constricting around the words. "The only part of her my father got to bury was her severed hands. I need to see her grave for myself. Then, I need to burn the whole fucking place to the ground."

The air turned brittle, and Darce fought the urge to shiver. "And him?" he asked, nodding at Sébastien.

"Séba has never met an Admiralty throat he didn't want to cut," Jacques said. "He's rather good at it, too."

Sébastien folded his arms across his lean chest. His daggers glinted in the moonlight, their pristine points thirsty for blood. Darce didn't doubt they'd be put to good use against the Admiralty. He just wasn't sure if he was willing to risk finding one of them in his own back.

"Well?" Jacques met his gaze steadily. "What will it be?"

Darce stiffened. These men were strangers. A shared enmity towards the Admiralty wasn't enough for him to trust them, not when so much hung on Cunningham's death. If this chance slipped, he'd never get another.

Before he could answer, Featherblade cawed and leapt from its perch, flapping into the night sky until it was a faint silhouette against the moon. Darce waited for it to return to the mast, but it remained above the waves, circling the gaping mouth of the harbour.

Nishi moved beside him, tracking the gannet across the sky. "It's unwise to ignore a guidebird when it's telling you to get underway. If Featherblade is content to sail with them, that's enough for me. It should be enough for you too."

The waves lapped against the soulship's hull. There was still a stirring in his veins, but it was no longer agitated. Instead, it felt like a current, promising to carry him where he needed to go.

The tides had taken him this far. Who was he to ignore their will?

He turned to Jacques. "Burn the whole fucking place to the ground, you said?" A grim smile unfurled at the corners of his mouth. "Then I suppose we better get started."

CHAPTER ELEVEN

ISLA

Though Storwick and the last lingering traces of the haar were far behind them, Isla couldn't help but shiver as she climbed the stairs from her cabin to the *Red Gale's* deck. The morning sky was pale and bright, but that wasn't enough to defuse the tension that had hung over the ship ever since they'd returned.

Not for the first time, she found Ruairidh glaring at her from the helm, the scar behind his eyepatch twitching. Cam had spent the last few days fighting off a wretched cough, and Ruairidh's mood had grown fouler every hour the young Sea Kith sentinel had been confined to their cabin.

"It will pass," Isla had assured him. "The haar doesn't afflict humans the way it does selkies. Its touch is cold and cruel, but it won't drag Cam to the fathoms."

His only reply had been a curled lip and a threatening hand on the hilt of his dirk. Isla had kept her distance since then.

Now, she found Cam by the bow once more, weaving wards above the waves. Their dark brown skin had recovered from the ashen pallor that had settled over it, but the lingering rasp of their cough scratched as they called out to Isla in greeting.

"The winds are with us this morning," they said with a grin. "I've never known the *Red Gale* to cut through the waves so cleanly. Perhaps it's because Swiftclaw has returned."

"Swiftclaw?"

Cam gestured to the sky, and Isla followed their gaze to find a sea eagle circling above them. The bird was huge—twice the size of Featherblade, at least—with speckled grey-brown plumage and a flash of white tail feathers. Even from this far below, she could make out the deadly curves of its yellow talons and hooked beak as it rose higher, wings stretched wide.

"It's a wild spirit, even for a guidebird," Cam said. "Often stays away for weeks at a time. But it always comes back when we need it."

As if it had heard them, the eagle pierced the air with a piping cry, leaving Isla's ears ringing. "You think we need it now?"

"After what we saw in that village? I'd say so." Cam shook their head, sombre-eyed. "I'd heard stories about the haar before. But until I felt its touch, I never realised I could feel so cold. It was like the fathoms themselves spilled into my lungs. Part of me fears they're still there, waiting to drag me under." They sent Isla a sidelong look. "Is it true what they say about the mist sickness? That it can infect a selkie with so much despair they lose all sense of who they are?"

Isla flinched, the words striking close to the bone. Thinking about Eimhir brought an ache she couldn't easily bury, no matter how hard she tried. "It's not something you need to worry about."

"Aye, see, that's where ye might be wrong." Cam pulled the brim of their hat further over their face. "I probably should have mentioned this before, but...well, there's a reason the cap'n didn't want me going to shore. I don't just have the auld blood. I've got selkie blood too."

"Selkie blood?" Isla startled. "But you're..." The words died on her lips. No pelt hung around Cam's shoulders in rippling folds of sleek fur. No salt scars crawled across their skin from a soul stripped from them.

They didn't have a pelt. They'd *never* had a pelt.

Just like her, not so long ago. She remembered the hole in the hollow of her chest, the absence of something she'd never known she'd lost. She'd never understood the ache of that missing part until she'd taken Mara's soulskin as her own.

"It was my father," Cam supplied, their gaze drifting to the water. "I never knew him—never got the chance. One day, when my mother was carrying me in her belly, he took to the waves and didn't come back. She feared he'd been captured and killed. Perhaps that was easier to believe than the other fear, that he'd left her to return to his people—left us both. Only the tides ken the truth, and they're not for talking."

"I…I'm sorry." Isla curled her hands, nails digging into her palms. "I know the agony of not having the answer to who you are. The pain of feeling unmoored, adrift from who you think you should be. I wish there was more I could give you than words that will never be enough."

"I don't need answers, not anymore," Cam said. "I learned too sore a lesson in chasing them. It cost me everything."

There was a weight to their voice that seemed too raw, too heavy, for someone barely free from the lingering touches of adolescence. But Isla had heard that kind of brokenness before. She'd seen it in the shadows that haunted Nishi's face.

"Your captain," she said. "Ruairidh said you were a sentinel, but not *his* sentinel."

Cam nodded. "When my mother died, my aunt took me on board her ship, though it was no place for a bairn. It was the first place I started to feel…*me*. Barely a week later, we were set upon by storm harpies, and she fell defending me. Their screeches rattled in my ears as I knelt to the *Red Gale's* deck and made the blood oath to save her. From then on, she wasn't just my aunt, she was my captain." A rueful smile tugged at their lips. "I was twelve years old. I had no idea what the oath meant at the time, but my aunt was bleeding from a harpy claw meant for my throat and I knew couldn't lose anyone else I loved. Not that day, anyway."

Isla swallowed. "What happened?"

"She saw the pain pulling at me every day, the slow rot inside me from not knowing who I really was. She did everything she could to heal me from that wound. And she paid the price for it." Cam closed their eyes. "I didn't know she'd been trying to find the Selkie Isles until their raiders boarded and started slaughtering us. They didn't want to hear our reasons for being there. They didn't care."

Isla's blood turned cold. She knew how fiercely her people defended the waters around Eileanan Selch. No ship that set its sights upon selkie shores could be allowed to leave. The price of safety was the annihilation of any ship that strayed too close.

"One of them killed my aunt in front of me." Cam's voice was thin. "As her blood washed across the *Red Gale's* deck, I felt my oath break, and I was ready to follow her to the fathoms. But then the skinchanger looked at me. He stared into my eyes, and something changed in him. It was like he *knew* me. Perhaps he recognised some reflection of my selkie father in my features. Whatever it was, it was enough to stay his hand."

"He let you go?"

"He spared the few of us that were left," Cam said. "Including my aunt's first mate."

Realisation flooded Isla's chest. "Ruairidh."

"He loved her. He loved her enough to keep living after his own sentinel was butchered and flayed." Cam lifted their chin, meeting Isla's gaze with wet, shining eyes. "I'm not Ruairidh's sentinel. It is not a blood oath the cap'n and I share, but a promise to my aunt's memory. One we both swore to keep."

One of your people's chieftains owes me a debt, Ruairidh had told her. *When you get your pelt back, you'll make sure I'm given the chance to settle it.*

"The selkie who killed your aunt," Isla whispered. "The one who let you go. Do you have a name?"

Cam shook their head. "Only a face. An umber-eyed man, his pelt black as night. I'll remember him until the day my blade meets his heart."

Duncan. It hit her like a blow, knocking the air from her lungs. Part of her had known before the truth left Cam's lips. It had to be him. There was nothing Duncan wouldn't do to protect Eileanan Selch.

Nothing, perhaps, except lay a hand on the child of a friend.

You still don't understand, do you? he'd said to her once. *You're Mara's wee girl. You were never in any danger from me.*

When Isla met Cam's eyes again, their tears were gone, leaving only steel behind. "I don't mourn the loss of a pelt I never had. The only part of my soul that ever mattered is already with the fathoms. All I care about is killing the man who sent it there, so I can join my captain again."

The weight of her conversation with Cam sat heavy in Isla's chest over the next few days, like a dragging anchor she couldn't cut herself loose from. Though her lungs yearned for the crisp bite of sea air, she remained below deck as much as she could bear, preferring the stale confines of her cabin to the scrutiny in Ruairidh's one-eyed gaze.

He wanted Duncan. And Isla had given her word to deliver him.

A bitter taste rose in her throat. It was a betrayal she'd never intended, one she didn't know if she could follow through on. Duncan had let her go back in Arburgh. He'd given up the soulship without a fight for the sake of Mara's memory. For *her.* She'd spent months fearing him, waiting for a betrayal that never came.

At least, not from him.

It was too much. The red-stained timber closed in around her, threatening to suffocate her if she stayed down here any longer. She needed to see the blue-green stretch of the horizon again. She needed the freedom of the waves, even if she could no longer reach them.

She leapt up the stairs two at a time and rushed to the gunwale, fingertips digging into the wood as she sucked in one breath, then another. The frantic thumping of her heart bruised her ribs, leaving her aching.

This was a mistake. She should never have come aboard this ship. She'd thought this was where she needed to be, but she felt more adrift than ever.

"There you are." Lachlan hauled himself towards her, crutch under one arm and a rolled-up sheet of parchment tucked under the other. "I've been looking for you everywhere. You can't keep avoiding me forever."

Isla stiffened. "I wasn't—" The rest of the lie died on her tongue. The tension between them had thickened again since Storwick. The only reason it hadn't suffocated her yet was because she'd been doing her damnedest to act like it didn't exist.

Lachlan motioned to the navigator's table, clearing a space to unfurl a large, ink-stained map. "Turns out the Sea Kith don't put much stock in charts. They prefer to let the tides take them where they please. But they let me rake through some of their prizes, all the shite they've not got around to selling yet, and I found this."

Isla brushed her fingers over the parchment. The smooth sheepskin surface left her hands tingling, reminding her of another life, the life she'd chosen when she'd first left Silveckan all those years ago. Even then, she'd felt the stirring of the sea deep within her bones. She just hadn't understood what it meant.

"We know they hit Storwick," Lachlan said, trailing his finger across the chart until it landed on the small inlet on the west coast. It sat above Arburgh, hiding in the capital's shadow.

All the horror from that night hit Isla anew as she stared at the rough mark on the chart. Here, it was a village not of stone and timber and people, but a scratching of ink against parchment. Storwick didn't exist anymore. The village was lost. The charts just didn't know any better.

"One of the Sea Kith ships sent word of an attack on Shielness a few days ago," Lachlan continued, tracing the coastline further north. "It's a quiet place, mostly known for its kelp harvesting. And then..." He tapped a small spit of land jutting out. "Carroncross. There are only whispers, but all the signs point to—"

"A pattern," Isla said. "They've been moving north ever since Arburgh. These villages, the distances... Eimhir is only resting long enough to regather her strength before striking again. With each village that falls, the haar spreads further. Before long, there will be no safe ports left on the west coast."

Lachlan pored over the chart. "If they keep heading north, we might be able to catch them at—"

"Wait. They didn't hit Kinraith?" Her eyes fell across a narrow bay guarded by fierce rocks. The ink bled across the parchment in jagged letters, spelling the port's name. But Kinraith wasn't just a name. She'd been there; she'd seen its bustling docks, its sprawling markets, the fearsome sea stacks rising around the harbour, ready to impale any ship that drifted off course. It wasn't as large a port as Arburgh, nor as formidable. The rocks might have provided protection against ships, but they wouldn't stop a selkie attack.

So why had Eimhir avoided it?

A crease formed between Lachlan's brows as he examined the chart again. "The Sea Kith haven't mentioned anything about Kinraith. But you're right—it falls directly in the path of Eimhir's attacks. If she left it alone, there must be a reason." He lifted his gaze. "You know her better than I do. What do you think?"

It was difficult to tell whether his words were a peace offering or an accusation. She *did* know Eimhir better than him, better than anyone. Or she'd thought she did. Now, she wasn't sure how much of her cousin was left and how much the mist sickness had gnawed away, leaving nothing but the husk of who she once was.

"Eimhir wants Silveckan to suffer like her people—*our* people—have suffered." The words wrenched from her throat. "The only reason she'd spare a place like Kinraith is if it was a fight she couldn't win."

"Kinraith isn't the capital," Lachlan said. "She risked more in Arburgh."

A scoff carried across the wind behind them. "Then you need to ask yourselves what might be waiting in Kinraith that's enough to keep her away."

Isla turned to find Ruairidh watching them, his mouth stretched into a humourless smile. His long red braid shifted over his shoulders as he crossed the deck, each stride slow and purposeful.

He cast his eye over the chart. "You won't catch her following ink on parchment. I thought a selkie would understand that."

"I understand fine," she said curtly. "But if we can use her movements to establish a pattern, we might be able to—"

"You're trying to hunt her." Ruairidh regarded her with a scathing look. "That's a mistake. Those creatures know what it's like to be hunted. They won't let themselves be caught easily. Instead of chasing her down, you should be drawing her out."

"If it were that simple, do you not think I would have—"

Ruairidh's hand flew to his belt, and he drew the long, serrated blade of his dirk. Iron glinted in the morning light as he held the dagger aloft, then plunged it into the middle of the parchment. It trembled there, blade wobbling back and forth in the wound it had ripped through the sheepskin surface.

Isla looked back to the chart, where the dirk perfectly split the inked letters spelling Kinraith.

"Think about it, selkie lass," Ruairidh said. "What would be enough to keep her away from there? What would keep *you* away?"

Though the sky was clear, her skin prickled with a shadow she couldn't escape. It was a ghostly breath on her neck, an echo haunting her footsteps. "The Admiralty," she said. "That's what's waiting in Kinraith."

The moment she spoke the words, a cold grip wound its fingers around her heart, squeezing until she could barely breathe. She tried to push it away, willing the frantic thrumming in her chest to settle. If she let herself feel the fear, she'd drown in it.

This isn't a problem you can ignore, Muir had warned her.

"It makes sense," Lachlan said slowly. "The Grand Admiral would have needed to find somewhere to regroup and consolidate what's left of the fleet. Still, I thought they might've headed southeast and gathered at one of the lowland ports. Kinraith lies too close to the capital, too close to where the haar first started spreading."

"That's why he chose it," Isla said despite herself. "His pride won't allow him to abandon Arburgh. That city was a symbol of the Admiralty's might. He wants to find Eimhir as much as we do."

Lachlan fixed her with a measured gaze. "And if he finds her first?"

The question cleaved deeper than she expected, paring away her attempts at denial until all that remained was a truth too painful to consider. If Cunningham found Eimhir first, if he stripped her pelt from her corpse and took it for himself, Isla would be left with only one choice.

"Then I'll go back," she said, the admission sour on her tongue. "I'll submit to his every condition. I'll be the caged daughter he wants me to be. As long as I can clear the haar, it will be worth it. It has to be."

Lachlan baulked. "You can't seriously... Galbraith would never let you—"

"*Don't.* Not now." She turned to Ruairidh, who was watching her with an inscrutable expression. "Even if the Admiralty has berthed in Kinraith, I fail to see how that helps us in drawing Eimhir out like you suggested. The fleet's presence is precisely why she's avoiding it."

"A fight she couldn't win, that's what you said." The pale grey tattoos around Ruairidh's eye shifted as his mouth curled into a smile. "But what if we tipped the scales in her favour?"

Isla stilled as the implication behind his words washed over her. "You want to strike at the Admiralty? In Kinraith, of all places?"

"I don't see why not." Ruairidh shrugged his huge shoulders. "It wouldn't be as much of a risk as engaging the bastards in open waters. They'll be pinned behind those rocks, and we have no need to take prizes.

We just need to make them scream loud enough that your selkie friends come swimming."

Something twisted in the pit of Isla's stomach. Eimhir was no fool. She wouldn't risk rushing into anything she sensed might be a trap. For Ruairidh's plan to work, Kinraith's harbour would have to run red with Admiralty blood. It had to be real. Only that would be enough to draw Eimhir out.

"If we do this, we're no better than the selkies," Lachlan said heatedly. "The fighting won't be contained to the harbour. It will spill into Kinraith itself. Its people will be caught up in this, just like Storwick...just like Caolaig."

She tried not to wince at the way his voice cracked, the way the memories of that night broke off from his words like shards burying under her own skin. "If we do nothing, Kinraith may survive a few more weeks, a few more months. But Eimhir won't stop. She'll hit another fishing village instead, another port. And *that* will be just like Caolaig." She met his gaze. "I want this to end. But no matter what we choose here, more blood will spill before it's over."

As she spoke the words, she hated herself for them. They were nothing but another excuse, another justification for the violence they couldn't find a way free from. So long as they continued to partake in the bloodshed, there would be no escaping it.

"I..." She shook her head, swallowing the grief and guilt. "I don't know what other choice we have."

"Neither do I," Lachlan said. "I only wish it wasn't this."

The truth hung there, raw and ugly. For a moment, she thought Lachlan might recoil from it, leaving her alone to carry the weight of what they had to do. But when she met his eyes, she saw the same burden, the same bleak shame that blackened her own heart.

"Eimhir needs to be stopped," she said.

"Aye," Lachlan replied defeatedly. "That she does."

The understanding stretched between them, ripening with all the things left unsaid, all the unspoken horrors of what they'd done. It smelled like blood in the air, filling her lungs with a coppery tang.

She turned to Ruairidh, steeling her nerves against the weight of a decision made. "Are you truly willing to go through with this? If we go after the Admiralty, your people will bleed too."

"Our blood belongs to the fathoms," he said. "If the tides grow thirsty for it, who are we to deny them?" He cast his gaze up to the *Red Gale's* scarlet sails, a melancholy look falling across his hard features. "There is worse to fear from this world than joining those we've lost below the waves."

Dread whispered at Isla's neck, filling her ears with the echoes of what Cam had spoken of before. She knew now what Ruairidh wanted from her. More than that, she understood. That kind of loss, that kind of anguish...it sickened the soul as much as the haar did.

More pain. More violence. More vengeance.

Unless we end the cycle, it will be the end of us, Duncan had told her once.

Across the waves, the horizon seemed to darken, though the morning sky was bright and clear. A bitter wind nipped at her neck, bringing with it a chill she couldn't shake.

If there was an end, she couldn't yet see it. Only the blood it would take to get there.

CHAPTER TWELVE

DARCE

The blade of Muir's fishknife glinted under the moonlight, and Darce held his breath as he waited for its teeth to find flesh.

A full day had passed since they'd sailed away from Île de Durgavie and returned to the open water stretching between Breçhon and Silveckan. Muir had already made several attempts at reopening his sentinel bond, but each time the knife scored his palm, it drew forth nothing but droplets of blood. The sea spirits that once sang to him had fallen silent, and no amount of coaxing on Muir's part was enough to stir them.

The tip of the blade wavered against Muir's palm. A thin line appeared beside the one he'd carved a few hours before, splitting apart his skin as blood welled to the surface.

"Anything?" Darce asked.

Muir curled his hand into a fist, squeezing until the red droplets trickled through the gaps and fell to the deck. "The tides truly have forsaken me, it seems."

Featherblade let out a low, mournful cry and Darce slumped against the mast, disappointment filling his chest. Even with the vast stretch of the sea between them, he still felt Isla through the oath he'd made, the part of his soul he'd given her. It was difficult to imagine burying that ache so deeply he'd never be able to dig it back up.

Perhaps that was why Muir was suffering for it now. Perhaps some bonds were never meant to be severed, no matter how painful they were.

"I never wanted this to work," Muir said, breaking into his thoughts. "I would have happily gone to the grave never hearing the call of the tides in my veins again. But I *needed* it to work, for Isla." He choked out a harsh, bitter laugh. "I couldn't protect Mara. Perhaps I was a fool for believing I could do any more for her daughter."

"This isn't over yet. We can still—"

"No, Sergeant," Muir said shortly. "I'm not the man I was before. I don't *want* to be, and the tides fucking know it."

He closed his fingers around the fishknife and flung it over the side. The blade hit the waves with a splash, disappearing into the depths before Darce could speak another word.

"If we're to find this prison, we'll have to do it another way," Muir said. "There's nothing more my blood can give us but wasted time."

His footsteps faded across the deck as he walked away, leaving Darce with nothing but the weight of despair sinking into his bones. Featherblade gave another cry, the sound rattling through the night sky like a lament.

"He's a dour old bastard, but I didn't think it was in him to give up so easily." Nishi joined him at the gunwale, her hair flying in the breeze. "He's got salt in his blood, whether he wants to believe it or not. I wager the tides aren't done with him yet."

Darce looked out over the swell, searching the waves for an answer they couldn't give. "Did you clear out the stores before we left port?"

She quirked an eyebrow. "Sold most of what we had to an Îleanach liquor merchant and dumped the bottles he wouldn't take. You think the poor sod is going to break?"

"I think we're long past that."

The wind dropped, leaving the air unnaturally still. The swell had settled too, lapping against the soulship's hull in a gentle rocking motion. Darce had never felt the deck so steady. It was as though...

A memory flashed through his mind, turning his blood cold. The *Vanguard*, dead in the water, becalmed by a stillness he couldn't explain. A long, lithe shadow passing under the ship's keel. An oily, serpentine whisper in the base of his skull.

"Nishi," he said, throat dry. "How well do you know these waters?"

She shot him an affronted look. "You're talking to a Sea Kith. These swells and currents are my home."

"I didn't mean—" He grimaced. "I'm not talking about the currents. I'm talking about what lurks beneath them. Are there sea serpents in these parts?"

"There are sea serpents everywhere," she said. "But they're standoffish creatures. They prefer to keep to the depths, out of the way of those who disturb the sea's surface. We've nothing to fear from them, so long as we're not foolish enough to attract their attention."

Darce closed his eyes. "Such as tossing a fishknife covered with auld blood into the depths?"

"Aye, now that would be unwis—" Nishi stilled, her brown skin draining of colour. "Fuck. Tell me that irritable old sod didn't..."

The deck lurched, and she stumbled, catching herself on the gunwale. Darce's legs buckled too, sending him staggering before he found his balance again.

He met her gaze. "I think that answers your question."

Featherblade jerked its head towards him, the gannet's blue eyes fierce and knowing. There was no escaping the chill that entered his lungs. The magic in his blood thrummed with the presence of scale and sinew. He felt the twists of the creature's coiled body and rippling hide as if they were gliding through his own veins.

He could barely make out anything below the waves, but he sensed the serpent as it circled the soulship, knocking its tail against the hull with a detached kind of curiosity.

The deck pitched again, spray crashing over the side at the violent motion. Darce wrapped his hands around one of the lines running from the mast, holding himself upright until the ship settled once more.

"Perhaps it will lose interest," he said, mouth dry and stale. "That's what happened last time on the *Vanguard*. If I can calm it with my magic—"

"It's not going to lose interest." Muir emerged from the hold, eyes fixed on the eerily still water. A haunted look had fallen across his features, deepening every crease in his weathered brow.

He pressed his fingertips to his forehead. "It's not going to lose interest," he repeated. "I feel it in my head. Slipping into every crevice, filling my skull with its whisper."

Darce froze. "You can feel it? How—"

The rest of his words were lost as the waters around the soulship started to churn. Whatever calm had besieged the waves had been disturbed by something underneath, sending ripples across the surface. The water frothed as it climbed the side of the hull.

Nishi turned to him, her jaw set. "I need you to call the tides to our side. There's only so much I can do at the helm of a ship with no sails. We'll need your sentinel blood to get us out of here. See if you can find that Îleanach friend of yours, too."

"I'm here." Jacques climbed the quarterdeck stairs two at a time, cheeks flushed. Sébastien followed close on his heels, hands closing around the ornate hilts of his daggers as his keen gaze swept across the breadth of the ship.

"*Marées*, I thought we'd run aground," he said, the Breçh in his accent thickening. "We felt something scrape the hull. What's happening? Why did you call for..." He slowed, raising his eyes skyward.

Darce already sensed the shadow falling over him, the shiver burrowing through his woollen cloak into the depths of his bones. It wasn't the same kind of chill that the haar carried. This was something more ancient. Something more terrifying.

He inched around slowly, holding tight the breath he had left in his lungs.

The serpent rose out of the water, as black as the night sky. Darce had never seen a creature so huge, so utterly dominating of its surroundings. The beast stretched as tall as the soulship's mast, its scales glittering like jewels under the glow of the moon. Patches of sinewy hide were hidden beneath clusters of seashells and barnacles, encasing the creature in a kind of armour. Swathes of green and yellow kelp hung from the ridges between its scales, slipping into the roiling waves as it coiled its huge neck.

Featherblade gave a bloodcurdling shriek and leapt from the deck in a flurry of white feathers.

"Move back," Nishi hissed. "Away from the—"

The rest of her words were swallowed by a baleful roar from the serpent's gullet.

A rush of warm air hit Darce's face, and he braced himself as the force of it carried him backwards. The hot, briny stench of the serpent's breath burned his eyes and his throat, making him splutter.

He shielded his face with one arm as salt and spittle flew from the serpent's needle-like fangs. The awful roar persisted, tearing through his remaining eardrum until he thought it might deafen him.

"Sergeant!" Nishi's shout carried over the din. "You need to get us out of here. Summon those mists and take us back into the soulless realm. It's the only chance of escaping that thing."

He reached for the magic singing in his blood. The soulship's bones thrummed into life with the faded voices of the sea spirits that had made their home in them. The haar didn't answer to him, but to them. It was a promise of protection, a promise that their sacrifice would be honoured.

The chill that flooded his veins was a strange thing to welcome, but welcome it he did. As spray filled his lungs, it chased away the burning of the serpent's breath. This was a current he knew how to navigate, a cold he could survive. He only had to let it carry them to the other side.

Ice crusted around his lips as he sucked in a painful breath and willed the mists to spread. Already he could see the shroud winding along the masts, forming sails of salt-thick fog. The moon's glow had been snuffed out, lost behind the dense haze surrounding them.

Across the deck, Muir choked out a rasping cough, his braids glittering with frost. Jacques extended a hand, sweeping his fingers through the swirling mist. "What is this place? Why does my soul feel like it's in shadow?"

Darce knew exactly what he meant. Every time they crossed between their world and the soulless realm, he felt the weight of it on his heart. The sky had turned an unnatural, tenebrous shade of red, coating the horizon in its oily wash. The waves lay still, absent of the spirits that gave them their yawning sigh, their heaving crash. None of it felt real. None of it felt alive.

The sails hanging from the soulship's mast billowed with a wind that wasn't there, carrying them across the glassy black water. There was no flutter of canvas, no clapping in the breeze. Just the haar, taking them where it willed.

Nishi glanced to the helm. The wheel was slowly spinning of its own accord, uttering a creaking groan as it shuddered one way, then the other.

"If I never see this wretched realm again, it will be too soon," she muttered darkly. "No ship should sail without a captain at its helm. Not even one made from selkie bones."

"You could take the wheel."

She snorted. "Aye, right. I know better than to piss off whatever forces are at work here. If the mists want to take us somewhere, let them. As long as it's far from that serpent, I've no complaints."

The mention of the serpent brought a shiver to Darce's spine, and he cast his eyes towards Muir. He was standing in the middle of the deck, shoulders stiff, legs planted wide. The low burr of his voice carried through the thin air in mutterings.

"What happened back there?" Darce asked, pulling his shoulder around. "What did you mean about—"

Muir wheeled to face him. His eyes had gone slack and distant, the brown of his irises lost behind a blue-green film that bled into his capillaries and turned the veins around his temples dark. For a horrifying moment, Darce thought of Cunningham's appearance after the twisted blood oath revived him. Muir had the same ashen pallor, the same bloodshot gaze.

"Easy, Sergeant." When Muir spoke, his voice was his own. "If you get twitchy, you'll only startle it."

"Startle...startle *what?*"

The answer came in the slow churning of the black, soulless sea. Every drop of blood in Darce's body turned to ice as a flash of shimmering scales crested through the surface, then disappeared again.

"It's back," Nishi said. "It must have crossed the haar after us. But...*how?*"

"There are creatures in these waters far more ancient than selkies," Muir said, his eyes clouded with the blue-green film. "They roam where they please, paying no heed to magic or mists."

Something burst from the water in a scything arc, sending a shower of spray across the deck. Darce barely had time to catch the glint of shells and scales in the dim light before the serpent's tail coiled, then came crashing towards the ship.

"Watch out!" he yelled, lurching for the nearest line. It was too late. The serpent's sinewy tail thundered into the waves at the soulship's port side, cleaving through the water like it had split the sea in two. The ship rolled violently, and Darce stumbled, losing his footing on the slick deck.

His chin hit solid bone, and his mouth filled with blood as teeth met tongue. Beside him, Jacques and Sébastien slid towards the port gunwale, unable to stop themselves against the smooth, slippery surface. The three of them tumbled into each other, limbs colliding as they came to rest perilously close to the edge. Below, the waves frothed and spat in the serpent's wake, ready to swallow them whole if they fell.

A shrill shriek pierced the air, and he caught sight of Featherblade circling the mast, its wings flapping agitatedly as it cried out.

"*Du calme*," Jacques said, barely breathing. "Wait for the ship to settle."

Darce stilled. The tides had fallen silent, their fickle will beyond his grasp here in the soulless realm. He couldn't summon them to calm the waters. He couldn't do *anything*.

A guttural roar filled his head, stiffening every hair on the back of his neck. Another hot wash of breath rushed over the deck as the soulship slowly righted itself. When Darce looked up, he was faced once again with the wide, dripping maw of the sea serpent.

He pushed himself onto his elbows, scuttering as far back as he could drag himself. Beside him, Sébastien clambered to his feet, hands whipping to the daggers on his belt. But they would be no use, not against the monstrous creature towering over them. Its fangs dripped saliva and seawater onto the deck. Its ink-black scales glittered like diamonds, protected by the layers of barnacles and shells armouring its underbelly. Every movement was made of coiled power and rippling sinew.

There was no escape.

"Isla," he murmured, her name spilling from his lips like an apology. Would she feel it when the tides took him? How long would she last without the sliver of his soul protecting her from the gun-anam?

Whatever happens, you have to live, Muir had said. *For her.*

Muir.

He had fallen like the rest of them, but now he stood at the gunwale, hands spread wide as he stared down the serpent's quivering gullet. Blood crusted around the cuts he'd made in his palm, his failed attempts at reaching for the sea spirits that once called to him.

Something stirred in Darce's veins, like the faintest ripple stretched across a great distance. It wasn't his own magic—that was out of reach. He glanced at Jacques, who shook his head, his face stark.

Then, Muir raised his hands and twisted them into a ward.

Darce stilled. All he could see were the serpent's gaping jaws and the oily wash of the sky behind. And there, in the middle of it all, was Muir.

Streams of seawater rose from the deck, droplets glistening as they spiralled around Muir's outstretched arms. He was calmer than Darce had ever seen him. The spirals of water shifted as he formed more wards with his fingers, muttering a cantrip too deep and low to hear.

The serpent's scaled throat fluttered again, but this time, no roar erupted from its gullet. Instead, it released a mournful wail, the sound shuddering deep into Darce's bones. The cry was unlike anything he'd heard before. It held the depths of the sea itself, its discordant tones shifting like the currents.

"The mad bastard is doing it," Sébastien said, hushed. "I've seen sentinels calm the swells, subdue a raging tempest...but to quell a sea serpent?"

A thin smile pulled at the corner of Jacques' lips. "They recognise one of their own, it seems."

Time slowed. Each breath Darce drew felt fainter than the last, the air lost to the tension of the stalemate between Muir and the serpent looming over him.

Then, with a juddering sigh, the creature slowly sank beneath the surface, leaving no trace behind but a small cluster of bubbles on the waves.

"Fuck." Muir staggered back, hitting the deck with a thud as his knees gave out. He stared at the oozing wounds on his hands with an expression Darce couldn't decipher. His eyes were back to normal, their deep brown colour returning as the film disappeared. Whatever had taken hold of him had slipped away as easily as the serpent.

"What was that?" Darce asked, voice tighter than he'd intended. Though the serpent was gone, the cold grip of fear lingered. Not for the creature, but for the man in front of him.

"He called it here." Nishi adjusted her tricorne hat, watching Muir warily. "Serpents can smell blood in the currents from miles away. The moment that damned fishknife hit the waves, it was only a matter of time."

"It was hardly on purpose," Muir groused. "I wasn't thinking. Still..." He frowned, tension returning to his brow. "Shite, maybe you're right. Perhaps I did call it here, whether I meant to or not. I had to do *something*. The tides refused my call."

"And this was the best way to get their attention?" Darce glanced at the water, the waves calm once more. "You've done this before, haven't you? You knew how to calm it."

The ghost of a smile flickered across Muir's face. "Cirein-cròin, they used to call me. You didn't think there was a reason for that? Aye, I've done this before. But I was younger than you the last time I shared my mind with one of those creatures. I'd forgotten what it felt like."

"Shared your *mind?*"

"Don't give me that look—it's no different from what her lot do with those bloody seabirds of theirs." He gestured bullishly towards Nishi. "The Sea Kith aren't the only ones with salt in their blood."

"Maybe not, but we know better than to engage in a battle of wills with a sea serpent, of all creatures," Nishi shot back. "It almost had you, you foolish old prick. We all saw it. A minute longer, and it might have drowned you in its resolve. Bonding with a guidebird is one thing"—Featherblade let out a self-satisfied squawk—"but to have the gall to think you can survive a mind that ancient—"

"But he *did* survive it, didn't he?" Jacques tilted his head, staring at Muir with something akin to reverence. "Few of us would be able to say the same."

Darce shivered. He remembered the encounter with the sea serpent back on the *Vanguard*. The creature had brushed his mind for only a moment, but its rattling whisper had echoed in his skull long after, its touch chilling his temples. For Muir to have withstood the creature's presence for so long, to have matched it in will...

He chuckled weakly. "Isla always did say you were a stubborn old bastard."

"Where do you suppose she gets it from?" Muir's lips twitched, then he grew sombre. "The tides wanted to test me. They sent me that serpent to remind me of what I was, what I walked away from. Seems they know me better than I know myself."

Darce's heart quickened. "What are you saying?"

Muir raised his arm, uncurling his fingers to examine his hand. The dried gashes scoring his palm had left behind a crisscross of scars. A far-off whisper stirred in Darce's veins, sighing like the break of the waves. The tides were calling them back.

Calling *all* of them back.

"You did it," he said hoarsely. "You reopened your bond with the Grand Admiral."

Muir's face was grim. "Aye, so if we want to find this tides-damned prison, we better move quickly. Because now, he'll be coming for us."

CHAPTER THIRTEEN

ISLA

The pinprick lights from the stars were already visible in the gloaming as the *Red Gale* crept up the coast towards the port of Kinraith. The hazy purple sky hadn't quite surrendered to the cloak of night yet, but it would soon be upon them, and with it, the darkness they needed to slip in unseen.

Isla leaned over the gunwale, arms resting on the red-stained timber. The ship's huge sails were full with the Silvish southwesterly harrying them over the waves. Spray leapt from the choppy waters, and she licked her lips, savouring the brackish taste.

She missed it, she realised with a twinge. It wasn't just her soul Eimhir had taken when she'd stripped her pelt from her; it was her *home*. No longer could she expel the air from her lungs and plunge so deep that the water squeezed her muscles and organs. No longer could she feel the currents flicking at her whiskers, guiding her to where she needed to go. There was an entire world below the waves, one that *belonged* to her.

One she might never return to.

The thought was too much to bear. Even now, the glittering trails across her skin bit deeper, trying to gnaw to a part of her they couldn't yet reach. The patterns held a morbid kind of beauty in the waning light, swirling across her pale flesh like Sea Kith tattoos. But these marks didn't carve out the places she'd sailed, the people she'd loved and lost. Instead, they were a sobering reminder of what she might become.

Gun-anam. The word rang in her head like an invocation. She could almost see the wraiths drifting across the waves towards the unsuspecting port, ready to sate their endless hunger on the blood waiting to be spilled there.

And there *would* be blood. For this to work, there had to be.

She tensed as Ruairidh joined her. The Sea Kith captain surveyed the waves, the scar behind his eyepatch twitching as he frowned.

"Having second thoughts?" she asked.

He grunted. "I know you don't hold me in any particular esteem, but I don't relish the thought of sending my crew into a fight that will certainly claim some of their lives. Even if each of them would gladly give it." He shifted so his blue eye was fixed on her, keen and discerning. "Cam talked to you."

"They did." Isla pressed her lips tight.

"That's it? Nothing you want to say?"

She let out a weary sigh. "I know as well as anyone how the grasp of vengeance can suffocate a person. I know what it can drive them to."

He turned to the waves. "Then you understand."

Her fingers drifted to the salty ridges around her wrists. Aye, she understood. That was the worst part. It would have been easier to hate Eimhir, easier if her betrayal had severed Isla's love for her like the swift stroke of a blade.

"I pity her," she murmured, not meaning to speak the words aloud. "My heart aches for what she must bear."

"Your pity is wasted. Would you want it, if you were her?" Ruairidh shook his head. "It cuts as painfully as a blade, and the wound only festers with resentment. We're past the point of pity, all of us. Best you learn that soon, so you can do what you need to do when the time comes."

Isla ran her thumb across the edge of the sgian dubh in her coat pocket. Eimhir had turned the blade against her so easily. The scar in the crook of her elbow still remembered the bite of steel, the rush of blood. Would Isla be able to do what Eimhir had done? Did she have a choice?

This violence belongs to all of us, Eimhir had told her once. *It will continue as long as we let it.*

A low whistle came from the crow's nest, breaking into her thoughts. Ruairidh straightened, a slow smile unfurling as his gaze found the horizon. "Now there's a sight."

Rising from the waves were the fearsome rocks that guarded Kinraith's harbour. The teeth, the locals called them, referring to the old legend that said they'd once sat in the maw of the Cirein-cròin itself.

Looking at them, it was easy to understand why. As the last sliver of sunlight slipped away, the rocks were bathed in a carmine glow, as if the jagged limestone jutting out from the water had gorged itself bloody. It would be easy to drift into their waiting jaws, for the hull to be chewed up and spat out in scraps of floating timber.

"There's nae need for us to venture into the harbour itself," Ruairidh said, as if he'd heard her thoughts. "We'd only get pinned between the rocks and the Admiralty's cannons. But we can do some damage from out here. I'll send my best throatslitters into Kinraith ahead of time, quiet like. They'll take advantage of the chaos and put down any shoreside Admiralty officers distracted by the fighting."

"Just make sure they stick to the Admiralty," Isla said. "Lachlan was right to fear the people of Kinraith getting caught up in this. I don't want them to pay the price for us bringing bloodshed into their home."

"And where is your brother?" Ruairidh glanced around. "You said he was rather close with the Admiralty. Seems to me he might have some knowledge we could use."

"I don't—" She broke off, his words hitting her with a sudden realisation. "I'll see if I can find him."

"Best you do. It won't be long until night falls." Ruairidh's mouth pinched into a tight smile. "Then the fun begins."

Isla left him, fighting to keep her expression smooth even as her heart hammered against her ribs. She'd done it again—lost sight of what mattered to Lachlan, let him slip through her fingers once more. It wasn't just the people of Kinraith who were in danger tonight. If the *Vanguard* was moored at Kinraith, then it was almost certain Blair Cunningham would be with it. He was the Grand Admiral's nephew. Her cousin, by blood if nothing else.

And, if her suspicions were correct, the man Lachlan loved.

She quickened her step, eyes flitting across the deck for a glimpse of his golden hair and rosewood crutch. The sun was below the horizon now, and darkness was drawing in. No oil lamps or braziers would be lit this time. The *Red Gale* would wear the night like a cloak, slipping up to the waiting Admiralty fleet until its cannons were pointed at their throats.

A frustrated sigh tore loose from her lips, and she came to a halt, taking a second to gather her racing thoughts. What if it were Darce in danger? What would she do in Lachlan's position?

The answer didn't take long to come to her. The memories were raw: the mahogany box pressed into her hands, her blood turning cold when she found Darce's ragged ear inside. She'd left Eileanan Selch without a second thought. She'd left *Eimhir*. There was nothing that could have kept her from him.

She turned abruptly on her heel, leaving behind the bustle of the main deck to find the lower platforms where the tenders hung on knotted lines. All seemed quiet as she made her way around, until she caught sight of a familiar figure working at the ropes of one of the boats rigged near the stern.

"You're a bloody fool, you know that?"

Lachlan jumped, spinning around with a flustered expression. "I wasn't—" He stopped when he saw it was her, eyes narrowing. "Oh, it's you. What are you doing here?"

"I've come to stop you doing something incredibly unwise, it seems."

She cast her eyes over the tender. "What were you thinking? Even if you made it past the rocks and avoided the Admiralty, there's still the small matter of the attack the Sea Kith are planning. You'll get yourself killed."

He gave her a stony look. "I didn't ask for your counsel."

"No, you never did like being told things you didn't want to hear." She tried to keep the irritation from her voice. "I know why you're doing this. If Blair is in Kinraith—"

"Then he'll likely be killed, thanks to this plan of yours." He glared at her. "I'm going to find him, to warn him. He won't be able to prevent what's coming, but at least it will give him a chance to escape. If you try to stop me—"

"Lachlan." She reached for his arm, trying to ignore the painful twinge in her heart when he stiffened at her touch. "I didn't come here to stop you. I came here to *help* you."

He stilled, the anger in his eyes yielding to wariness.

"I didn't ask for your help, either," he said, but there was no heat behind the words. Instead, she heard a trace of something she'd feared lost, something she was still afraid to reach for.

"You didn't ask for any of this," she said softly. "Least of all me. I know you'll never forgive me for coming back, but—"

"No." His throat clenched around the word. "That's not it, Isla. All those years I spent in your shadow, waiting for the day I'd be free of it... But when I finally was..." He looked away, knuckles white as he gripped the handle of his crutch. "That's what I'm trying to forgive you for. Not for coming back, but for finding it so easy to leave."

Her fingers tightened in the woollen sleeve of his coat. This time, he didn't pull away.

"You never did like my shadow, but it will always watch over you," she said. "No matter where I am, no matter *what* I am, that will never change...brother."

Her words lingered in the air, waiting for him to grasp at them or push them away. All the old resentment balanced on the edge of a blade, ready to slip and wound them both.

Eventually, he met her eyes. She was half-afraid to look too closely, dreading what might have changed. What might *not* have changed.

"Thank you," he said. "For being here."

Something burst loose behind her sternum, releasing her of the pain and tension coiled around her. It was still too raw to acknowledge, too soon to inspect the damage that had been done, but it was enough. For now, it was enough.

"Come, then," she said. "Let's go."

They slipped away from the *Red Gale*, oars sliding through the choppy water under the cover of night. By the time Ruairidh noticed one of the tenders was missing, they'd already be ashore. All they had to do was find Blair before the fighting started.

The rocks glowered at them through the darkness, promising retribution if they drifted too close to their hackles. But even without her pelt, Isla knew the shape of the currents beneath the waves. She worked her oar with deft caution, whispering instructions to Lachlan as he rowed beside her. Before long, they'd found a narrow scrap of shoreline half a mile from the main port, and the tender crunched into the shingle as they made berth.

Isla glanced towards the glow of the harbour, trepidation curling in her chest. "Perhaps it would be best if I went ahead. There are many among the Admiralty who would recognise you, and if we happen across them before we find Blair, it could mean trouble."

"And you're in no danger at all, I suppose?" Lachlan snorted. "The Grand Admiral managed to sway a crew of Sea Kith to his side in his attempts to bring you back. If we're to worry about anyone being recognised, it's you."

"Together, then." Isla gritted her teeth. "As long as we both keep our guard up."

They trudged along the shore, hoods low over their faces. Despite the hour, Kinraith was as alive as Isla remembered it, narrow streets bustling with animated chatter and the musk of ale. The daytime fish markets had closed, replaced by stalls boasting glittering trinkets and selections of wine and whisky. The briny stench from the morning catches lingered in the air, but it was dampened by the fragrance of burning clove and lavender, of grouse and hare roasting on the spit.

"Everything seems so normal," Lachlan said, eyes glinting beneath his hood as he surveyed the markets. "You'd never know Arburgh had fallen, that the coastal villages were being swallowed by the mists. Say what you like about the Admiralty, but at least their presence here has kept this place from the same fate as the capital."

Only for now, Isla thought grimly. This was only a breath of calm before the storm about to break. It wouldn't be long until Kinraith's streets bled with the same kind of violence Arburgh had suffered only a few short weeks ago.

And this time, Eimhir wouldn't be the one to blame for it.

Shame pulled tight in her stomach. Back on the *Red Gale*, it had been easier to tell herself that this was what they needed to do. The truth of it hadn't changed—if they didn't find a way to stop Eimhir, more villages and ports would suffer. The mists would spread. Blood would spill.

But knowing the truth didn't make facing it any easier. Not now that she walked Kinraith's cobbled streets, meeting the eyes of passersby who would soon find their home under attack because of her.

Her ears pricked at a short burst of laughter carrying across one of the squares, and she caught sight of a group of young Admiralty officers wandering through the markets with easy smiles and curious eyes. Their jewel-toned cloaks stood out against the muted grey and brown garb of the locals, drawing attention as they strode through the crowd.

Ruairidh's throatslitters would find their targets all too easily when they arrived.

She motioned for Lachlan to follow, then slipped through the bustle of bodies. Snatches of conversation filled the air in a low burr, but she ignored the background noise and focused on the casual chatter between the officers.

"I still don't like it," one of them said. "We're exposed here with the *Vanguard* gone."

"You worry too much," his companion replied, clapping an arm around his shoulders. "The *Vanguard* may be a monster, but it's just one ship. Besides, do you really think the Grand Admiral would have left his nephew behind if he was concerned about an attack? Kinraith is probably the safest place we could find ourselves."

Isla exchanged a look with Lachlan. Blair was here, but the *Vanguard* wasn't. Something had caught Cunningham's attention, drawing him to the open seas.

"Blair is a good lad," the first officer conceded. "But he's only a lieutenant. He's not a captain—never will be, without a sentinel. And after the losses we took at Arburgh, we need captains more than ever."

His friend guffawed. "Aye? Why don't you go back to the tavern and tell *him* that? Better yet, let me watch. The lad might not be his uncle yet, but he's got a mettle of his own. I wouldn't fancy being the one to test it."

"I didn't mean it like that. I was only..."

Their voices faded as they disappeared around the corner, and Isla drew back, heart racing. Something didn't feel right. The *Vanguard's* absence should have come as a relief, but instead, a cold trickle of dread ran down her spine. Cunningham had gathered his forces at Kinraith for a reason. Whatever had stirred him to leave, it must have been enough to justify taking away the fleet's most fearsome protector.

If he was hunting her, he'd picked up a false trail. But if it was something else, some*one* else...

"There's a tavern in that direction," Lachlan said, breaking into her thoughts. "If that's where those officers came from, Blair might still be there. We'd best move quickly—we don't want to be here when the fighting starts."

She nodded, following him through the cobbled streets towards Kinraith's bustling centre. Past the market quarter, they came across a tavern on the corner of a narrow wynd. The wooden sign above the door was worn and peeling from the sea air, but a warm glow came from inside, spilling onto the street as the door creaked open to let out a group of sour-faced patrons.

"If he's here..." Lachlan paused. "Be careful how you approach. Whatever the Grand Admiral has done, he's still Blair's uncle. And you've tried to kill him twice."

I've failed twice, Isla thought darkly, though she kept her words to herself. "You'd like me to let you do the talking, I presume?"

"I'd like it better if you agreed to stay outside. But since we both know that will never happen, then aye, let me do the talking. This will be difficult enough as it is."

A worried crease appeared between his brows, and she fought the urge to reach for his arm again. There were some things she couldn't protect him from. Some pain that was his to bear alone.

Eventually, Lachlan pushed through the tavern door, shoulders tense. Isla slipped in behind him, keeping her head down as she followed. The tavern was quieter than she'd expected, the barstools empty. Only a small group of locals sat in the corner by the hearth, dice and cards strewn beside their tankards. They glanced over at a booth in the opposite corner, lips curling in an obvious display of distaste.

Isla followed their gazes, and her heart lurched.

It was Blair.

He was sitting alone, his cloak loose and his Admiralty bonnet lying discarded on the table. His light brown curls fell loose across his forehead as he stared stone-faced at the pewter tankard between his hands.

She felt Lachlan stiffen. He must have seen it too: the grief haunting

Blair's downturned mouth, the exhaustion written in the shadows ringing his sombre eyes.

"Go," she said gently. "There may not be time to make things right, but there's time to save his life. That's what we came for."

She thought she'd spoken quietly, but at the sound of her voice, Blair's head snapped up.

For a moment, she thought he might be drunk. His blue-grey eyes were distant and glazed as he stared at them without blinking. His mouth formed the shape of a word that refused to come forth, leaving his jaw hanging open.

The colour drained from his face, and he rose from the table with his hand wrapped around a polished rosewood pistol.

"Traitor," he hissed, and levelled the barrel directly at Lachlan's head.

CHAPTER FOURTEEN

DARCE

A new sense of urgency filled the soulship's misty sails as fiercely as the wind, carrying them from something they could not outrun.

It was a race, Darce realised. One where they couldn't see their opponent, but felt their breath on their necks all the same. Wherever Cunningham was, it didn't matter. Now that Muir had opened himself to the blood oath once more, their souls were tethered. One way or another, they would find their way back to each other again.

Not even the tides could save them from that.

"This doesn't feel right," Nishi said, picking at a stubborn knot on the seaweed-encrusted line she was working to untangle.

"It's our only chance of finding that prison," Darce said. "We had to do it, even if it means bringing the Admiralty down on us."

"I'm not talking about *that*." Nishi snorted. "You think I fear facing the Admiralty? I owe the Grand Admiral a debt for what he did to Kerr. The sooner I see that bastard again, the sooner I get to kill him." She dropped the rope, then gestured to the helm with a disgruntled scowl. "No, what doesn't feel right is giving the wheel over to a washed-up old seadog who hasn't commanded a ship in more than twenty years."

Darce followed her gaze to where Muir stood on the quarterdeck, hands resting lightly against the soulship's wheel. His dark brown skin might have been etched with crinkled lines, but he held himself with the same strength Darce imagined him carrying decades ago. The Cirein-cròin, he was called. A sea serpent so ferocious they had to bestow upon it a name to match their terror.

He'd never seen it in him before. But the grim determination burning in Muir's eyes, the huff of defiance in every breath as he guided the wheel through his hands, showed Darce a glimpse of the man Muir had once been. The man he needed to be again, if any of them were to survive this.

"He sails well," Nishi said grudgingly. "That just makes it all the more galling."

The days passed quickly as they cut through the Strait of Silveckan, following the faint thread Muir had found in the calling of his blood. The trail took them north, past the great sea stacks and bird colonies of the Drift, until all that lay ahead of them was the great, empty stretch of the ocean.

"Difficult to believe there's anything else out there," Darce said. "We've not seen a spit of land in days. It's like there's no end to it."

"There's not," Muir said from the helm. "At least, not until you reach Skallenar, and that would take the best part of a month, even for a ship with proper sails." He glared at the clouds wisping around the bone mast, as if the absence of billowing canvas was a personal affront.

"Skallenar?" Darce said, startling. "That's where the Admiralty prison is?"

"It can't be," Nishi cut in. "It's a dead land, a frozen graveyard. Nobody has settled there since the Great Winter wiped out the Skalls a century ago."

Muir rolled his eyes. "Of course we're not going to bloody Skallenar. But before the Skalls died out, they used to sail across the ocean in their hundreds, raiding and pillaging the north coast of Silveckan. The Admiralty built watchtowers on remote islands in the middle of the sea to spot them coming so they could give the northern settlements forewarning. Most of them fell to disrepair and ruin after the Skalls stopped coming, but there are a few outposts still standing. Used by smugglers, mainly. Or so I thought."

"That's where you think he's keeping his prisoners?" Darce asked. "In one of these old watchtowers?"

Muir nodded. "The nearest one is Baininch Rise. Supposedly its ruins crumbled into the sea some half a century ago, but I'm beginning to suspect that's a convenient lie. The truth, well..." He tapped his chest. "That's in here, isn't it?"

The gruff edge to his voice wasn't enough to mask the bitterness, or the pain. Not for the first time, Darce felt a twinge of sympathy. Being separated from Isla was like a dull ache behind his sternum, an emptiness waiting to be made full again. But Muir's connection to Cunningham...that was a blade between the ribs, the twisting of a knife. Muir had buried it for decades before tearing the wound open again, and the suffering was plain to see on his face.

"How did you do it?" Darce asked, the words slipping from his mouth before he could take them back.

Muir gave a dark chuckle. "How did I turn on the man I swore my soul to, you mean? The worst part was how easy he made it, in the end. He'd become something I couldn't bear. He'd turned *me* into something I couldn't bear. When I tried to break the oath, I didn't expect to survive it. Perhaps I didn't want to. But the tides, cruel as they are, saw fit to keep me alive. They quietened me to their roar, slipped out of my grasp. I thought they'd abandoned me, but the sea is a patient beast. All it had to do was wait."

"If the tides kept you alive, it was for a reason," Nishi said. "They knew Isla would need you again one day." Something softened as she looked at Muir. "I know what it's like to yearn for the relief of the fathoms. But they're not ready for us yet. Not while Cunningham draws breath."

"That's why we're here, isn't it?" Muir spun the wheel through his hands and the soulship answered, listing to one side as it cut through the leaping waves. "The only reason Alasdair has lived this long is because of the oaths he's perverted, the stolen blood spilled in his name." He glanced at the horizon, eyes glinting with an unspoken promise. "We'll see how his sentinels' loyalty lasts when the bastard no longer holds their leash."

When Baininch Rise climbed out of the water before them a few days later, the island's crags were barely visible through the thick veil of rain sweeping across the waves. It wasn't a storm—not yet—but the darkening horizon felt like a threat all the same.

"Here, take a look." Nishi lowered her spyglass and handed it to Darce. "Tell me what you see."

Darce lifted the brass instrument and peered over the waves. The rain crawled towards them, obscuring Baininch Rise behind a dreich haze. The island was little more than a scrap of limestone jutting though the grey-green waves. But there, nestled in the middle of the steep crags, was the façade of a watchtower.

He was about to hand the spyglass back to Nishi when something made him hesitate. The metal bit against his cheekbone as he pressed harder, focusing on the water dashing off the rocks, the spray flying into the air.

"There are no ships," he said. "No jetty. There's...nothing."

"There's something." Muir's voice was low, his eyes moody. "I can feel the blood wards under my skin, even if you can't. Alasdair's fingerprints are all over this place. In the stone, in the fathoms below the rock and sediment. It's like he was just here. Like he's *still* here."

"Well, he's not, is he?" Nishi said. "Like the sergeant said, there are no ships. And you can bet your arse he's not sailing anywhere without that monstrosity of his. Calling it a man-o'-war doesn't do it justice. It's an abomination."

She was right. The *Vanguard* was nowhere in sight. No shadows darkened the hazy line between sky and sea. They were the only ones out here.

"It makes sense." Jacques emerged from the hold, his hair tied back in the wind. A loose strand of grey whipped free at his temple, and he tucked it behind his ear as he narrowed his eyes on Baininch Rise. "That's the place?"

Darce couldn't mistake the undercurrents of rage and grief in his voice, rising from where they'd once been buried. How long had it been since Maggie Grier died here? How long had Jacques imagined laying eyes on his mother's grave?

"That's the place," Darce said. "What do you mean, it makes sense? Why wouldn't there be an Admiralty presence here?"

"I didn't say there wasn't an Admiralty presence. But it stands to reason that there are no ships." He folded his arms, contemplating the waves. "This place is supposed to be in ruins, isn't it? Any ships berthed alongside a deserted scrap of rock would only draw the wrong kind of attention if they were spotted. It's likely this place is garrisoned by a small rotation of guards. The only time a ship will breach these waters is when it comes to retrieve them and bring their replacements."

"Seems like a risk."

"Does it?" Jacques gestured to the island. "Even if the prisoners managed to break free and kill their guards, where would they go? There's no shoreline within a hundred miles. Remember, the Grand Admiral only gets away with this because so few know about it. He disposes of those he no longer needs, severs loose ends before they can talk." His jaw clenched. "This isn't a prison. It's a grave. Those inside just aren't dead yet."

His words hung heavy in the air, weighing around Darce's neck like a noose. He knew the feeling of being caught in Cunningham's grasp.

There had been a time he'd wondered whether he would ever be able to escape it.

"We'll get them out," he said. "That's what we came here to do."

He lifted his chin as the first droplets of rain reached the soulship. Within seconds, the deck was soaked, rivulets running down the bone. Darce closed his eyes and felt the water trickling through the grooves, dripping through the cracks into the hold. Before it fell from the sky, it had come from the sea, and now it rushed to return there. It hummed in his veins, turning his blood cold.

When he opened his eyes again, the haar was closing in, covering them in its cloak. By the time they reached Baininch Rise, they would be shrouded by a veil no spyglass could pierce.

"I'll ready the tender," Nishi said as she observed the mist creeping across the deck. "The haar should give us enough cover to slip onto the isle without alerting the Admiralty. After that, well..."

She didn't need to say any more. The way her hand drifted to the hilt of her rapier spoke loudly enough.

The haar clung close as the soulship cut through the waves. Each passing second felt colder than the last. But this time, when the oily red sky of the soulless realm began to bleed above the masts, Darce pulled them back towards the living world again. Crossing over completely would turn them into shadows that would leave no mark on the world they knew.

This was a mark they needed to leave.

The waves slapped the side of the tender as they pushed off from the soulship and sailed into the mists surrounding Baininch Rise. They'd scavenged the rickety boat from Caolaig with little time to fix it up, and now flakes of periwinkle paint peeled from its wooden hull, floating away with the seafoam. It was a tight squeeze with the five of them, but nobody wanted to stay behind. The soulship would be safe enough in the haar, waiting for them to return to its bones once more.

Darce met Featherblade's keen blue gaze from its perch at the bow and gave the gannet a silent nod. For once, the bird didn't shriek a haughty reply, just spread its huge wings and took off over the waves.

"A useful scout to have," Sébastien remarked. "Though I must say, I'll be disappointed if we manage to sneak in undetected. I was looking for an excuse to open a few Admiralty throats today."

"I have no doubt you'll get your wish," Jacques replied dryly. "Getting in is one thing. Getting out with all the prisoners is another matter entirely."

On the other side of the tender, Muir was uncharacteristically quiet. His brow was furrowed, his eyes focused on something the rest of them couldn't see.

"Blood wards," he said, voice low. "Crude, but effective. They were meant to be used for protection, but Alasdair twisted them like he twists everything."

"You warded the compass," Darce said. "The one that led us to Mara's pelt."

Muir nodded. "I was his sentinel. He trusted me like no other. He had me imbue my own compass with his blood so it would only ever point to Mara. After I helped her escape and went slinking back to him like a dog, he tried to use it to find her. He bled his palms over it a hundred times." He examined the scars on his own hands. "But it just kept leading him back to that tides-forsaken island where he'd sealed her pelt. He had no use for it after that, so I took it for myself before I left the Admiralty for good."

"And this place?" Darce peered at the watchtower looming out of the haze. "What kind of protection has he put in place here?"

Muir's face was grim. "I'd say we're about to find out."

A few minutes later, Featherblade returned, letting out a hushed caw as it landed on the side of the boat. Its beady eyes carried a glint of triumph, and Darce couldn't help the rush of anticipation that flooded his veins as the tender found the gravelly shore. This was the chance they'd been waiting for. If they freed the prisoners locked in this wretched hole,

Cunningham would no longer have leverage over his sentinels. He'd no longer have their protection.

They hauled the tender out of reach of the hungry waves and looked around. A narrow stretch of shoreline snaked along the fearsome crags, the rocks half-submerged under the encroaching waves. Darce edged cautiously across the slippery surface, following Featherblade through the mist as the guidebird led the way. The air was damp and fetid with the stench of rotten kelp. It was too gloomy to see much past the end of his nose. He had to trust Featherblade.

Eventually, the trail opened up, and Darce found himself staring at the seaweed-covered stone at the bottom of the watchtower.

He let out a breath. Muir was only half right—the tower may not have been in ruins, but it was far from intact. The stone was crumbling in places, dripping with sediment and slime in others. A section halfway up had fallen away entirely, leaving a gaping hole like a wound in its side, rain and wind howling through the gutted carcass.

There couldn't be anyone here. They were in the wrong place.

His dismay must have shown, for Featherblade fluttered to his shoulder, giving his cheek a nip.

He whipped a hand to his face, fingers coming away bloody. "You wretched wee—"

Nishi laughed. "You deserved that. Sea Kith don't doubt their own guidebirds."

"I'm not a—" He broke off at her smile, a strange, uncertain warmth rising in him at the meaning in her words. When he glanced at Featherblade, he found the gannet watching him with its intense stare. "You're right, I'm sorry. It's just this place..."

He'd spent time in an Admiralty sea cliff prison. He remembered the bite of wind creeping in through the cracks in the rock, the ache in his lungs from the damp air, the constant dripping from the roof of the cell. But that paled in comparison to the decrepit ruin before them.

"Staring at it won't make it any more inviting," Muir said. "We'd best move. I don't know where the *Vanguard* is, but I know it's coming for us."

The low note of warning in his voice was enough to prickle the hairs on Darce's neck. Cunningham's shadow was impossible to forget. It darkened every step, lurked in every corner. Muir was right. They didn't want to be here when the Admiralty arrived.

Featherblade hopped off his shoulder again, spreading its wings to glide to the moss-covered ground. Darce followed it around the watchtower, heart leaping when he saw a hole in the crumbling stone, the gap large enough for a person to squeeze through.

They had their way in.

Jacques flexed his fingers into a ward, clearing his eyes of the rainwater streaming down his face. "Keep the tides close at hand, if they'll allow it. There may only be a token force of guards here, but we don't know how many might be sentinels themselves."

"A sentinel bleeds like any other," Sébastien said, thumbing his daggers. "We can handle whatever is in that tower."

Darce slipped through the hole first, blinking as he waited for his eyes to adjust. No oil lamps hung from the walls, no braziers lit the way through the gloom. The only source of light came through the cracks in the stone, and even that was dim and grey.

He crept forward, following Featherblade's light hops along the slippery ground. The reek of damp was more pungent inside, and he fought to suppress a cough. Any sound would give them away, so quiet was the tower.

A screech echoed from up ahead, and Darce's hand flew to the straps holding his claymore in place between his shoulder blades. A second later, he relaxed. It was only a herring gull. The bird had likely been startled by Featherblade's baleful glare as it swooped forward, leading them to a narrow, spiralling stairwell.

"Looks like we're going up." Nishi drew her sword from her belt. "Not much room to swing a blade if it comes to it."

"Featherblade will alert us if there's anyone ahead," Darce said. Still, he followed suit, silently unsheathing his own rapier. The weight of Laird Cormick's claymore rested on his back, promising it would be there if he needed it, but the stairwell was too narrow to wield the two-handed sword. Darce had little doubt the time for its brute strength would come soon enough.

They climbed the winding steps, shoulders brushing the walls on either side. Trails of cobwebs clung to the corners of the low, sloping ceiling. From the stairwell, the howl of the wind sounded more eerie than ever, whistling through the weather-beaten tower with a high-pitched, breathy wail.

"This doesn't feel right," Sébastien muttered behind him. "The Admiralty are snakes and cowards, but they are not stupid. We shouldn't have made it this far without coming across some kind of resistance."

Darce couldn't find it in himself to disagree. A sense of dread grew in his chest, turning him cold. He knew how ferociously, how *violently*, Cunningham guarded what was his. They were walking wilfully into a trap, knowing its jaws would snap shut around them. He felt like the stone steps might crumble at any moment, burying them in the bowels of this place.

After a few more turns, an arch opened in the side of the stairwell, leading into the middle of the watchtower. Featherblade gave a low trill and hopped through, craning its long neck to make sure Darce was following.

"This is it," Muir said, moving alongside him. "I can feel the wards stronger here, like the pulse of something that should be long dead. It has the taint of his corruption all over it."

A chill crawled down Darce's spine at his words, and he willed his breathing to steady as he entered the room. Part of the watchtower's wall had broken away, leaving another hole for the raging wind and battering rain to pour through. But through the hole also came a beam of waning daylight, casting a dreary glow across something glinting in the corner.

It was the rusting iron bars of a cell.

Darce edged forward, keeping himself close to the wall as more cells came into view. The perimeter of the room was lined with them, a dozen or more in total. All he could see behind the bars were shadows, but he already feared what they'd find inside.

The scar around his missing ear burned, and he pressed his fingers against the reminder. He knew first-hand how Cunningham treated his prisoners.

A pallor fell across Nishi's skin. She was no stranger to Cunningham's cruelty either. She'd seen what his torturers had done to Kerr.

"You go ahead," she said, rasping. "I...I can't."

Darce squeezed her shoulder, then crept closer to the first set of bars. The cell reeked of piss and filth and stale blood. No light crept in through any cracks in the wall. It was a hole shrouded in utter darkness.

"Is anyone there?" he asked softly.

There was no answer. Then something shifted, and a gaunt figure crawled towards the bars.

It was a young lad, barely more than a bairn. His cheeks had lost the fullness of youth, hollowed by squalor and starvation. Bruise-coloured shadows circled his deep-set eyes, and when he opened his mouth, Darce caught a glimpse of broken, rotting teeth.

"You're not one of them," the lad whispered. "You can't be new, either. Rotation doesn't happen for another week. I count the days, see? I'm canny like that. Ma always said I was a canny thing."

"That's right." Darce tasted bile at the back of his throat. "We're no friends of the Admiralty. We've come to get you out of here, get you back to your family. What's your name?"

The lad looked at him, head tilted as if he was trying to remember. "Tam. My name is Tam."

"Well met, Tam. I'm Sergeant Galbraith." He extended his hand towards the bars, flinching when Tam skittered back with frantic eyes. "I'm not going to hurt you, lad. I'm here to help."

"Don't touch the bars," Tam hissed, his face chalky. "You can't pass through the bars. Not if you don't want to drown."

"Drown?" Darce stepped back. "What are you talking about?"

"The wards." Muir joined him, a dark look on his face. "Alasdair must have placed some kind of seal on the bars that only his blood can open."

Tam peered up at him, nose wrinkling. "The cage opens. But if we cross, if anyone crosses..." He buried his head between his knees, matted hair spilling across his shoulders. "The sea fills them up. It comes out of their eyes and ears. They choke on salt and seafoam. I've seen it, I have."

Darce stilled, horror turning him to stone. This was why they hadn't seen any guards on patrol. Cunningham's wards were all that was needed to ensure there would be no escape for the prisoners. The guards were only here to keep them alive.

"Can you break them?" Darce kept his voice low as he turned to Muir. "You were his sentinel. Surely you can—"

Muir shook his head. "Only Alasdair's blood can do that."

"There must be another way. *Look* at him." Darce curled his hands into fists, trying to stop the tremor in his arms. "We can't leave him in this place."

"You think I want to?" Muir glared at him. "If we're to get these prisoners out of here, it won't be through those bars." He ran a hand through his sailor's braids. "Come on, let's keep moving. Perhaps we'll find something we can use."

The tone of his voice told Darce he held little hope, but there was nothing else to do but follow him around the rest of the room. Each cell they peered into brought a new kind of suffering, a new kind of horror. A woman with empty, gaping holes instead of eyes. A man so thin the shapes of his bones protruded from his pale, sallow skin. The prisoners looked out from the shadows, faces bleak and empty.

There was no hope here. Only pain.

"There are at least a dozen cells on this floor alone," Jacques said. "How many more levels does this cursed place have? How many others are…"

His words faded into the wailing wind whistling through the tower. Something had caught his eye. Something had drained the blood from his face, leaving his cheeks white and stricken with terror.

Darce followed his gaze to the cell ahead. It was as wretched as the others, reeking of decay and strewn with filth. Only a small crack let in any kind of light. It wasn't enough to illuminate the cell, but it fell across the figure chained in the corner.

Her legs were bare and thin, bloodied where the iron manacles had bitten into her ankles. Her weathered skin was so pale it seemed translucent, stretched over her frail bones.

But none of that was what Jacques was staring at.

It took Darce a moment to see it. Then he realised the poor woman had no shackles around her wrists. She had no *need* for shackles. All that remained at the ends of her forearms were two ragged stumps.

His chest seized. He knew who she was.

Silveckan's most renowned shipwright. The woman who'd built the *Vanguard of the Firth*. Jacques' mother.

Maggie Grier was alive.

CHAPTER FIFTEEN
ISLA

Before Lachlan could speak, before he could do anything, Isla pushed forward, putting herself between her brother and the barrel of Blair Cunningham's pistol.

A dry laugh spilled from Blair's lips as he cocked the hammer with a staccato click. "You think that will stop me? You may be my cousin by blood, but I owe you no loyalty on the account of family. Not after what you've done to mine."

"I warned you," Isla said calmly. "I gave your uncle the chance to do what was right. Instead, he let Arburgh fall. The capital's gutters run with blood, and he is as much to blame for that as Eimhir."

"Blair, please." Lachlan tried to move around her, but she kept her feet planted firm, shielding him from the pistol. "I know I'm the last person you want to see—"

"Oh, so you *do* remember?" Blair shook his head. "The only reason I helped free your sergeant and uncle from the gallows was because I couldn't bear to see you in pain. Though it seems you're quite unaffected when it comes to mine." His mouth tightened into a bitter smile. "I risked everything to spare you seeing your family hanged. All I asked in return was for you to spare me the heartache of laying eyes on you again, but here you are."

Lachlan's face clouded. "I only came so that I might have the chance to save your life. It's not safe for you in Kinraith tonight. You need to get out of here while you still can."

Blair held the pistol steady, its barrel pointed at Isla's chest. There was no tremble in his hand, no sliding of his grip, just a glimmer of understanding in his eyes. "Your selkie friends are coming to finish us off, then? Arburgh wasn't enough?"

"It's not the selkies," Lachlan said. "It's the Sea Kith."

For the first time, Blair's composure slipped, and he flicked his gaze to Lachlan. "The Sea Kith? But why would... How would you know of their intentions?" When Lachlan didn't reply, a hollow laugh tumbled from Blair's throat. "Another blade in the back. Now you've thrown your lot in with brigands and pirates? Tides, I can't believe I ever thought I knew you."

"That's enough," Isla snapped. The wounded look on Lachlan's face sent a rush of anger through her, flooding her cheeks with warmth. "You know as well as I do the Admiralty is not the victim here. If I could lay waste to the entire fleet without risking the lives of the people in this port, I'd do it in a heartbeat." She gathered her breath. "As it stands, a crippling blow will have to do. It's the only thing that will draw out Eimhir. That's the reason we're here."

"Is that what you're telling yourself?" Blair's mouth twisted in contempt. "Because it seems like you're doing the skinchangers' dirty work for them."

"Don't you *fucking* dare." She stepped towards Blair, ignoring the barrel pressing against the bone armour covering her sternum. "You've been tucked up here in Kinraith, safe from everything that's happening out there. You haven't seen what they've done to the villages and ports up and down the coast. If you escape here with your life, go to Carroncross. Go to Storwick. Go to Caolaig, where all of this started. You'll see for yourself the kind of suffering we're trying to spare this island."

She didn't look down at his finger coiled and ready around the trigger. She didn't care about the threat of sparking flint and burnt powder erupting against her breastbone. Instead, she found the blue-grey of his gaze, the eyes that looked so much like his uncle's but held the promise of a different man. A *better* man.

"Blair," Lachlan whispered behind her. "Please."

The seconds stretched thick and uneasy, each longer than the last. Finally, Blair released the barrel from her chest and slid the pistol into its holster, his expression unfathomable. He turned to Lachlan, and the gleam of hurt resurfaced.

"You need to leave," he said, wrapping his hand around his tankard as he sank down to the table. "If anyone recognises you, I won't be able to protect you."

"You think I care about being recognised?" Lachlan pulled out a chair and sat opposite him. "I came here to protect *you*."

Blair stared at the tankard. "I don't blame you for choosing your family. I understand exactly what it feels like. I lost my parents too. My uncle... Whatever he is, he's all I have left."

"That's not true," Isla said.

He glanced up at her, his stare hard. "I told you, whatever blood we share—"

"It's more than blood we share." Her eyes drifted to Lachlan. She knew the look on his face, and what it meant.

Blair followed her gaze, cheeks flushing. "That's not... *We're* not..."

"He came here for you. He chose you." She waited until his eyes met hers again. "Back on the *Jade Dawn*, I held a blade to your neck and offered your life for Kerr's. Your uncle killed him anyway. He didn't care what happened to you. If I'd opened your throat that night, it wouldn't have been Cunningham that suffered. It was for Lachlan's sake I stayed my hand."

The furrow in Blair's brow deepened. The anger had slipped away, leaving behind a grief she recognised well. "You expect me to turn traitor like it's only my uncle I stand to lose. The Admiralty is more than a single man. I won't abandon my shipmates and scurry off into the night like a rat because you tell me to."

"Then you will die," Isla said, patience fraying. "There's no time for this, Blair. You have to—"

"She's right, you know," came a smooth drawl behind them. "As much as I loathe to find any kind of commonality with this salt-sullied former friend of mine, she does have a point. If you stay here, you'll pay for it."

Isla stilled. She knew that voice. Precise, clipped, every syllable as sharp as the tongue that spoke them.

She turned slowly, nails digging into her palms. There he stood, tall and resplendent in a cobalt-coloured velvet coat that brought out the red in his coiffed hair and the cunning gleam in his eyes.

Quinn. Nathair *fucking* Quinn.

Her mind clouded, like she'd lost herself in a fog as thick as the haar. But instead of salt rot and damp, every breath drew in the suffocating heat of rage.

She flew at him with a snarl. She didn't need a weapon; she just wanted him to bleed.

Before she could reach him, a strong arm wrapped around her waist to haul her back, and Lachlan's voice broke through the pounding in her skull. "*Don't* draw attention to us."

She wrestled against him, fighting to break loose. Quinn was as placid as ever, amusement curling at the corners of his lips.

"Nishi will kill you," she spat, panting. "She'll *burn* you for what you did to the *Jade Dawn*."

Quinn arched an eyebrow. "It was the Admiralty who hunted down the pirates. All I did was my civic duty by alerting our fine officers to where the ship might be found. Any law-abiding citizen of the capital would have done the same."

"You slithering, sanctimonious *bastard*. I swear to you, I'll—"

"Enough." Lachlan tugged her to her chair, barring her way back to her feet with the length of his crutch. He looked up at Quinn, an inscrutable expression settling across his features. "What are you doing here, Nathair?"

If Quinn was surprised by his coldness, he didn't show it. He only clicked his tongue and offered another mocking smile. "No pleasantries? Have you cast my friendship aside so quickly?"

"You did that yourself when you sent my uncle to the gallows," Lachlan replied curtly. "You almost got him killed."

"I sent the *Eel* to the gallows. A piece of southside smuggler scum that nobody would ever miss. That he and your uncle are one and the same is a failing of character on his part, not mine."

Isla glared at him. "It's never your fault, is it? It's so easy for you to wash your hands of the strings you pull, the machinations you put in place. I hope I'm there the day it all catches up to you. I hope—"

Lachlan squeezed her arm in warning, then turned to Quinn. "You've still not explained why you're here."

"The same reason as you, it seems." Quinn flicked his eyes to Blair. "When Arburgh fell, I decided my best chance at protection would be staying close to the Admiralty. And while I had to abandon my home, I still had my rats and birds. Imagine my surprise when one of them whispered to me of a Sea Kith ship waiting out past the rocks, cloaked in the cover of night. With the *Vanguard* gone, I thought it only right to warn the lieutenant here. It would be a shame to lose the port his uncle left him in charge of, after all."

Blair stiffened. "That seems charitable of you. Uncharacteristically so."

"You wound me." Quinn lowered himself into a bow. "Have I not proven myself a servant of the Admiralty?"

"A servant to whatever benefits you most, more likely." Blair folded his arms. "The last I heard, your merchant fleet went up in flames on the Eel's orders. How did you scramble together the coin to buy passage with the Admiralty, let alone bribe your rats and birds?"

Quinn chuckled softly. "Muir made a mistake, as fools and drunks often do. The moment he revealed his blackmail was the moment he lost his leverage over me. Investments can be made and unmade easily, especially in a place as rampant and ravenous with greed as the capital. By the time his smuggler friends set those ships ablaze, I'd already sold their deeds to a consortium of magistrates. They thought it was quite the bargain at the time."

Isla fought to swallow her rage. It was always the same with Quinn. No matter how tightly he was cornered, he managed to find a way out. He was like a growth that would keep coming back unless it was ripped out at the roots.

She flicked the sgian dubh into her palm, the dagger's handle cool against her skin. All she had to do was get past Lachlan. One stroke, and she could open Quinn's throat. She could watch his smirk die on his lips and be rid of him for good.

He met her eyes with a knowing smile. "I wouldn't, were I you. Not if you ever want to go back to that miserable, windswept estate of yours."

"What are you talking about?"

"Why, leverage, of course." He reached into his coat and produced an envelope bearing an ornate wax seal. "The magistrates didn't just give me coin in return for my merchant fleet. I requested an additional kind of payment." His teeth flashed. "The deeds to an estate forfeited to the capital due to the untimely deaths of its former custodians and the traitorous actions of their first-born heir."

Isla stared at the envelope. He was bluffing. He couldn't have.

"Blackwood Estate?" Lachlan's voice grew cold with rage. "You swept in and snatched my family's home for *leverage?* My mother and father are buried there, you conniving, heartless prick. If you think for a second I'd ever let you—"

Quinn stepped back, pocketing the envelope as quickly as he'd produced it. "I make no apology for doing what is necessary to survive in these times. Should we all come out on the other side of this, I'll gladly enter negotiations for the return of your home. If anything happens to me, however…" The corner of his mouth quirked. "I have made it explicitly clear that upon my death, Blackwood Estate will be torn down, with a new Admiralty outpost constructed in its place. One can never take too many measures when it comes to the skinchangers, after all. If Caolaig is ever to be resettled, it seems only fitting it should receive the protection your family were unable to give it."

Isla barely heard him. A foul taste rose at the back of her throat. Whether it was from grief or shame or rage, she couldn't be sure.

"It's just a piece of parchment," she said, half to herself. "It doesn't mean anything."

Even as she said it, she knew it wasn't true. She recalled how tightly she'd clutched her mother's letter all those months ago, scrunching the parchment until the ink bled and the edges tore. It had brought her back to Silveckan when nothing else could. It had started all this.

A promise, especially in death, always meant something.

When she met Quinn's eyes again, she forced herself to remain steady. He'd taken too much from her already. She wouldn't let him take the last shreds of her dignity along with it.

He smiled, as if to show he'd seen through the bluff. "It's not such a terrible bargain, in truth," he said. "All you have to do is keep me alive. Now, let's talk about arranging passage out of here before—"

The words were still slipping from his mouth when a distant whistling sound rushed in through the tavern windows, and a hurtling monstrosity of cast iron and black powder tore through their midst in an explosion of fire and blood.

CHAPTER SIXTEEN

DARCE

Darce froze in horror as Maggie Grier stared back at him from the shadows of her cell, the stumps of her arms hanging limply at her side.

Then, she started to wail.

The low-pitched noise burrowed into Darce's bones. Every second, the groan grew louder and more agitated, thick with too many years of pain and torture to imagine.

Jacques rushed forward, but Muir caught him by the collar before he could get close. "The bars," he warned. "It wouldn't do to come all this way just to get yourself killed."

"Let me go." Jacques struggled, but Muir's grip was strong. "I won't touch the bars, all right? Just let me go to her."

Muir released him, watching grimly as Jacques crashed to his knees in front of the cell. Even in the darkness, Darce saw his cheeks draining of colour, the stricken look haunting his face. Jacques had come here to lay eyes on the place his mother had died. This was a fate much crueller.

"Ma?" Jacques edged closer to the rusting bars, hands trembling as he held them short of the blood-cursed iron. "It's me, Hamish. I'm here."

Maggie looked at him blankly and mumbled something Darce couldn't hear. Another wail tore from her throat, shuddering through the air. Then, a shout went up from one of the other cells, and more voices joined the din.

"*Merde,*" Sébastien muttered. "If there are any guards here, that racket will bring them running. I think we lost any chance of getting out quietly." He unsheathed his daggers with a flourish, then glanced towards the stairwell. "If you have a plan to free these people, I suggest you get started. I'll go to the lower levels and buy you as much time as I can."

"I'll come with you," Nishi said, still lingering in the shadows of the archway with a haunted look on her face. "I wouldn't mind making a few of those bastards pay for what they've done here."

"You should go too, Sergeant," Muir said. "We already have two sentinels here, and your gifts might be needed."

"But..." Darce looked back at the cell. Jacques was on his knees, shoulders shaking as he leaned as close as he could without touching the iron bars. Inside, Maggie Grier's face was contorted in misery, tears streaking through the blood and filth caked across her lank cheeks.

Darce couldn't help her. He couldn't help any of them, not as long as the wards held.

"Find a way," he said, grasping Muir's arm. "You were his sentinel. You *must* be able to break them."

Muir didn't say anything, but the look on his face left Darce only with despair as he followed Nishi and Sébastien into the stairwell.

A strained silence hung between them as they hurried down the steps as quickly as the narrow twists would allow. The horror of what they'd seen in the cells remained unspoken, but was no quieter for it. Darce heard it in each ragged breath, every frantic thump of their boots.

The first guard appeared from nowhere, emerging around the corner in a flash of sapphire and emerald. Before Darce had time to gather himself, Sébastien leapt, drawing one of his stiletto daggers across the guard's throat in a perfect line. The laceration was thin but deep, and the guard dropped to his knees, blood spilling across the jewel-toned fabric of his cloak.

Sébastien inspected his dagger. "Just a wee taste, *m'ami*. Plenty more to come."

"Care to explain what it was that made you hate the Admiralty so much?" Nishi asked, arching an eyebrow. "We all have our reasons, of course, but yours seem particularly...enthusiastic."

"My reasons are my own," Sébastien said. "All you need to know is if I see one of those cloaks, I'll cut it down. That should be good enough, no?"

Nishi gave a hard smile. "I agree."

A shout carried up the stairs, echoing off the damp stone walls. More guards must have been gathering below. It was difficult to tell how many there were, but as long as they remained in the stairwell, it didn't matter. The narrow steps would funnel them close, preventing them from using their numbers to their advantage.

"We can hold them here," Darce said. "We'll block the way up to the cells and give Muir and Jacques as much time as we can."

Sébastien tilted his head. "They're not coming up. I think...I think they're going further *down*."

Darce stilled. They hadn't thought to search for what might lie below the tower, they'd just followed the stairwell up. If there was an undercroft, it could hold more cells. It could hold worse. "Shite. I'll go after them. If they're retreating, they must have a reason. I don't want to be caught out by any nasty surprises."

"At least take the Îleanach," Nishi said, glancing at Sébastien. "His daggers seem drawn to Admiralty throats. I'll stay here to cut off anyone who tries to head up to the cells." She tugged down the brim of her tricorne hat, copper eyes turning sombre. "Watch yourself, Sergeant. We've lost too much already. Would hate to tell Blackwood we lost you too."

Her words pressed heavy on Darce's mind as he continued into the stairwell. It wasn't just the prisoners he'd fail if he got himself killed. His soul was the only thing tethering Isla to this world. If he died, he'd die knowing he'd condemned her to the haar, to the gun-anam. He could risk almost anything, but not that. Not *her*.

"We'll get you back to her." Sébastien's mouth lost its usual wry twist. "This lass of yours. She'll see you again, I promise."

"I—" Darce stopped, surprised. "Thank you."

Sébastien gave a tight nod, then ducked under a cobweb-shrouded archway leading deeper into the tower. The musty air thickened with the rotten stench of brine and kelp, burning Darce's throat as he edged carefully down the steps. The slick stone was strewn with moss and seaweed. One slip would send him and Sébastien tumbling to the bottom and whatever awaited them there.

The muffled echo of raised voices floated up the stairs. Darce tilted his ear towards the sound, but he couldn't make out the exchange, only the fraught tension in it. The guards were panicking about something—*arguing* about something.

When he reached the bottom of the steps, he saw what it was.

The stairwell opened into a huge undercroft, its vaulted arches looming over the vast space. The watchtower's foundations were built into the rocks, jumbled together in a patchwork of smooth limestone and red brick. Placed around them, coated with grime and a carrying stench so familiar it made Darce's stomach churn, were dozens of barrels of black powder.

"*Merde*," Sébastien muttered again. "These fucking…"

The guards looked up, faces caught somewhere between fury and defiance. There were only two of them—not enough to put up a fight. But they didn't need to put up a fight. Not when those barrels would do the job for them.

It was like Jacques had said—Baininch Rise was never meant to be a prison. It was a grave. And with a single spark, they'd all be buried in it.

"Do it!" one of the guards barked. His hair was flecked with grey, and he bore a nasty scar on his cheek. "Our orders were clear. If this place was ever discovered, we were to topple it into the sea."

"And us along with it?" The woman he'd snapped at folded her arms. "Ye might be keen to die, but I've nae desire to meet my end in this shitehole. We don't have to blow ourselves up if we kill the bastards who found us."

She shot Darce a hateful look, the venom in her glare burning through him. There was something odd in the way she spoke. Her voice, her expression...everything about her struck something discordant inside him. Like he was seeing someone who shouldn't exist. Like he *knew* her.

It hit him like a wall of grief.

"Rhona," he said, her name sharp with regret.

The woman jolted, eyes widening. "What the fuck did you call me?"

"You're her sister, aren't you? You..." He shook his head. "I don't understand. He *took* you. He used you to break her. He held your life over her head to force her to serve him."

The first guard glanced between them. "What's going on here? Do you know this prick, Evie?"

"No, I don't. And it's clear he doesn't ken me, either." The woman's eyes flashed dangerously. "Rhona? That bitch stopped being my sister when she gambled our family's lives away with that nasty wee card habit of hers. We lost *everything* because of her. That's why I'm here."

A cold realisation gripped Darce's chest. "All this time she thought she was keeping you alive...but you were never one of his prisoners. You're here by choice."

"After an apology, is she?" Evie snorted. "The Grand Admiral gave me another chance, a chance to make something of myself. Guarding a musty old tower one week out of the month isn't so bad when you spend the rest of the time wanting for nothing. Maybe ye can pass on the message to Rhona the next time she ends up kneecapped for her debts."

"Tides take you—she's fucking *dead* because of you!" Darce snarled. "She ran her captain through with her own blade because she thought she was saving you, then turned a dagger on herself because she couldn't live with it."

Something flickered across Evie's face. Whether it was grief or guilt or an old, buried resentment, Darce couldn't be sure, but it contorted her sharp features into something pained. Then it was gone, and she curled her lip into a sneer. "I don't know how ye ken my sister. I don't much care, either. If she's dead, ye'll be joining her soon enough."

The coldness in her voice twisted his stomach. He should have remembered Muir's warning from all those months ago. Not all loyalty needed to be bought with blood. For some, coin would do the job just fine.

He eyed the barrels, heart pounding. There was still a way out of this. There had to be. "If you bury us here, Cunningham is the only one who wins. Are you so eager to die for him?"

"I don't need to die for him," she said. "Not if I kill you first."

She moved quicker than he could blink, wheeling around to snatch a small crossbow from the table behind her.

Darce never saw it coming. She loosed the bolt, and he felt a punch in his shoulder, warm blood splattering his cheek. The bolt hit its mark, tearing through flesh and muscle before lodging in the wall somewhere behind him.

He doubled over, clutching a hand to his blazing shoulder. Blood seeped through his fingers, dripping onto the stones with a relentless *tip-tip*.

A muttering of Breçh curses filled his ear, and he vaguely became aware of Sébastien moving beside him, stiletto daggers glinting in his hands. The swish of steel sliced through air, and when Darce lifted his head, Evie was lying across the table, crossbow slipping from her hands as one of Sébastien's blades quivered in the hollow of her throat.

Darce stared at her blank, glassy eyes, so deep a brown they were almost black. In death, she looked just like Rhona. A scraped-out shell of everything she'd once been. A woman gutted not only by Cunningham, but what she'd done in his name.

He staggered to his feet, only to be met with the unmistakable sound of flint striking against steel and the warmth of a naked flame.

"The Grand Admiral gave us our orders," the first guard said. The gnarled scar across his cheek danced in the flicker of the torch he held in his hand. "A quick death here is preferable to what he'll do if I fail to see them through."

Darce couldn't move. The pain in his shoulder rooted him to the spot. The guard was already heading for one of the barrels, his boots splashing through the puddles. There was nothing on his face but grim resolve. The man had made his choice. He'd see it through, even if it meant his end.

An agonising heat seared through Darce's shoulder as he lunged for him, but the effort brought him to his knees. He'd never make it. The barrels were only a few short strides from the torch. All it would take was a lick of flame, and the black powder inside would ignite, blowing them all to pieces in a grave of smoke and stone.

Then came another whistle of steel. Sébastien moved with a desperate, deadly grace, leaping across the uneven ground towards the guard. His dagger had missed its mark this time, only nicking the guard's wrist instead of burying itself deep in sinew and flesh. But it was enough to make the man falter. Enough to give Sébastien time to fly at him.

Then the crack of a pistol tore through the undercroft, and Sébastien staggered back, his shirt blooming red. His eyes widened as he touched his fingers to his ribs.

"Drown it!" he spluttered, blood spraying from his lips as he stumbled towards the guard. "Drown it all!"

The guard swung the torch wildly, almost striking Sébastien's head, but the cutthroat ducked under the blow and scrambled to wrestle the wooden handle from his grasp. The flames lapped at his flaxen hair, searing his skin pink as he fought to prise the guard's fingers away. But the blood still seeped from the red stain in his shirt. He wouldn't be able to hold on much longer.

Neither of them would.

The floor was cold and hard beneath Darce's knees. All he could feel was the burning in his shoulder. Pain blurred his vision, turning everything dark. His palms scraped against the ground, finding slimy seaweed and puddles of water.

Salt water.

Drown it. Sébastien's cry echoed in his throbbing skull, and through the haze of pain, Darce understood.

He reached for the tides. The heaving swells around Baininch Rise crashed through his ear, but slipped through his fingers. He felt the spray on his skin before it shrank away again, leaving him fumbling in the dark.

Please, he begged. *Not for me. For Isla.*

Blood gushed from his shoulder, trickling into the shallow pools of seawater scattered through the undercroft. The sea's touch surrounded him: the acrid stench of rotting kelp, the erosion on the limestone walls, the soft lapping of water coming from a small underground lake.

This place knew the sea. It led to the sea.

He reached out again, and this time, a wave rose within him. His blood sang with the tides' roar, deep and furious. They'd heard him, and they'd answered.

Across the room, Sébastien was wrestling for the torch. His skin was blistered, his flaxen hair charred from the flames, but he hadn't fallen yet. He was still fighting.

Darce raised his arm with as much strength as he could muster, gasping in relief as a blue-grey wall rose from the edge of the cave. The wave rushed forward, crashing over a dozen of the barrels, drenching their pine and willow casings along with the black powder stored inside.

"Not...enough," Sébastien choked. "You have to drown it, all of it."

Tides, he was trying. But blood poured from the crossbow wound, leaving his head reeling. He could barely hold his weight off the ground. All he wanted to do was close his eyes and surrender.

The sea raised its voice in fury, crashing off the inside of his skull. It wouldn't let him rest. It rushed to his blood, and he was at its mercy.

He lifted his arms again, pulling another wave towards him. The icy water sprang from the stone, bursting from every crack and fissure. It soaked more of the black powder barrels, scattering Darce with spray as it washed through the undercroft.

But it didn't reach the guard. The grizzled man still had one hand wrapped around the handle of his torch. The other found Sébastien's throat, shoving him to the side as he staggered the last few metres to one of the dry, untouched barrels.

It happened in a heartbeat. The scrape and clatter of the lid falling to the floor. The sharp intake of breath as the guard plunged the torch into the barrel's maw. The bright, raging glow that lit up Sébastien's horror-struck gaze right before the barrel exploded, bringing the wretched bones of this place down around them.

Water rushed into Darce's lungs, turning his chest to ice. He couldn't see anything, couldn't feel anything but the churning sea dragging him to the depths.

Something plunged through the water next to him, leaving a trail of bubbles—part of the crumbling watchtower. It had almost crushed him, but the currents had pulled him to safety at the last second, spinning him head over heels.

His chest burned, begging for precious air, but only the sea was waiting to rush in. If he surrendered, the ripples of his death would carry across the waves until they reached Isla. He couldn't let himself drown here. He had to *live*. There was more than his own life at stake.

He twisted his body and tried to make sense of which direction the surface was in. The sea closed in, weighing down his sodden clothes. Salt stung his eyes as he peered through the water, but he only saw darkness.

Perhaps he was trapped. Perhaps the tower had collapsed on top of him, cutting off any hope of escaping.

No, he thought. There had to be a way to the open water.

He let his muscles relax, ceasing his struggle. As he quietened, the call of the tides rose from the magic in his blood. He didn't need to fight it. He needed to lose himself in it.

A rush of cold seeped through his veins, and it took all he had not to gasp. The sea poured through him, funnelling into every crevice, surging around his organs like the waves eating at a cliff. The tides had claimed him as their own, and he'd given himself to their mercy.

A fierce current wrapped him in its grasp, propelling him through the darkness. Through his water-clogged ear, he heard the muffled thumps of more chunks of stone plunging through the surface. How much of the tower had been blown apart in the blast? Had Muir and the others escaped, or did they lie crushed and buried under the rubble?

He cracked open an eye and was met with the sting of seawater. A faint light broke above. If he could only reach it...

His lungs ached as he thrashed towards the distant surface. Even now, he feared it was too far, that the fathoms would drag him back and hold him until he drowned. But the light was brightening, so close he could almost taste the sweet relief of air on his tongue.

He crashed through the surface, chest seizing as he sucked in a breath. The relief was almost enough to turn his vision hazy, and it took all he had to cling to consciousness as the waves leapt around him. Every breath burned his tender lungs, but he relished it all the same. No matter how painful it was, he was grateful for it. It meant he was alive.

A shrill caw pierced the air. Featherblade must have been looking for him. He couldn't see the gannet, but knowing it was near was comfort enough.

His drenched hair fell across his eyes, and he fought to hold himself above the waves. The watchtower was barely visible. He couldn't see how much of it had crumbled into the waves. Part of him didn't *want* to see. There was no telling how many prisoners had been caught in the explosion, how many had been swallowed in the falling stone, crushed in the tower's bowels.

Just like Sébastien. Darce blanched as he remembered the flash of the black powder igniting under his face, his wide-eyed look of realisation.

It would have been over quickly. But knowing that was no comfort at all.

He dragged himself through the waves as best he could, salt water stinging the hole the crossbow bolt had left in his shoulder. Each stroke sent a fresh burst of pain up his arm, but there was nothing else to do but push through it. Pain, he could deal with later.

The tender was still sitting high on the gravelly shore when he stumbled out of the water. Nobody had taken it yet. He wasn't sure whether that was a good thing or not. If the others had been buried under the rubble...

Another shriek tore through the air, and Featherblade swooped through the mist, white wings splayed as it flapped to a halt in front of him. Behind the gannet, several figures limped through the drizzly haze.

Darce caught sight of a familiar tricorne hat, and his heart leapt. "Nishi?"

She winced, carrying her weight gingerly on one leg. When she saw him, her eyes went slack with shock. "Sergeant? But you were... How the fuck did you get out?"

"By the will of the tides, and nothing else." He glanced at the strangers behind her. Prisoners, by the looks of them. Cheeks gaunt, eyes hollow. "What about Muir and Jacques? Did they—"

"They're alive. Helping get as many prisoners out as they can. That blast tore through half the tower—took one of the walls clean down and collapsed half the floors in on themselves. Turns out the Grand Admiral's cursed cells don't mean much when you can walk out through the big bloody hole in the wall." Nishi's jaw tensed. "Not everyone made it. Some of the cells are still intact. Others are buried under stone. I heard them screaming."

"We lost Sébastien too. I need to find Jacques. I—"

"Séba's gone?" A faint voice came from the mist, and Jacques emerged, eyes bleak. His arms were wrapped around his mother's frail shoulders as he coaxed her along, but at Darce's silence, he stopped dead. "What happened down there?"

"The Admiralty happened," Darce said, grief and anger rising in his throat. "Cunningham happened. He'd rather lose this place to the bottom of the sea than let the people in it walk free. We should have known that."

"Would it have made a difference?" Muir joined them. "You're bleeding, in case you hadn't noticed."

Darce pressed a hand to his shoulder, his fingers coming away wet and red. "Thanks for the reminder. And aye, it would have made a difference. We could have—"

"Even if we'd known, it would have changed nothing," Muir said, cutting him off. "We had to come here. We had to try."

"And the ones we're leaving behind? The ones we got killed?"

"Surely this isn't the first time you've failed someone, Sergeant." Muir's voice was hard, but the bitterness seemed directed as much inwards as it was at him. "Mourn them, if that's what you need to do. Then set the guilt aside before it drowns you."

Like it did me. The unspoken words filled the air, all the more painful for being swallowed. They all had their own ghosts, their own mistakes whispering at their ears. Mara. Cormick. Kerr. Sébastien. The wretched souls they were leaving behind in this place would haunt them too.

His gaze found Maggie Grier. Her achingly thin arms were rigid with gooseflesh as she trembled in Jacques' grasp. But though her expression was blank and confused, there was a light to her green eyes that hadn't been there before. A sliver of understanding that the walls holding her for so many years had been torn down.

Aye, they'd failed. Darce would carry that with him, no matter what Muir said. But he'd carry too the souls they'd managed to save. He'd carry them away from here, and hope that one day, he might be forgiven for the cost.

CHAPTER SEVENTEEN

ISLA

Isla scrambled to her feet, ears ringing, throat thick with smoke from the fire blazing through the tavern.

Heat burned her cheeks as she tried to find her bearings. The cannonball had ripped through the front window, sending a shower of glass across the tables. One of the beams had caved in, partially collapsing the roof. Now, the tavern was aflame, crumbling around them.

She found Lachlan on the floor, panting hard as he shielded Blair with his body. His rosewood crutch lay beside him, cracked in half. It would be no use to him now. She needed to find something else for him to use, anything else...

"Leave it," he said. "We need to get out of here."

She nodded, lips pressed tight. There was nothing she could say. She'd agreed to this. She'd *invited* it. The Sea Kith may not have intended for one of their shots to miss its mark, to go hurtling past the fleet and tear through Kinraith instead, but she'd known it might happen.

That was the thing about violence: after it was unleashed, there was no controlling it.

Smoke filled her lungs, and she coughed until her chest ached. The tavern's doorway was ahead, half-blocked by a fallen beam. She ducked through, waiting for Lachlan to follow. He emerged a moment later coated in blood and grime, arm looped around Blair's shoulder as he limped on one leg.

She met his gaze. "Quinn?"

Lachlan shook his head. "I didn't see him. Maybe the cannonball took him."

Part of her wanted to believe it, but she knew Nathair Quinn better than that. If there was a way out, he was gone already, slithering away like the snake he was.

She pushed the thought aside. Whether Quinn was alive or dead didn't matter. Whatever noose he'd strung around their necks would fray to pieces if the haar continued to spread. She could only focus on stopping it.

"Take Blair to the tender," she said. "It could be hours before Eimhir takes the bait, and every second he stays here is another chance of getting caught in the slaughter. It's not safe to be Admiralty in Kinraith tonight."

Blair trailed his eyes over the burning tavern. "Seems to me it's not safe to be anyone in Kinraith tonight."

The accusation burrowed under her skin like a barb she couldn't dig out. There was no denying the truth of his words. The tavern roof was collapsing inward, flames burning through its shell. Pillars of smoke rose across the port, bleeding into the night sky. The air reverberated with the shrill echo of screams.

This was only the beginning.

Blair fixed Lachlan with a steely gaze. "I meant what I said before. I won't run to assuage your guilt for what you've done here. If the skinchangers come, the people of this port will need protection. *That* is what the Admiralty is for." A shadow fell across his face. "At least, that's what it should be. Even if my uncle has lost sight of that, I have not. I *will* not."

The stubbornness in his jaw made Isla want to punch it. "Then stay, if that's what you want. But I won't risk—"

"I'll help." Lachlan stared at Blair, steady and resolute. "You're right. The people of Kinraith deserve better than what we've brought on them. The least I can do is stand with them in the face of what's coming."

Isla opened her mouth to protest, then snapped it shut again. Blair held a part of Lachlan she couldn't reach, a part that ran deeper than the fractured bond she'd been working to repair. There was no use resenting it, not when she understood it so well.

"Fine," she said through gritted teeth. "But at least take that damn cloak off. It will only make us more of a target to Sea Kith and selkie alike. You won't be able to help anyone if you're dead in a gutter."

Blair gave a reluctant nod, shedding the sapphire folds from his shoulders and letting the cloak spill to the ground. Underneath, his woollen coat and white buckskin breeches were covered in grime and ash from the tavern. As long as nobody looked too closely, he might pass as a well-off local caught up in the chaos rather than the Admiralty royalty he really was.

The narrow streets were swarming as they left the blazing tavern behind and headed further into the port. Frantic locals hurried to their homes, fraught and fearful as they jostled past stiff-shouldered Admiralty officers. The air was thick with the stench of smoke, and Isla spotted more than one orange glow over the roofs. The *Red Gale* had hit the Admiralty with all it had, and Kinraith had been caught in its salvo.

I did this, she thought bleakly. *I let this happen.*

A thump of footsteps came from one of the narrow wynds ahead, and she tore herself from her thoughts to see a young Admiralty officer stumbling from the shadows, his forehead slick with sweat.

He stopped in front of them, and she realised with a lurch that it was one of the officers she'd seen earlier, laughing drunkenly as they traipsed through the night market.

"Lieu—Lieutenant Cunningham," he said, eyes widening in recognition. "Tides be praised, I found you. Something's happened. The pirates...they got Jack. They killed him dead, and—"

The rest of his words disappeared in the blood bubbling from his lips. Before Isla could make sense of what had happened, the lad slumped to the cobbles, cloak turning red.

Behind him stood a Sea Kith with a needle-thin blade, blood dripping from its tip. Her mouth widened into a cruel grin as she trailed her eyes over them. "Which one's the lieutenant, then? Not that it matters. I'll gut all three of you."

Lachlan stiffened. "We came here with you on the *Red Gale*. It's not us you're here for, it's—"

The pistol jerked in Isla's hand, and a shot cracked through the air. The familiar smell of burnt powder singed her nostrils as the plume of smoke cleared, leaving her only with the sight of the Sea Kith falling to her knees, chest blooming with red.

A strangled silence stretched between them. Then Blair gave a hollow laugh. "If that's how you treat your allies, perhaps I was safer as your enemy."

Isla looked down at the pistol. The stock pulsed in her hand like a heartbeat. She hadn't even realised she'd drawn it.

"You're neither ally nor enemy," she said tightly. "You're family."

She ignored the disconcerted look on his face as she shoved the pistol back into its holster, her palm burning. It was too easy. It always was. Blood demanded blood, over and over until they were all fucking drowning in it. Even when it felt necessary. Even when it felt right.

You're family, she'd told Blair. The moment the Sea Kith had threatened him, she'd had no choice but to act.

At least, that was the truth she told herself. The only truth she could live with.

As they rounded the next corner, Isla's heart stilled. The cobbles were stained bloody, leaving a smeared trail to a broken body lying in the corner of the street. Bones jutted out from flesh, their ends snapped and shattered. Limbs twisted in unnatural angles, crushed by the huge iron ball that lay on top.

She could see no Admiralty cloak, no Sea Kith tattoos. Just a pair of blank, glassy eyes.

Blair muttered something under his breath, then turned to her with a sickened look. "How long is this supposed to last?"

"Long enough to wound the Admiralty, no more." She squirmed. "A barrage of cannon fire aimed at drawing attention to the harbour while the throatslitters cut down as many officers as they can. They're meant to fall back before the selkies close in."

"*If* the selkies close in, you mean." Blair's eyes were cold. "There's no guarantee Eimhir will take the bait. You've traded the lives of everyone in this port for a chance you don't know you'll get."

"She'll come. She has to." The words were empty, tasting like ash. This was the only way to draw Eimhir out, the only language she understood now the bloodlust had her in its grip. There had been no other choice.

This violence belongs to all of us. Eimhir's voice echoed in her ears like a ghost. *It will continue as long as we let it.*

Someone had to let go. Someone had to break the hold of this cycle that had caught them in its currents.

Isla had thought it could have been her. But as Kinraith burned, she looked down and found her hands as bloody as the rest.

By the time the sky brightened with the pale grey of morning, Isla feared the night's horrors had been for nothing.

Word travelled quickly on the waves. She knew how swiftly the selkie scouts bore tidings to the clans. If any of her people had witnessed the Sea Kith's assault on the Admiralty, they would have reported it. But hours had passed, and still there was no sign of Eimhir.

Blair was right. She hadn't taken the bait.

Kinraith's townsfolk began to emerge, assessing the scars left on their home. Screeches echoed overhead as the gulls and crows fought each other for a chance to scavenge at the scraps left behind.

As Isla walked the narrow streets, she was drawn to flashes of sapphire and emerald splayed across the cobbles, the fabric stained red from opened throats. Ruairidh's crew had done their work well. The Admiralty had been dealt a blow, leaving them bloodied.

It was what they'd come here to do. Strange, then, that the sight of her enemy lying like carrion for the crows should leave her so empty.

Blair left them at first light, returning to the docks to assess the damage to the ships moored in the harbour. All Isla could see past the Admiralty fleet were the jagged ridges of the rocks rising from the waves. There were no crimson sails on the horizon. The *Red Gale* had slunk away before dawn, just like they'd planned.

She and Lachlan should have been on it. Instead, they were stranded here in the trap they'd failed to spring.

After a while, their aching bellies persuaded them to take respite in one of the port's inns. A subdued atmosphere hung over the tables as they ate, weighing on Isla's heart as she pushed a warm hunk of bread around her milk-sodden porridge. The honey they'd sweetened it with couldn't relieve the bitter taste on her tongue. It felt like everyone knew what she was, and what she'd brought here.

She tugged down her sleeves, concealing the scars circling her wrists. She didn't want to look at the reminders any more than she wanted prying eyes to take notice of them.

Lachlan chewed his porridge, glum and distant. They'd managed to scramble enough coin to buy a worn hazelwood cane for him to use in place of his crutch, but the stick was stiff and awkward in his hand when he walked.

When he glanced up at her, his gaze was mild, but Isla couldn't mistake the familiar glint of accusation.

"She didn't come," he said flatly. "This was all for nothing."

There was no use denying it. "So it would seem."

His eyes hardened at that, like he'd been waiting for an argument she'd refused to give him. Then he sighed, the tension loosening from his shoulders as he slumped against the threadbare cushions propped against his chair. "I thought you knew her."

Isla flinched. Without meaning to, her fingers found the salt on her skin again, running over the rough trails biting into her flesh. "I thought I did, too."

"Do they…" He trailed off, gaze lingering on her sleeves. "Is it true what Galbraith said? That if you don't get your pelt back, you'll turn into one of those wraiths?"

"It would have happened already if it wasn't for him. When he made the blood oath, when he gave me part of his soul…" The words lodged painfully in her throat. "I never wanted him to chain himself to me. I wanted him to have a choice. But if he hadn't…"

"It was his choice. *You* were his choice." Lachlan shook his head, a rueful laugh spilling from his lips. "Tides, I was jealous. When you left all those years ago, I started looking to Galbraith like an older brother. He became family to me. And then you came back, and it felt like another thing taken from me."

"Lachlan, I—"

"I'm not blaming you. Not anymore, at least." The corner of his mouth twitched into a smile. "I know he loves us both. But back then…something changed, and suddenly I was on the outside. He'd never looked at you like that before."

Isla smiled despite herself. "Probably for the best. Our father would have hanged him."

"He'd never have got the chance. Mother would have gelded him first." Lachlan chuckled, then grew sombre again. "Everything happened so fast. I lost them both in the space of a week. You came back, but you weren't the same person I'd waved goodbye to at the docks all those years before. I felt Galbraith drawing closer to you, and I thought that meant he was slipping away from me. And I'd changed too. I don't think I understood that before." He met her eyes steadily. "I understand now. I know what's important. And I don't want to lose sight of that again."

She wrapped her fingers around his. His hand rested against her skin, pulse beating with the blood she'd once thought they'd shared. The blood they'd never needed to share. "I told you before, you're my brother. Nothing will ever change that. If there's one thing I've learned over the last few months, it's that we choose our family."

He squeezed her hand, looking out the window towards the docks. "You already know I won't leave him here. I can't."

"Aye, I know. I just need you to promise me you'll be careful. He might be able to protect you for now, but his uncle branded you a traitor. If the *Vanguard* comes back—"

Before she could finish, the inn doors burst open, rattling on their hinges. The morning light spilled into the dim room, and in the middle stood Blair, face pale and curls dripping seawater.

"The docks," he panted, breath sharp and ragged. "You have to hurry."

Lachlan was already pushing himself upright, hand clenching around his cane. "What happened?"

When Blair's eyes found hers, they held no ire or resentment, just desperation. She'd seen that look before. She knew the kinds of horrors held in that reflection.

Caolaig. Arburgh. Storwick. This was how it started: with a ripple in the waves and the glint of a selkie axe hungry for flesh.

It seemed the violence they'd been courting had decided to answer.

CHAPTER EIGHTEEN

DARCE

It took the best part of an hour to ferry everyone from the bleak, shingle-covered shore to the waiting soulship. The tender was small, and in the end, more than three dozen prisoners had escaped the watchtower's ruins. It didn't feel like enough. Not after seeing the horrors inside Baininch Rise. Most of the rescued were half-starved, broken in body as much as in mind. Some had been mutilated like Maggie Grier. Others bore the scars of time and neglect: long nails and filth-matted hair, blackened gums and sallow skin. Yet in each of their gazes, Darce saw the same glimmer of something too desperate to put a name to. Something that swelled in his own chest.

Even here, in the shadow of the Admiralty's terror, there was hope.

He stood on the shore, waves lapping at his boots as he waited for the tender to return. The watchtower loomed over him, loose chunks spilling from its crumbling innards. There was little left of it but its bones.

Jacques wanted to search for Sébastien's body, but Darce had gently dissuaded him. Even if the depths of the tower hadn't collapsed, he'd seen how close Sébastien had been to the barrel of black powder. There would be nothing to find in that undercroft. Nothing left to bury.

His shoulder twinged, and he let out a hiss. The blood loss had left his head heavy. He had to get patched up soon or he'd be no use to anyone.

"Are you doing that?" Muir asked sharply.

Darce looked up. It was only the two of them left on the shore. The prisoners had been carried across to the soulship, and all that was left was for Nishi to return and row them back. But there was no sign of the boat, no splash of oars.

"What are you talking about?" he asked.

Muir gestured to the waves. "*That*."

It took Darce a moment to realise what he meant. Then it hit him: the hum of magic had slipped from his veins, and with it, so had the haar. Whether it was from the pain of his wound or the exhaustion seeping into his bones, he'd lost his grasp on the tides.

Across the waves, the mists were clearing, scattering into spray. He could see the glistening sheen of the soulship's mast winking like the torch from a lighthouse.

Then he saw the shadow on the horizon, sails full and black against the clouds.

The *Vanguard*. It had found them.

Muir's mouth tightened. "We knew he was coming for us. It was only a matter of time."

"I'll bring the mists back. Just give me..." Even as Darce spoke, he knew it was no use. When he reached for the tides, they slipped away from him, distant and elusive. He couldn't summon the haar, not in the state he was in. And without it to shroud them, there would be no escaping the *Vanguard*.

"There's our Sea Kith friend." Muir squinted across the waves to the approaching tender. "She's got strong arms, not that it'll do us much good. By the time we get back on board, Alasdair will be all but on top of us." His hand drifted to his chest, fingers curling around his heart. The beat of the blood oath, pulsing stronger each second. A wound ripped open after decades of denial.

"Like poison," Muir muttered, answering a question Darce hadn't dared ask. "Like I can feel his corruption in my own blood, my own soul. Or perhaps it's mine, and I never had to face it until now. Either way, it's rotten. It needs to end."

The crossing to the soulship passed in a haze, as if the haar that had slipped from Darce's grasp now seeped into his skull, turning his head heavy. He only heard echoes of Nishi and Muir's muffled voices.

The shadows in the corners of his eyes bled across his vision, and he found himself drifting to a place where the pain could no longer reach him.

How long the slumber held him, Darce couldn't be sure. Voices swirled around him, muttering things that didn't make sense, filling his dulled head with noise. He felt the fabric of his shirt ripped away and the sting of a needle entering his shoulder, but it was so distant it didn't seem real. The only thing that broke through his heavy stupor was the slap that cracked across his cheeks, jolting him to his senses.

Muir offered an unapologetic shrug. "Sorry, Sergeant, but I can't let you sleep any longer. Not if any of us are to get out of this alive." He helped him sit upright against the base of the mast, and Darce groaned as a fresh pain lanced through his shoulder.

"Aye, that'll be the stitches." Muir grimaced. "Would have given you a dram of something to take the edge off, but apparently you and the Sea Kith gutted our stores back at Île de Durgavie. So it serves you right, I say. But a wee bit of pain is no bad thing. It might keep your senses sharp, keep you alive."

The deck lurched, hitting the bottom of Darce's spine with a bruising thump as he struggled to sit straight. He couldn't see over the top of the gunwale, but the spray flying into the wind was wild and fierce. They were cutting through the waves at pace, battering through with brute force.

"We're calling the tides to carry us as best we can," Muir said by way of explanation. "But Jacques is used to more subtle manipulations than the yoking of the waves, and I'm...out of practice, to say the least. We need your help. We need the haar."

He offered a hand, and Darce took it, hauling himself to his feet. His shoulder twinged, but he pushed the pain away and tried to focus on getting his bearings. The rain was falling harder, sweeping across the horizon. They'd lost the light, and the waves frothed dark and angry, crashing against the hull with so much ire Darce was surprised the bone didn't splinter.

He turned to Muir. "How long?"

Muir nodded towards the aft, where the churning foam of the soulship's wake trailed into the waiting jaws of the monster hunting them.

The *Vanguard of the Firth*. A man-o'-war with no equal.

It was bearing down on them faster than Darce could believe, its huge black sails fully set to catch the wind raging across the waves. Every sentinel on board would be channelling their magic towards the swell, urging it to carry them to their prey.

They'd never stood a chance.

A familiar screech rattled through the air, and he craned his neck to see Featherblade circling the empty mast, flitting through the spaces that should have held sails of mist and spray. The gannet knew what the soulship needed. Darce knew it too. There was only one thing that could save them.

He closed his eyes, trying to push away the image of the *Vanguard's* towering masts, its billowing sails. The ship was like a storm rolling in, promising to break upon them with all its wrath. He needed to take them to a place it could not strike.

Somewhere in his chest, he felt the soulship call to him. He'd given part of himself to its bones. His blood had sated its deck. Now, it cried out in terror, aware of what hunted it.

He reached for the tides. The shiver in his veins was faint, but it was there. He waited for the brackish taste to rise in his throat, for the frost to crawl up the hairs on his arms as the haar thickened and closed in around them. Instead, there was silence. Even the soulship's screams faded.

Fickle be the waves, Nishi had told him once. Nobody, not even a sentinel, could command the will of the tides. All he could do was reach for them, and pray they decided to answer.

"Twenty metres wide, eighty-five metres in length. Not including the bowsprit, of course."

Darce opened his eyes. Standing beside him, blue-lipped and glassy-eyed, was Maggie Grier. Her grey hair whipped her gaunt cheeks as she stared out over the waves, the stumps of her forearms resting on the gunwale. Her gaze was fixed on the *Vanguard* as she let loose more mutterings like half-whispered curses.

"Oak and Silvish pine. Cedar, in places. Keeps the rot out." A garbled hum rose from her throat. "A first-rate ship of the line, make no mistake. Do you see the cannons?"

She pointed her arm, but all Darce could see through the rain was the *Vanguard's* looming shadow.

"A hundred and twelve," she said. "Fifty on each broadside. Three forward cannons, nine chasers on the stern. More than a hundred tonnes of cast iron waiting to bite through our bones."

"Ma, you shouldn't be up here." Jacques appeared at his mother's side and slipped his arm around her frail shoulders, coaxing her away. "Let's get you out of this rain before you catch a chill."

Maggie ignored him, still fixated on the *Vanguard*. "A crew of eight hundred, along with a dozen sentinels and their captains. And one..." She hesitated, trembling.

"One admiral," Darce finished for her.

"Aye," she whispered. "One admiral."

She allowed herself to be ushered to the shelter of the hold, but the haunted look never left her face. Her suffering was written in lines and shadows, clinging to her like a pall. It wasn't just Maggie Grier's body that Cunningham had broken. Wasn't just her mind, either. It was her spirit.

"She's not wrong, you know." Muir joined him, his lambswool cloak sodden. "As soon as that bastard gets us broadside, we're done for. Those guns will shred this ship to splinters."

"He won't fire on us," Darce said. "Not if he believes Isla might be on board."

Muir's lips stretched into a thin, humourless smile. "You still don't know him at all, do you? Don't make the mistake of thinking he loves her the same way you do. Alasdair believes that because his blood runs in her veins, she belongs to him, and *only* him. He cannot stomach the thought of losing her like he lost Mara—losing her to the sea, to the salt, to her people. He'd sooner crush her in his grasp than let her slip free of it."

The cold edge of his words pared to the bone. Muir was right. He knew the horrors Cunningham was capable of. He'd witnessed it first-hand with Mara all those years ago.

"There's nothing of a man left in him, is there?" Darce asked.

Muir stared at the clouds as the rain beat down, clinging to the crown of his white braids. "There hasn't been a trace of a man left in him in a long time. Of all the mistakes I've made in this wretched life of mine, my worst is not recognising that sooner."

Across the waves, a blinding flash of lightning tore across the sky. It lit up the clouds behind the *Vanguard*, turning the hazy outline of its sails into a stark silhouette. Before long, the ship would be upon them.

"It'll be over quickly," Muir said, eyes distant. "He can't risk his sentinels discovering what we found at Baininch Rise. If they knew we had their families on board, his hold over them would be broken. They'd turn on him like beaten dogs on their master, and he'd be out of sacrifices."

Sacrifices. The word struck a memory in Darce, a revelation murmured through salt-scarred lips pressed against his. He'd bound his soul to Isla, but he wasn't the only one on this ship who knew what it was to give up part of themselves. To have part of themselves *taken.*

This time, when he reached for the haar, it wasn't only his blood that stirred. He felt it in the sewn-up stumps of Maggie Grier's arms, severed of the hands that had built so many monuments to the waves. He felt it in the hollowed cheeks and wasted muscles of the young lad, Tam, starved of body and bairnhood. So many scars, so many wounds, all of them carved by Cunningham's hand to bind the ones they loved to his will.

When the sea spirits in the soulship's silent bones raised their voices again, it was not in cries of fear. Instead, they called out in mourning, in *rage.*

His blood thrummed. The sea crashed in his veins, stronger than it had ever been. It seeped through him, trickling its icy waters into parts of him he didn't know the cold could reach. He tasted salt on his tongue and nearly choked on the briny stench that filled his nostrils. It was enough to drown him, if he let it. The fathoms were at his fingertips, ready to swallow him whole.

The blanket of fog swept around the soulship's mast in swathes of white. A familiar sting nipped at Darce's cheeks as the frost began to form, sinking icy teeth into his flesh, turning his lips dry and cracked. Across the horizon, the storm clouds disappeared, and the deep rumble of thunder faded in his eardrum.

The sky turned red once more. They were back in the soulless realm.

Darce collapsed, his mouth dry. He'd done it. *They'd* done it. All the suffering, all the pieces torn from body and mind...the soulship knew that kind of pain. Its bones understood that kind of loss. And in their most desperate need, its spirits had answered. They'd summoned the haar.

Muir's hand dug into his uninjured shoulder. A sombre look flitted across his eyes, a shared understanding of what this had cost. "Cormick knew what he was doing when he trusted his family to you."

A bittersweet swell of emotion rose in Darce's chest, but before he could dwell on it, the monstrous shadow of the *Vanguard* emerged from the mists.

The haar had fallen on them not a moment too soon. It swirled around the soulship, shrouding it from the living world. On the other side, the *Vanguard* was a haze, its fearsome hull bleeding into the gloom. It didn't know they were there. They'd slipped out of sight, beyond its reach.

All the same, Darce couldn't help but hold his breath as it crept closer. His chest constricted, like a weight was pressing against his ribs, squeezing the air from his lungs. The sweeping curve of the *Vanguard's* hull towered over them, so close he could see the individual gunports and the muzzles of the cannons waiting inside. *This* was how close they'd been—a whisper away from a barrage of iron and black powder that would have sent them to the fathoms.

He wasn't sure what made him look up. A brush of dread, perhaps, carried by a non-existent wind. A twist in the pit of his stomach, warning him of something he couldn't yet understand. Whatever it was, it compelled him to turn to the *Vanguard's* deck.

Alasdair Cunningham stared back with steely eyes and a cold smile.

For a fleeting second of horror, Darce thought he could see them, that the haar had failed them somehow. Then his frantic heart slowed, and he realised the Grand Admiral hadn't moved. But there was a knowing glint in his eye that sent a chill down Darce's spine all the same.

Cunningham might not have been able to see them, but he knew they were there.

Beside him, Muir stiffened. "Alasdair..."

It wasn't even a murmur. Barely more than a breath, lost to the damp smothering them.

But Cunningham's smile widened.

It happened too quickly for Darce to understand. The *Vanguard* was already slipping past them, leaving them in its wake. Cunningham stood at its stern and pulled a dagger from his jewel-toned cloak, steel flashing in his hand.

Then he turned the blade inwards and buried it in his own heart.

Darce froze in horror as Cunningham slumped to his knees. The ghost of his smile lingered as he fell to the deck and the *Vanguard's* stern disappeared behind the haar.

What had he done? What the *fuck* had he done?

"Sergeant..." Muir was staring at him, eyes slack.

He fell, clutching his chest, and Darce finally understood.

"No!" The word tore from his throat as Muir slumped to the deck. There was no red stain blooming across his shirt, no blood pouring from a wound in his chest. No blade had touched his skin.

The blood oath is a powerful bond. Muir's voice echoed in his ear, fading fast. For years, Muir had cut himself off from the call of the tides. He'd buried whatever promise had once existed between him and Cunningham. Now, he was tethered to him again. Their souls were bound, and only one thing could sever that thread.

"What happened?" Nishi rushed over, placing her fingers over Muir's chest. "His heart. I can't feel it."

"The Grand Admiral," Darce said. "He buried a blade in his own chest. He's—"

"Dead." Nishi moved her hands over Muir's sternum. "He must be. It's the only thing that could do this. This is the cost of a blood oath breaking."

"There must be some way to keep him alive. You didn't die when Kerr..."

"You really believe that?" Nishi gave a dark chuckle. "I'm on borrowed time, Sergeant. The only reason I didn't follow Kerr to the fathoms that night was because I had a promise to keep. I swore I would make that bastard pay. It's the only thing anchoring me to this world."

"But Muir—"

"He came here to stop the Grand Admiral. If he's done that, there's nothing left keeping him here."

Darce looked down at Muir's ashen face. His forehead was free from creases, his sailor's braids spilling around his shoulders. There was no trace of the decades-old suffering that had marred his brow with its weight. In a way, he seemed almost at peace.

It would not last, he realised. Cunningham would not *let* it last.

Seconds passed, then minutes. Darce waited, knowing what was about to happen, *hoping* it would happen.

Everything was still. The air was dead and quiet, the black waves eerily calm under the red sky.

Then Muir's chest spasmed, his limp body jolting against the deck.

Nishi sprang back in horror. In front of her, Muir seized violently, his eyes rolling so far back only the whites were exposed. The veins around his temples bulged like they were trying to escape his skin.

Darce held him steady, waiting for it to pass. "And so it happens again. Another betrayal. Another broken oath."

"His sentinels." Nishi stilled. "One of them brought him back. This was no accident. Cunningham *meant* to do this." She looked down at him, eyes bleak. "Why? What could possibly be worth this kind of torment?"

Muir thrashed again, then fell limp, his breathing coming in ragged gasps. For a moment, it seemed like they'd lost him after all, that whatever bargain had paid for Cunningham's life on the other side of the haar hadn't been able to reach Muir here.

Then Muir's eyelids fluttered and he stared at the starless sky above, pupils as black as the waves. "A warning," he answered, voice thin. "He wanted to show me what I stand to lose."

His words rang painfully in the silence. Not even the haar could swallow them, not when the truth was so clear, so cutting.

If Alasdair Cunningham was to die, he'd take Muir with him.

CHAPTER NINETEEN

ISLA

It was happening again. The haar was rolling in, and Isla couldn't do a damn thing to stop it.

Even before they reached the docks, she felt the change in the wind, each gust sinking its spiteful teeth into her. The chill burrowed bone-deep, claiming her for its own, promising it would never let her go.

If she'd had her pelt, she might have been able to disperse the gathering shroud. But Eimhir had taken that from her. That, and much more.

"Do you think she's here?" Lachlan asked, peering into the mists.

Isla nodded. Eimhir was here. She had to be.

She pulled tight the burgundy lapels of her father's old dress coat, forgetting that her fingers brushed soft wool and silk brocade, not the dense depths of fur. The weight of the long-tailed coat hanging loose over her shoulders was a borrowed comfort, but it wasn't *hers*.

She turned to Blair, who was staring rigidly ahead. "What should we expect when we reach the docks?"

"You should know better than any of us. You're one of them, aren't you?" His jaw tightened, and he pushed his wet crop of curls from his forehead. "It's bad. There are bodies littering the jetty, and not just

Admiralty officers. The local dockworkers are caught up in the fighting. Some have been dragged to the waves and drowned. The others..." He shuddered. "I've seen too many flayed bodies to speak of what's happening down there. I don't imagine you need me to describe it."

No, she didn't. Isla remembered too well the sight of flesh stripped from muscle and bone, the metallic stench of blood and tissue. She knew exactly what was happening at the docks.

Worse than that, she'd *invited* it here.

"I thought if they came, they'd attack with the cover of night," she mumbled, half to herself. "To come ashore in daylight...it's not like the selkies. It's not like Eimhir."

"She saw a chance and she took it," Blair said. "Three of our brigantines left at first light in pursuit of the Sea Kith vessel that attacked us last night. No doubt she was watching, waiting for the right time to strike. We were weakened, wounded. We never saw it coming."

"You can't blame yourself. Eimhir—"

"I *don't* blame myself," Blair shot back. "You were the one who wanted to draw her out. Well, it seems you succeeded."

Isla pressed her lips together. There was nothing she could say. Blair was right; this was her doing. Back on the *Red Gale*, filled with fear and desperation, it seemed like the right choice. It was only now, standing at the outskirts of the docks, that she realised how wrong she was.

The cobblestone gutters ran red, splashing colour onto the mist-thick streets. Bodies scattered the way ahead, a bloody trail leading towards the docks. Some of them bore the mark of a clean death: an axe to the skull, a throat slit to the bone. But others carried a message, the same message selkies always left when they took vengeance on those who wronged them.

Woollen cloaks torn open. Shirts ripped at the seams. Backs flayed until there was nothing left but ribbons of flesh exposed to the salty air.

Isla pushed the images from her mind before she retched. They were almost at the docks, and as she looked over the moored ships, an unpleasant shiver crawled down her spine. The last time she'd been in Kinraith, Eimhir had been by her side. They'd carved out a tentative truce, agreeing to sail to the capital together. It wasn't friendship, not at the beginning. Just the hope that something in this tides-forsaken world could be saved.

If we are to trust each other, we must bury what came before.

Grief clawed at her heart, digging up the pain she'd tried to bury. They'd never stood a chance. Too much blood had been spilled, too much lost on both sides. She'd tried. They'd *both* tried. And in the end, it had brought nothing but hurt.

She turned to Blair. "Do you have a ship under your own command?"

He bristled. "I am no captain, if that's what you're asking. Without a sentinel, I'm not—"

"I'm not talking about Admiralty law. Do you have a crew willing to follow you and a ship you can escape on?"

His brow furrowed as he looked between her and Lachlan. "Aye, I do."

"Good." She let out a breath, keeping watch on the haar creeping across the docks. "You're going to take my brother and get out of here."

Lachlan's face was stony. "If you think I'm going to run away like a feart bairn while you martyr yourself—"

"I can't do this. Not while you're still here." She averted her eyes from the bloodied corpse propped up against the doorway next to them. "I need to face Eimhir. I need to find the strength to take back what she stole from me. But if she gets to you first, if she tries to use you against me..." She shook her head. "Tides forgive me, but I'd sacrifice this whole port to the mists to keep you safe, wee brother. And I don't think you want that."

Lachlan faltered. "We came here to stop her. Together. How can you hope to find her alone?"

"I don't need to find her. She'll come to me." Isla slipped her shoulders, letting the long burgundy coat fall to the cobbles. Underneath, her bone armour glistened. She touched her hands to her ribs, fingers brushing over the last gift Mara gave her. "Blair is right. I wanted to draw her out. This is the only way to do that."

"But—"

"*Please*, Lachlan." She held his gaze. She didn't want this either, but he was an open wound Eimhir would find easy to strike at. She couldn't risk it, couldn't risk *him*.

It was Blair who reached him in the end. A gentle touch, a squeezing of the shoulder both hesitant and achingly raw. "The *Midnight Crest* is rigged and ready for sail. I can't promise a warm reception, but you'll come to no harm as long as I stand on its deck."

Lachlan's grip tightened around the handle of his battered hazelwood cane. The seconds stretched, each more strained than the last. Then he nodded stiffly. "I know you need to do this. Just...come back, Isla. Whatever it takes, find a way home."

"I always do." She brushed her hand against his cheek. "Find Darce. Tell him...tell him I'll see him soon."

She watched until they disappeared, her chest tight with worry. Then she reached for the seal-skull mask hooked onto her belt.

The bone was cold between her fingers, the empty sockets so dark she feared she might lose herself in their void. It was a mask that had haunted her for months with its rotting, blackened bone, its stench of decay. So many nights she'd awoken drenched in sweat, the nightmare lingering over her. She'd never known what she was running from, not until she'd gone to meet it.

Now, her màthair was one with the sea. The bones she'd passed on to Isla gleamed white, free at last from the haar's corruption.

Go, nighean. Take back what is yours, and do for our people what I could not.

Isla pulled the seal-skull mask over her head. The haar's depths were waiting for her, and so was Eimhir.

The cobbled streets and wooden jetties sprawled like a patchwork of capillaries across Kinraith, but for Isla, they only led to one place. Even stripped of her soul, the sea called to her, beckoning her home. She slipped through the mist like a ghost, navigating through the fallen bodies. Each one was a reminder of what she'd brought on this place, what reclaiming her pelt would cost.

She rounded the corner and ran into a grizzled Admiralty officer, his face scratched bloody. When he noticed her bone armour, his eyes widened, and he slashed at her with his cutlass.

Her pistol was already warm and waiting in her hand. One squeeze of the trigger, one crack of flint, and the officer crumpled to the ground, blade clattering against stone as he landed in his own blood.

She fumbled in her breeches for another shot, fingers closing around the cold lead spheres. It was unlikely this sorry bastard would be the last to try to kill her. She had no friends here, selkie or human. She had to stay alive until she found Eimhir, no matter what it took.

Something curled inside her at how terrifyingly easy it was to justify another life taken. To justify more blood spilled, as long as it was spilled serving *her* purpose. It was little fucking wonder they'd ended up where they had. Nobody wanted to be the first to lay down their weapon. Nobody could afford to.

Ahead of her, the mists thinned, and the sounds of a scuffle reached her ears. She hurried forward to see two men in Admiralty cloaks wrestling with a third figure, fists flying as they knocked him to the jetty's wooden surface. They were pulling at his shoulders, tugging loose something sodden and russet-brown.

Isla stilled. She recognised that colour of fur, just as she recognised the long-limbed, red-headed selkie it belonged to.

Angus.

She lifted her pistol, clenching her teeth at the crack as she fired a shot through one of the Admiralty officer's backs. Before the other had time to react, she stowed the gun and charged at him, wrapping her arms around his waist to tackle him to the ground.

The officer grunted, striking her ribs on the way down, but the bone cuirass shielded her from the worst of the blow. Before she could scramble away, he drew his fist back again, but he never got the chance to land it on her.

Steel winked through his throat. A fishknife, plunged into his neck.

Blood poured from the wound, staining her bone armour red. She pushed the officer's weight off and tried to haul herself back to her feet, but she'd barely lifted her knees when something else hit her, knocking her to the damp wooden planks again.

It was Angus. He clamped one hand around her throat, and with the other, he tore the seal-skull mask from her face.

His icy blue eyes met hers, and he stilled. "Fuck. I *knew* it." The weight of his hand around her neck didn't tighten, but he didn't release her either. He held her against the jetty, breathing hard through his nose. "What are you doing here, aineol?"

Hearing the word from his mouth stung more than she expected. He'd never called her that before, not even the first day she'd arrived on Eileanan Selch.

She pushed him away. "You should know better than anyone why I'm here. You were there when she took my soul from me, after all."

A flicker of shame fell across Angus's freckled features. Then it was gone, and his eyes hardened as he sat back on his haunches and allowed her to rise. "I don't condone what Eimhir did. No selkie would. But she was mist sick. Once it was done, there was no taking it back. All I'm trying to do now is what's best for my people."

"They're my people too," Isla shot back. "I'm fighting to keep the promise I made the chieftains on Eileanan Selch. Eimhir's bloodlust won't deliver the future our people deserve. It will only carry us to our end."

"Are you so sure it will be *our* end?" Angus's eyes gleamed. "Or will it be humankind's?"

"If the haar continues to spread, it will be the end for us both. Or do you believe our people can survive a world drowning in that kind of pain?" She shook her head. "You've seen what mist sickness does to a selkie. Eimhir won't be the last. Even if you slaughter every human on this island, it won't turn the haar back to what it used to be."

There it was: a trace of doubt casting his eyes in shadow. Part of her wanted to reach for it, to tear it out of him and force him to look at it. But she knew how blind a person could be to a truth they didn't want to see. The half-healed gouge in the crook of her elbow and the salt scars around her wrists were all the reminders she needed of that.

"The gun-anam deserve more than the violence she's feeding them with," she said. "Those tortured wraiths can be put to rest by someone willing to bear their pain for them. If you won't listen to me, then look upon these bones and let them tell you. No longer do they carry the blackened rot of the haar's corruption."

Angus pursed his lips. "Duncan said you'd found Mara. But that doesn't mean anything. You could have stolen those bones from her like you stole the anam-long from under us."

"You think I stole the soulship?" A wry laugh caught at the back of her throat. "Ask Duncan about that. Ask your brother why he let me go."

Angus opened his mouth, then faltered, his freckled forehead creasing as he turned away. "You won't find what you're looking for here. Eimhir is our aislingeach, our dreamer. What she carries is too precious to risk. She knows better than to come anywhere near Kinraith."

The twitch in his jaw was barely discernible, but Isla was watching for it. The lie hung between them, so fragile that either of them could have shattered it by acknowledging it for what it was.

Eimhir *shouldn't* have been here, but she was.

"I'm going to find her," Isla said evenly. "Do you intend to stop me?"

Angus picked up the seal-skull helm he'd wrenched from her face, looking into its empty sockets like he was searching for answers. Then he handed it to her, fingers steady as he pressed it into her waiting grasp.

"Aye," he said, the word heavy with regret. "I'm afraid so, aineol."

He waited until she pulled the mask back over her head, the bone snug against her temples. Through its empty eyes, she watched as he picked up the fishknife from where it had sunk deep into the Admiralty officer's throat.

More blood, then. She shouldn't have expected anything less.

She braced herself, but she wasn't quick enough. Angus charged towards her in a blur of pale limbs and russet fur, knocking her to the ground. Her back hit the wood with a thump, and she rolled out from under him before he could bring the fishknife down on her throat.

He was quick, and stronger than she'd ever been, even with her pelt. The muscles she'd developed from plunging through the depths in her sealskin had wasted away, leaving her with little but skin and bone. It was all she could do to scramble away from him, keeping clear of the hungry edge of his blade.

She tried to climb to her feet, but he shot out a hand and grabbed her ankle, hauling her back to the jetty. Through the gaps in the wooden slats, the waves heaved, filling her ears with their crash. He'd drag her down there if he could, and the tides would finish her for him. The sea was no friend to her now. It would fill her human lungs with salt, drowning her with no regret.

But Angus shirked back, his palm smeared red, blood dripping between his fingers. He must have torn his hand open on the serpenthide scales of her boot when he'd dragged her down. The gashes looked deep, with ribbons of skin hanging loose.

He grimaced, pressing his hand to his mouth to suck the blood, and Isla took the chance to thrust herself backwards out of his reach. Her hands slipped against the wooden planks. There was nowhere else to go.

The only thing behind her was a short drop to the waiting waves, and as soon as she plunged beneath them, there would be no coming back up.

Angus's expression softened. "I'll make it quick. Eimhir would want that for you."

Her hand drifted helplessly towards her pistol. She'd already used the shot on the Admiralty officer who'd attacked Angus. By the time she slid another lead ball into the barrel, it would be too late. Angus would drag her into the swell and hold her until under her lungs filled with the sea she'd so desperately yearned for ever since losing her pelt.

But not like this.

He stalked towards her, and Isla shifted her fingers to curl around the handle of the sgian dubh instead. The small knife glinted, its silver edge imbued with the blood of all those it had drunk from.

Angus stilled. "You would threaten me with the dreamwalker blade? You should not even carry it. By rights, it belongs to the aislingeach."

"It belongs to me," Isla said, voice steely. "As it belonged to Mara, and all those who wore the dreamwalker pelt before us. It knows the taste of blood spilled in sacrifice. And it knows the poison of blood taken forcefully. It will never belong to Eimhir, and neither will my pelt. That stolen soul she wears will haunt her like I warned her it would."

The words hit their mark. She saw it in the flash of doubt in his eyes. It was only a slight hesitation, but it was enough.

She leapt at him, arm outstretched as she thrust the sgian dubh into the russet folds of his pelt. The blade sank deep through the fur, buried to the hilt. She felt it biting through skin and muscle, and when she lifted it away again, blood streamed from the wound she'd carved into his chest.

Angus roared and reached for his own dagger, but she pressed her weight on top of him, holding the sgian dubh's blade to his throat. A vein pulsed in the side of his neck. All it would take was a flick of her wrist, and it would be over.

Her fingers trembled around the engraved hilt. This wasn't what the sgian dubh was meant for. It was a ceremonial blade, a blade crafted for sacrifice, not slaughter.

She had no choice. Angus would have done the same to her.

"Stop." A low, rasping voice cut through the air. "Let him go."

A prickle chased down Isla's spine. She knew that voice. She heard it every night in her memories. It was as familiar as she'd ever remembered it, yet carried all the coldness of a stranger.

She withdrew the blade from Angus's throat. His blue eyes were bright with pain as she lifted herself off him, but he was still breathing.

"Stay where you are," she told him. "This isn't your fight."

She turned slowly, gripping the sgian dubh in one hand. She already knew what she was about to face, but that didn't make it any easier.

Eimhir stood on the edge of the jetty, barefoot and dripping with seawater. Her ragged brown-blonde hair flew wildly in the wind. When she met Isla's eyes, there was no warmth behind her gaze, just a steel so sharp it threatened to cut them both.

The haar wisped around her, drifting from the dappled grey fur of the pelt hanging around her shoulders.

"Cousin," Eimhir said, the word colder than it had any right to be. "I hear you've been looking for me."

CHAPTER TWENTY

DARCE

There was nothing Darce could do but wait.

The long, gleaming blade of his claymore lay across his knees as he wiped the oil-soaked rag over it again. It didn't need to be cleaned. It hadn't drawn so much as a drop of blood since Isla pressed it into his hands back at Blackwood Estate. But polishing the steel until it shone gave his hands something to do.

Cunningham was out there. Now that they'd emerged from the haar, the *Vanguard* would find them again. When that happened, he had to be ready.

Darce ran the rag down the edge one last time, blinking as a rare ray of sunlight bounced off the steel. It gave him some comfort to know the sword was waiting as much as he was. The chance would come for both of them. Of that, he was certain.

He glanced at the sky, savouring the faint warmth on his cheeks. For once, there were no storm clouds shrouding the horizon—no clouds of any kind. The wash of endless pale blue lifted his spirits, loosening the tightness that had clutched at his chest ever since fleeing Baininch Rise.

"Don't get used to it," Muir said, appearing beside him. "Fair weather only means the next storm will break harder."

"Is that an old sailor's superstition?"

"More like a lifetime of experiencing things going to shite." Muir sighed. "I don't know if you can call what happened back there a victory, but we came away with more than we lost. We have a chance at turning the *Vanguard's* sentinels. Alasdair won't take that lightly."

"Came away with more than we lost? Sébastien is dead. Half the prisoners ended up trapped or buried. And you..." Darce broke off, the truth bitter on his tongue. "You just learned that Cunningham's death will mean your own."

Muir didn't reply. The creases around his eyes deepened as he surveyed the rolling waves. There was no stiffness in his jaw, no weight deepening his brow. He looked as at peace as he'd been the night before, when Cunningham had taken him over the brink of death and brought him back.

"I'm not afraid of what has to happen," he said quietly. "Never have been."

Darce stilled. "You knew."

"I suspected. It was generous of Alasdair to confirm it, all the same." Muir shrugged. "I told you I'd pay whatever price was asked of me if it meant Isla getting her freedom. I knew what the blood oath meant when I made it. I knew the cost of reopening it."

His words hung between them, refusing to be carried off in the breeze sweeping over the deck. The truth wouldn't go away just because Darce didn't want to face it. It was like a shadow over him, a darkness he couldn't see a way out of.

"There must be something we can do," he muttered, half to himself. "This never happened to you any of the other times he was struck down and brought back. You buried the bond once; you can do it again."

Muir snorted. "Spoken as if it's as simple a matter as the opening and closing of a door. You of all people should understand it's more complicated than that. It took nearly everything I had to sever the bond between us twenty years ago, and the rest of me to open it back up. This is a *wound*, Sergeant. And this time, it cannot be stitched back together. Whatever happens next, both Alasdair and I will bleed for it." He let out a long breath. "Which is why Isla cannot know."

"You can't keep this from her."

"Aye, I bloody well can. And you will too." Muir glared at him. "She won't have the mettle to go through with killing him if she learns it will mean my death too. She doesn't let go of the people she loves, not when she believes there's a chance she can save them."

"You think I don't know that?" Darce shot back. "We're talking about a woman who walked into Arburgh alone and surrendered herself to Cunningham without a second thought, all because he cut off my ear. But that was Isla's choice to make. So is this. Don't ask me to take that away from her. I won't."

"And what about my choice?" Something in Muir's voice cracked, and his weathered hands tightened around the gunwale. "I'm ready to do this. I *need* to do it. The last thing I want is to lose my niece because she can't accept that. You know the truth of it is well as I do: Alasdair must be killed."

"And you can count on me to see that through. If you need me to swear it to you, I will." Darce fixed him with a solemn gaze. "But I won't keep the truth from Isla. She deserves to know what she's losing. She deserves the chance to say goodbye. You both do."

Muir stared doggedly ahead at the gentle heave of the waves. For once, the swell was not green or grey, but a deep, shimmering blue under the clear sky. For all the wrath and terror the waves held, there was beauty in them, too. This was Isla's home. The place Darce was fighting for her to return to.

A place where he could not follow.

"I don't want to lose her either," he said. "But I won't let that fear turn me into Cunningham. Perhaps she's not the only one who has to learn how to let go."

Muir dipped his head between his arms, his breathing fraught with pain. When he resurfaced, his eyes were bleak and bloodshot.

"Aye," he said, voice strained. "Perhaps you're right. At least...at least let me be the one to tell her. When the time is right, I'll say goodbye to her in my own words. I swear it on Mara's memory."

Darce nodded. "Don't leave it too late."

"I won't." Muir turned to the soulship's deck, taking in the unfamiliar faces scattered from prow to stern. "Whatever is waiting for us is beyond the horizon. Our more immediate concern should be what to do with these prisoners. We can't turn them loose with the Admiralty out there. As callous as it sounds, we need them to bargain with. The *Vanguard's* sentinels will remain beholden to Alasdair as long as they believe he has something over them."

In the middle of the main deck, Maggie Grier was circling the mast, her haggard face set with a frown as she peered high and low, as if inspecting it for some kind of flaw. She rapped the bone with the stump of one of her arms, then jumped back, her expression lighting up with joy.

"This is the first time in years they've found themselves outside the walls of that place," Darce said. "We can offer them refuge, but we can't force them to stay. We'd be no better than Cunningham."

Muir muttered something that sounded dangerously close to '*idealistic prick*', then folded his arms and turned to the waves. "In any case, it won't do them or us much good if we're caught out here with our breeks down. This ship has no weapons, and I doubt the *Vanguard* will be so sloppy as to let us slip its nets twice. We need to find the Sea Kith again."

We need to find Isla, Darce thought, but he kept the longing to himself. His chest tightened with the tug of their bond, the oath they'd made to each other. He didn't know where she was, but he knew how to reach her. That was where the soulship was carrying them. He didn't need to harness the waves. He didn't need to think about it. The ship knew where it belonged.

"It disturbs me to find myself in agreement with the Admiralty cur," Nishi said, trudging down from the quarterdeck. She hadn't spoken much since Baininch Rise, preferring to leave the helm to Muir while she tended to the prisoners. Darce could only imagine the memories they must have stirred in her, the reminders of the torture the Admiralty had inflicted on Kerr.

"How are you holding up?" he asked.

There was a fresh gleam in her copper eyes, like part of her had been sparked back to life. "It's difficult to look at what he's done to them. I see Kerr in each of their faces. But it reminds me of why I'm still here, why I chose not to follow him to the fathoms. Someone has to give these people their vengeance. Someone has to make that bastard pay."

"It disturbs me to find myself in agreement with the boorish pirate," Muir said dryly. "But if we want to make Alasdair pay, we'll need a force that can stand up to the *Vanguard*. That ship won't go down without a fight."

Nishi tilted her head towards the mast, where Featherblade perched high above, preening its brilliant white plumage under the sun. "We're passing close to the Drift, and Silvish shores lie none too far behind. If the sergeant sends his guidebird out, I wager we'll find the *Red Gale* soon enough. And Blackwood with it, if tides be kind."

A cold knot tightened in Darce's stomach. He didn't know what was waiting for them back in Silveckan. There was no telling how much further the haar had spread, how many more villages had been swallowed by its rotten chill. If Eimhir was out there, if Isla hadn't managed to find her, or worse, if she *had*—

It's not up to the fucking tides. Isla's voice filled his head, as urgent as the day he'd left her. *I need you to tell me this isn't the last time we'll see each other.*

He'd promised her. He'd drunk in every part of her, committed the softness of her skin and the echo of her heartbeat to memory. With every lingering kiss, every desperate touch, he'd sworn to find his way back to her side.

When he looked up at Featherblade, the gannet was already spreading its wings, swooping from the mast in a flash of feathers. No words needed to be spoken. The bird knew as well as he did where to go.

"I'm coming," he murmured, and prayed the tides would carry the words to her before it was too late for them both.

Later that day, Jacques approached him at the bow, eyes shadowed with dark circles. Darce knew too well how grief could weigh a person down. He'd seen the loss on Jacques' face in his own reflection more times than he wanted to think about.

"How long since you were last in Silveckan?" he asked.

Jacques grimaced. "Too long. And in other ways, not long enough. I never wanted to flee my home, abandon my family. But neither could I live knowing one day I might be called upon to sacrifice my own captain. Now, Ben is gone, Sébastien is dead, and my mother…"

"Your mother is alive."

"Is she?" Jacques' voice was hoarse. "I'll never know half the things she suffered in that prison, and perhaps that's for the best. When I think about all those years I spent in Île de Durgavie, believing she was dead… I could have been looking for her. I should have—"

"He sent your father her severed hands," Darce said gently. "You didn't have reason to believe anything other than that he killed her to punish your desertion. The blame for what happened lies with Cunningham, not you."

"And Séba? Who do I blame for his death?" Jacques shook his head. "He followed me to that place, and I left him buried in its bowels."

"Sébastien knew what he was doing. He gave his life to save the people in that tower, to save you and your mother."

"Leave it to him to turn noble right at the bloody end." Jacques laughed weakly. "He was born to Breçh pirates, you know. The Admiralty caught his parents' ship when he was a bairn. Slaughtered the crew and threw him into a workhouse back in Arburgh. He killed the foreman on the first day, then stowed away on a ship bound for Breçhon. By the time I met him, he was—" He broke off, a shadow falling across his face. "No, never mind. I didn't come here to wallow in what I've lost, not when so much remains at stake. I was hoping you might join us at the stern. There's something I wish to show you."

"Us?" Darce raised an eyebrow.

"Muir is waiting. Impatiently, I might add. Shall we?"

Darce followed him the length of the ship to the quarterdeck. Muir was leaning against the gunwale with crossed arms and a scowl, while Nishi watched from the helm with mild curiosity.

"What's going on?" Darce asked. "What did you want to show us?"

"Well, that rather depends on you," Jacques said. "And the tides, of course. We can't do much out here without their will, but they seem to favour you. And we've already seen what the old Cirein-cròin here can do."

Muir's expression only grew more disgruntled. "Is that meant to be flattery, lad?"

"It's an invitation," Jacques said. "The *Vanguard* has a dozen sentinels serving on its deck at any given time, all working to yoke the tides to its might. We can't match that power. But if the three of us were to combine the strength of our own gifts...we might stand a chance, if nothing else."

Darce glanced at Muir, expecting him to dismiss the suggestion out of hand, but a contemplative look settled over the older man. "What did you have in mind?"

"Well, seeing as the waves are as calm as they are..." A slow smile tugged at the corner of Jacques' mouth. "How about we see if we can summon a storm?"

Despite Nishi's protests, the three of them soon stood at the gunwale, hands resting on the bone-hewn surface as they stared at the soulship's wake. The sky was bright. The waves leapt playfully alongside them, tamer than Darce had thought possible.

That would soon change.

He closed his eyes and reached for the tides, their ice rushing through his veins without hesitation. Where their whims had once been fickle, they now answered him more often than not. Perhaps he did have their favour, as Jacques said. Or perhaps they too knew what would happen if the haar spread. He'd seen the waters of the soulless realm—black and opaque, eerily placid. No sea spirits lurked in those depths, only an empty, endless ache.

Muir and Jacques stood either side of him, still and silent. He couldn't hear them breathing. But as he reached out with his magic, he felt a stirring in theirs, too.

"It's working," he murmured, closing his fingers around the small nick he'd made in his palm. The three of them bore the same wound. Sentinels and selkies alike could sense the spilling of auld blood, even from the slightest of cuts, and Jacques had suggested it might help them channel their magic as one.

Now, he felt it. As the tides rose within him, so did the ripples from Jacques and Muir. He sensed the deft manipulations coming from Jacques, altering the currents with a subtle touch that might stir a storm surge fifty miles away. On his other side, Muir was a foaming vortex, drawing water from depths Darce couldn't imagine.

He cracked an eye open. "Try not to summon any sea serpents this time, will you?"

Muir's only response was two fingers forked in his direction.

"Concentrate," Jacques urged. "The sentinels on the *Vanguard* have sailed together for years. We don't have that time."

Darce focused on the waves again, shivering as the chill in his blood grew sharper. He didn't want to summon the haar. The sea fog might help them flee the *Vanguard*, but it wouldn't help them fight it. For that, he needed the wrath of the waves, the spite of the storm they were trying to call.

A fierce swell rose within him, and he tasted salt water on his tongue. The waves were restless, yearning to churn. The depths stirred far below, sending a shudder through the sea itself.

The tides heard them, and they were answering.

"I hope you know what you're doing," Nishi said. "I'm no stranger to sailing through a squall, but I'm not so foolish as to invite one onto me."

The sunlight warming Darce's skin disappeared, and when he looked up, he saw clouds knitting together like a shroud. As if in response, the sea surged, sending spray flying over the gunwale. The rich, shimmering blue had darkened into a tumultuous grey-green, frothing and spitting like the waves had taken some kind of insult.

This was the sea they needed, with all its dangers and all its wrath.

He stumbled to keep his footing as the deck lurched under the force of a cresting wave. Water broke against bone with a roar that left his ear ringing. They'd invited this, just like Nishi said. They'd stoked the tides into a temper, and now they rose, throwing themselves against the soulship's hull in a ceaseless, foaming rage.

"Together," Jacques said. "Call them higher."

Darce extended his reach, blood turning to ice as he allowed the magic to rush through his veins. If he lost his grip on its power, it might drown him. But he wasn't alone. He sensed Muir and Jacques beside him, their magic mingling with his own. The humming in his blood joined with theirs, entwining until they were one. He felt *everything*: the crushing weight, the frantic swell, the spray disappearing into the wind. It all rose within him, spiralling from his core.

Behind him, Nishi released a breath. "That's...that's not possible."

The waves leapt. But this time, they didn't crash back into the sea. Instead, they hung in the air, caught by the swirling wind. A grey-green wall surged in front of them, rippling in the dreich light.

Then, it began to climb.

Darce didn't know what was happening. The swell in him was rising, and so were the waves. They swirled into a funnel, twisting as they writhed towards the clouds. It was like the pillar of water he'd summoned on the shore all those months ago when he'd first drawn on his sentinel blood. But that had been a small, fleeting surge of power. This...this was different.

The waterspout continued to climb, searching for the storm. When at last the spiralling waves touched the sky, the sea roared in triumph, spitting and frothing around the swirling base. Darce watched as the funnel grew thicker, drawing more of the sea into its midst. All he could hear was its deafening roar. All he could feel was his soaked skin caught in the backwash.

It was monstrous. It was magnificent.

A disbelieving laugh spilled from his throat. His hands were so numb he could no longer feel them, but it hardly mattered. Not in the face of what they'd summoned.

"Main mast stands two-hundred feet above the waterline. Predominantly Silvish pine, provides flexibility in high winds."

Darce turned to find Maggie Grier behind him, a look of wonder plastered across her pale, bony face. Her eyes shone with fervour as she stared up at the waterspout.

"It's a sturdy mast. Bends, doesn't break. Survived an Adrenian cyclone once." Her mouth stretched into a wide smile. "Won't survive this."

The meaning of her mumbled words took root in Darce's chest. Maggie Grier knew the *Vanguard* better than anyone. Her fingerprints were all over its hull. Her mind was behind every carefully laid section of deck, every fastening holding the ship together. She knew what it could withstand.

She knew what could break it.

A hushed murmur broke loose, mingling with the waterspout's roar. More of the prisoners ventured onto deck, struck with fear and awe.

They exchanged pointed glances, whispering words to each other that Darce couldn't hear through his muffled ear.

He turned to Muir. "What are they saying?"

"The same thing we're all thinking." The funnel churned, reaching the black clouds above, and Muir drew his mouth into a grim smile. "That we just might stand a fucking chance of winning this fight."

CHAPTER TWENTY-ONE

ISLA

Isla stood across from Eimhir, her hand closed around the sgian dubh's engraved handle. She'd imagined this a thousand times, but there was nothing that could have prepared her for pain that lanced her heart, the rush of grief that filled her chest. Her cousin. Her caraid. The stranger who'd buried a blade in her arm and ripped her soul from her in a swift, bloody betrayal.

Eimhir laid a hand on Angus's wounded chest. "Gather the others and head back to Eileanan Selch. There's nothing left for us to do here. I'll be right behind you."

Angus nodded, his face contorting as he hauled himself to the edge of the jetty. As the russet-brown fur of his pelt spread over his freckled skin, he gave Isla one last look, his expression unfathomable. Then his human features yielded to black selkie eyes, and he was gone, his lithe shape disappearing beneath the waves.

Eimhir released a heavy breath. "All is well. Our work here is done."

Isla glanced across the docks. The haar clung to every corner, thick and damp. A coppery tang cut through the stench of rot and salt in the air. Kinraith had met the same fate as Storwick, as Arburgh. The mists would not clear when Eimhir left. They would linger, infecting the cobbled streets and bloodwashed docks until the soulless realm and all its horrors began to bleed into the world.

"There was a time I'd never have believed you wanted this," Isla said. "Now, I wonder if I ever knew you at all."

Eimhir blanched, but her eyes turned flinty. "I might say the same. After all the Admiralty has done, here you are in its service."

"You think I'm here with the Admiralty?" Isla gave a hollow laugh. "I *used* the Admiralty. I used this port, tides take me for it. I invited this blood and death because it was the only way to call you to me."

A flicker of realisation crossed Eimhir's face. "You are responsible for the Admiralty's losses here? You set the Sea Kith upon them?" A cold smile curled at the corner of her lips. "Perhaps you are still one of us after all."

The gentle mocking twisted the blade deeper, but Isla met her with a cold stare. "I always was. You lost sight of that. You lost sight of everything."

"I suppose it's easier for you to believe that, isn't it? Easier to blame the mist sickness that infected me, rather than blame yourself." Eimhir shook her head. "It was not I who lost sight of what mattered. Even now, when you bear the salt scars, when you know the pain of what it means to be gun-anam, you would still withhold their vengeance from them. They *deserve* this."

"They deserve to rest from the violence they've suffered. *Look* at me, Eimhir." Isla spread her arms, exposing the gleaming white bones of the cuirass around her ribs. Even in the gloom, they held an ethereal sheen. There was no lingering trace of the haar's corruption. No slime or rot in the hairline cracks, no staining or decay. "This is what our people deserve. A chance to be at peace, like Mara is. Please, caraid—"

"*Don't.*" Eimhir's voice was like stone. "Don't call me that. There can be no friendship between us, not when you insist on standing against what I must do."

"Perhaps you're right." Isla swallowed, her chest tightening. "For all I loved you—for all I love you still—I cannot let it stop me from doing what *I* must do."

Her eyes dropped, trailing to the pelt spilling over Eimhir's shoulders. She wanted to bury her hands in its thick folds. The soft lustre of fur, the dappled markings rippling across the grey, the familiar scent of sea and salt and *home*. It was hers, all of it.

When she met Eimhir's eyes again, all traces of cordiality had disappeared from her cousin's gaze, replaced by cold steel. "Do not test me, Isla. I was glad when I learned the auld blood saved you from becoming one with the salt and spray, but if you try to take what is mine, I'll send you to the fathoms myself."

Isla reeled, cheeks flushing like she'd been slapped. "This is what it's come to? After everything we've been through, everything we fought for?"

"So it would seem."

The sgian dubh was warm in Isla's hand, her fingers tight around the small handle. All she had to do was leap forward and let the blade find flesh. It didn't matter where the steel cut; Eimhir would bleed all the same. And then...then she could take her soul back. That was what mattered, wasn't it?

Still, she couldn't move. Her feet remained rooted to the spot. In the hollow of her chest, her heart ached, bruised by Eimhir's words.

"Please," she whispered. "If there is any part of my cousin, my friend, left...don't make me—"

The rest of her words were lost to a gasp as her head snapped back, caught by a blow she hadn't seen coming. Eimhir's bare foot connected with her chin, sending her staggering. By the time she caught herself, Eimhir had darted to the edge of the jetty, knees bent and ready to spring.

A rueful smile twisted the corner of her mouth. "I'll see you again, you know. When your sergeant dies and the gun-anam claim you as one of their own, I'll be there to welcome you to my side. Perhaps then, you'll understand what it is I'm fighting for."

"Eimhir, stop!"

It was no use. Eimhir leapt into the waves, plunging below the surface in a streak of dappled grey fur.

Isla dropped to her knees, puddles dampening her blood-soaked breeches. She'd *lost* her. Everything she'd done...all the blood on her hands, all the deaths she'd caused to draw Eimhir here, and she'd let her slip through her fingers again. All because she'd hesitated. All because Eimhir had *seen* her hesitate.

"Tides fucking take you!" Her strangled scream ripped from her throat, vanishing into the howling wind.

It was over. This had been her only chance, and she'd cast it away. There was no way to follow her, not without...

Isla stilled. Her selkie form was lost to her. She had no pelt. But she had Mara's bones, her final gift. They had carried her all this way. Perhaps they would carry her a little further.

"Màthair," she said. "I need your help."

The waves crashed over the end of the jetty, showering the wooden planks in seafoam. Whether it was an answer to her desperate plea, Isla couldn't be sure. But if nothing else, it was an invitation.

She secured the sgian dubh on her belt, then pulled the seal-skull mask over her head again. It settled into place around her temples, its cool touch a comfort. Through the skull's empty eyes, she watched the waves leap again, dashing over the docks with the same fury she felt in her own bones.

They were calling her.

Her serpenthide boots bit into the slippery wooden surface of the jetty as she broke into a run. All she heard was the pounding in her ears, the echo of each breath she sucked into her lungs. The docks faded into nothing. There was only the end of the jetty and the churning waves waiting below it.

She leapt.

All at once, the shock of cold hit her, squeezing the air from her lungs. Icy seawater closed around her, seeping through her skin. She'd forgotten how merciless its touch could be. She had no fur to protect her, no layer of blubber to keep her muscles and organs warm. She was a human in a place she had no right to be, and the sea would punish her for it every second she lingered here.

A fierce current dragged her down, and she resisted the urge to thrash against it, even as the light from the surface grew dimmer. Her lungs burned as the weight of her drenched clothing pulled her further out of reach.

There was no going back. She'd offered herself to the tides, and it was for them to decide what to do with her.

Please, màthair, she thought as darkness swallowed her. *Help me follow her. Help me put an end to this.*

At first, there was only silence. Then came a rushing from the depths, a surge of angry bubbles that shot past her flailing limbs and encircled her in rippling streams. A shape began to form beneath her, lithe and equine. The ripples grew into strong, watery muscles. The bubbles frothed into a foaming mane.

The kelpie let out a furious bray, jets of water streaming from its nostrils.

It seemed the tides had answered her.

She leaned forward and sank her numb fingers into the water horse's icy mane. It jerked its head, blinking through eerie green eyes that glowed in the murky depths. Part of her wondered if there was a remnant of Mara that lived on in the creature, or whether her heart simply yearned to seek another lost part of herself.

The kelpie pawed a hoof through the water, tossing its head impatiently.

Go, Isla urged. *Find her.*

She'd barely finished forming the thought when the kelpie reared, its haunches coiled and eager. It dipped its watery head and charged through the currents, carrying her on its back. Isla clutched its mane and leaned into its strong, flowing strides. Her lips strained from the effort of holding her breath. Her hands were numb from the sea's unforgiving chill.

None of it mattered. Not if it meant catching Eimhir.

The kelpie burst through the surface, and Isla filled her lungs with air, gulping it down in greedy gasps. She blinked away the sting of seawater and focused on the horizon. The worst of the haar was already behind her, and in front, it thinned to reveal a pale blue sky. She could see the glimmering sea stretching in front of her, the water bright and clear.

More than that, she could see a familiar shape darting through the currents.

"Eimhir," she muttered, hot anger rising in her throat. "Eimhir!"

The dread mount charged, hooves thundering across the waves. Eimhir was fast, but the kelpie was one with the sea itself. It leapt through the swell, its powerful legs churning with the waves as it ploughed through the spray.

Isla clenched one hand around the sgian dubh on her belt. There could be no hesitation this time. No doubt, even if it tore her apart. She knew what she had to do.

But as the last of the haar dissipated around her, the kelpie began to slow.

"No..." She scoured the waves for Eimhir. A grey ripple shot ahead, disappearing into the depths. "No, we have to go after her!"

The seafoam under the kelpie's hooves washed away until all that was left was the sigh of the waves. She felt the mount's watery hide diminishing beneath her, returning to the sea.

It was a creature of the haar, like the gun-anam. It could not stray beyond the mists' reach.

The kelpie tossed its head, droplets from its mane splattering across her cheeks. It craned its neck to look at her, glowing green eyes offering a gleam of apology. Then, it released a final watery bray and sank into the waves.

Water rushed up Isla's nostrils as she plunged below the surface. The depths pulled at her, and she kicked furiously, summoning all her strength to drag herself back above the waves. When she felt the bite of air on her face again, she sucked in a desperate breath, fighting to keep her chin above the heaving swell. The kelpie had taken her away from Kinraith, far past the jagged rocks that protected its bay. There was no land in sight.

It was over.

The thought numbed her. There was nothing else she could do. She was alone out here, the weight of her sodden clothes tugging her towards the depths. It was only a matter of time. The fathoms would welcome her into their arms and claim her for their own.

I'm coming, they whispered.

When the next wave crashed over her head, the currents swirled around her, dragging her through the water. She thrashed her limbs, but there was nothing she could do to escape. The sea had hold of her, and it would not surrender her easily.

She tumbled, unable to discern where the surface lay. Darkness seeped into the corners of her vision, turning her head heavy. Every so often, she felt the relief of sea air on her cheeks, and she gulped down a breath. Sometimes, it was enough. Other times, she only swallowed water, filling her chest with ice and brine.

After some time, exhaustion took her, and she slipped in and out of consciousness as she drifted with the waves. Each breath ached like a weight bearing down on her bruised lungs. She saw nothing but darkness, heard nothing but the crash of spray and the distant mewling of seabirds.

Then, something changed. The pressure lifted as her body was dragged out of the water. Light broke through, burning her salt-raw eyes. The bite of the breeze nipped at her dry, cracked skin.

Through the haze, she glimpsed a fluttering of red sails. Hushed voices murmured around her, muffled and distant. Warm hands swathed her limbs in wool. She tried to focus her vision, but it was too painful.

"Easy, selkie lass. You need to rest."

Words formed on the tip of her tongue, but her throat was too dry to give voice to them. The darkness was coming for her again, beckoning her into a peaceful slumber. She couldn't fight it. She didn't want to fight it.

The last thing she saw was the huge, majestic shape of a sea eagle coming in to land on the mast, and the pristine white feathers of the gannet that swooped down beside it.

INTERLUDE

She doesn't stop swimming until she reaches Eileanan Selch. It's the only place that's safe for her, the only place she can't be followed. Caim is a sanctuary, protected on all sides by fearsome rocks that would gladly tear a ship to splinters. The only way to reach it is through the snaking underwater caverns, where no human can breathe.

Eimhir doesn't breathe either. Not until she reaches the end of the tunnel and comes out the other side. She can't help but glance at the pool behind her. She knows Isla can't follow. She knows she is safe. But that doesn't stop the prickle at the back of her neck, the unmistakable feeling of being watched, being *haunted*.

By the time she trudges down the cliffside to the crannogs, she's ready to collapse. It's not just the exhaustion, though her burning lungs and aching limbs are ready to give up on her. It's the pain of seeing *her* again. It gnaws through the numbness, finding weakness in the cold resolve she's buried herself in ever since claiming the dreamwalker pelt. It reminds her of who she was *before*.

The chieftains' enclave waits for her atop the loch's grey surface. She crosses the wooden bridges linking one crannog to the next until she reaches it, pausing at the sturdy oak doors. It's the only chance she has to gather her breath. A fleeting respite before the next fight. Sooner or later, it all will catch up with her. But she cannot stop. Not when they are so close.

The doors swing open with a creak, and she strides into the room, shoulders square. The warmth from the firepit should stoke colour back into her pale cheeks, but that kind of comfort is beyond her now. She has paid the price for one too many brushes with the haar. She belongs to the mists, and their chill is not easily chased away.

"Aislingeach." Angus climbs to his feet, pelt loose around one freckled shoulder. His exposed chest bears a deep, nasty gouge near his heart, and Eimhir realises with a shudder just how close she's come to losing another friend.

"I'm glad to see you made it back," he tells her. "I feared…"

He doesn't need to say the rest. She sees it in the relief in his eyes, the fear in his pale, hollowed-out cheeks. It's not just about losing a friend. It's about losing their aislingeach, their dreamer. This is the burden she chose when she claimed her pelt. This is who her people need her to be.

Of the six chairs, only three are clad in their wolfskin regalia. The others lie cold and bare, their chieftains lost. This fight has cost them much already, as she knew it would. It will cost them more before it ends.

Beside the fire, two of the chieftains kneel by a woman Eimhir recognises as one of their scouts. Her eyes are glazed with agony, and she writhes on the bed of heather next to the flames, a moan escaping her lips. She is naked, stripped of her pelt, and though Eimhir can see no trails of salt marring her skin, she knows it is only a matter of time.

Before she can say anything, Duncan is in front of her, his umber eyes dark and questioning. "What happened?"

That's not what he's really asking, and Eimhir knows it. So she replies, "Isla lives. I already swore to you I would not kill her unless she left me no choice."

How close was it? she wonders. She remembers Isla's hand tightening around the sgian dubh, the muscles in her forearm twitching. If not for that hesitation, that sliver of doubt, what might have happened?

"I asked her about the anam-long." Angus turns to his brother. "She said you let her go back in Arburgh."

He's trying to keep the accusation out of his voice, but Eimhir hears it all the same. It doesn't matter, not to her. She feels no rush of anger, no sting of betrayal. Somewhere, in the part buried so deep it's lost to her forever, she already knows what Duncan has done. She understands what it's like for love to linger in the most unlikely of places.

"Isla came for the soulship, and I did not stop her," Duncan says, the low timbre of his voice offering no apology. "She wore Mara's bones, bones that would have found their resting place in the hull of that ship in another time. It was not my place to deny her that. Not if it meant staining the deck with her blood...Mara's blood."

"She is not Mara," Eimhir replies. "And do not forget, she is as much the Grand Admiral's daughter as she is the daughter of a selkie."

The words sound forced to her own ears, even with everything that has passed.

Duncan must realise it too, for he looks at her evenly and says, "Yet you love her still."

There is no denying it, not when she feels the truth like a blade buried in the place she once had a heart. A fresh pain breaks through the numbness, reminding her of all she has lost.

But she's not the only one fettered by a love she cannot let go of. She has seen it in Isla—the agony clouding her eyes as she clenched the sgian dubh, the stiffening of her spine as she baulked at what she needed to do. She faltered. She will falter again, if Eimhir can give her reason to.

The selkie across the room is still thrashing, agitated moans spilling from her throat. It will be a drawn-out death, one filled with agony as the salt sinks deep into her flesh, gnawing through organs and tissue until there is nothing left. Eimhir doesn't pity her. There is no room left in her heart for such things. But that doesn't mean she can't offer this woman a reprieve from her suffering.

She walks to the other side of the room and unclasps the bolts of the sturdy lockbox nestled in the corner. Inside lies a bundle of fawn-coloured fur, speckled with gold and brown.

It's odd how something that once held her soul feels so unfamiliar, like a skin she has no memory of slipping into. The pelt in this box is no longer hers, not since she claimed the folds of dappled grey that hang around her shoulders now.

As she pulls it from the chest, Angus tenses. "You mean to... Are you sure that's wise, aislingeach?"

"It's what I have to do," she replies.

The two chieftains part to let her through as she approaches the stricken selkie woman. Their faces flicker with fear and reverence, but Eimhir ignores them and kneels beside the woman, pushing her sweat-soaked hair from her clammy forehead.

"I pass to you the blessing my ancestors once bestowed on me," she murmurs. "You will not join the gun-anam today."

The woman's eyes widen as Eimhir pulls a small dagger from her pelt and opens a bright red line down the crook of her forearm. Blood gushes from the wound, spilling across the fawn-coloured fur she clutches in her hands. She smears her arm across her old pelt, releasing it to the other woman like a breath she'd been holding.

When the fur is stained red, Eimhir places the pelt across the woman's shoulders like a shroud. The woman closes her eyes and stops writhing, her crinkled brow smoothing into a deep, tranquil peace. When she wakes up, she'll be whole again.

Eimhir stands, wiping dribbles of blood clean from her forearm. Her pale skin is marred with crimson streaks, but it's nothing the cleansing touch of the sea won't wash away.

Duncan fixes her with a sombre look. "You've removed any chance of compromise."

She knows. She meant to.

There is no going back from what she has done. If she loses her pelt, she'll no longer have the safety of her old soulskin to slip into. She will become gun-anam.

If Isla finds her again, she'll be met with a choice that will break her.

Understanding dawns across Angus's face. "You trust her that much? To give up her hopes of reclaiming the dreamwalker pelt to save you?"

"It's not a matter of trust," Eimhir replies. "It's a matter of pain, of grief. Isla could never bear seeing someone she loves suffer. She takes their sorrow into her, carries it as her own. She's not strong enough to do what must be done. She never has been."

Her words echo on her tongue for hours after she leaves the crannog and makes the long climb to the top of the crags. They taste of fear and doubt, but she cannot swallow them down again. This is the choice she has made. She *knows* Isla, knows her deeper than the currents of their shared blood. There is only one way for this to end.

When she reaches the summit, she takes in the stretch of water surrounding the island. The rolling waves are peaceful, but they will not remain so for long. Sooner or later, the bloody violence with which she's been flaying Silveckan will return here, like Isla promised it would. And when it does, Isla will return too.

Eimhir stares out over the waves and smiles.

Come, cousin. Condemn me, if you can. I'll be waiting.

CHAPTER TWENTY-TWO

DARCE

A hot flash of pain burst across Darce's knuckles as they connected with bone. Blood splattered across the deck, but his grim satisfaction was buried under the rage building in his chest.

"You *left* them," he said, the words a snarl. His hand throbbed, but he balled it into a fist again as the other Sea Kith closed in.

Ruairidh stepped back, pressing his fingers to his tattooed cheek. When they came away bloody, he guffawed. "Didn't expect such fierce teeth from such a wee sprat. But I'd caution you against trying it again, lad. Bigger fish than you have found themselves gutted for less."

"I don't give a—"

"Easy, Sergeant." Nishi placed a steadying hand on his arm. "We have enough enemies to worry about. Let's not give ourselves any more. Isla is alive. That's all that matters."

"No thanks to him." Darce glared at Ruairidh. The Sea Kith captain seemed unconcerned by his outburst, which only angered him more. There was no remorse on his face, only a maddening glint of amusement in his single blue eye.

"No thanks to me?" Ruairidh licked the blood off his fingers. "She and her brother were the ones who skulked off in the night. It was never part of the plan for them to infiltrate Kinraith, much less for her to end up in the fucking water. She was lucky Cam had Swiftclaw keeping watch on the waves, or she'd have drowned."

A pealing cry rang out from the mast above, and Darce lifted his head to see the huge sea eagle glaring down at him with fierce yellow eyes. The bird was twice the size of Featherblade, with curved talons and a hooked beak that looked like it could take someone's arm off.

He clenched his fists. "Don't pretend you did it for Isla's benefit. This was about your bargain, nothing more. She can't deliver you the selkie chieftain if she's dead, can she?"

"Does it matter why I did it?" Ruairidh shrugged. "Your selkie lass is alive. If I were you, I'd spend less time haverin' to me and more time getting the colour back in those bonnie cheeks of hers, if you ken what I mean."

He winked, and Darce was ready to lunge at him again before Nishi guided him away with a firm hand.

"The bastard has a knack for getting under the skin," she muttered. "Don't be so foolish as to give him an excuse to cut your throat. We'll need you in the storm that's coming. And as much as I hate to admit it, we'll need him too."

Darce took a steadying breath, willing his anger to subside. When Featherblade had led them to the *Red Gale*, he'd expected to find both Blackwoods waiting for him. Instead, Isla was shivering in the hold, half-drowned and dead to the world, and Lachlan was missing.

He climbed down the stairs and followed the hallway until he found the room where Isla was sleeping. The glow from the oil lamp cast shadows across her pale skin, dancing across every vein, every line of salt biting into her flesh. Her lips were dry, her hand like ice as he gathered it in his. It seemed impossible that the tides had returned her to him a second time.

He brushed his hand across her forehead, sweeping away a lock of hair brittle with salt. She stirred at his touch, her bruised lids fluttering open to reveal bloodshot green eyes.

"Darce," she whispered, his name like a question on her lips. "I saw Featherblade. Thought it was a dream."

"It was no dream," he said. "I'm here. I promised I would find my way back to you."

A rasping cough shuddered through her. When it subsided, she asked hoarsely, "What happened?"

He told her, pausing between recollections to help her tilt back the honeyed concoction the Sea Kith had brewed to soothe her aching throat. When he finished talking, she took over. A burst of relief rushed through him to hear Lachlan had escaped Kinraith, but Isla's brow creased with worry.

"I told him to find you," she said. "You've not seen him?"

"Not yet. As soon as Featherblade picked up the *Red Gale*, we came straight to you."

She chewed her lip. "I left him with Blair. I hope that wasn't a mistake. If he hands him over to the Admiralty..."

"I don't believe he would do that," Darce said. "He's a better man than his uncle."

"And what about us?" She fixed him with a desperate look. "After what we've done, are we any better than the Admiralty, than Eimhir?"

"I..." Guilt rose in Darce's throat, sharp and pungent. He still saw Baininch Rise in his dreams, the watchtower disappearing into the mists as they sailed away from those they'd buried, those they'd left behind. "We didn't have a choice."

"Is that true? Or is it merely a lie we tell ourselves to justify the blood on our hands?" She leaned back in the cot, tears glistening in the corners of her eyes. "Do you not suppose Eimhir thinks she's doing what needs to be done? That Cunningham believes his violence is necessary? Why should we be any different?"

"Because we're trying to make things right."

A bitter laugh spilled from her throat. "Ask the people of Kinraith if we made things right. What we did to that port... I was so caught up in doing whatever it took to find Eimhir that I couldn't see the shadow of her growing in myself."

The silence was so heavy Darce feared it might smother them. There was nothing he could say, nothing he could do to ease her pain. Not when the same doubt seeped through his own heart. He could only bear it with her, his fingers closing around hers as he traced the scars on the back of her hand.

After a while, she spoke again, every word aching with despair. "I'm *tired*, Darce. It never ends, no matter what we do. We cannot help but add to it, over and over and over again. It won't stop." A tear trickled down the side of her face, leaving a salty trail in its wake. "I couldn't kill Eimhir. I didn't *want* to kill Eimhir."

She doesn't let go of the people she loves, not when she believes there's a chance she can save them. The echo of Muir's words swam through his head. It wasn't just about Eimhir. Isla deserved to know what would happen to her uncle if the Grand Admiral was killed. But Darce couldn't tell her, not like this. He would keep his word to Muir, at least for now.

He pressed a gentle kiss to her lips, tasting the lingering sweetness of honey and lemon. "You need to rest. We can worry about what comes later after dawn breaks."

As he lifted himself from the chair, her hand tightened around his. "Please, Darce. Stay."

There was more in the tremor of her voice than the meaning of that single word. It was layered with grief, with need.

"Always," he said, and lowered himself back to her side.

It wasn't until the following evening that Isla regained the strength to pull herself from her bed and join the rest of them for supper. Darce watched as she slipped into the room, purple shadows of exhaustion ringing her eyes. Part of him wanted to rise to help her, but her grim resolve told him he wasn't needed. Not for this.

She lowered herself into an empty chair, a shimmering fishscale cloak fastened across her shoulders. Its silvery folds spilled over the bone cuirass around her ribs, casting the armour in a ghostly sheen.

At the opposite end of the table, Ruairidh's face split into a wide grin. "Good to see you up and about, selkie lass. Would be a shame to have gone to all that effort to save your life only to have you succumb to bloodlung."

"I appreciate the concern. And the rescue." She turned to Cam, giving the young Sea Kith sentinel a solemn nod. "I'm glad you were watching the waters."

"Ye saved my life from those wraiths when I froze back in Storwick," Cam said. "The auld ways demanded I return the favour." They waved towards the table. "Go on, ye should eat. You'll need your strength for what's coming."

As they tucked into the spread, a stilted silence fell across the room, punctuated with the scraping of cutlery and the sloshing of wine and ale. Out of the corner of his eye, Darce saw Muir reach for a decanter of amber-coloured whisky, and he quickly replaced it with a jug of water.

Muir scowled. "Thought you'd be more understanding, given my condition." He glanced at Isla, then lowered his voice. "Can't blame a man for wanting to take the edge off the thought of his imminent passing."

"You're not dead yet." Darce tore a hunk of bread and ladened it with strips of salted pork. "When do you plan to tell her?"

"When the time is right," Muir said. "But I'll do it on my terms. Don't take that from me."

At the far side of the table, Ruairidh popped a pink octopus leg into his mouth and wiped his lips clean of grease and crumbs. He sat back in his chair with a satisfied sigh, observing them through his keen blue eye as they finished.

"It's time we discuss what to do next," he said. "Some of the other Sea Kith crews feel emboldened after the blow we struck the Admiralty at Kinraith. They're ready to join the fight."

Nishi twirled her fork, mouth drawing into a troubled line. "I've tangled with the *Vanguard* enough times to know we'll need more than ships to stand against the Grand Admiral. He has a hold over the tides in a way I can't understand. He corrupts the auld blood, twists the sacred oaths, yet the waves bow to his sentinels' command. We cannot win as long as he draws breath." She slammed the fork into the table, watching it quiver on its prongs. "And all of us here know how little he likes to stay dead."

Ruairidh raised an eyebrow. "Isn't that what the hostages are for?"

"They're not hostages," Nishi snapped. "They're wretched souls who have been through enough at the hands of the Admiralty. Aye, they could be our hope of turning the sentinels, but the *Vanguard* will blow us out of the water before we get the chance to try. We can't risk meeting the Admiralty head on."

"Then you'd do well to cut me loose at the first chance." Muir crossed his arms. "There's nowhere I can go that Alasdair won't follow. The blood oath will lead him to me, and whoever I'm with."

"And if you get captured or killed? What good would that do us?" Isla spoke for the first time, her voice stubbornly unyielding. "We need you, uncle. More than you know."

Muir's expression was as surly as ever, but there was a flicker of regret in his eyes, a twist at the corner of his mouth that might have been guilt or grief or both.

Tell her, Darce thought. *Before I have to.*

"By all means, if you have a better suggestion, let's hear it," Muir said, returning Isla's gaze. "I, for one, would delight in settling on a course of action that doesn't result in the deaths of everyone at this table."

If his forced glibness stung her, Isla didn't show it. Instead, she looked around the rest of them, hands shaking as she laid her palms flat against the crimson tablecloth. "I need to return to Eileanan Selch."

Darce felt the unease rippling across the room as her words washed over them. He'd been expecting it, but he couldn't suppress the dread worming into his heart.

The Selkie Isles. She wanted to walk into Eimhir's waiting jaws.

A dark look fell across Ruairidh's face. "There's no good that can come of going to that place. If the rocks don't get us, their raiders will."

"You don't have a pelt anymore," Cam added. "You cannot reach her."

"I don't need my pelt. The tides will carry me, like they did at Kinraith." Her hand drifted to the gleaming bone around her chest. "All I need is the haar."

A chill crept down Darce's neck at her words. The kelpie. She was asking him to summon the mists so she could ride to whatever was waiting for her on that island. She was asking him to carry her there, as only he could.

He swallowed, wishing with all his heart he could refuse her. "Aye," he said. "If that's what you need."

Ruairidh gave a derisive snort. "You think you can take on an island of selkies? I'd wish you luck, but it would be a waste of breath."

"I have no intention of taking them on," Isla said. "They are my people. My fight is not with them. And if the Sea Kith plan to stand against the Admiralty, there are no better allies to be found than on Eileanan Selch."

"Allies?" Ruairidh's braid spilled across his shoulders as leaned forward, fixing her with a dangerous glare. "You forget, selkie lass, I know what happens when a ship strays too close to your people. I've already borne the cost of that once in my life. I have no desire to do so again."

"I haven't forgotten anything," Isla replied. "And I understand your grief better than you know. Long before I knew I was one of them, the selkies raided my home. They killed my father, slaughtered the people of our village. There's not a day that passes that I don't think about what they took from me."

"And you never tried to find the skinchangers responsible?" Ruairidh prodded. "Never thought of hunting them down?"

"Would that have brought back those I lost?" Isla countered. "Perhaps I could have found them and killed them. Then their family could come and kill me, and this whole fucking thing could go on and on. Someone has to be the first to put down their weapon. And after what we did to Kinraith, I've decided it will be me."

She rose from the table, pale cheeks flushed pink, eyes bright with unspent tears. Darce wanted to reach for her trembling hands, but any comfort he offered would only be a lie. The truth was already out there, ringing in the raw echo of her voice.

Ruairidh grunted, the furrow in his tattooed brow softening as he leaned back in his chair. "Aye, well, not all of us can be as noble as you."

"Noble?" A pained laugh spilled from Isla's lips. "If you think I'm claiming some moral superiority here, you've misunderstood. My hands are as bloody as everyone else's, and they'll be bloodier still by the end of this. But there *can* be an end to this. If we stop chasing vengeance. If we break the cycle."

Darce glanced to the corner of the room. His claymore stood propped against the wall, bound in its cloth wrappings. The blade was a reminder of the promise he'd made to Cormick Blackwood, the sworn oath to keep his children safe. He'd been ready to drench the sword in blood in the name of that promise, but beneath the wrappings, the steel was clean. Was it possible that the best means of honouring his word was to keep it that way?

Ruairidh shook his head. "There are some wounds that cannot be forgotten. What you're asking is—" He stopped abruptly, cut off by the thud of footsteps hurrying down from the deck above. The oak doors burst open, and a red-faced deckhand stumbled into the room.

"Sails," she said, gasping for breath. "Emerald and sapphire."

Jewel tones. A shiver crawled up Darce's spine. Whatever plans they'd been trying to decide on, it was too late.

The Admiralty had caught up to them.

CHAPTER TWENTY-THREE

ISLA

Isla stared across the waves, ignoring the pain in her fingertips as she squeezed the edge of the gunwale. The last vestiges of daylight slipped beyond the horizon, darkening the purple-streaked sky. But there was still enough to see the approaching sails, the reminder of the net tightening around her.

The Admiralty would never give up. Cunningham would never give up.

"We need to get back to the soulship so I can summon the haar," Darce said, following her gaze. "Whoever that is, they're moving fast."

"Go," she said. "I'll be right behind you."

He gave her a reluctant nod, then hurried off. Isla's fingertips dug deeper into the gunwale, snapping off loose splinters of wood. Frantic shouts from the *Red Gale's* crew rang in her ears as the deck bustled with movement, but she shut out the commotion, focusing on the billowing sails.

It wasn't the *Vanguard*. This ship was smaller, cutting through the waves with a lithe hull and narrow prow. As the cloak of night fell across the waves, she could make out the rich tones of emerald and sapphire hanging from the twin masts. The ship sailed towards them with furious purpose, undeterred by the *Red Gale's* hull drifting broadside.

"Prepare the cannons," Ruairidh bellowed, his braid flying in the wind as he marched along the deck. "As soon as that ship is in range, I want the full might of our portside unleashed."

A shriek came from overhead, and Isla looked up to see Featherblade circling the masts, its wings a flash of white. It soared into the clouds, then returned with Swiftclaw. The huge sea eagle let out a cry of its own, and both birds peeled off from the *Red Gale* to skim across the waves towards the approaching Admiralty ship.

Isla glanced at Cam. "What's going on there?"

"The guidebirds must know something we don't." Cam's mouth tightened. "This doesn't feel right."

A chill swept across the deck, and silvery droplets wound around the soulship's mast as its sails began to form. The smaller ship rolled restlessly on the waves alongside the *Red Gale*, eager to slip into the haar. Already Isla felt the nip of frost on her skin, the sting of salt thickening in the air.

"You should get over there," Cam said. "Leave the Admiralty to us and get away while you can."

"I will," Isla said. "It's just—"

A piercing screech tore through the sky, and she snapped her head around to see two shapes returning from across the waves. Featherblade and Swiftclaw were racing towards them, wings scattering the spray as they flapped relentlessly.

"That was quick." Cam peered out from under the drooping brim of their hat. "Look, Swiftclaw has something in its talons."

The guidebirds burst into chatter as they drew near, Featherblade's raucous caws mingling with a piping cry from Swiftclaw. They swept low over the deck, barely clearing the gunwale, and Isla jolted as something landed with a thud behind her.

She stooped low, curling her fingers around the object.

It was a cane. A battered hazelwood cane.

Ruairidh stalked the quarterdeck, roaring orders into the wind. The *Red Gale's* stern had drifted, baring its broadside to the approaching Admiralty ship. Every cannon was ready to fire. All it would take was a signal to the gunners, and they would erupt in a salvo of cast iron and black powder.

"Wait!" Isla hauled herself up the wooden steps and tore across the deck. She had to reach Ruairidh before he gave the command. The Admiralty ship was coming at them head on. Even if it manoeuvred now, it would never get broadside fast enough to fire a volley of its own. It would be blasted into pieces, taking with it everyone on board.

She rushed forward, darting between the bustling crew. "Captain, you have to hold. Don't fire on that ship."

Ruairidh turned, the scar behind his eyepatch twitching. "It's bad enough you've gone soft when it comes to those skinchanger friends of yours. But asking me to spare an Admiralty ship? I'm starting to question whether you and I are on the same side."

"It's not the Admiralty." She braced her hands on her knees, fighting to regather her breath. When she lifted her head, she met Ruairidh's questioning gaze with a weak smile. "It's my brother."

It wasn't until she was fixing the wooden gangway from the Admiralty schooner onto the soulship that Isla allowed herself to breathe normally again. The haar had retreated, leaving nothing but a clear sky and the canopy of stars above them. The glow from the moon fell across the ship, giving the bone an eerie sheen as she stood at the end of the gangway and waited for her brother.

Lachlan hobbled carefully down the wooden walkway, arm looped around Blair's shoulder for balance. Neither of the men looked at each other. There was a strain between them that stifled the crisp air.

When Lachlan reached the deck, Isla started forward. "Are you—"

"Still in one piece. Relatively speaking, of course." A hollow smile tugged at the corner of his mouth.

She pressed the hazelwood cane into his hands, and he accepted it gratefully, wincing as he steadied himself on the handle. He didn't look as comfortable with it as he had with his crutch, but for now, it was all he had.

As Blair extricated his arm from around his shoulders, Lachlan paused. "You won't change your mind, then?"

Blair paused, eyes fixed firmly on the wooden walkway beneath his feet. "I told you I would return you to your family. But my place is with the Admiralty."

A loud snort came from behind them, and Isla saw Muir standing with his arms crossed. "Do you know what it is you're scurrying back to, lad?" he asked. "Or did your uncle keep you in the dark about what he was doing out at Baininch Rise?"

Blair's mouth pulled tight. "I have no idea what you're talking about."

"Would you like us to tell you about the horrors we found there? Or would you like to see the prisoners we rescued with your own eyes?" Muir's voice was cordial, but Isla didn't mistake the dangerous undercurrent rumbling through each word. "Perhaps you can explain to them why you're so eager to return to the man who locked them up in a wretched hole and kept them alive only so they could be used as leverage against his sentinels."

Blair squared his jaw. "You expect me to believe the word of a traitor and a drunk, a man who turned on his own captain?"

"You don't need to." A voice cut through the air behind them, and Isla turned to see Darce and Jacques emerging from the hold, shepherding a frail woman with bright green eyes and stumps in place of hands.

Blair observed them. "I remember you. You deserted the same month I joined the Admiralty. Hamish Grier, wasn't it?"

"It used to be. Now, it's Jacques." He nodded to the woman beside him. "This is my mother. You may have heard of her. After all, she built the very ship your uncle terrorises these waters with."

Blair paled. "That's not—Margaret Grier died in an accident years ago out at the Corran shipyards. All they found of her body was…" Something strained in his voice as he looked at her, his eyes darting to her ragged arms. "She was given an Admiralty funeral. I was *there*."

"*Midnight Crest*," Maggie Grier mumbled, surveying the Admiralty schooner bobbing on the waves alongside them. "Thirty-six metres. Pine decking, oak hull. Original mast snapped in a winter squall. Restored it myself. Better now."

"My mother never worked a day in the Corran shipyards," Jacques said coldly. "All that time, she was holed up in Baininch Rise to keep me in line. To ensure that if the Grand Admiral ever had need of me, I would answer. And when I snapped my leash, he had her mutilated to punish me for it." He shook his head. "I spent years believing she was dead because of me. Somehow, the truth was worse."

"There are others," Darce added quietly. "You have no idea the suffering that exists in that place. There were more we couldn't save, more we had to leave behind."

Blair swallowed. When he glanced at Maggie Grier again, something in his expression changed. There was no denying the similarities between her and Jacques: their hawkish looks, their green eyes.

"Please," Isla said. "This isn't the Admiralty you want to serve."

When Blair made no reply, Darce walked towards him, a rolled-up sheaf of parchment between his fingers.

He held it out, hand steady. "This contains the names of everyone we rescued from Baininch Rise. If you find your way back to the *Vanguard*, tell its sentinels what we did. Let them know they're no longer bound to serve him, that they have a choice."

Lachlan stiffened. "Galbraith, if he gets caught—"

Blair's hand closed around the parchment. He stared at the rolled-up letter with an unfathomable expression, then pocketed it, turning towards his ship with a troubled weight on his brow.

At the foot of the gangway, he paused. "Before I go, there's something else. When we fled Kinraith, we took as many refugees as we could hold. It wasn't until we were halfway to the next port that we realised Nathair Quinn was amongst them."

"Quinn?" Isla stilled. "You're certain?"

"I've seen him," Lachlan said. "He's looking worse for wear, but it's him."

Nishi had been standing by one of the masts, talking in soft tones to Maggie Grier. Now, she approached, stiff and tense. "Did I hear you right? You have the bastard who sold out the *Jade Dawn?*" She closed her hand around her pistol. "That coward is *mine*. I'll send him to the fathoms myself."

"Nishi—"

"No, Blackwood." The captain shook her head, eyes glittering under the brim of her tricorne hat. "You don't get to take this from me, not after what he did to my crew. You weren't there. You didn't watch their bodies char and burn. You didn't hear them screaming through scorched lungs. If you want to set aside vengeance, that's *your* choice to make. This is mine."

Isla's throat constricted. "It won't bring them back. It won't make any of this easier to bear."

"If you're right, that will be my burden to carry." Nishi set her jaw, her gaze unmoving. "After all we've been through, I consider you kith. But you can't change my mind, not on this."

Isla's chest turned cold. "I...I understand. Better than I want to admit."

Blair glanced between them, shifting uncomfortably. "I can bring him aboard, if that's what you wish. But first...he requested to speak to Isla. Alone."

Darce stepped forward. "That's not going to happen, Lieutenant."

"It's all right, Galbraith. She'll be fine." Lachlan gave her a sombre nod. "I had the chance to make my peace with what's to come. You should, too."

His words rang around her head as she followed Blair onto the Admiralty ship. The lieutenant led her to the brig and pointed towards a familiar figure slumped in the corner, shackles around his bruised wrists.

Isla took a sharp breath. Whatever happened to Quinn back in Kinraith had left its mark. Yellow-green bruising ran down one side of his jaw, and a nasty cut bisected his eyebrow. His once-coiffed hair sat limp and dishevelled, and though he wore an exquisite silk doublet and velvet cloak, no amount of finery could hide the fact that this was a man beaten, a man broken.

He looked up as she approached, his blue eyes glinting with his usual mixture of amusement and contempt. "Well, dear Isla, isn't this a familiar sight? Though I must confess, I rather preferred it last time, when I was on the other side of the bars."

Blair leaned in and spoke quietly. "I'll let you talk. Come and fetch me when you're done."

He slipped away, footsteps fading into the hallway behind her. There were no other prisoners in the brig. The cells were empty, save for Quinn. It was just the two of them.

She moved closer to the bars, taking in his bruised face, his cool expression. He was still wearing a mask. She doubted she'd ever truly known the man beneath it. Now, she'd never get that chance.

His mouth stretched into a disdainful smile. "Is that pity I see? Please, spare me. This is humiliating enough already. Of all the ships I could have crawled onto to escape that tides-forsaken port..."

"You're lucky to be alive."

"Am I?" His smile turned bitter. "We both know what happens next. Your Sea Kith friend wants my head, and you're going to serve it to her on a gilded platter. Don't deny it. I saw the truth on your face the moment you walked in."

Isla tensed. "It didn't have to end like this. But you couldn't help yourself. You needed *more*. Nothing was ever enough for you—not my friendship, not my brother's. Not when there was a chance for you to claw more power for yourself."

Quinn shrugged. "It was never personal, old friend. Lachlan was simply too attached to you. You became a piece on the board I had to remove."

"And Blair? Did you plan to remove him too?"

His expression soured. "The lieutenant was a distraction I didn't anticipate. One that proved to be my undoing, in the end."

The sting of his words lingered. Isla could almost smell the reek of death in the brig. It clung to the air, a noose around Quinn's neck. There was no escape for him, and they both knew it.

He lifted his gaze, almost contrite. "I was just the messenger, you know. It was the Admiralty that hunted down the Sea Kith ship. It was the Admiralty that watched it burn, flesh and timber alike."

"That doesn't mean your hands are clean."

A harsh laugh tore from his throat. "I've never killed another soul in my life. Not directly, anyway. I'd say my hands are cleaner than most." He fixed her with a shrewd look. "Let me go, Isla. I'll tear up the deed to Blackwood Estate and return your home to you with no conditions attached. I'll disappear to Breçhon or Vesnia, and you'll never have to see me again."

Something in her chest constricted. "You should have made that offer to Lachlan before you got here, before it was too late."

"I did. He said it wasn't his place to accept. You are the Blackwood heir, after all. Trueborn or not, it didn't matter to your parents. They put you first, in everything." Quinn curled his lip. "No wonder he withered in your shadow all those years."

Isla moved closer, kneeling by the bars until she was level with Quinn. Usually, it gave her some satisfaction to see his mask slip. But this time, under the cruel contempt, all she could see was the fear of a man who knew his time was up. And that was no kind of victory at all.

"I spent so long hating you," she said softly. "But now, at the end, I only find myself wishing you'd found another ship to stow away on."

His face hardened. "Don't. If this is to be done, let it be done. I have no need for you to pretend at sorrow for my sake."

Isla turned away, leaving him to the darkness of the brig as tears stung the corners of her eyes. "There is no pretence, Nathair. But whatever sorrow I feel for what's about to happen, it isn't for you."

There was no breath of wind to sway the long wooden plank jutting over the waves. It waited steadily, patiently, every knot and splinter anticipating what was to come. At the other end, the abyss waited. There was no returning from that kind of drop.

A hush rippled through the crew, and bodies parted to let Nishi past. The captain held Nathair Quinn by the bloodstained lapels of his fine velvet coat. His eyes were dead and dull, but a familiar sneer lingered on the upturned corners of his lips.

Nishi shoved him towards the plank, then turned to Ruairidh. "By rights, he should be meeting the fathoms from the deck of the *Jade Dawn*. I thank you for offering your ship in its stead."

For once, there was no levity in Ruairidh's expression, no wry twist of his mouth. He stared at Quinn from behind his eyepatch, cold as the grave. "For all our differences, we are kith, and the *Red Gale* knows what it means to lose a crew. You don't need to thank me, Captain. Not for this."

Nishi turned to Quinn, her copper eyes glittering as she pushed him onto the plank. The board shuddered, but it held steady as Quinn stumbled, catching himself before he slipped over the edge.

He straightened, hair falling across his forehead. There was no way back to the *Red Gale's* deck. Nishi had closed it off, blocking his path with a rigid spine and a scowl. At the other end of the wooden plank, the fathoms waited. All that lay ahead was a sharp drop to the rolling waves.

For the first time in his life, Nathair Quinn had no way out.

The same thought seemed to cross his mind, for the sneer wavered enough for Isla to see the terror. He could see his fate in front of him, waiting at the end of the plank.

"Walk," Nishi said tightly. "While you still can."

The pale glow of moonlight shattered off the waves like glass. There was no swell tonight. It would be easy. It would be peaceful.

Still, Quinn didn't move.

"You salt-shy coward," Nishi snarled. "This is a more honourable death than you deserve. I should burn you piece by piece for what you did. Now *walk.*"

The barest measure of a smile curled at the corner of Quinn's lips. He closed his eyes to the sea stretching in front of him and stood as still as stone. Even now, he couldn't bear to lose. He would pull the strings until the end, until they snapped between his cruel fingers once and for all.

Nishi's jaw clenched as she drew her pistol from her belt. "Fine," she growled, voice burning with loathing. "Have it your way."

He always does, Isla thought.

The shot cracked through the crisp night sky. Quinn staggered, blood and bone bursting from the hole in his temple. His body slumped across the plank, draped over the edge like it was caught between worlds.

Then, slowly, it slid, and the waves swallowed it with a gentle splash.

Nobody spoke. Nobody dared breathe. The gunshot echoed, stale and unfulfilled.

Nishi pocketed her pistol and stalked back to the soulship, the shadows on her face darker than before. An uneasy murmur followed her as the gathered crowd dispersed.

"Bad luck to shoot someone who already has one foot over the fathoms," Cam explained. "Not that he gave her much choice."

"There's always a choice," Isla replied. "Quinn made his. Nishi made hers."

Cam peered at her from under the low brim of their hat. "I thought you'd have made more of an effort to talk her down after your speech earlier."

"I wanted to. But taking this away from her wouldn't have changed anything. If she's to live for more than vengeance, Nishi must decide that for herself." Isla took a steadying breath. "So will you, when the time comes. One day, not too far from now, you'll find yourself face to face with Duncan."

"Duncan? Who is—" Cam stilled. "You...you knew? When I spoke to you of the bastard who killed my captain, my aunt, you knew who it was?"

"He was my selkie mother's closest friend," Isla said. "He loved her, even when he couldn't forgive her. He saved my life when my own cousin betrayed me." She paused, meeting Cam's eyes. "And he'd do anything to protect his people against those who might threaten them."

Cam flinched. "He *killed*—"

"I know. And I understand why you hate him for it. But he is more than what he did that day." She closed her eyes. "We all are. We *have* to be. Or this will never end."

The waves lapped gently against the *Red Gale*, caressing its hull with their constant motion. Moonlight glittered off the water, leaving no trace of where the sea had swallowed Quinn's limp, lifeless body. It was quiet, as death often was.

"This...Duncan...slaughtered almost everyone on this ship," Cam said. "He only stopped when he saw me. He let me go. Do you think it was because he knew my selkie father?"

"That seems likely."

Cam gave a pained laugh. "Were it not for the fickleness of the tides, I might have had a pelt of my own, a chance to know the place my father called home. I might have called this Duncan kith." Their face contorted, though whether it was in longing or disgust, Isla couldn't be sure. "I could have learned to live with the ache of that part of me forever being missing. But when I lost my aunt, when Duncan ripped that piece of my soul from me...it left an emptiness I'd never felt before. Ever since, I've held on to the thought that killing him would fill that hole. But I saw the look on Nishi's face just now. It didn't mean *anything*."

Isla shook her head. "No, I don't think it did. Losing Kerr, losing the *Jade Dawn*...the grief of such things cannot simply be undone. Nishi knows that now. I think you know it too."

A shadow flitted overhead, blocking the pale glow of the moon. Shortly after, a mournful cry tore through the air and Swiftclaw landed on the gunwale, talons goring the wood as it stared at Cam with keen, unblinking eyes.

"Ye talk of things that cannot be undone, yet you're resolved to rid the haar of its corruption," Cam said after a moment. "Ye believe it can be returned to what it once was. If there's hope for that..."

Isla thought of Mara, the way her ghostly, shimmering form had dissolved into the sea like an aching sigh. "I cannot save the gun-anam, not any more than you can raise your aunt from the fathoms. Nothing will bring back what was taken from those wraiths. But we can end their suffering, their ceaseless torment. We can give ourselves the chance to heal."

"Then that will have to be enough." Cam's eyes took on a sheen. "Whoever my father was, he's gone. But if he lost himself to those mists all those years ago, it gives me some comfort to think that even if I cannot give myself peace, perhaps I can at least do this."

The knot in Isla's chest pulled tight, then loosened with her next breath. *You will bear it*, Mara had told her. *For as long as you are able to.*

Aye, she thought. And she would not be alone.

CHAPTER TWENTY-FOUR

DARCE

A faint, shimmering mist clung to the cresting waves like dew in the morning light. It wasn't the haar—not this time, at least. Just the traces of a cool, crisp night yielding to dawn as the sun fought to break through. But Darce could take no joy in the day's quiet beauty. For once, he needed the blanket of salt and fog.

"I can't make you do it," he said, fighting to keep the impatience from his voice. "The deck won't drink blood spilled unwillingly. It has to be your gift to give, your sacrifice."

Jacques grimaced, the needle-like blade of his rapier poised to prick his palm. But before the tip could pierce flesh, he withdrew it again, a shadow falling across his face. "It's not right. Everything you've told me about this ship, about the bones it was built from... You forget, I once served in the Admiralty by *choice*. I killed selkies because I believed they were a threat to our ports and villages. My blood is no gift to these bones. It's poison."

"Why not let them decide whether or not to accept it? Isla gave you leave to try," Darce said. "The survivors from Baininch Rise don't want to move to the *Red Gale*. For better or worse, this ship is their home, at least for now. If anything happens to me, they'll be stranded. Someone else needs to be able to summon the sails."

"It doesn't have to be me," Jacques countered. "What about Muir?"

Darce bit back his retort. He had no idea where Muir had got to, though it wouldn't have surprised him if the stubborn old bastard had found himself at the bottom of a bottle again. He'd been more dour than ever since their tangle with the *Vanguard*, and he still refused to tell Isla the truth about what Cunningham's death meant for his own fate.

Time was running out for all of them. If Muir wanted to run from that, the tides could bloody well take him.

"Forget about Muir," he said tersely. "This is about you. If you would only—"

"I can't."

"You haven't even—"

Someone cleared their throat behind him, and Darce snapped his head around to see Lachlan watching them, a smirk on his lips. "As congenial as ever, Galbraith. Truly, with a disposition like that, it is a wonder my father didn't appoint you his ambassador instead of his swordmaster."

Darce gritted his teeth. "Now is not the time, little laird."

"For your persistent hounding? I quite agree." He shifted his weight on his cane as he glanced at Jacques. "He was the same in the training yard. Never satisfied until you were bruised and bringing up breakfast. Don't take it personally."

Jacques fixed him with an appraising look. "You're the brother."

Darce couldn't help but stiffen. There was a time not so long ago when Lachlan would have bristled at that. When the simple reminder of Isla—who he was to Isla—would have burrowed under his skin, prickling his resentment.

Now, the wry smile on his mouth sharpened, but there was no bitterness behind his eyes. "Aye, I'm the brother. And I know a thing or two about sacrificing something you were never willing to give."

Lachlan shifted his weight on the cane and made his way to a nearby barrel, hoisting himself onto it with a grunt. He rolled back the pinned-off ends of his breeches to reveal the stump of the leg he'd lost—the leg Eimhir had taken from him to save his life.

Darce couldn't help the bile on his tongue as he looked at the sewn-up skin, the scars marring Lachlan's pale flesh. There had been no other choice. The infection from the poisoned selkie bite had spread too quickly. Everyone else in the room that night had known it, had accepted it. Everyone except the one person who mattered.

"I hated Isla for letting it happen," Lachlan said evenly. "I think there will always be a part of me unable to forgive it, no matter how deep I bury it. But I can't take that back, and neither can she. The only thing I can do is make it *mean* something."

Something glinted in the palm of his hand, and before Darce could move or cry out in protest, Lachlan scored a deep line through one of the scars snaking across the stump of his leg.

Blood welled from the cut, dribbling around the end of the stump and falling to the deck with a patter. The crimson droplets quivered against the bone as if they were waiting for something. But Lachlan wasn't a sentinel. The auld blood didn't run through his veins.

The deck began to drink.

It happened slowly at first: a gentle lapping up of the falling droplets. Then the bone grew hungrier, drawing the blood into its marrow, gorging itself on what Lachlan was providing.

"Losing my leg wasn't a sacrifice," Lachlan said. "It was something stolen, something taken from me. But this...*this* is something I can give."

His eyes trailed over the trickling stream as it sank into the deck, swallowed by the bone. No resentment clung to his features. Instead, Darce saw the stiff resolve of the man he'd always hoped Lachlan would grow into.

"You think this is the answer?" Jacques' expression twisted in anguish. "More blood? Hasn't there been enough spilled already?"

"Aye," Lachlan said. "But this time it's different. These wounds have a chance of healing."

A snort came from behind, and Darce turned to see Nishi watching them. For once, there was no wrath burning in her copper gaze when she looked at Lachlan, only the gleam of something like a truce. "Tides help us all if the Admiralty lapdog is starting to make sense."

She pulled a dagger from her belt, then tugged the cords around her shirt collar loose, revealing the faded scar running down her breastbone. The raised skin stood out against the swirling ochre and terracotta tattoos across her chest, and Darce recognised it at once for what it was.

The lasting memory of her bond with Kerr. The would-be fatal wound she'd taken to save his life, before he'd tethered his soul to hers.

She drew the blade down the length of the scar, wincing as it welled open. Then she pressed a hand to her bloodied chest and held her fingers out. The droplets trembled against her warm brown skin before falling to the deck with a light *tip-tip*.

"There's not a soul on this ship who hasn't lost part of themselves," she said. "It's not possible to walk away from such things unchanged, unmarked. We all have scars, and many of them. But they are a sign that we survived. I wager that's something these bones understand."

A murmur rippled across the deck, and Darce noticed for the first time the crowd gathering. The prisoners...no, that wasn't right. They weren't prisoners anymore. They'd left Baininch Rise behind them. They'd chosen the soulship as the place they wanted to be, even with the dangers that lay ahead. Somehow, they'd found a way to belong here.

Nishi was right. They were survivors. All of them.

The first to step forward was Tam, the young lad Darce had spoken to through the rusting bars of the watchtower. His gaunt cheeks had filled out a little, his broken-toothed smile stretching wider across his narrow face. There was a spark of something in him, so alive Darce could feel it.

"Ma always said to repay a deed done right," he said, looking up at Nishi with imploring eyes. "These bones did right by me."

"Aye, they did," Nishi replied gently. She flipped the dagger in her palm and held it out to him, the blade stained with her blood.

Tam hesitated, then wrapped his scrawny fingers around the hilt. He drew a steady line down the callused pad of his finger and watched, half-dazed, as a single drop of blood oozed forth and dripped to the deck.

The bone drank again.

As the murmurs spread, so too did the dagger, changing hands faster than Darce could keep up with. It found old wounds, reopened gashes and gouges long scarred. More blood spilled across the deck, the bone quenching its thirst on what was offered.

Jacques furrowed his brow. "I feel something. Like the echo of a sound not meant for my ears."

"That doesn't mean you shouldn't listen," Isla said, emerging from the hold. The crowd parted to let her through, and she moved into the middle of the deck, taking in the crimson stains underfoot. "My ancestors built these ships to carry the grief of what they'd lost. They saw their pain as something to be honoured, not avenged. That is the lesson we must learn from these bones. And for all our faults, they're willing to show us how."

She moved to the gunwale, trailing her pale fingers across the smooth white surface. "Mara told me I had to take the gun-anam's suffering into my pelt, make it part of me," she said, half to herself. "Just like these bones are doing. *This* is how we move past the bloodshed that has been killing human and selkie alike. We need to know each other's pain if we're ever to have a hope of letting go of it."

Darce slipped his hand around hers, squeezing her fingers. The scar on his palm tingled as it met her skin, pressing so close her pulse beat against his.

She was right. The blood spilled across the soulship's deck wasn't violence. It was a promise that this time, when the skin knit together and the scars closed over, their wounds would truly heal.

"Twenty metres. Single mast, no sails. Not yet."

Maggie Grier shuffled across the deck, eyes shining as she lifted her chin towards the empty yards, like she expected the sails to appear with the quiet burr of her words. When they didn't, she looked down again, unperturbed.

"Bone-hewn hull, blood-quenched deck," she continued. "An old ship. A ship that remembers. And..." She trailed off, turning to Isla with a questioning gaze. "Home?"

Isla stared back at her. "Home," she echoed.

Maggie's cracked lips split into a smile. Then she raised the stump of her right arm to her mouth and sank her teeth into her own skin.

Jacques let out a startled cry and moved towards her, but Maggie didn't blanch. She pulled her arm away and let a slow trickle of blood fall from the nip she'd made.

"Your turn," she said softly. "The sails."

A sharp breath escaped Jacques' throat as he moved back to the gunwale. His neatly tied hair flew in the wind as the breeze picked up, whipping loose strands of black and grey.

Something in the air changed. A shudder rippled through the water, stirring the waves into restlessness as they heaved against the ship. Darce felt the familiar rush of magic coursing through him, but this time, the tides were not rising at his behest.

Jacques paled, but he kept his arms steady as he lifted them, calling the haar to him. The mist clinging to the cresting waves thickened, crawling towards the soulship with all its rot.

"There." Maggie craned her neck towards the mast. "Now, we can sail."

Darce followed her gaze to the spirals of salt and spray winding along the yards. They unfurled into shimmering sheets that fluttered in the wind, promising to carry them across the waves and through the haar.

Isla squeezed his fingers. "Cunningham kept these people locked up for years. They don't have anywhere else to belong. If we can give them this..."

He brushed his thumb over her hand. "*You* gave them this. You found the soulship."

"Mara led me to it," she said, pointing to the glistening bone cuirass around her ribs. "She believed the anam-long could give us a chance for peace. Give *all* of us a chance for peace." She paused, releasing a slow, shaking breath. "I once asked Eimhir if she thought friendship between human and selkie was possible. She wanted to believe it. So did I. Seeing these bones accept my brother's blood, accept the offerings from those who should have been their enemy…" A sombre look fell over her face. "Mara led me to this ship for a reason. If it can forgive the wrongs that were done to it, maybe there is hope for the rest of us."

She pressed her lips against his cheek, soft and fleeting. Then she untwined her fingers from his and slipped through the crowd towards Lachlan, a faint smile stretching the corner of her mouth.

The tension loosened in Darce's chest. The Blackwoods had each other again. Whatever was coming next, they would face it together. And Muir…

He frowned. The stubborn old bastard still hadn't shown his face. If he was avoiding Isla, perhaps he'd ventured over to the *Red Gale*. The gangway hung between the two ships, disappearing into the mist. It wouldn't have taken much for him to slip away unseen.

As Darce climbed the steps leading to the quarterdeck, the haar retreated across the waves as Jacques released his grip. The towering hull of the *Red Gale* emerged from the haze once more, and Darce crossed the gangway to the ship's bustling deck, keeping his eyes trained for any sign of Muir.

Before he'd made it ten paces, a Sea Kith deckhand strode in front of him. "Sergeant Galbraith?"

Darce stilled. "Aye, that's me."

"I've got something for you." She shoved a leaf of parchment against his chest. "Auld fella with white sailor's braids asked me to pass it on."

Before Darce could say anything, she stalked off, leaving him with nothing but the folded letter and a racing heart. He peeled open the corners, dread turning him cold before he had the chance to trail his eyes over the splotched ink.

Muir must have been hurried when he'd written the note, or perhaps drunk again. Each word was drawn in sharp edges and jagged lines, like his hand hadn't stopped shaking enough to form the letters smoothly.

By the time you read this, you'll likely have surmised what it is I've done. I would have preferred to say my goodbyes in person, but you'd have only tried to stop me. At least this way, it's too late for that. At least this way, I can help you get where you need to go. The Admiralty will follow wherever I go now that the blood oath between me and Alasdair has reopened. If Isla is to reach the Selkie Isles without drawing them down on us all, I must be gone.

I suspect you understand that, Sergeant, even if you don't agree with it.

Tell Isla the truth, if you wish. It may not be what she wants to hear, but she can't stop it. I'll face my reckoning with Alasdair, as I should have done twenty years ago. What she needs to do is get that pelt back and finish what Mara started.

I know you'll look out for her and Lachlan. I wouldn't be leaving if I had any doubt about that. If tides be kind, you'll all live to see the kind of peace you deserve. If I can give you that...well, it would be nice to meet the fathoms with one less regret.

Take care, lad. You've done Cormick proud.

Darce stared wordlessly at the letter, his mouth dry as the words seeped in and took hold. Part of him wanted to tear the missive into pieces and scatter it into the waves. But that wouldn't undo what Muir had written. Nothing would. It was already too late.

He lifted his head. Now that the mists had cleared, the soulship was visible alongside the *Red Gale* once more, its deck gleaming in the pale morning light. Isla and Lachlan sat in the shadow of the mast, heads bowed in quiet conversation. For once, there was no stiffness in either of their shoulders, no tension weighing their brows. Just a shared understanding, a semblance of a peace painstakingly rebuilt.

A peace Darce had no choice but to shatter.

He closed his hand around the parchment and stalked back to the gangway, Muir's words haunting his every step.

CHAPTER TWENTY-FIVE

ISLA

"Let me see it." Lachlan snatched the letter from Darce's hands, brow furrowed as he perused the crumpled parchment. His lips moved soundlessly, his hands trembled. Isla knew the look on his face. She'd lived this once before.

It was unnerving how quickly she could be whisked back to that moment as if no time had passed. The warmth of the Vesnian sun beating down on her cheeks. The cool surface of the coin she'd pressed into the dispatch lad's hand in exchange for the missive he held. The nausea twisting her stomach as the words unfurled before her, setting all this in motion.

Come home, my child. Allow me to give you the gift I have kept from you for too long, before it is too late for us both.

But she *had* been too late. Lady Catriona had surrendered her grip on life before Isla could reach her, leaving nothing behind but the words in that letter and the will-o'-the-wisp's ghostly light.

Now, Muir seemed determined to do the same.

Lachlan paled as he lifted his gaze from the letter. "That stubborn bastard. What was the fucking point in saving him from the gallows if all he was going to do was throw his life away?"

"You risked everything to save him back in Arburgh," Darce said. "Muir believes he's doing the same."

Lachlan stared at him incredulously. "Don't tell me you think he's right."

"Right? No. But I understand why he might think so. Cunningham will find him eventually. The blood oath makes that inevitable." Darce shook his head. "I know you'll resent him for it, but he's doing this to protect you both. To give you a chance."

A wave of grief rose in Isla's chest, quickly overtaken by the hot anger roiling beneath her skin, flushing her cheeks. All her life—before she'd even been *born*—her family had protected her. And one by one, she'd lost them for it.

She couldn't lose anyone else.

"How long did you know?" She tried to keep the accusation from her voice, but there was no holding back the sorrow that spilled over. "When did you discover my uncle's fate was bound to Cunningham's?"

Darce lowered his gaze. "Shortly after leaving Baininch Rise. I wanted to tell you, but Muir asked for the chance to do it on his terms. I felt I owed him that."

"And *this* is what he calls his terms?" She gestured to the letter in Lachlan's hands, a harsh laugh ripping from her throat. "A scrap of parchment left behind while he steals away without a word?"

Darce flinched. "Isla, I—"

"No." She waved him off as he approached, then stopped as the hurt flashed across his face. "Shite, no, Darce. I'm not angry at you. I don't blame you for keeping his confidence, for trusting that he would do the right thing. But I'm *furious* at him. For taking the easy way out. For not having the courage to tell us."

"You wouldn't have let him go."

"I—" She bit off the rest of her protestations. "No, I wouldn't. I'd have found another way. I'd have knocked some sense into that thick skull of his."

Her breath burned in her lungs as she tried to settle her racing heart. She wrenched her gaze from Darce and turned to the gangway bridging the gap between the soulship and the *Red Gale*, where Nishi was hurrying towards them with a grim expression.

"I spoke to Ruairidh," she said. "Seems the sly auld dog scared some twitchy deckhands into rigging the *Gale's* cutter for him. It's a wee single-mast boat, more suited to making runs between larger ships in a convoy. But it's seaworthy enough, and if the winds are with him, he'll already be well on his way."

"Did they take a heading?"

"South-southeast." Nishi frowned. "You're not going after him, are you?"

"Of course we're going after him," Lachlan said shortly. "A boat that size on these swells? He'll be lucky if he survives long enough to get captured by the Admiralty."

"I've seen him sail. He's as fine a helmsman as any Sea Kith I've crewed with, and that's not praise I give lightly." Nishi's brow furrowed deeper. "The *Red Gale* is setting a course to regroup with the other crews and decide whether to sail for the Selkie Isles." She chewed her lip. "I had expected the soulship to be amongst them."

"It will be," Isla said. "I won't risk losing it to the Admiralty. But I'm going after Muir."

Understanding dawned in Darce's eyes. "The kelpie. If I summon the haar, we can ride through it to reach Muir." He pulled her close, fingers winding around hers. "We'll find him. We'll bring him home."

Home. The word filled her with a bittersweet ache, and she leaned into the comfort of Darce's chest, fighting to blink away the tears.

Lachlan cleared his throat. "As much as it pains me to impose my company upon you both, Muir is my uncle too. I won't stay behind." He cut Isla off with a sharp look as she peeled away from Darce's embrace. "We're family—all of us. I've been guilty of forgetting that. I won't make that mistake again, and you shouldn't either."

His expression was as unyielding as when they were bairns caught in a squabble neither of them would back down from. But they weren't bairns anymore. So much had changed since then. It was a comfort, of sorts, to know some things hadn't.

Isla turned to Nishi. "Take the soulship. Jacques can summon its sails now. When the time comes to face the Admiralty, I hope we'll find you at Eileanan Selch."

Nishi stood stiff and still, giving nothing away. Then she marched forward, pulling Isla into a one-armed hug. "I'll make sure the Sea Kith are ready to play our part. You better be there, Blackwood. I don't have it in me to say goodbye to another friend."

Isla squeezed her back. "You said before that the tides had a strange way of bringing us together. I refuse to believe they're done with us yet. We'll be there, Captain. You can count on it."

She caught Darce's eye, and at once, she sensed the change in the air. No flag flew atop the soulship's mast, but the wind gusted across her cheeks as it abruptly changed direction. It stirred the tips of the waves, making them restless and choppy. Her breath clouded as it left her lips, caught in the chill that swept across the deck.

The kelpie was a creature of salt and spray, like the gun-anam. She needed its swift speed across the waves, and it needed the haar.

"Màthair," she whispered, casting her eyes over the waves. "Carry me to Muir, the way he once carried us both from the capital. Help me save him."

The waves leapt against the hull with a deep, watery roar. Isla braced herself as the deck rocked, then settled again. The tides were agitated. Perhaps they sensed the storm coming as much as she did. Perhaps they knew what was ready to break on them all.

Another wave rose high, crashing over the edge of the gunwale. This time, the spray didn't scatter into the wind. It hung in a shimmering haze, forming rippling haunches and a foaming mane. A series of thin splashes echoed in her ears as the creature's watery hooves met the deck, and when it tossed its head, it let out a wet bray.

Lachlan recoiled, colour draining from his cheeks. "It looks like those wraiths. You're sure we can trust it?"

Isla reached out and brushed the kelpie's snout. Her fingers passed through it like she'd plunged them into an icy pool, leaving her hand white and coated in frost. "The haar isn't the only thing the gun-anam corrupted. But this kelpie is more than the rot and pain lingering in the mists. Mara summoned it to carry me from the fathoms. Every time I've needed it—needed *her*—it has appeared."

The kelpie fixed her with its ghostly green stare. Seafoam spilled down its back, the stench of it brackish and foul. A dread mount, indeed. But there were far worse monsters in the world.

She turned to Lachlan. "You don't have to—"

"I do." He met her gaze. "I'm with you, sister."

A swell of emotion rose in her throat, and she swallowed it down before climbing onto the kelpie's back. Her legs prickled with gooseflesh as she slid into place, breeches already soaked through with icy water. But the kelpie held firm, even as it churned like the roiling waves.

As Darce and Lachlan climbed up behind her, she wrapped her fingers around the seal-skull mask. Once they left the soulship behind, it would be these bones alone that carried them through the haar. Mara's parting gift. A promise that she would always be within reach.

The skull was cool and smelled like seawater as she pulled it over her face. Through its empty sockets, she peered at the horizon and the clouds gathering above it.

"Ride," she urged.

The kelpie leapt.

They'd been riding for almost an hour when the rain started to fall. It descended on them quickly—a distant pattering of droplets on the water that grew louder and louder until it became a roar in Isla's ears. Within minutes, the rest of her clothing was as sodden as her breeches, making her shiver as she clung to the kelpie's mane.

Through the haar, she saw the storm clouds overhead. They clung together thick and black, hanging so low it seemed they might touch the tips of the cresting waves.

"If the dread mount scatters, we're done for," Lachlan yelled over the roaring wind. "We won't last five minutes in this."

Isla bit her tongue. He was right. When she'd last ridden the kelpie, it had dissolved beneath her, surrendering her to the wrath of the waves. This time, if things went wrong, there would be no Sea Kith to come to her rescue. They were at the sea's mercy.

"As long as the haar holds, so will we," she called back. "We can't be far from Muir."

Unless the swell already claimed him, a voice in her head whispered.

She pushed the thought away. This couldn't be for nothing. Muir was one of the greatest seafarers the Admiralty had ever known. He knew how to survive a storm. Part of her believed he could survive anything.

"Hold on, uncle," she said, lips stinging from the salty air. "We're coming for you."

As if it heard her, the kelpie dipped its head and charged, hooves thundering through the waves. She buried her fingers in its icy mane, ignoring the bite of spray against her cheeks.

"There!" Darce's voice was sharp at her ear, and his hands tightened around her waist. "Do you see it? Its sails are stowed, but it looks like a single mast—too small to be a sloop."

Isla narrowed her eyes at the hazy shape in the distance, shrouded behind the relentless downpour. If she'd had her pelt, she could have dived beneath the swell and observed the boat from under the surface, sensing the currents on her whiskers. But she only had her weak human eyes and the desperate hope squeezing her heart.

It had to be him.

"Go," she said, coaxing the kelpie on. "Take us to him."

The cutter was less than fifty metres away; she could see its narrow prow, its sails stowed along the yards. There was only a solitary figure on deck: a man hunched over the wheel, his white braids drenched.

"Muir!" she yelled.

As the kelpie leapt, it dissolved into spray, scattering into the sea. Isla landed with a clatter, bracing her fall with the heels of her hands.

When she lifted her chin, Muir was staring down at her with a stunned kind of horror.

"What have you done?" he croaked. "Tides take you, Isla—what have you bloody *done?*"

She scrambled to her feet and wiped the seawater from her face. "What have *I* done? I should be asking you the same damn thing. Slipping away without so much as a word... I knew you were a reckless fool, but I never thought you a coward."

Muir's face darkened. "Call back the dread mount and get out of here while you still can. All of you."

"Not without you." She grabbed his arm, squeezing until her fingers ached. "Darce told me about the blood oath, about what it means for you. But we're in this fight together, until the end. You don't have to do this alone. You don't have to protect me anymore."

"You think I don't know that?" He shook his head. "I see Mara's strength in you. I see Cat's spirit. *You're* the only one who can stop Eimhir. *You're* the only one who can stop the gun-anam. I didn't come out here to protect you. I did it to give you a chance of winning this fight. And now, you've doomed us all."

"What are you..." She trailed off. She couldn't swallow, couldn't *breathe*. All she could see was the red smear across the fishknife Muir held by his side and the puddle of blood forming underneath it. "You've called him here. You might as well have lit a fucking beacon and shown him exactly where to find you."

"Aye, I did. Because *this* reckless fool had a plan. Or he did, until the other one"—he brandished the fishknife at her—"decided she knew better."

"You never told me—"

"And this is why." He ran his bloodied hand through his braids. "You're clinging to the hope that there might be a way out of this, a way to stop Alasdair and save me at the same time. But there isn't, Isla. Just like there isn't a way to save Eimhir. You have to stop fighting for those of us who are lost and fight instead for those you can save."

He cast a pointed look across the deck, and a painful ache pulled at Isla's heart as she followed his gaze towards Darce and Lachlan. Both were watching like they could see something she was blind to. Like they understood something she didn't.

"You can't expect me to give up," she said, the words hoarse in her throat.

A rueful smile flickered across Muir's lips. "It's not about giving up, lass. It's about knowing when to let go... Knowing *how* to let go."

He paused, shoulders rigid. The haar had dissipated with the kelpie, but a murky gloom clung to the waves. There was no sign of the horizon, no trace of the Sea Kith ship they'd left behind. But something had caught Muir's attention.

"He's here," he murmured. "I can feel him."

Isla's blood turned cold. "How long do we—"

The deep, resonating blast of a ship's horn tore through the damp air. The sound squeezed like a vice, stealing the breath from her lungs. When the piercing bellow ended, its echo lived on.

Cunningham had found them.

Her mouth turned dry as the fog stirred over the port side, drifting away to reveal a looming, monstrous shadow. Through the darkness, she could make out the jagged prow, the wolven figurehead carved into the wood.

It was too late to run. Muir's blood had drawn the *Vanguard* here like a current pulling the ship towards them. There was no escaping it.

Lachlan's hazelwood cane scraped across the deck as he hobbled towards her. His hand found her shoulder, fingers pressing so tight she was sure they'd leave bruises behind. Darce drew in by her side, his touch achingly soft as he brushed her knuckles with his own. He didn't say anything. If this was the end, the beat of his blood against hers was all she needed.

Muir's face twisted in what might have been ire or contrition or both. "This wasn't what I wanted. You were never meant to be here for this."

"Yet here we are, together." She reached for him, taking his callused palm in hers. "I wouldn't have it any other way, uncle."

The words left her with a tremble, the false bravado lingering in the air. She lifted her chin, shivering as she stared at the *Vanguard's* towering hull. Somewhere on deck, Cunningham was waiting. There was nothing she could do to chase away the terror of seeing him again, this monster who called himself her father. She had to go to him, her ears ringing with the inexorable clang of a cage closing shut.

CHAPTER TWENTY-SIX

DARCE

The cold bite of metal shackles chafed against Darce's wrists as he stood on the *Vanguard's* deck, awaiting his fate. Laird Cormick's claymore had been stripped from his back, his rapier snatched from his belt. All he had left was the faint call of the tides singing in his blood, but a nudge from Muir was enough to quell that impulse.

"It's not the time, lad," he muttered, eyes flitting across the deck. "Not yet."

Darce followed his gaze. There, standing before them with a look that could sink an entire fleet, was the Grand Admiral.

The cost of each corrupted blood oath had left its mark. Snaking veins protruded from his neck, stretching his deathly pale skin over his bones. His eyes were glassy, irises darker than the fathoms themselves. There was no flicker of humanity left in them, only a reflection of the monster that had always lain underneath.

When he saw Isla, his lips tightened. "Daughter. I knew the tides would bring you back to me."

A shudder rippled through Isla's body beside him. Darce felt the stiffness in her spine, the hairs on her arms standing on edge.

Protect my children, Cormick had told him. *Swear to me you'll keep them safe.*

There was only one thing he could do, one thing that might give them a chance.

He turned to the sentinels flanking the Grand Admiral. He recognised their faces from the time he'd served on the *Vanguard*, but he didn't know their names. They'd kept to themselves, carefully guarding a secret he hadn't known existed. A secret their captains knew nothing about.

"He'll never let them go," he said, gaze flitting between them. "Those he's taken from you, the people you love. No matter what you do, their lives are forfeit. You must understand that."

A shadow fell across the Grand Admiral's face. "Hold your tongue, or I'll have it taken from you." He signalled to a group of Admiralty officers. "Take the traitor to the brig. He can rot with the bilge rats before he meets the noose."

"I've been to Baininch Rise," Darce said sharply. "I've seen the blood-cursed cages. We rescued as many as we could. Maggie Grier. Young Tam. Dozens more. I can tell you—"

His chin rocked back, caught by a swinging fist. The coppery tang of blood filled his mouth as the Admiralty officers closed in, the butts of their muskets raining down on him. One caught him in the temple, and he collapsed to the deck, head reeling. The rest of the officers fell on him, their boots finding his spine, his ribs, his skull. He flattened himself against the deck, his good ear squashed against the damp wood as he tried to shield himself from their blows. All he could hear through the ragged hole on the other side of his head was the muffle of raised voices, and through them all, Isla's furious scream.

"You're a traitor and a fool," the Grand Admiral hissed, cutting through the air. "Your lies have no power over my crew. They know to whom they owe their loyalty."

Two Admiralty officers grabbed Darce's shackled arms and hauled him to his knees. He squirmed under their grip, finding the eyes of the gathered sentinels.

"You aren't bound to him any longer," he spluttered. "You don't have to betray your oaths to your captains. If you could only—"

One of the officers threw a heavy blow, crashing a fist into his jaw. Darce's head snapped to the side, blood and fragments of broken tooth splattering across the deck. He slumped, blinking away the blurriness that set in around his vision. His skull throbbed so violently he feared it might burst. Bile rose in the back of his throat, threatening to choke him.

"Stop." Lachlan's voice rang across the deck. "He and Isla are bound by the blood oath they made to each other. You know what will happen if you kill him. Are you willing to risk her death?"

Darce clutched his head, waiting for the next blow. But it never came. The Admiralty officers drew back, and when he lifted his bruised, battered face from the deck, Cunningham was staring at him, his hand raised in a gesture of restraint.

"I don't need his death," Cunningham said, voice dangerously soft. "There are far worse things I can do to make him suffer. But as for you..." He turned to Lachlan with a steely gaze. "What consequence would come from your death, I wonder? The Blackwoods' second son, cast to the side in favour of a daughter who was never theirs to claim. So insignificant, so...unremarkable." His lips stretched into a cruel smile. "Will anyone mourn you when you're gone?"

Isla thrashed against the officers holding her back, her cheeks white. "Don't you *dare* touch him. He is my brother."

"He is a traitor. Just like the sergeant. Just like my old friend here, even before he succumbed to the filth of the canals." Cunningham's gaze trailed from Lachlan to Muir, cold and unforgiving. "If I could send the three of you to the fathoms, I would. As it turns out, the Blackwood boy will have to pay the price for all of you."

"No, he won't." A murmur rippled through the gathered officers as a lone figure pushed through, his sapphire cloak furling around him.

Blair Cunningham met his uncle's steel-eyed glare with his own, his hand tightening around his cutlass as he moved in front of Lachlan. "This has gone far enough. I won't let you corrupt the Admiralty any more than you have already." In his other hand, he drew out a familiar piece of parchment. "Do you recognise these names? They are the prisoners you kept in that forsaken tower out in the northern seas. I didn't want to believe it at first, but then I asked around." He turned to a small group of sentinels watching on. "Everything Sergeant Galbraith said is true. Some of you know it already. No matter what my uncle tells you, he'll never—"

Cunningham lunged, cuffing him around the jaw with such force Blair stumbled back. "My own nephew, poisoned by the lies of traitors. If you are so foolish as to believe their claims, you can join them." He motioned to the Admiralty officers. "Take these wretches below. I'll deal with them once I've had a long-needed conversation with my daughter."

Panic seeped through Darce's chest. "*No.* Isla, don't let him—"

A foul-smelling rag was wedged between his teeth before he could say anything more. He gagged against the fabric, fibres scratching his tongue as he fought in vain against the officers grabbing his shackled wrists. Every time he tried to wrestle free, he was met with another blow to the face, another swift kick to the ribs. There was nothing he could do but allow himself to be dragged away.

The last thing he saw before he disappeared into the hold was the way Isla flinched as Cunningham offered his hand with a cold, uncompromising smile.

The *Vanguard's* brig wasn't as unpleasant as some of the other Admiralty prisons Darce had found himself in over these last few months, but that didn't make his cage any more of a comfort. The bite of the irons chafed his wrists raw and bloody, and his body ached all over from the beating he'd taken.

It was impossible to tell how much time was passing. No light crept in through the hull. No oil lamps flickered on the walls. He could barely see the hunched outlines of Muir, Lachlan and Blair. He sat on the damp, squalid floor, his spine resting uncomfortably against the metal bars at his back.

Muir grunted. "Neither of you should be here. If you'd only had enough bloody sense to let me go—"

"Drop it, uncle." Lachlan's voice was heavy. "You know damn well we'd never abandon you. If you're expecting an apology for us trying to stop you getting yourself killed, you'll be waiting a long time."

"I don't think any of us will have the luxury of seeing a *long time*, not after this." Muir shook his head, the gesture barely visible through the darkness. "You're lucky you're alive. I suppose cosying up to the young lieutenant had its benefits after all."

On the other side of the cell, Blair stiffened.

"That's not what any of this was about, and you know it," Lachlan snapped. "Tides, Muir, do you have to be such a prickly bastard all the time? Is it beyond the limits of your imagination that I might actually... That we..."

Darce chuckled. It was too easy to picture the flush rising up Lachlan's neck, the heated indignation in his eyes. "Peace, little laird. You should know better than to get caught on the end of his line. He's only trying to piss you off because he's knee deep in his own shite and can't see a way to climb out of it."

"I *would* have had a way to climb out of it if you hadn't been so bone-headed as to follow me." Muir's voice lost its edge. "I told you, I had it under control. But risking my own life is one thing. Risking your lives...that was never part of the plan."

Darce straightened, pain shooting across his ribs as he shifted his weight. "What plan is this, exactly? Because I don't see how you could ever hope to—" He broke off at the thud of footsteps coming from the corridor outside the brig. "Quiet. Someone's coming."

He waited as the oak door shuddered open with a low, drawn-out creak. For a moment, there was only silence, and perhaps the echo of someone breathing. Then, the muted glow of a lantern stirred in the shadows, and a solitary figure slipped into the room.

The woman in front of him must have been in her early forties. The lamplight illuminated strands of silver in the golden coils of her hair. Her mouth was pinched, her forehead wracked with worry as she cast her eyes over them, wary and desperate all at once.

"The list," she said. "Do you have it?"

Blair shook his head. "One of the officers confiscated it. I imagine it's ashes now."

The woman's brow furrowed deeper, the hope in her eyes dimming as she drew back from the bars. She didn't say anything, but Darce saw her swallow hard.

"You're a sentinel," he said. "You had someone at Baininch Rise."

"Aye." Her voice trembled. "You said you'd been there. You said you'd got some of them out."

"Not enough."

"Tam." She stared at him, searching for something he could give her. "Young Tam, that's what you said on deck. Is he... Did he..."

"A canny lad," Darce whispered. "That's what he said you called him."

She let out a cry, then pressed her hand to her mouth, stifling the sound. When she spoke again, her voice was raw. "You were there. You saw him."

"He's with friends," Darce said. "People who will protect him and the others who made it out of that place. Whatever horror he suffered, he's free of it now. And so are you."

The sentinel jerked back, doubt falling across her features. "Only if what you are saying is true."

"I think you know it is."

Her jaw quivered, fear written in every line on her face as she glanced at the corridor. "Not all of us sentinels are bound to the Grand Admiral through fear. Some are bought with coin, with the promise of power. They will not turn on him. If I approach the wrong people... I cannot risk it."

"Heather." Blair shifted on the other side of the brig, irons clinking around his wrists. "It is Heather, isn't it? I may not have the list, but I committed every name on it to memory. I've carried them with me ever since I learned the truth. Please, help us."

She flicked her eyes towards him. "You expect me to trust you? You're his family."

"Aye, and because of that, it took me too long to see him for what he truly is." Blair swallowed. "None of us will ever be free until he's stopped. But we can't stand against him alone. We need the sentinels on our side."

Heather pursed her lips. "I don't know if I can do what you're asking of me."

"Do it for Tam," Darce said gently. "He's out there. Once this is over, you'll see him again."

"I..." She let out a heavy breath. "I cannot promise you anything. I must speak to my captain, tell her the truth of all this, and pray she forgives that which I cannot forgive myself." She retreated into the shadows, the lantern light fading with each step. When there was nothing left but a muted glow around her bleak, hopeless gaze, she paused. "For weeks, the tides have been stirring in my blood. I fear we are on the edge of a storm unlike any these waters have seen. If I come back, you must be ready."

The last of the light disappeared, leaving nothing behind but suffocating darkness and the omen ringing in her parting words.

CHAPTER TWENTY-SEVEN

ISLA

Isla brought her fork to her mouth and forced herself to bite into the steaming flakes of trout clinging to the tines. The fish was too sweet and mild to sate the hunger in her. It had come from the fresh water of a loch, and she yearned for salt.

Across the table, Alasdair Cunningham drew his oily lips into a smile. "I remember bringing Mara urchins from the market. She'd scoop out the roe with her fingers and devour it like she'd never tasted anything as sweet."

Bile rose in Isla's throat. Mara's name was like poison from his lips, a word he had no right to utter. Her chest grew hot with rage, the flush creeping up her collar until her cheeks were aflame.

She dropped her gaze, unable to stomach Cunningham's maudlin expression. There was nothing left in his features but the marks of the monster he was. Congealed blood gathered in the corners of his eyes. His pallid skin stretched over bone like a living corpse. His soul was rotten, and there was no hiding it anymore. Not after the blood he'd spilled to keep it intact.

The gilded chain between her wrists clinked delicately as she placed her cutlery on the table. The cuffs were lined with velvet, set with sapphires and emeralds and black pearls. When she looked down at her wrists, her pale skin glistening with trails of salt, she imagined Mara's hands bound in these same shackles years before.

Cunningham followed her gaze. "Your mother couldn't see the beauty in them either. Nor their necessity. But I would do anything to keep you safe, Isla. Even if it means protecting you from yourself."

She pushed away the half-eaten plate of food. "You don't want to protect me. You want to possess me like you did Mara. You held her in your grip so tightly that the only way she could escape it was by forfeiting her soul, forfeiting her *life*. You might have forgiven yourself for that, but I never will."

He touched his pale, skeletal fingers to his breastbone, lingering over the place Isla had plunged the sgian dubh only a few short weeks ago. "This is the second time you've tried to kill me. There is nobody else in Silveckan or its waters who could do such a thing and be forgiven. But this must be what it means to love one's child. It is unconditional."

His words curdled her blood, stiffened the hair on the nape of her neck. She wanted to squirm in her chair. She wanted to throw the plate against the wall and storm out. Anything but suffer the treacle-thick sentiment of his words a minute longer. She was drowning, hands bound by her gilded shackles.

"What happens now?" she asked tiredly. "Will you keep me locked up on this ship while Silveckan falls to the haar? Do you even care about what your crusade has brought upon this island?"

His gaze turned cold. "The skinchangers will pay for what they have done. Too long have I met their viciousness with restraint. I won't suffer it any longer. I'll bring the entire might of the Admiralty to bear on those savage creatures. Our shores will finally be free of them. Every last one."

A trickle of dread seeped into her heart. "You'll never find them."

"Perhaps not. But you will." He surveyed her coolly. "You know the waters in which they dwell. You know how to reach them. Take me to them, my dear child, and I'll see your pelt rightfully returned to you."

Without thinking, she clasped her hand around her forearm, fingertips brushing over the crystalline trails biting into her flesh. The skin was pink and raw, stinging every time her clothing snagged on the scars. The fragment of Darce's soul she carried might have saved her from fading into salt and spray, but that didn't mean she felt the loss of her pelt any less. It was an ache she carried every day, a pain burrowing bone-deep.

"I would rather surrender myself to the fathoms than give up my people to you," she said, tugging her sleeves down. "You will not have them. You will *never* have them."

Cunningham didn't flinch. She'd expected the shadow of rage to darken his features, for his lips to draw into a cruel sneer. Instead, he looked at her with something akin to pity.

"Their poison runs deeper in you than I ever imagined," he murmured. "To choose these creatures, these monsters, over those you call family..."

"You are *not* my family." Venom rose in her throat. "You have no to right to call yourself—"

"I wasn't talking about me."

His words turned her blood cold, and she stilled. The threat hung in the air like a blade waiting to fall.

"What do you mean?" Her mouth ran dry around the question.

He leaned back in his chair, steepling his fingers. "I never wanted it to come to this. But I must have the heading of the selkie colonies, Isla. For your own good as much as Silveckan's. If you feel so beholden to them that you cannot give me their location, you leave me no choice but to tear it from you piece by piece."

Before she could say anything, he pushed himself from the table, stalking its length to crouch by her side. His hand smoothed the tangled mess of her braid, fingers brushing delicately against her cheek.

"I'll start with the Blackwood boy," he whispered against her ear. "He won't even remember the agony of losing his leg by the time I'm through with him. Every time I bury my blade under his skin, every time I carve part of him away, his eyes will be fixed on you, knowing *you* did this to him. Knowing you chose those creatures over him again."

Isla's throat constricted. "Please...he doesn't have anything to do with—"

"And the sentinel, the *sergeant...*" His voice was rancid, dripping with loathing. "I can do far worse than take his ear. I may not be able to kill him without risking your life, but I will make him yearn for death. I'll make him regret every moment he spent with you, until all he sees when he looks at you is pain."

She couldn't speak. She couldn't breathe. Horror took root deep in her chest, binding her in place, paralysing her with a fear she'd never felt before. If she gave him what he wanted, she'd be condemning Eileanan Selch and its people to the Admiralty's wrath. But if she remained silent...

His hand clenched in her hair, fingers rough at the roots. "The choice, daughter, is yours."

There was no choice. There was nothing she could do.

She closed her eyes, fighting to keep the tears from spilling as she brushed her hand over the bone armour encasing her ribs. *Forgive me, màthair.*

"All right," she whispered, the sting of betrayal on her tongue. "I'll tell you everything."

The next few days passed in a dull stupor, each waking hour thicker and more oppressive than the last. Her limbs turned to lead. Her heart became a hollowed-out shell in the cavity of her chest. She walked the length and breadth of the *Vanguard* like she was one of the gun-anam, drifting through the world with no hope, leaving only wretchedness and despair in her wake.

An Admiralty guard followed her like a shadow. The golden chain linking her shackles clinked between her wrists, reminding her of the cage that had closed around her. The brig was off limits. So was straying too close to the gunwale, to the irrevocable way out the waves might have tempted her with.

Not even the salt in the air and the spray against her cheeks provided her any comfort. Their taste was bittersweet, the ache of a hunger that would never be sated. She'd *lost*. There was no going back, not after what she'd done.

When at last the silhouette of Caim's jagged peaks rose on the horizon, she bit her tongue until her mouth filled with blood.

"There it is." Cunningham drew alongside her, eyes cold in the shadow of his tricorne hat. "The heart of the Selkie Isles, as you promised." He turned to her with a tenderness that churned her stomach. "You did well, Isla. I'm proud of you."

She spat out the lingering blood on her tongue, spraying the deck with scarlet. "Your approval is poison," she said hoarsely. "This empire you've built on the waves…I'll scratch and claw and bite it bloody until I tear the whole thing down. I'll fight you until my last breath, until the fathoms show me mercy and claim me for their own."

His expression remained as serene as ever. Not even the slightest twitch appeared in the hard line of his jaw. It was as if she hadn't spoken at all, as if her words had gone unheard, unrecognised.

"Things will be different soon," he murmured, half to himself. "When the skinchangers are gone, the hold they have over you will be gone too. I can free you from their torment, child."

Isla buried the scream rising in her throat and turned to the horizon, blinking away stinging tears. Caim loomed closer every minute, its crags and ridges disappearing into the clouds. There was no approaching it from the water. The rocks surrounding the island were too hungry, too fierce even for the *Vanguard*. If they drew too close, the jutting fangs of limestone and basalt would tear the hull to pieces and gorge themselves on the splinters.

Part of her wanted Cunningham to try it. She'd rather take her chances with the tides than with him.

"My sentinels have traced the currents here. They tell me there is no way through." He pursed his lips. "I am no stranger to a siege at sea. If these creatures wish to cower on this forsaken rock, so be it. But any selkie that leaves will pay the price in blood. I will not retreat, not until the sea runs thick with their corpses."

"You can't win. These waters belong to them."

"These waters belong to *me*." His voice was like a cord about to snap. He loosened his shoulders, and a thin smile appeared. "Why don't you take a look for yourself and tell me what you see?"

He drew an ornate silver spyglass from the sweeping folds of sapphire brocade around his shoulders. Isla took it, holding the metal to her eye as she peered through the lens.

Ahead, Caim seemed closer than ever. Her heart lurched at the familiar sight of it: the proud cliffs carpeted in green, the kittiwakes and guillemots flitting from their nests, the wall of seafoam dashing against the rocks. She hadn't realised how much she'd missed it. But the island was no longer hers to call home. She'd sworn to the chieftains she'd protect it, and she'd betrayed them.

"No, not that way." Cunningham guided the spyglass towards the stern. "There. Now you'll see."

Her fingers trembled, terror turning her to ice. *Ships.* Dozens upon dozens of ships spread across the horizon. They rocked restlessly on the waves, like hungry beasts waiting to be unleashed from their chains. Sleek brigantines slicing through the swell. Mighty galleons with rows of gunports. Men-o'-war almost as huge and monstrous as the *Vanguard* itself, their sails filling the sky.

These waters belong to me, he'd said.

Tides help them, he was right.

She tore the spyglass from her eye, letting it slip through her fingers to clatter to the deck. Each breath came sharper than the last, but no amount of salt air would be enough to quell the panic rising in her. Eileanan Selch couldn't stand against this. She'd wanted to stop the bloodshed; instead, she'd delivered it to her people's shores.

"Please," she said, straining. "Mara would never have wanted—"

Cunningham wheeled on her, a storm gathering in his eyes. "*Don't* tell me what she would have wanted. She made her choice when she left me, when she ripped you from me before I had the chance to call you my own." He grabbed her, fingers bruising her jaw. "If anyone is to blame for the blood and pain of these past twenty-five years, it is *her*. You would do well to remember that, lest you follow in her wake."

His fingers loosened and she stumbled back, cheeks throbbing from the callous force of his grip. She pressed her fingers against her skin, not daring to meet his eyes.

The heavy rasps of his breathing quietened. "Isla. Look at me."

Slowly, she lifted her chin.

"You are all I have left of her," he said, his voice low. "Don't make the same mistakes she did."

"That's not true. There is something else left of her. Something we both lost." Holding his gaze was torturous, but Isla forced herself to keep steady as she summoned what nerve she had left. "Mara's pelt is still out there. I know how much you treasured it. As delicate a grey as the morning cloud. Patches that ripple like ink of midnight blue. Eimhir stole it from us both. If you would let me go to her—"

His eyes hardened. "My sentinels told me there is no way through."

"Not for a human." She swallowed. "Please. Only I can take it back."

She held her breath as he surveyed her, his expression as dark and uncertain as the churning waves. *This* was what he wanted—not her, but the last surviving piece of Mara. If she could only convince him...

He regarded her with a smile. "How desperate you are to be whole again, my daughter. How eager you are to risk it all to reclaim what she stole from you." He took her hand in his, thumb brushing her skin where the golden cuff clung to her wrist. "I swear to you, the pelt will be yours once again. When I recover it, I'll allow you to clad yourself in your skin as often as you wish. All you have to do is ask."

"But—"

"Patience, Isla. I will not lose you to reckless folly, not when we are so close to ridding these waters of the skinchangers." He dropped her hand, glancing at the quarterdeck. "I must make preparations. If you wish to stay above deck, you'll remain where I can see you. Where I can protect you."

He stalked away, leaving her with her Admiralty guard and the ceaseless waves for company. She couldn't venture close enough to the gunwale to feel the spray on her skin, not without the officer hauling her away. Instead, she closed her eyes and imagined the droplets showering her cheeks, the sting of salt gathering around her lashes, the damp strands of hair clinging to her forehead. She imagined the wind whipping around her exposed limbs as she leapt. She imagined the crushing pressure of the sea's embrace as she plunged below the waves, back in the place she belonged.

When she opened her eyes again, she saw a horizon dark with Admiralty sails.

She squeezed her hands. It was hopeless. There was no sign of the Sea Kith. Perhaps Ruairidh had deemed it too much of a risk. Without them, without their ships, there was nobody to stand with Eileanan Selch. Her people were on their own.

Something warm and runny dribbled down her lip, and she pressed her hand to her nose to stop the streaming.

It wasn't from the cold. Her hand was smeared with blood.

She glanced at the sky. Something was stirring in the dense, dreary clouds. The pressure in the air dropped; she felt it in the throbbing in her temples, a dull ache against her skull. A change in the weather this swift...it wasn't natural, even for Silvish waters.

The sky darkened quicker than she'd thought possible, storm clouds gathering in swathes of grey and black. Already, the rain had begun to fall, pattering against the deck.

Then, without warning, the *Vanguard* lurched portside.

Isla stumbled, barely managing to catch her balance. The golden chain binding her wrists clinked like windchimes heralding an approaching squall.

Something had rocked the *Vanguard*. Not a selkie; the ship was too large, too monstrous to be jostled by anything that size. Neither were they close enough to Caim to have run aground on the snarling rocks jutting up from the seabed. This was something else, something that filled her with a primal fear of the waves and what lay beneath them.

The ship jolted again, keeling so violently the hull let out a deep, agonised groan. She felt the wood straining, ready to break.

Behind her, the Admiralty officer tasked with watching her turned pale. "Tides, protect us," he whispered. "These waters are not meant for us. What manner of creature have we—"

His voice gave way to a strangled gasp and he shrank back, his frantic features falling into shadow.

When Isla turned around, she saw why.

A serpent was rising. Its long, lithe neck arched from the waves in a perfect loop, seawater cascading down its scales. She couldn't yet glimpse its fearsome jaws—its head was buried beneath the surface, but its curved spine stretched towards the clouds, colossally thick. Each of its scales was the size of a shield, encrusted in limpets and barnacles. Strands of kelp clung to its hide, fluttering in the swirling wind as it climbed towards the sky.

She stared up at it, dazed. All the air seemed to evacuate her lungs at once, leaving her breathless and lightheaded.

Then, at last, the creature lifted its head from the waves.

Fear rooted her to the deck. She couldn't have run if she'd wanted to. Her lungs seized, refusing her scream. All she could do was watch as the serpent rose to its full, monstrous height.

It hung there amongst the gathering storm, looming over the *Vanguard*. Its huge serpentine head was almost the size of the ship itself, its hide armoured with shells faded from years of erosion. This was no mere sea serpent. This creature was *ancient*. A monster of the depths, born of a place so beyond reach she couldn't fathom its existence.

The Cirein-cròin.

The serpent trailed its abyssal gaze over the ship to rest on her. Its beady eyes were like two whirlpools, drawing her into their boundless depths. For a moment, she wondered if she saw something there—a glimmer of recognition in the face of a monster.

Then, the creature opened its yawning gullet and bellowed, and the hot spray of salt water began to burn.

CHAPTER TWENTY-EIGHT

DARCE

Darce hadn't realised he'd fallen asleep until the floor lurched beneath him, jolting him back to consciousness. He shot upright, straightening his spine against the bars. The brig was as dark as ever, but he didn't need to see to know something wasn't right with the *Vanguard*. The floor was listing so steeply he feared the ship might keel over. Seawater seeped in through the cracks in the hull, running in hurried rivulets as the ship slowly righted itself again.

"What was that?" he asked, throat dry. They hadn't been given fresh water since the previous day, and there was no sign Heather or the other sentinels were coming to help. The irons around his wrists had chafed his skin bloody, and his legs had been bitten to pieces by bilge rats as hungry as he was. Every part of his body ached.

Through the darkness came a muffled groan, followed by the thin rasp of Lachlan's voice. "That shudder through the ship? I thought I dreamed it. Do you think it's the selkies? If they've come for Isla..."

"It's not the selkies." Muir sounded strange. Each word was oily and garbled, like he was speaking underwater.

A chill crawled down Darce's spine. "What did you do?"

When no answer came, he peered through the darkness, finding Muir's shadow. A glassy film coated the whites of his eyes, turning them a deep blue-green. His skin had taken on an ashen hue as the colour seeped and spread. It was like the sea itself had leached into his veins, rippling through them until they were black beneath the skin.

It was exactly like before. Muir had called another serpent, yoking himself to an unfathomable mind through the auld blood running in his veins. Now, the tides were taking their due, claiming him for themselves.

Darce shook him. "You need to sever the connection. Whatever manner of beast you've summoned, it's going to drown you if you don't free yourself."

Muir coughed, seafoam bubbling from his throat. "I know what I'm doing. I just need to..."

A thud echoed through the floor above, and footsteps thundered down the wooden stairs at the other end of the corridor. Darce held his breath as the muted glow of a lantern cast away the shadows and Heather strode into the brig, her pale cheeks flushed pink.

"This is your chance," she said. "For all our sakes, I pray you take it."

The pristine folds of her emerald cloak spilled across the floor as she knelt by the bars, a rusted key in her hand. A dull, metallic clunk rang through the brig, and the cage door opened.

She moved swiftly, twisting the key into Darce's shackles. The irons fell apart, freeing his aching wrists, and he rubbed the raw skin gingerly as he climbed to his feet. Heather freed Blair and Lachlan, then stood over Muir, tensing at his sea-infected features. "Is he safe?"

"I'll do it." Darce took the key and knelt by Muir's side, prising the cuffs from his wrists. He looped the older man's arm around his shoulder, hauling his weight off the floor with a grunt.

Heather stepped back, gesturing to a sturdy oak chest in the corner of the room. "You'll find your effects in there. It's chaos up on deck. If there was ever a hope of..." She closed her mouth around the rest of the words, fear creeping into her expression. "I do not have the courage to take up arms against the man who held my chain for so long. But I promise you, I will not defile the oath I made to my captain, not now I know Tam is free."

Darce clasped her arm. "Thank you, Heather. Even if you can't fight with us, it's enough to know you won't try to bring the bastard back."

"There are others who would," she warned. "I cannot account for them."

"I understand. Whatever happens, I hope the tides are kind to you."

Heather nodded, then disappeared into the corridor. Darce hurried to the chest she'd pointed out and swung the lid open to find a bundle of confiscated swords and pistols. He plucked them out, passing them back one at a time, making sure to slip Isla's sgian dubh safely into his pocket.

Eventually, he caught the gleam of his rapier's needle-point blade and slid it into the loop on his belt. There was only one thing left.

He leaned further into the chest, raking until his hands met a familiar bundle of cloth.

Lachlan hopped forward, grasping the door frame for balance without crutch or cane to steady him. "Are you ready?"

Darce peeled back the wrappings. The claymore looked up at him patiently, its broad edges glinting in the dim light.

"Aye," he said, taking the hilt in two hands. "I think I am."

The deck was in chaos, just as Heather had warned. Rain thundered off the surface, splashing underfoot as Darce scrambled down the stairs to the main deck. The *Vanguard's* officers were little more than hazy shapes as they rushed around him, barking frantic orders over the wind.

Something wasn't right. A foul, pungent stench hung in the air. It wasn't like the rotten chill that crept in with the haar—this reek was hot and oppressive. It was *alive*.

That was when he noticed the deck steaming.

He stood dazed as wisping vapour rose from the wood and evaporated. It was as if the deck was burning, but there were no flames. Only a stifling warmth and the sharp stench of brine.

"It's rising portside!" someone bellowed behind him. "Watch out!"

Darce peered through the downpour. A squall had closed in around the ship, whipping up the wind, drawing together tumultuous black clouds above the *Vanguard's* masts. And there, bursting through the waves in the middle of it all, was the serpent.

He'd known it from the moment Muir's eyes had turned filmy with seawater down in the brig. But it wasn't until now he realised what the mad bastard had summoned. This wasn't like the sea serpent that had harried them through the mists. This was something else entirely.

Footsteps splashed behind him, and he turned to find Blair staring up at the creature, his cheeks pale. Lachlan leaned at his side, arm slung around Blair's shoulder for balance.

"Fuck," he muttered. "This was his plan all along, wasn't it?"

"Aye, it was." Muir staggered forward. His eyes were as fathomless as the depths, like Darce might drown in their pull if he stared at them too long. But when Muir turned to him, his smile was as maddening as ever.

"Dark be the water, and darker still the creatures that lurk within," he said. "We needed a monster beyond magnitude, and the storm that follows in its wake. There is only one serpent that could ever answer such a summons."

Darce swallowed. "The Cirein-cròin."

Muir nodded. "Long have I felt its mind in the depths of my own, calling me to it. I was always too careful to listen. All these years the auld blood lay silent in my veins...I'd forgotten what it sounded like."

"It's killing you. It's pulling you to depths you can't possibly survive."

"I'll take my chances," Muir said gruffly. "Now, let's find that niece of mine and get off this ship before the serpent takes it to the fathoms."

Darce drew a steadying breath. Isla was close; he felt her as surely as the aching beat of his own heart. But the *Vanguard* was a huge ship, and the rain hammering down made it difficult to pick out an individual amongst the chaos sprawling across the deck.

He started forward, summoning his magic to shield his eyes. He kept his hands tight around the claymore's hilt, holding the huge sword steady by his waist. If he needed to use it, he wouldn't hesitate. Not if someone stood between him and Isla.

But the sentinels and captains paid little attention to him as he strode through their midst. They were focused on the Cirein-cròin looming above, its coiled neck a silhouette against the sky every time the lightning flashed. It let out another bellowing roar from the depths of its gullet, and hot sea spray and brackish saliva lashed across the deck, sending more steam into the air as the residue burned through the wood.

"It's not attacking," Blair said, glancing at Muir. "Not directly, anyway. Are you holding it back?"

Muir blinked, wiping an oily tear. "As much as I can, but it won't last. It wants to feast on the *Vanguard's* bones, and as soon as the gunners get those cannons going, its appetite will only get bigger. We don't want to be here when those jaws close around the hull."

Darce looked up at the serpent's colossal head. Each fang in the creature's mouth was as long and deadly as the serrated rocks jutting through the waves around Caim. Even from this distance, the reek of its hot breath was overpowering, thick with fish rot and salt and timber. He didn't want to think of its cavernous gullet looming over the ship, the stifling darkness rushing towards them as it swallowed its prey.

"Darce!"

He tore himself from his thoughts at the sharp cry of his name, searching the fray of bustling bodies to find where it came from. Finally, his eyes fell on a lone figure pressed against one of the *Vanguard's* towering masts.

Isla. The left side of her face was pink and scalded, and flecks of dried blood trailed around her nose, but it was her.

She rushed towards him, hands chained in golden shackles. "How did you—"

"The sentinels," he said, taking her face in his hands. "Some of them have come to our side. What happened here?"

She winced as he touched his fingers to her cheek. "I got caught in the serpent's spit. The steam was so hot I could barely breathe." Her eyes flitted to Muir. "I suppose I have you to thank for that, uncle? A wee bit of warning would have been nice."

"Summoning it to save our sorry hides wasn't enough? You always were an ungrateful brat." Muir sniffed, his eyes seeping oily tears. "Where's Alasdair?"

"I don't know. I managed to slip away from his guard in the chaos, but I've not seen him since the serpent rose." She turned to Darce. "I need to get to Caim. This may be the only chance I have to find Eimhir and take my pelt back. But even if I summon a kelpie, it won't be able to reach the island without the haar. I need you."

"I know." He stepped back, letting his hands fall from her face. This was how it would always be. To love Isla was to love the tides, the way they returned to shore only to retreat again. She was a current he'd follow, a wake he'd never leave. But he couldn't contain her, not any more than he could contain the sea itself. All he could do was carry her where she needed to go.

When he reached for the tides, they answered without hesitation, their roar crashing through his veins. Never had he felt them so keenly, so furiously. They poured their chill into his blood, turning his lungs to ice, filling his capillaries with salt.

"Galbraith?" Lachlan's voice was distant, muffled by the waves breaking through Darce's ear. "Are you all right?"

He didn't answer. Part of him feared he was drowning. Part of him wanted to, if this was the rush that came with it. Magic thrummed through him, its call more ferocious than ever before. More *beautiful* than ever before. He closed his eyes and felt the heaving swell against the

Admiralty fleet, the individual droplets of rain lashing against the deck, the wind billowing in the sails. It was him, all of it.

When the air turned dense and cold, he barely noticed. The haar held no fear for him now. When the mists crept in, leaving his hands glistening with frost, he didn't flinch.

He opened his eyes to find Isla staring at him, mouth half-open. "I never realised how much of the sea is in you," she said breathlessly.

"Neither did I. Not for years. Not until you came back to Blackwood Estate." He moved closer, taking her hands in his. "You called to something in me I'd tried to keep buried. You awoke this gift in me. Now, I don't know how I ever survived without it, without you."

She pressed her lips to his, so gentle he thought he might break beneath her touch. Her taste was softness and salt, a warmth that left him hungry for more. He'd drown in her, no matter what it cost him.

Lachlan gave a pointed cough. "Forgive me for returning us to the urgency of the situation at hand, but there's still the small matter of those shackles. Isla, if you try to fight Eimhir like that, she'll kill you."

A haunted look fell across Muir's face. "I've seen these chains before. There is only one key, and Alasdair won't give it up easily."

"There's no time for that. I need to go to her." Isla glanced at Darce, eyes shining with desperation. "Can't you cut through them?"

"Steel can't cleave through steel like that, lass," Muir said gently. "He'd be more likely to take your hands off."

The haar swirled around them, prickling every hair on Darce's neck. It spread across his skin in icy fractals, turning his breath cold and damp inside his lungs. The sensation stirred a memory in him from months ago. The *Jade Dawn* fighting through a storm. A lone wraith advancing on Isla with a wisping, spectral hand. A shattered blade, lying in pieces.

"I can do it," he said.

Lachlan looked at him in alarm. "Galbraith, what are you—"

"You know I'd never do anything to endanger her, little laird. I'm telling you, I can do this." Darce reached for the tides again, drawing the haar close. It swirled in silvery tendrils, answering the magic thrumming in his blood.

He focused on Isla's shackled wrists. The mist coiled around the chain as it spread from one wrist to the other, its unnatural chill percolating into the metal.

Isla looked up at him, calm and trusting. In the reflection of her gaze, he saw himself lift the claymore, holding the blade poised and ready. The mist crawled up the formidable length of steel, coating it with frost.

As he readied his grip, a flicker of doubt stilled him. This was Cormick's blade. Isla had trusted him with it.

She gave him an imperceptible nod, the permission he needed to do what must be done.

He brought the claymore down.

The roar of the sea filled his ears as the steel met the shackles. The shudder of the impact ran through his hands, and a blast of cold stole his breath from his lungs.

The cuffs shattered. So did the blade.

He watched, mouth dry, as shards of broken steel fell to the deck. All that remained was the onyx handle, the crossguard bare and empty without the rest of its blade. Ever since Isla had placed it into his hands, he'd waited to use it. And now, the first time would be the last.

"A promise kept," Isla said, so soft it might have been a whisper. She rubbed her fingers over her bare wrists, her skin glistening with streaks of salt. "I never needed you to kill for me, Darce. If that sword has given me my freedom, that is all the purpose it ever needed to fulfil."

"It's what our father would have wanted." Lachlan squeezed a hand around his shoulder. "It's why he chose you to protect us."

Darce stared down at the remnants of the claymore. The pieces of steel glinted up at him, silent in their judgement. He waited for the guilt to rise, the shame to coil in his chest. Instead, he felt a sense of calm, like he'd been relieved of a weight he hadn't realised he'd been carrying.

A promise kept, Isla had said.

Perhaps she was right.

"The mists have reached the island," Muir said, peering through the shroud. "You can loosen your hold, Sergeant, before this chill sets in permanently around these old bones."

"I'm not..." Darce trailed off. Around the *Vanguard*, the haar was growing thicker, its stench burning his throat. The hum of magic coursed through his veins, growing colder by the second. He wasn't drawing the tides to him anymore, but still they surged in his blood, stirred by a familiar presence. "This isn't me."

A rattling screech tore through the air, stabbing his remaining ear. Elation rose in his chest as a huge white shape burst through the mist, shrieking wildly.

Featherblade.

The gannet soared above the *Vanguard*, its blue eyes and yellow-crowned head providing a flurry of colour amongst the bleak haze. It spread its wings, sweeping around in a wide arch before disappearing into the fog once more.

Darce held his breath, waiting. Then a ship broke through, leaping across the waves with sails of salt and spray.

It was the soulship.

"Nishi," he said. "Jacques. They came for us."

He'd barely finished speaking when another shadow darkened the fog, and the *Red Gale* loomed out of the haar behind the soulship, crimson against white.

"And not alone, either." Lachlan flicked his eyes over the ships, a satisfied smile tugging at the corner of his mouth. "Seems the Sea Kith are ready to join the fight after all."

More ships emerged from the gloom, following the soulship and the *Red Gale*. This was the best chance they'd get to strike at the Admiralty—perhaps the only chance. None of them could let it go to waste.

Darce turned to Isla. Her hands were cold as he took them in his, but he was used to the chill. He ran his thumbs over the delicate trails of salt, tracing every brittle line on her skin, committing every part of her to memory, even the scars.

"I'll be waiting for you when you return," he said, low and rasping. "I always will."

She leaned towards him, closing the space between them with a kiss. His lips brushed hers for only a moment, but it was enough.

"You have my heart, and my soul," he whispered, pressing her sgian dubh back into her hands. "Now, go and find yours."

The water churned, forming a familiar equine shape. The kelpie rose from the swell, tossing its shimmering mane, pawing its watery hooves against the waves.

Isla took one final look at him, the resolve in her gaze giving him more comfort than parting words ever could. She leapt onto the dread mount's back and charged into the waves, leaving in her wake the irreparable fragments of the shattered golden shackles he'd freed her from.

CHAPTER TWENTY-NINE

ISLA

Every breath felt like drowning as Isla clutched the kelpie's mane and rode through the spray. The swell seethed around them, crashing over her head, drenching her clothes. Her teeth chattered and her arms shuddered from the haar's deathless touch, but there was no turning back.

Caim was ahead.

She couldn't see the island, but she knew it was there. Something in her chest was anchored there, calling her home. Not the barren crags or the shores of the inland loch, but the part of herself that Eimhir had taken from her.

She might have left a piece of her soul behind with Darce, but it was safe in his hands. The rest was up to her to reclaim.

When the island's silhouette loomed through the mist, Isla braced herself for the plunge. The only way to reach Caim was through the sea caverns, and no human could hold their breath long enough to navigate those submerged, snaking tunnels.

Aineol. The old taunt whispered in her ears over the roaring wind, reminding her of what Eimhir had taken from her. Worse, reminding her what she'd walked away from.

She shook her head. No, even if she'd lost her pelt, she was no human. She had the tides on her side, a dread mount to carry her home. She'd made a promise to her people. Perhaps there was a way she could keep it.

The kelpie gave a watery snort, then leapt over a surging wave. Isla barely had time to suck in a breath before the wind and rain disappeared and she plunged into the sea's unforgiving embrace.

Though her clothes were already soaked, there was no preparing for the cold. All the precious air she'd drawn into her lungs threatened to be squeezed loose by the vice-like grip around her ribs, crushing her with its icy touch. Her eyes stung as she tried to peer through the gloom, but she had no selkie vision down here. All she could see was a green-grey blur, a world that no longer belonged to her.

She squeezed the kelpie's mane, its currents turning her fingers numb. If she surrendered her hold on the creature, she'd be lost to the depths. Already, she felt the sea pressing around her fragile human body. She no longer had the protection of a fur-coated hide and layers of blubber to stave off the cold and the crushing pressure.

Her lungs burned as the kelpie charged deeper, leaving the surface behind. The haar swirled around them, saturating the murky water with wisps of ghostly white mist. They had to be close to the cavern.

Ride, she willed silently. *As fast as you can.*

The kelpie tossed its head and thundered forward with all the fury of the tides. Isla pressed her lips tight, her chest seizing. She couldn't hold on much longer. The ache was too painful. But if she opened her lungs to the sea...

Suddenly, the pressure lifted. The kelpie's watery hide dissolved into droplets, and Isla landed against the cold, damp rock in a tangle of limbs. The cavern air was stale with must and kelp, but she breathed it in like it was the sweetest thing she'd tasted, filling her stinging lungs until she became dizzy.

"I knew you'd find a way back. As soon as I saw the haar reach our shores, I knew."

The voice was low and calm, rumbling from the other end of the cave. Isla lifted her chin off the rock, droplets of seawater trickling down her nose as she peered through the darkness.

Duncan stood at the foot of the steps leading out of the cavern, arms folded across the ink-black fur of his pelt. He surveyed her with a gaze that held no malice, but no warmth either.

She slowly climbed to her feet and wrung the water from the ends of her coat. "Mara gave me the means to return here without my pelt." She pulled the sodden lapels aside to reveal the bone cuirass underneath. "She wanted me to come back."

"That's the only reason I haven't killed you where you stand." A shadow fell across Duncan's eyes. "You made the chieftains a promise—made *me* a promise. You swore you'd protect these shores from the Admiralty. Instead, you've led them right to us."

"I know," Isla said. "And if I must answer for that betrayal, I'll gladly face the chieftains when this is all over. But I didn't come here alone. The Sea Kith sail with us. The Admiralty is weakened. If we fight together, we have a chance to end Cunningham's reign over these waters."

"The Sea Kith are human."

"That doesn't mean they're your enemy." She tried to blunt the sharpness on her tongue. "And neither am I."

The silence was suffocating, broken only by the lapping of the cavern's pool. All Isla could think about was every distrusting look Duncan had given her, every cold condemnation he'd uttered.

And still, he'd saved her. Still, he'd let her take the soulship and sail away, knowing she would come back here to reclaim what Eimhir had stolen from her.

"You told me to prove you wrong," she said. "I came here to do that. I'll defend our people from the Admiralty. I'll give the gun-anam the peace they deserve. But first, I need—"

"I know what you need," Duncan said. "I was there when Eimhir took your pelt from you. I saw her standing over you, sgian dubh stained red, your bloodied soulskin in her hands. That was the moment I knew she was beyond reach. Beyond hope."

"Would you..." Isla bit her tongue. "Would you have stopped her, had you reached us in time?"

He met her eyes. "You carried the only piece I had left of my dearest friend. I would have done anything to protect Mara. It took me too long to realise that should have meant protecting you." He turned away, anguish darkening his features. "You'll find Eimhir at the top of the crags, watching the storm that's about to break. But there is something you should know before you go to her. She has passed on her old pelt, given another selkie the gift of her blood and soul. When you take yours back, there will be nothing left for her but the fathoms. She will be gun-anam."

Isla's breath caught in her throat. "Why would she—"

"To shatter any hope of compromise. If you wish to be whole again, you must condemn her to the same torment she would have inflicted on you." Duncan gave her a sombre look. "She doesn't think you're strong enough. She believes this will stay your hand."

"It can't," Isla said, the words like poison on her tongue. "I *have* to."

Even as she spoke the words, part of her wondered if she believed them. Eimhir had given up her pelt. The speckled, fawn-coloured fur that once hung around her shoulders was no longer hers to inhabit. All she had was a stolen soulskin. *Isla's* soulskin. And if Isla took it back...

Duncan's gaze was steady. "Do what you need to do, but don't forget that which you owe our people...*your* people. Let Eimhir's mistake not be for nothing. Let this pain mean something."

"You believe she is beyond saving?" Isla asked, desperation seeping into her voice. "She is my cousin. Mara's blood runs in her as it does in me. Part of your friend lives on in Eimhir, too."

"Mara surrendered her soul to save your life. Eimhir would have killed you to take it from you." Duncan shook his head. "Letting go of those we love leaves a break that is slow to mend, a scar that is loath to fade. I learned that with Mara. If you want to save our people, you must learn it too."

He moved to let her pass, and she started up the steep steps, seawater dripping from her clothes. The truth was a cold, heavy thing, sitting in her heart like a stone she couldn't dig out. It was hers to carry—she'd been doing so for weeks. But only now did she truly feel the dull ache of its weight.

She paused, turning back to Duncan. "You spoke to me of a debt owed. I should warn you, there is a ship amongst the Sea Kith with crimson sails and a captain with one eye. He sails with a half-selkie you spared when you defended these waters against their ship years ago. You owe them a debt too, one they are keen to see paid in blood. How you answer it is your choice."

A flicker of recognition danced across Duncan's features. Then it was gone, yielding to a troubled frown. "Sometimes I fear we are forever fated to reap the violence of our choices. That whatever future we hope to carve out is already written in the blood of our past."

"It can change." Isla's voice caught in her throat. "It *has* to change. I have to believe that."

A rueful smile tugged at the corner of Duncan's mouth. "Sometimes, you're just like your...just like Mara. Go, eileanach. Before it's too late for us all."

Islander. The word echoed through her ears, resounding in every thump of her heart as she climbed out of the cavern. She clutched it close, afraid to let it slip through her fingers lest it be carried away on the wind. It was *hers*, finally. This acceptance, this belonging. As much as the tides crashing against the cliffs. As much as the pelt she was fighting to reclaim.

The hillside trail emerged through the overgrowth, gravel snaking through swathes of lush grass and bracken. If she followed it, she'd find herself at the crannogs sitting atop the serene waters of Loch Mòr. But Eimhir wasn't there, not anymore.

Instead, she climbed the cliffside path, grimacing as the wind whipped across the exposed ridge. Crumbling stone shifted beneath her feet as she edged carefully along the trail. On her right side was a drop so sheer it made her stomach lurch. Far below, foam churned at the foot of the cliffs, spray leaping against the rocks.

Each footstep felt familiar. She'd seen this ridge in her selkie memories—no doubt Eimhir had too. But it wasn't just her cousin she was following; it was every soul who'd inhabited the pelt before her. A sense of *knowing* tugged at her, beckoning her forward. It wasn't the same as the ache she felt from Darce. This was something more urgent. Something calling her to it.

As she climbed towards the summit, she glanced across the water. The haar shrouded the island. The only trace of the ships within its midst were shifting shadows too distant to make sense of. Across the wind, she caught a muffled crack of cannon fire followed by the air-shattering roar of the Cirein-cròin.

That wasn't her fight. This was.

Eimhir stood where Duncan said she'd be, looking out over the waves. Her brown-blonde hair spilled down her spine, flying wildly as the wind swirled. Around her shoulders was her pelt. *Isla's* pelt.

The dappled fur shone with a lustre that seemed impossible in the dreich grey light. Flecks of ink blue and pale lavender rippled through the folds, making Isla's stomach clench. It was so close she almost believed she might reach out and snatch it from Eimhir's shoulders.

If only it could have been as simple as that.

Eimhir turned slowly, her expression hard-edged. When their gazes met, Isla saw nothing of the woman she knew in Eimhir's eyes, only a gathering storm. The mist sickness had hollowed her out, leaving behind nothing but a husk.

"Cousin," Isla said. Then, one last, desperate time, "Caraid."

The coldness on Eimhir's face didn't yield. All Isla found in her features was rage. The bloodlust that had taken hold of her left no room for regret, no room for love.

"All the mistakes you have made, and still you have learned nothing," Eimhir said, a bitter smile twisting her mouth. "But it seems there is time for one last failure. Welcome home, *aineol*."

CHAPTER THIRTY

DARCE

"You need to get off this ship."

Muir's terse words tore Darce's attention from the fog Isla had disappeared into on the back of her charging kelpie. Wherever she was now, it was beyond his reach. The only thing he could do was make sure the rest of them escaped the *Vanguard* with their lives.

The distant crack of cannon fire echoed through his ear, and he ducked as the gunwale exploded in front of him, sending shards of wood flying. He shielded his face from the splinters and stumbled towards Lachlan, who had taken shelter behind a barrel.

When he saw Darce, his face twisted into his customary scowl. "Would have been nice of the Sea Kith to wait until *after* we made it off before they opened fire."

"They saw an opening and they took it." Darce offered his hand, hauling Lachlan up off the deck. "Can't say I blame them. I doubt they know we're on board."

"All the more reason to get off this bloody ship." Muir limped over to them, eyes glistening with the oily film from his bond with the sea serpent. "If the sergeant here dies before Isla can reclaim her pelt, all this will have been for nothing. We need to give her the time she needs, and that means getting you to safety."

Darce knew the logic in Muir's words was sound, but something in his chest seized at the thought of running. "The Grand Admiral. Someone has to—"

"Someone, aye. Doesn't have to be you." Muir nodded to Lachlan and Blair. "The two of you best be going as well. You'll stand a better chance of surviving what's coming if you're with the Sea Kith."

Darce stilled. "What do you mean to do?"

"What I've been waiting to do for more than twenty tides-forsaken years." Muir gave a grim smile. "Don't concern yourself with me. Just make sure you're still breathing when my niece returns. She'll need you before this is over."

Another barrage of cannon fire rocked the *Vanguard's* hull, chewing a hole in the side of the main mast. Somewhere through the haar, the Cirein-cròin let loose a watery roar, the hot stench of its breath rushing across the deck like a brackish wind. The last time Darce had caught a glimpse of the creature, its fangs had been strung with jewel-toned cloaks and shards of bloodied timber.

Muir was right. They couldn't stay here.

The waves battered the *Vanguard's* hull as Darce peered through the hole that had torn through the gunwale. It was a steep drop, and if the shock of icy water didn't kill them, the swell most likely would. Jumping was a death sentence.

"We need to find a tender," he told Lachlan. "Stay here and keep your head down. I'll head to the aft deck and—"

"There's no time." Lachlan hobbled beside him, appraising the churning seafoam. "I admit, swimming was never my favourite pastime, even when I had both my legs. I can't say I particularly like my odds. But you're a sentinel, Galbraith. If there's anyone who can keep the tides from taking us, it's you."

Darce opened his mouth to argue, but a shrill screech cut him off.

He lifted his head to see Featherblade soar overhead, white wings stark against the storm clouds. The gannet darted between the *Vanguard's* towering masts, releasing another rattling caw from its beak. Then it skimmed low and shot towards the sea like an arrow unleashed, wings folded against its streamlined body as it plunged below the waves.

It's unwise to ignore a guidebird when it's telling you to get underway, Nishi had told him. If Featherblade wanted him to follow, he could do nothing else but trust it.

Blair moved forward, placing a hand on Lachlan's shoulder. "Promise me you'll do whatever it takes to reach your ship. I need to know I'll see you again when this is over."

"When this is..." Lachlan's face fell. "You can't be serious. You're not staying here—you'll be killed."

"We asked the *Vanguard's* sentinels to stand with us. I can't abandon them. It would make me no better than him." Blair's gaze was resolute. "You saw me as something more than my uncle. You believed I could be a better man. Thanks to you, I've seen what the Admiralty could be without him. If I leave, that will never happen."

Something in Muir's face twitched, a flicker of emotion clouding his eyes. Then, as suddenly as it appeared, it was gone. "I'll do my best to watch out for the lieutenant here," he said gruffly. "You need to go, both of you."

"But—"

"Go, Lachlan." Blair's voice was tight. "Before it's too late."

Before Lachlan could protest any further, Darce placed a strong hand around his shoulder and ushered him to the edge of the ship. The waves roiled and crashed, their grey-green depths almost black under the pall of storm clouds. The swell was waiting for them, hungry to swallow anything that plunged below the surface.

Darce squeezed Lachlan's collar. "Are you ready?"

Lachlan said nothing, but he nodded stiffly.

Thunder rumbled through the clouds. Barely a second later, a spear of blinding white light forked through the sky, illuminating shadows in the mist.

Darce sucked in a breath and pulled Lachlan over the side.

It took a lifetime to hit the water. The wind whipped around him as he fell, stinging his cheeks raw. The pit of his stomach gave way to nothingness. The air roared as he plummeted towards oblivion.

The sea slammed into him like a vicious blow, sending a shock through his legs. All the air in his lungs abandoned him as his chest seized from the cold. He tumbled through the currents, limbs flailing, fingers numb as he desperately clung to the collar of Lachlan's coat.

A fierce undertow sucked him down, dragging him away from the surface. The depths wanted to claim him. They wanted to starve him of his precious breath, crush his organs in their relentless grip. As he thrashed his legs, the pressure closed in, drawing him towards the fathoms.

Help me. He reached for the ebbing magic in his veins. *Take us back to where we need to be.*

Something stirred, turning his blood to ice. His lungs burned with the effort of holding his breath, so painful he thought they might burst.

Then, something surged beneath him. A jet of water rose from the depths, snatching him in its swirling stream. He tightened his grip around Lachlan's shoulder and braced himself as the current pushed them towards the surface. They were almost there. A few more seconds, and...

He burst through the waves with a gasp. Cold, salty air hit his lungs, and he gulped down a mouthful of seawater in his desperation to draw breath. All he could see through his stinging eyes was the might of the swell heaving and crashing. It wouldn't take much for it to swallow them again.

"Lachlan?" he choked. "Are you all right?"

Lachlan sucked in a shuddering breath, his lips blue as he nodded in reply. "Do you see it? The soulship?"

Darce darted his head around, searching for the bone hull. The haar was as thick as ever, clinging to the tips of the waves. He couldn't see the *Vanguard* anymore.

"It can't be far," he said, spluttering through another mouthful of seawater. "We have to—"

A piercing cry cut off the rest of his words, and Featherblade emerged from the mists, flapping furiously. When it saw them, it swooped around in a wide circle, yammering a series of urgent shrieks.

Another wave crashed overhead, dragging him under, but when he fought to the surface again, he saw something stirring in the haar. The mists parted, and a pointed white prow slowly emerged from their depths.

The soulship.

As it drew nearer, Featherblade gave another shrill cry, and a familiar ladder shimmered into being from the spray dashing against the ship's hull. Silvery droplets clung together, winding into watery rungs like they had during their escape from Arburgh.

Darce reached it first, fingers slipping as he pulled himself towards the deck. Lachlan followed close behind, his breathing laboured. When at last they reached the top, they spilled over the gunwale, landing on the deck with a thump.

All Darce could hear through his water-clogged ear was his own ragged breathing. Then came the click of serpenthide boots, and he lifted his head to find Nishi standing over him.

"I've never met anyone who has known as much favour from the tides as you, Sergeant. I'm not sure if that makes you special, or if you're just the luckiest bastard on the seas."

Featherblade cackled, then hopped down to the deck and nipped Darce affectionately on the ear. He touched his fingers to his skin, but the gannet had apparently decided not to draw blood this time. "If it's luck, I can only hope we've not used the last of it. I have a feeling we'll need more before this is all over."

"We don't always get the luxury of a favourable wind. A good captain knows how to sail with what she's got." Nishi offered an outstretched hand, and Darce took it, hauling himself back to his feet. Behind him, Lachlan climbed upright, balancing on his one leg as he leaned against the gunwale for support.

Nishi glanced between them. "Blackwood?"

"She's gone to face Eimhir." Darce swallowed the tightness in his throat. "Whatever happens next, it's in her hands. There's nothing more we can do."

"I fear you may be right." Nishi's eyes darkened. "We caught the Admiralty by surprise, but the fleet outnumbers us four to one. It's only a matter of time before they gain control of the battle. When that happens, they'll tear our ships to pieces." She shook her head. "I've seen guidebirds flying back and forth with messages. Some of the captains want to retreat. But we'll never get a shot like this again. It's our only chance of sending that bastard to the fathoms once and for all."

Darce exchanged a look with Lachlan. "Muir stayed behind on the *Vanguard*. He intends to kill Cunningham, whatever the cost."

Nishi snorted. "The auld seadog has more to him than I thought, I'll give him that." She glanced up at the soulship's wisping sails, the silvery shrouds rippling in the wind. "This could be the end of my people. There's no sign of the selkies coming to fight with us. The Sea Kith can't stand against the Admiralty alone."

"You're not alone." Lachlan met Nishi's eyes with a steady gaze. "Isla is out there fighting for you. Muir is fighting for you. Blair..." He grimaced, shifting his weight. "They'll come through for us. But we have to give them the time they need."

Nishi twitched. For a moment, Darce expected an angry flush to rise in her cheeks, a sharp rebuke to spill from the tip of her tongue. Instead, she gave Lachlan a long, measured look, and something yielded in the crease of her brow.

"Aye," she said slowly. "We can do that. I know a thing or two about catching the Admiralty's attention. If the fleet is focused on our broadside, they won't be looking for the blade slipping between their ribs." She turned to Darce, eyes clouding with uncertainty. "You believe she's coming back?"

Something raw tugged at his heart, and he fought to keep the emotion from his voice. "Aye. I have to."

Nishi nodded. "Then we'll buy her every minute we can. Send Featherblade to the *Red Gale* and tell Ruairidh we're making a stand. Then, find Jacques and prepare to sail. There's a storm breaking, and I mean to be at the centre of it." She strode to the main deck and took her place at the helm, the white bone of the wheel glistening beneath her hands. "The Admiralty may think it knows these waters, but the sea is not home to them like it is to us. It's about time we showed them that."

CHAPTER THIRTY-ONE

ISLA

The woman in front of Isla was a stranger.

She still looked like Eimhir—her damp blonde tresses, her hard-edged features, her stormy eyes. But under her flinty exterior, there had always been warmth. Now, there was only a callousness that turned Isla's blood to ice.

"Nothing to say?" Eimhir's voice was low, each syllable sounding like it had been dragged over stone.

"I didn't come here to talk," Isla replied. Her hand shifted around the sgian dubh tucked in her coat. She brushed her thumb over the engraved patterns on the hilt, trying to ignore the way her heart thumped at the sensation of the steel against her skin. She'd come here to take back what was hers, what Eimhir had stolen from her. She had every right to reclaim her soulskin. And yet...

A wry smile curled at the corner of Eimhir's mouth. "Will you do it, cousin? Do you believe you can make yourself whole again, knowing what it will cost?"

Guilt lodged in Isla's throat, and she swallowed painfully. "Passing on your pelt was your choice. You gave it up willingly."

"And now you have a choice." Eimhir's smile was cruel. Cold in a way that made her unrecognisable.

"Aye," Isla said softly. "It seems I do."

Even now, there was a place deep in the hollow of her chest that trembled with indecision. Part of her knew she would break if she did this. It would leave a scar that would never heal. She looked to the clouds above, willing them to split open and let the light through, to give her some kind of sign that there was another way this might end.

Instead, she felt the sting of rain against her cheeks.

The sgian dubh shook in her hand as she slowly drew it from her coat. There was no going back—not for Eimhir, not for her.

Eimhir's face fell. "So, this is how it is to end, is it? In blood, like everything else."

"You knew that when you gave up your pelt," Isla said. "Perhaps you convinced yourself otherwise, counted on me being unable to bear the weight of one more regret. But I will bear far more than that by the time this is over. I will carry the pain of our people everywhere I go. I would carry yours too, if only you would let me. Or we can finish this with the blood you've been craving ever since the haar took you from me."

She thought she might have imagined a flicker of uncertainty across Eimhir's stony features. A glimpse of something lost, a ghost half-forgotten. Then it was gone, and the only thing left was the snarl on her lips.

"It is *mine*," Eimhir said, burying her fingers in the grey fur.

Then, she leapt.

Isla darted to the side, but she wasn't quick enough to escape the blow. Eimhir's elbow cracked against her temple, sending her spinning to the ground. Her spine hit the stone with a bruising thud and she groaned, breath knocked from her lungs.

Before she could do anything, Eimhir was on top of her, reaching for her neck. Isla scrambled for the sgian dubh, bringing it around in a wild strike. The blade slashed Eimhir's palms, sending a splatter of crimson across them both and drawing a guttural cry from Eimhir's throat.

The distraction wasn't much, but it was enough. Isla pushed Eimhir away and staggered to her feet. A vicious pounding rattled through her skull from where Eimhir had struck her, and she blinked away the muddy haze seeping in at the corners of her vision.

Eimhir slowly climbed to her feet too, cold and impassive as she stared at her bloodied palms. "It seems you mean to finish what the Grand Admiral started."

Hot rage rose in Isla's chest. "I'm not the one wearing a stolen soul-skin. You're so lost to the mist sickness you can't see what you've become."

Eimhir charged, but Isla was ready this time and slipped to the side, boots crunching against the rain-soaked gravel. The loose stone at her feet shifted, tumbling over the ridge to the nothingness below. She had to get away from the edge. She knew how sheer the drop was, how fearsome the rocks were that jutted through the waves. If she fell, not even the tides would save her.

She wrapped her fingers around the sgian dubh, circling Eimhir cautiously. Close-quarters scraps had never been her strength. She preferred a comfortable distance, a pistol in her hand. But with Eimhir, there was no choice. Her pelt, her *soul*, hung around Eimhir's shoulders. There was no escaping the intimacy of this fight, cousin against cousin, blood against blood.

Thunder tore through the air, so loud it shuddered through Isla's bones. The sky lit up in a brilliant flash, turning the black clouds into ghostly silhouettes across the horizon. The squall was on top of them. She felt it in the rain lashing her skin, the wind biting her cheeks.

"This is what you brought upon us," Eimhir yelled over the roar. "We could have kept Eileanan Selch safe from the storm, but you couldn't face what needed to be done. You've *never* been able to face it."

Isla lunged, driving the sgian dubh into Eimhir's shoulder. The blade bit through her pelt, raking through fur and flesh. A terrible scream ripped from Eimhir's throat, and Isla barely managed to duck out of the way of the furious blow that followed.

She stumbled back, the blade warm in her hand. Eimhir's strong, wiry shoulder was exposed through the bloodstained fur, a deep gash running down it. Something twisted in Isla at the sight of what she'd done, the damage she'd inflicted on her own soul.

This wasn't right. This wasn't what she wanted. There had already been too much violence, too much blood spilled. She *had* to find another way.

Steel rattled against stone as she let the sgian dubh fall.

Eimhir pushed away the soaked strands of hair clinging to her forehead. "I was right," she whispered. "You can't do it."

Tears stung the corners of Isla's eyes, mingling with the rain streaming down her cheeks. She opened her hands, letting the blood from the sgian dubh wash away, leaving her fingers cold and empty.

Eimhir flinched as Isla moved towards her. But the sgian dubh lay discarded at their feet, its silver blade glistening with blood. It would not draw any more tonight. Isla was sure of that.

When there was no space left between them, she met Eimhir's gaze. Even now, she couldn't help but search for a trace of the woman who'd once called her kin.

Eimhir's arms closed around her. "This is why I had to take it, caraid. This violence belongs to us all. There is no escaping it. You never understood that."

Isla leaned against Eimhir's shoulder, pressing her cheek to ice-cold skin still wet with blood. The arms around her were those of a stranger. All they shared was the blood beating between them.

It was all she needed.

"I'm sorry, cousin," she said, her voice splintering. "But it was you who never understood."

Eimhir stiffened, but it was too late. Isla felt the blood smearing her face: Eimhir's blood, *her* blood, the blood they both shared with Mara.

It trickled through the grey fur around Eimhir's shoulders, stirring the pelt into life. Isla felt its folds shifting like the currents, finding its way back to her, coming *home*.

"No!" Eimhir thrashed, trying to break free, but Isla locked her arms and held her in a twisted embrace.

"Our magic is born not from blood, but from sacrifice," she said as Eimhir squirmed. "It never stopped being mine."

She pushed Eimhir away, gasping as they broke apart. The folds of her pelt spilled over her shoulders, hanging across the sodden lengths of her coat. She brushed her fingers over the fur, tracing the subtle ripples of colour, the dappled patches smattered through the grey.

It was hers. It had *always* been hers.

A shadow darkened Eimhir's face, and she lunged for the sgian dubh, but Isla was too quick. She snatched the hilt and staggered back, her heels perilously close to the crumbling edge of the ridge.

Eimhir stared at her, eyes empty, cheeks devoid of colour. "Do it," she said flatly. "Bury your blade in me and let this be the end."

Grief welled in Isla's throat. "And what good would that do? More killing, more blood spilled, more vengeance. It will never end, Eimhir. This has to stop. *We* have to stop it."

"I can't do that. This sickness is consuming. It's all I am, all that's left of me." Eimhir's fists tightened, her knuckles bloody. "You know what will happen to me without a pelt. You know what I'll become."

"I won't kill you, Eimhir."

"But you would see me suffer instead?" Eimhir took a furious step towards her, and Isla tightened her fingers around the sgian dubh. "I'll never forgive you for this. I'll go to the fathoms hating you with all I have left."

"Then I will bear that too!" A sob wrenched from Isla's throat. "I will bear it, because whether it is a year from now or a hundred years from now, you will know peace again. That is the legacy Mara left for me. *That* is why I took back my pelt. For every selkie lost to salt and spray. For you, caraid."

She edged back, her heel halfway over the precipice. Her ears roared with the crashing waves. The wind whipped around her face, hastening the tears spilling down her cheeks. This was what it had come to. There was only one thing left to give up.

The sgian dubh trembled in her hand, its engraved handle digging into her palm. She loosened her hold on it, letting her eyes fall across the blade one final time. The blade she'd plunged into Finlay's neck when his hands were choking the life from her throat. The blade that had failed to kill the Grand Admiral not once, but twice. The blade Eimhir had stolen to commit a betrayal beyond forgiveness.

And once, all those years ago, the blade Mara had used to cut her life cord and pass a newborn bairn into Muir's waiting arms.

"You were never meant for violence," Isla said.

The fur of her pelt ruffled with the wind, tickling her neck. She wasn't alone. It wasn't just her hand clutching the sgian dubh, it was the hands of every selkie who'd ever wielded it.

Together, they threw it over the ridge, returning it to the fathoms below.

Isla stared down at the water, the ache loosening in her sternum. She couldn't see where the blade had plunged through the waves. She didn't need to.

When she turned back, Eimhir was watching her, her eyes holding the death of something that had not yet come to pass. All Isla could see on her face were streaks of tears that would soon be lost to salt.

"What happens next?" Eimhir asked, voice hollow. "When you leave me to my torment, to the suffering you have condemned me to, where will you go?"

Her words buried under Isla's skin, promising to leave scars that would linger long after the memory of Eimhir's voice faded. She tried to swallow her grief and guilt, but tasted only salt on her tongue.

"I'll keep my word," she managed, throat tight. "To Mara. To our people. But most of all, caraid, to you. If despair takes everything else from you, don't let it take that."

She cast her eyes over the ridge one last time. The haar clung to the water, smothering the horizon. She couldn't make out anything past the mist. But she could see the heaving swell, its grey-green waves, its murky depths.

The sea called to her, and for the first time since Eimhir had ripped her pelt from her, Isla was able to answer.

INTERLUDE

The wind nips at her naked skin as she sways on the precipice, utterly, irrevocably alone.

She forgot what it feels like to be stripped bare. There is a cavity behind her ribs, cold and unfeeling. It's not pain that has taken root there; it is an absence, a loss she cannot hold. No matter how she tries to bear it, this hole won't go away. It will *never* go away.

The last time she was stripped of her soul, Isla was her salvation. Tonight, she's the one who stole it.

Her arms ache with the ghost of the embrace she should never have given. Her skin crawls with betrayal, its tendrils burrowing under her flesh, biting her to the bone. She had been so *certain*. She had been so wrong.

The hairs on her arms stiffen. Each icy gust of wind raises more goose-flesh across her exposed skin until her entire body is rigid. She examines her pale chest, the webbing of veins running under the surface. Before long, scars will form. Salt will sink its teeth into her, drying her out, devouring what is left of her. Her skin will peel and flake. Her organs will wither and die. And when she can suffer no more, she will give herself to the fathoms.

Gun-anam. The name doesn't hold as much fear as it once did. She's walked with them too often for that. She's felt their excruciating pain, their ceaseless torment. She *knows* them. And soon, she'll know them even better.

Wet stones shift beneath her toes as she forces one foot in front of the other. Each step is slow, agonising. There's no need for her to hurry. Isla is too far out of reach to follow, even if she wanted to. All that's left for her is this lonely ridge, the roaring wind, the crashing waves.

She follows the trail down through a narrow gully, the cliff pressing in on both sides. Rain lashes down, stinging her eyes, and she blinks it away as she emerges onto a familiar ledge overlooking the sea.

It stirs something in her, this place. It reaches through the numbness around her heart, pushes past the rage coursing in her veins. There are memories here, half-forgotten flashes of a simpler time. No rocks await her below the edge of the smooth, flat slab overlooking the drop. The waves churn, thick with seafoam, and she remembers the exhilaration of falling through the air with nothing to catch her but the shock of water.

The last time she came here, it was with Finlay. They'd leapt together, screaming like bairns as they fell through the sky, hearts racing, limbs flailing. They'd waited until the last moment, then plunged through the waves in their selkie forms, returning to Caim through the underwater cavern to do it all over again.

There will be no returning for her now. This leap will be her last.

The wind raises its voice in protest. It howls through her skull, urging her to give in to the boiling beneath her skin, the bloodlust that has led her to this precipice.

It wants her to fight, but she lost this battle long ago. There is no escaping the shadow, no warming herself from the cold buried bone-deep. There is only the hope of it ending.

She edges to the end of the slab, toes curling around the rock. The rain has made the surface slippery, but she won't let herself fall. If this is to be the end, it will be an end she has chosen. Perhaps she should be grateful for that.

Her cheeks thrum with the vibrations of raindrops hitting her skin, and she closes her eyes against the downpour. There's a peace in letting go.

She can't recall the last time she felt peace.

Before she knows it, she's falling again. This time, there is no pelt around her shoulders to slip into. Perhaps that's why it's over quicker than she remembers. There is no stretching of time to ponder the fall, just the wind whipping through her hair and the sea's grey-green maw opening to greet her.

The water hits her like a thousand knives. It's never been so merciless, so unforgiving. It sinks its cold teeth into her over and over again, until she wants to scream with the agony of it, the *injustice* of it.

But she can't scream. If she screams, she'll let it in. The fathoms will pour down her throat and fill her lungs with salt. She'll sink like a stone, a hollowed-out husk, until the crushing depths devour what is left of her and leave only bones behind.

That's what you want, isn't it? She opens her eyes to a white haze as the haar swirls around her, pulling her into its icy tendrils. At first, she tries to thrash free from its deathless embrace. Then, she remembers why she jumped.

Aye, this is what she wants. This is where she belongs. With the pain of her people.

The last thing she lets go of is a promise half-swallowed by the wind. An anguished cry, an oath made through tears.

You will know peace again.

She doesn't know if she believes it. But her caraid has always had a stubbornness about her, a will capable of defying the tides themselves.

So she finally lets go, and breathes the sea home.

CHAPTER THIRTY-TWO

ISLA

I t was time.

Isla tucked her clothes into the corner of the cavern and set her serpenthide boots by the edge of the pool. She didn't need them anymore. Fabric and leather didn't matter, not now she had her soulskin back.

The only armour she wore was the glistening white cuirass and the seal-skull helm. Mara's bones. The sacrifice that had carried her back from the abyss. The bones encircled her ribs, sitting against her own. The mask lay against her temples, cool and comforting.

She took a breath and readied herself for the change.

Her pelt stirred. Its grey folds spread across her shoulders, soothing her skin with its touch. The damp fur melted into her, becoming one with her flesh. It was like she'd never lost it, like this separation had been but a fleeting moment.

She lowered herself into the pool, a hiss escaping her still-human lips as the water hit her. It wouldn't feel cold for much longer. Already, her fur was thickening, a layer of blubber spawning underneath.

Her nose and mouth jutted outwards, elongating into a rubbery snout. At the same time, she felt the grinding of her human bones shifting inside her, rearranging themselves into her selkie skeleton. Beneath her pelt, she sensed Mara's bones changing too, wrapping themselves around her new form in a fierce, comforting embrace. They knew this transformation well. They were as much a part of her as her pelt.

When her vision turned grey, she let herself sink. Her flippers twitched, eager to propel her through the gloom. She was where she belonged. Here, amongst the salt and the swell, she was home.

The currents brushed against her whiskers, guiding her towards the winding tunnel, the open sea waiting for her on the other side. Now, all she had to do was get there.

She thrust forward, her enlarged heart thumping with exhilaration as she shot through the water. The currents rippled over her lithe body, parting for her as she charged with all her might. Every swish of her tail and flick of her flippers brought a new joy, so pure it was painful to remember a time without it.

As she reached the end of the tunnel, the world opened for her. An endless expanse, a promise of freedom. The icy currents grasped at her, pulling her in a hundred different directions.

Isla knew where she had to go. She sensed the disturbance in the water from a distance. Huge hulls of oak and cedar cutting through the waves. Muffled cannon fire echoing above the surface. Bodies flailing and thrashing until they sank, swallowed by the hungry fathoms. The sea carried it all to her, caressing her whiskers, rattling through her ear holes.

Through it all, she searched for Darce. But the tug of his soul was lost amongst so much blood. She couldn't tell where he was, or if he was one of those bleeding.

She burst through the surface, sucking in a lungful of salty air. A cluster of silhouettes bucked and heaved on the waves, but there was no way to tell whether they belonged to the Sea Kith or the Admiralty.

The haar's icy, rotten breath trawled across her fur as she continued towards the ships, and the human part of her shivered at its touch. The mists had already taken Eimhir from her. There were only so many encounters a selkie could withstand before they succumbed. If Isla couldn't find a way to rid it of its corruption, her time would come too.

A cry pealed through the air as a sea eagle soared towards one of the ships, circling the masts with powerful, heavy wings.

Isla's heart leapt. If that was Swiftclaw, then Cam was nearby. The huge brigantine ahead must be the *Red Gale*.

She dipped below the surface, flippers aching as she pushed her burning muscles as far as they would go. The hull loomed out of the darkness, its keel laden with strands of kelp and crusty barnacles. In her selkie form, she could only see grey, but something in her memory showed her the red paint the wood was stained with.

The ship was locked in a tussle with a galleon, the two hulls almost brushing. Isla swam between them, skirting a body that plunged in front of her. A cloak billowed around the man's shoulders as he thrashed, then fell still.

Isla didn't wait to watch him sink. He already belonged to the fathoms.

Poking her head through the waves again, she caught sight of a rope dangling from one of the gangways bridging the two decks high above. Whether the *Red Gale* was being boarded or doing the boarding, she couldn't tell. All that mattered was she had a way up.

She swam to the rope and slipped out of her selkie form, shivering as her pelt melted from her skin and let the icy seawater through. Mara's seal-skull mask sat over her eyes as she climbed. The sodden fur around her shoulders weighed her down, making her arms ache, but she pushed through the exhaustion and clambered onto the gangway, stomach pressed flat against the slick surface.

When she lifted her chin, she saw chaos. The *Red Gale* was swarming with jewel-toned cloaks, its ruby deck stained with more than paint. Clanging steel and muffled cries filled her ears, punctuated by the stutter of a misfired musket, its powder dampened by the pouring rain.

She pushed herself to her feet and ducked away from a cutlass aimed at her throat. Her pelt offered no protection here; she needed a weapon.

"Isla!" A familiar voice carried over the wind, and she saw Cam behind her, a rapier in one hand and a dirk in the other. The young Sea Kith sentinel gave a relieved bark of laughter, then stopped short, eyes widening as they fell across Isla's pelt. "Is that..."

"Aye." She motioned to the dirk. "Can I have that?"

Cam nodded, their gaze lingering on Isla's pelt as they handed over the short, serrated dagger. "What does it feel like?"

A wistful look fell over their face, and Isla felt a pang of sympathy. She knew that expression—the yearning for that which was missing, the feeling of not being whole. Cam was a half-selkie like her. But they didn't know what it was to have a soulskin. Perhaps they never would.

Isla placed a gentle hand on their shoulder. "It feels like home. Like the *Red Gale* is for you."

Cam wiped a trickle of blood from a nasty gouge above their right eye. "It won't be home for much longer if the Admiralty has anything to say about it. We're being overrun."

"No sign of any selkies?" Isla's heart sank.

Cam shook their head. "Just you."

"What about the soulship?"

"Causing trouble." A thin smile stretched Cam's lips. "It might not have cannons, but those sentinels on board are doing all they can to disrupt the Admiralty. Nishi is hitting its ships hard and fast, then vanishing into the mists before they can strike back. But she won't be able to keep it up for long. The Admiralty has too much firepower." They glanced at something behind Isla's shoulder, sobering quickly. "Best get that dagger ready. They're coming."

Isla turned to see a group of officers charging over the gangway, blades already bared. The first of them caught a Sea Kith deckhand unaware, steel plunging through the young woman's midriff until it appeared through the other side. He pulled it out with a wet squelch, then advanced on Isla, his sword dripping blood at his feet.

"Skinchanger," he said, lip curling.

Cam moved first, thrusting their rapier so fast Isla hardly saw them move. The Admiralty officer darted to the side, but he wasn't quick enough to escape the gash scored across his rain-soaked tunic.

A red line bled through the linen, and his face darkened. "Tides take you, pirate scum. By the time I'm through with you, you'll wish they had."

He charged forward with his cutlass raised, but before he landed a blow, a shrill screech rang out and Swiftclaw plummeted from the clouds.

A strangled scream tore through the air as the sea eagle's hooked talons raked across the officer's face, gouging his eyes. Then the guidebird was off again, powering to the sky with its huge, speckled wings.

Without hesitating, Cam leapt, burying their rapier in the middle of the officer's chest. The man let out a thin gasp, then crumpled to the deck, blood pouring from his mangled eyes.

The rest of the Admiralty officers stared at their fallen companion, white with shock. Then, their expressions slowly twisted into anger.

Isla squeezed her dirk as one of them lunged at her. She ducked under the furious blow, then spun around and slashed with the dagger in one fluid movement. The cut ripped the officer's cloak, but it wasn't deep enough to do any damage.

Before she could readjust, another Admiralty soldier grabbed her, grip digging into her collarbone. Isla ducked her head and bit as fiercely as she could, teeth sinking through flesh. The soldier whipped her fingers away with a howl and reached for her pistol with her other hand, but Isla was quicker. In less than a second, she was face to face with the woman, dirk buried to the hilt in the soft of her belly.

The woman's eyes went wide, then turned glassy. Isla slowly pulled the blade from her stomach and let her slide to the deck. A crimson puddle seeped out from under the woman's cloak, trickling through the cracks in the wood. There was a time the sight of it might have brought Isla relief. Now, there was only numbness.

When will it be over? she thought.

The wind roared in her ears, offering no answer.

Cam was trying their best to fend off three Admiralty officers surrounding them. A ribbon of water spiralled around their wrists, and they sent it towards the nearest officer, forcing the seawater down his throat. The man spluttered, weapon clattering to the deck as he clawed frantically at his neck. But the other two were on Cam in a heartbeat, cutlasses flashing with murderous intent.

Overhead, Swiftclaw gave an agitated cry, but the sea eagle was too far away. Cam slipped one sword, then took the other straight in the shoulder.

If they cried out, Isla couldn't hear it. Her ears filled with the muffled thump of her own heart, the gasp she sucked in as steel pierced flesh.

Cam stumbled back until they hit the gunwale, eyes wide. Blood poured from their shoulder, dripping onto the deck with a loud *tip-tip*. There was nowhere to go. The second officer was advancing, blade drawn, hungry for the killing blow.

Even as Isla started running, she knew she would be too late. She wasn't close enough. Even if she threw her dagger...

The officer's sword fell towards Cam. Then, it stopped.

A dark, towering shape stood between Cam and the Admiralty officer, sodden folds of ink-black fur rippling in the wind. The sword that had been aimed at Cam's heart wavered, caught on the edge of a huge axe.

Duncan lifted his head and drew his lip into a snarl. "These waters are not yours to bloody. They're *ours*."

He pushed against the sword with a ferocious shove, knocking the Admiralty officer into his own man. Before anyone had time to react, Duncan swept forward, bringing his axe around in a vicious arc.

The honed edge sliced through the air like a whistle, cleaving the officer's head clean from his shoulders.

The second officer stumbled back, face draining of colour. "No," he said, voice strangled. "I didn't want to come here. We were told every enlisted officer was needed. Please, I didn't—"

His words ended in a wheezing gasp as Duncan wrapped a hand around his throat, crushing the man's windpipe. He lifted the officer into the air, ignoring his clawing hands and thrashing legs as he carried him to the gunwale.

"You came here to hunt us," he said, voice low and gravelly. "Don't you want to meet your prey?"

The man scrabbled to free himself, but it was no use. Duncan hoisted him high, then released him over the edge, sending him to the churning waves.

Isla swallowed, mouth dry. "You came."

Duncan wasn't looking at her. Instead, his umber eyes were fixed on Cam. "I had to."

Cam pressed their hand over their shoulder to staunch the bleeding. When they caught sight of Duncan, they stilled, a shadow falling over their features. "I know you. It might have been more than ten years, but I'll never forget your face. You were there when the *Red Gale* was attacked in these very waters. You were the one who killed my aunt."

"I have killed many humans," Duncan said, as measured as ever. "I make no apology for protecting my people, my home, from those who would threaten it." He cast a slow, lingering look over the bodies of the fallen Admiralty officers, jewel-toned cloaks drenched with blood. "I suspect you understand that better than you want to admit."

Cam stiffened. "This is not the same. The Sea Kith are not the Admiralty. We posed no threat to your people."

"I'd have made a poor chieftain if I'd risked my people's lives on the chance that was true," Duncan replied. "We selkies have been hunted too often to live any other way."

Cam's hands curled into fists. "We were only there because of me. I wanted to find my father. His name was—"

"Harris." Duncan gave a heavy sigh. "I suspected the moment I saw you all those years ago."

A strangled cry escaped Cam's throat. "You knew him."

"We grew up together on Echlinn, one of the outer isles. He was my clanmate, my childhood friend. We lost contact when my father became chieftain of Caim. I'd heard he'd left Eileanan Selch, but…" Duncan shook his head, droplets flying from his coiled black hair. "When I saw you that day, I hadn't seen him in years. Suddenly, the face of a man I'd known as a bairn was staring back at me."

"That's why you let me go. Because of him." A pained look fell over Cam. "I never met him. Never knew I carried his face. I wondered if he'd returned here, if he'd left us to go back to his people, but…"

"Harris hasn't been seen around Eileanan Selch in more than twenty years," Duncan said. "If he is lost, our people are not to blame for it." A growl rumbled from his throat. "Humans are."

"The Admiralty is to blame. You know that as well as I do," Isla said sharply, moving between them. "That is the enemy we have in common, the enemy we've *always* had in common. Neither of us stand a chance unless—" She broke off at the sight of a huge longsword carving through the air towards them. "Watch out!"

Duncan leapt back as the blade fell, blood flying from its vicious, honed edge. Isla stumbled, heart hammering as she gathered herself to face their attacker.

She stilled. It was Ruairidh.

He clutched the monstrous sword in both hands, a revulsed look in his ice-blue eye. The red braid spilling down the middle of his head was matted with blood, and his lips were wet with hunger.

"Don't," Isla said desperately. "We can't afford to—"

A savage roar ripped from Ruairidh's throat as he charged, swinging towards Duncan's neck. The blow would have cleaved any other man's head from his shoulders, but Duncan was too strong. He rushed to meet Ruairidh, bringing up his axe to catch the furious weight of the Sea Kith's longsword. The two men locked together, snarling as they jostled, close enough to breathe the same violent air.

"I'll fucking kill you," Ruairidh spat. "I'll make you regret ever laying eyes on this ship, you wretched basta—"

Duncan threw his head forward, bone crunching against bone as his skull met the bridge of Ruairidh's nose. The Sea Kith captain staggered back, blood streaming from the gash. He barely had time to raise his sword again before Duncan fell on him, axe slicing through the air too fast to see.

Iron met steel again, the harsh clang of the two weapons ringing through Isla's ears. "Are you both so eager to die here?" she demanded. "You stubborn bastards. The Grand Admiral is still out there. *He's* the one we should be fighting."

"Stay out of this, selkie lass." Ruairidh whirled away, his huge shoulders heaving. "You did your part in bringing this scum here. Our score is settled. What happens next doesn't involve you."

He lunged, bringing his sword around with deceptive speed. Duncan leapt back, but not before the edge of the blade caught him across the chest. The deck splattered with blood and tufts of black fur, and Duncan's eyes darkened as he clenched the haft of his axe.

"I did not come here to kill you," he said, voice rippling with warning. "Isla told me of the debt I owed your ship. The auld ways demanded I pay it, and that is what I have done." He gestured to Cam, their shoulder bleeding, the decapitated Admiralty officer dead at their feet. "Your friend lives because of me. But if you still wish for blood, you'll have it, human."

"I don't give a fuck about the auld ways," Ruairidh snarled. "I intend to make you suffer for what you took from me, what you took from us both."

"Cap'n..." Cam strained as they clutched their shoulder. "He saved my life."

"That doesn't make up for—" Ruairidh cut himself short, the unsaid words ringing with regret. For the first time, an expression other than anger flickered across his face, and the scar behind his eyepatch twitched as he furrowed his brow. "Cam, I didn't mean..."

"Aye, you did." Cam hobbled towards him, wincing with each step. "You would trade my life for hers, even now. I don't blame you for it. How could I? You loved her, but she was *my* sentinel. When she died, part of my soul died with her. But I'm here. I'm alive. My home is the ship she commanded. My captain is the man she loved. Whatever I've lost, I still have that. And so do you." They glanced at Duncan. "Thanks to him."

Ruairidh shot a hard look at Duncan, his knuckles white around his sword. He took a slow step back, and something yielded in the stiffness of his shoulders.

"So be it," he said, rasping. "You saved one of my crew, selkie. That buys you your life today. But if I ever see you again, I swear by the wrath of the tides themselves I'll have your head."

Duncan pressed a hand to his chest, dabbing at the gash across his golden-brown skin. "Likewise, human. My people will fight with you against the Admiralty, but if your ship strays into these waters once this battle is over, we'll show you no quarter. Let that warning guard against any more blood being spilled on either of our accounts."

He gave Isla a sombre nod, then stalked towards the gunwale, his black pelt spreading across his shoulders. His seal form took over, and he disappeared over the edge, leaving behind nothing but a trail of blood and a splash.

Ruairidh stared after him, then turned to Cam. "If his people fight with us, we'll be able to drive the rest of the boarders from the *Red Gale*. You should head below and see the ship's doctor, get that wound tended to. I didn't let that selkie bastard go just to lose you to infection."

Cam smiled weakly. "Aye, Cap'n."

When Ruairidh left and it was just the two of them, Cam released a hiss and scrunched their fingers in the bloodied fabric of their shirt. A choking sob spilled from their throat, and Isla placed a hand on their back, feeling their shoulders heaving with each jerking movement.

Cam lifted their chin, eyes shining with tears. "I don't understand. A sentinel's life is tied to their captain's. When I survived my aunt's death, it was only because I had a reason to go on. I thought that reason was to avenge her, that when Duncan was dead, I'd finally know peace. But letting him go..." They shook their head. "What am I still doing here?"

"I can't pretend to understand the intricacies of the auld blood," Isla said. "Only that its magic is that of the tides, and they are capricious by nature. There must be reason yet for you to go on. Perhaps there is a part of you out there to find, like there was for me." She brushed her fingers over her pelt, smoothing the damp grey fur.

Cam swallowed. "I think...I think I would like to believe that." They turned to the staircase leading into the hold, then hesitated. "Are you heading back out there?"

The waves dashed against the *Red Gale's* hull, impatient and restless. If Isla answered their call, they'd take her to where she needed to go. The haar was impenetrable, but somewhere in its depths was a glimmer of bone and spray in the shape of sails.

"Aye," she said. "I'm going to end this."

CHAPTER THIRTY-THREE

DARCE

A deathless cold poured into Darce's lungs as the soulship plunged into the mists and crossed into the soulless realm once more.

He gripped one of the lines, fingers numb. It had been too close this time. A rogue shot from an Admiralty sloop had taken a chunk out of the stern, scattering the aft deck with splinters of broken bone. Another few seconds, and their entire starboard might have been decimated by the salvo that followed. Only disappearing into the mists had saved them, and that came with a price.

Behind the wheel, Nishi's brown skin took on a grey hue, her eyes shadowed with dark circles. Her jaw was set as determinedly as ever, but that didn't hide the exhaustion lining her face, the toll each crossing was taking on her. The haar was a veil between worlds, riddled with the festering echoes of violence and trauma. It might not infect humans the same way it did selkies, but it left a mark on them all the same.

"Everyone alive?" Nishi called hoarsely, spinning the wheel through her hands.

A half-hearted murmur of assent rippled across the deck. All around him, Darce saw the weary faces of the soulship's makeshift crew—the survivors of Baininch Rise. He was certain they'd endured far worse in that wretched tower, but he couldn't help but feel guilty for bringing them into this. They weren't soldiers, just pawns in Cunningham's insatiable need for control.

"Eyes portside. The serpent followed us through." Jacques stood near the bow, watching the water. The sky was clear on this side of the haar, free from the storm clouds and thundering rain. Its oily red colour washed across the horizon in a perpetual dusk.

Darce followed Jacques' gaze and caught the Cirein-cròin's lithe tail disappearing below the surface. The serpent didn't need the bones of the dead to slip between the living world and the soulless realm. It possessed a magic far more ancient than any of them understood. But though it had followed them through, it didn't seem to be paying them any attention. For now, at least.

Nishi trudged down from the helm, rubbing the back of her neck. "We can't keep this up much longer. We need to decide whether to take shelter amongst the Sea Kith ships or return to the *Vanguard* and hope we can reach Cunningham before we're killed."

"I say we go back." Lachlan approached, his arm tucked around a new crutch fashioned by a mellow-mannered carpenter they'd rescued from Baininch Rise. His golden hair was damp and dishevelled, but his gaze held a quiet resolve.

Nishi pursed her lips. "You were already forced to flee the *Vanguard* once. What makes you think it will be any different this time?"

"We have the selkies on our side," Lachlan said. "They're fighting with us. You know what that means. Isla must have—"

"We don't know anything, not for certain." Darce tried to quell the emotion rising in his chest. It was too dangerous to hope. It made him desperate in a way nothing else did. "But you're right—with the selkies, we might stand a chance of doing what we couldn't do before."

Nishi nodded. "We'll need to take the *Vanguard* by surprise. Make our approach in the soulless realm, then cross back through the haar at the last possible moment. Best send Featherblade to the *Red Gale* and let Ruairidh know our plan. We could use all the help we can get."

She turned to the helm, then paused, chewing the ring in her lip. "Sergeant, it's best I tell you this now. When you board the *Vanguard*, I won't be joining you."

Darce raised an eyebrow. "I thought you wanted to see Cunningham pay for what happened to the *Jade Dawn*."

"I did. I *do*. I want that sorry bastard to meet the fathoms in the worst way imaginable. I want him to fucking suffer." She let out a breath, clenching and unclenching her fists. "But I can't be there to see it. Not if it means leaving this ship."

Darce followed her gaze across the deck. Young Tam and a few other men gathered around the section of damaged gunwale, working to smooth out the broken bone. Maggie Grier hovered over them, nodding approvingly and babbling words Darce couldn't hear over the wind.

"These people, the ones we rescued from that tower...they are crew now," Nishi said. "And while I may not be this ship's true captain, I feel...I feel I could be theirs. It wouldn't be right for me to leave them. Kerr wouldn't want me to leave them."

Darce placed a hand on her shoulder. "They're lucky to have you. We all are."

She clasped his arm, then returned to the helm, leaving him to look out over the waves as the soulship slowly changed course.

The ongoing battle felt like a dream. Everything was beyond reach behind the haar's haze. Ships moved like shadows, pitching and heaving on a swell invisible to Darce's eyes. Columns of smoke belched from rows of cannons, but no sound reached his ears. In the soulless realm, they were cut off entirely. They were safe.

But that wouldn't be the case for long.

He joined Jacques at the bow, sensing the other sentinel's magic flowing into the soulship's billowing sails. "We could be coming out into quite the squall. Are you ready?"

"I don't doubt it. I wager we're about to brave the worst storm Silvish waters have ever seen." Jacques stared into the distance, a pensive look flitting across his face. "But that's the thing about storms, Sergeant: no matter how bad they are, no matter how much destruction they leave in their wake, there is always a clear sky waiting at the other end. A new day, a chance to start again. That's what I'm fighting for. That's what we're all fighting for." A thin smile pulled at his lips. "So to answer your question...aye, I'm ready."

The soulship cut through the water like a blade. No wind whipped around Darce's neck, no spray leapt over the ship's prow, but he felt the bone-hewn hull gathering speed all the same. They slipped past the ships on the other side of the haar like ghosts, weaving between the hazy shapes. No colours bled through the mist, only shadows. It was impossible to pick out any kind of detail.

He turned to Nishi. "We might need to cross back earlier than we'd planned. We'll never find the *Vanguard* in this."

"If we emerge from the mists too early, we'll never get close," Nishi countered. "The fleet's cannons will tear apart the bones of this ship."

"We don't have a choice. I can't tell apart any of these ships. We could be—" Someone brushed his arm, and he found Maggie Grier standing beside him with a crooked grin.

She gestured with the stump of her arm, her eyes fixed on something in the distance. A shadow loomed across the waves, its three masts towering against the sky. But the haze was too thick to see anything more than the ship's hazy outline. It might have been a man-o'-war, but there was no way to—

"Mine," Maggie said. The single word spilled from her lips softly, but it was wrapped in certainty. She *knew*. She'd built the *Vanguard of the Firth* with her own hands before Cunningham had taken them from her. She had a deeper familiarity with that ship than anyone, more even than the Grand Admiral himself.

Jacques looked at his mother, pride wrestling with sorrow on his features. He signalled to Nishi on the helm, then raised his arms, calling the sea spirits living in the soulship's bones.

"Mine," he echoed.

Darce joined him, reaching for the magic pulsing through his veins. It answered him with a gentle thrum, stirring from the depths of the hull, the surface of the deck, the highest reaches of the mast. The ship knew where it needed to go. It knew where to carry them.

The haar thickened again, turning the air damp and salty as it swallowed the dark red sky of the soulless realm. Darce coughed away the familiar taste rising at the back of his throat and tried to focus on coming out the other side. Once they were through, there would be nowhere to hide.

When the mists finally scattered, the storm hit.

Darce barely had time to steady himself before the soulship pitched forward, lunging over the crest of a wave that hadn't been there moments prior. The eerily placid waters of the soulless realm were long gone, replaced by a heaving swell. Waves half the height of the mast crashed over the prow, flooding the deck.

He spat out a mouthful of seawater and called on his magic to clear the rain from his eyes. Clouds knit together in a black shroud, so low they seemed to brush the soulship's mast. Lightning flashed overhead, jagged forks leaping between the swirling clouds.

This was more than a squall. It was a bloody tempest.

A shrill squawk rang through his ear as Featherblade shot off, fighting against the swirling wind. Wherever the *Red Gale* was, the gannet would find it. Darce only hoped Ruairidh wouldn't arrive too late to help.

"The *Vanguard* is changing course." Nishi gritted her teeth as she wrestled with the wheel. "The Grand Admiral must still have some sentinels doing his bidding—they're heading into the wind."

"Can we follow?"

"That depends on you." Her eyes glinted. "We're not just up against the Admiralty, we're up against the tides themselves."

His heart pounded as he staggered to the gunwale. On the other side, the waves seethed, showering the deck. Each flash of lightning illuminated the shadows in the depths.

Nishi was right. They had more than one fight on their hands.

"Jacques!" he yelled, voice muffled in the roaring wind. "We need to—"

"I know!" The other sentinel stumbled, gripping the gunwale for support. "I'm trying my bloody best here."

Darce concentrated on his own magic. There would be no taming the waves tonight—they were too enraged for him to dare. But perhaps he and Jacques could harness their fury to carry the soulship across the swell instead of letting it destroy them.

His blood turned cold, rushing through his veins like a current from the depths. Jacques' presence stirred alongside him as they worked to call the waves to their favour. But it wasn't just the two of them; Darce sensed more magic, singing as only the auld blood did.

Selkies, sentinels. All of them fighting. All of them dying.

He pulled back, loosening his hold on the tides before they drowned him. It was too much. He felt the blood spilled across countless decks, seeping into the water. What if it belonged to Muir? What if it belonged to—

Something seized in his chest, and he let out a choking breath. *Isla.* Her soul called out to him, anchoring somewhere deep beneath his sternum.

She was here.

Another wave crashed against the soulship's hull, and a lithe grey shape leapt from its midst. Darce's heart thumped as the selkie slid along the deck, its flippers splayed.

Then, in a fluid movement, it transformed, and Isla stood in its place.

He stared at her. Her hair hung drenched and loose, spilling down the small of her back. The salt scars had disappeared from her pale skin, leaving behind only gooseflesh. Around her shoulders once more was the grey fur of her pelt.

She was alive. She was whole again.

Her sea-green eyes met his, as fierce and beautiful as the waves them-selves. Then she was running, her bare feet slapping off the deck, her pelt shifting across her shoulders as she reached for him.

The moment her hands found his face, he was undone.

"I love you," she said, the words barely more than a breath. "With *all* my soul."

She pulled him close and parted her lips to meet his, kissing him with an urgency he'd never known. All he wanted was to take her in—the softness of her skin, the warmth of her mouth, the fierce grip of her hands around his jaw as she held him. The rain lashed down, soaking his skin, but he couldn't think about summoning his magic to shield himself from it. *This* was what he needed—the cold and salt and unbridled wildness of it all. He needed *her*.

He brushed his hands over the wet fur clinging to her shoulders. The lustrous folds were dappled with patches of blue so deep they were almost black. When the lightning flashed above, subtle traces of lavender rippled amongst the grey. She wore the pelt like a second skin, something so intrinsically part of her he didn't know how she'd ever survived with-out it. It was beautiful—*she* was beautiful.

"I love you too," he said. "When this is over..."

She drew back, a shadow falling across her face as she stared up at the *Vanguard's* looming hull. They both knew what awaited them on that ship. There was no escaping it—no escaping *him*.

"How are we to board?" she asked, appraising the height of the deck above them. "They'll cut our grappling hooks before we have a chance to climb up."

"We'll distract them. Jacques can—" Darce broke off, a flicker of movement catching his attention. He looked closer, and his heart leapt at the familiar sight of boyish curls and a tartan bonnet leaning over the side of the *Vanguard*. "Blair!"

The young lieutenant grunted, moisture dripping from his forehead as he heaved a length of knotted rope over the side. The coil unfurled and hit the waves with a splash, trailing alongside the *Vanguard's* hull.

"Come on!" he shouted. "They'll be on me the moment they realise."

"Isla, wait." Lachlan hauled himself towards them, fingers tight around the handle of his crutch. He stopped in front of Isla, eyes falling across her pelt. For a painful moment, a shadow flitted across his gaze, darkening his expression with the ghost of his old grief. Then it was gone, and Darce's heart leapt as Lachlan brought his sister into a fierce, one-armed embrace.

"I won't be able to make the jump," he said, voice muffled against her hair. "I can't come with you. I want to, but I can't. So I need you to know—"

"Wee brother." She pulled away, eyes shining. "There is nothing you can tell me that I don't already know. We're family. We always were."

Lachlan swallowed. "Blair..."

"I'll do whatever it takes to protect him." She glanced at Darce. "We both will."

Darce gave Lachlan's shoulder a rough squeeze. "You're my brother in all but blood, little laird. Make sure you're here when we get back."

"You too, Galbraith." Lachlan stepped away, his jaw clenched. "Now go, both of you."

The rope swung in the wind, its knotted length already soaked. Nishi had brought them as close as she dared. The gap between the two ships was narrow enough to leap, as long as they timed it right.

Darce took a shuddering breath. Below, the waves frothed, throwing themselves against both hulls with ceaseless fury.

"You have nothing to fear from them," Isla said. "They will not take you. I won't let them."

Her fingers brushed his as he climbed over, boots slipping against the rain-soaked ledge. The sea roared in his ear. Lightning flashed through the clouds. The ghost of Isla's touch was cold on his skin.

He pushed all of it to the side, and jumped.

CHAPTER THIRTY-FOUR

ISLA

"Where is Muir?" The question spilled from Isla's mouth as she clambered over the gunwale, fighting to catch her breath. It came out in a weak rasp, the words turning to mist in the frigid air.

The tension in Blair's jaw told her all she needed to know. "We got separated about an hour ago. I've not seen him since. The *Vanguard* is a big ship, but still…" He shook his head. "Whatever he's doing to control that serpent is taking its toll. Last I saw him, he was weeping blood and choking on seafoam. I don't know if—"

"He's alive," Isla said forcefully. "We'd know if he wasn't."

The reminder of the blood oath was like salt on an open wound. Grief and rage and resentment festered in the pit of her stomach, gnawing at her insides with nowhere to go. It shouldn't have to end like this. There *had* to be another way.

Darce glanced at her, pity aching in his eyes, and she knew it was no use. She understood better than anyone the power of a bond forged in blood.

"What about the Grand Admiral?" she asked, fighting to keep the tears from her voice. "If we're to end this, we need to reach him."

"He'll be at the helm," Blair said. "He won't trust anyone else in a storm like this. But getting to him won't be easy. Only some of his sentinels have turned, and even with the selkies on our side, we're outnumbered."

"We have no choice," Isla said. "If we don't stop him here, we won't get another chance."

The *Vanguard's* deck was awash with blood as they set off towards the stern. Trails of red trickled across the timber, mixing with puddles of seawater. The salty air and raging wind weren't enough to carry away the stench. It hung in the air, sharp and metallic, thick with rot and death.

Isla drew the dirk Cam had given her. Flecks of ragged tissue clung to its serrated teeth. Her hands were smeared red. But if this was the last time she stained herself with that kind of violence, it would be worth it. It *had* to be.

A yell carried from under one of the masts, and she turned to see an Admiralty officer wrestling with a selkie, tearing her pelt as he fought to rip it from her. The selkie thrashed and snarled, but the officer pinned her to the deck, hands buried in the white fur around her shoulders.

Before Isla could do anything, a crack tore through the air. She jerked her head to see Darce behind her, a plume of smoke wisping from the familiar pistol in his hand.

He looked down, fingers curling around the polished mahogany stock. "I forgot to mention I picked it up when the sentinels freed us from the brig." He held it out to her. "Sorry. I know the barrel only holds one shot."

Isla took the pistol, its stock warm from Darce's hand. Across the deck, the selkie scrambled to her feet, pulling her pelt around her shoulders. "It doesn't matter. You used it well."

She tucked it deep into the folds of her pelt, the fur holding it as tightly as a pocket. Then she lifted her head, taking in the chaos spilling across the *Vanguard's* deck. In front of them was a wall of jewel-toned cloaks and clanging steel. A wall they had to breach if they had any hope of reaching the helm.

"Selkie bitch!"

A blast of icy water hit her face, slamming her seal-skull mask against her cheekbones. The sea forced itself through her nostrils and into her throat, and Isla dropped to her knees, vision turning black. A sentinel—it could be nothing else. Seawater poured into her lungs as she desperately clawed at the funnel smothering her. She tasted salt and bile. She was *drowning*.

Suddenly, the pressure lifted, and Darce was in front of her, eyes dark with fury. He lifted his arms and blasted the wave back at the sentinel, sending the man flying across the deck. The sentinel hit the mast, head cracking viciously against the sturdy wood. Isla didn't need to see the lolling of his tongue and the unnatural angle of his neck to know he was dead.

Darce pulled her up. "Are you—"

"I'm all right. Thanks to you." The words came in a rasp, burning her throat. "We need to keep moving."

She glanced at the sentinel, his lifeless body propped awkwardly against the mast. How many others were willing to lay down their lives for the Grand Admiral—not because of his threats, but for coin and power? If one of them managed to bring Cunningham back from the brink of death again... No, she couldn't let it happen. She *wouldn't*.

Her stomach clenched, and she forced herself to look away. There wasn't time to dwell any longer. More Admiralty cloaks hastened towards them, steel bared. The only way to reach the Grand Admiral was to meet them.

Isla ducked under the first blow, the officer's sword skimming the top of her head. The red-faced, grizzled man tried to pivot, but he was too slow. Her dirk found its home between his ribs, sliding in so easily it brought bile to Isla's throat. When she tugged the dagger free, the officer slumped to the deck, a gurgling sound spilling from his throat as blood pooled beneath him.

Darce and Blair were locked in tussles of their own, darting around each other as they slashed and parried. She was used to seeing Darce with the formidable length of his two-handed claymore, but he moved more swiftly with his rapier, stepping lightly out of the path of a musket to draw a thin, bloody line across the gunwoman's throat.

Something knocked the back of Isla's skull, sending her stumbling. A selkie had barrelled into her before tumbling to the ground, limbs sprawling at all angles. She knelt to help him, but when she rolled him over, she was met with a vacant stare and a red stain blooming across his pelt.

She jerked back. She'd caused this. She'd brought the Admiralty here. Every time one of her people fell, every drop of blood spilled...she was to blame. Even if she killed Cunningham, what would be the cost?

"Robbie, where did you...*fuck*."

Isla lifted her chin to find a familiar figure before her, his russet-coloured pelt hanging loose around his shoulders. His face was smeared with blood, but there was no mistaking the blue eyes burning through the crimson mask.

"Angus," she said softly, his name leaving her lips like an apology.

He stiffened, gaze trailing from the fallen selkie to the folds of her pelt. "Duncan told me you'd gone to face Eimhir. I didn't think you'd actually..."

"Neither did I," Isla said thinly. The wound was too raw to bear. Eimhir's voice echoed in her ears, howling accusations over the wind. Isla couldn't forget the look of betrayal behind her eyes, the hatred twisting her expression. "I never wanted it to come to this."

Her voice sounded frail to her own ears, and Angus blanched. "Aye, well, it's come all the same, hasn't it? It doesn't matter what any of us wanted—this is what we got."

Isla eyed him warily as he wrapped his fingers tighter around the handle of his hunting dagger. "I'm not your enemy," she said. "I never was. Eimhir understood that, before..." Grief thickened in her throat, strangling the rest of her words.

"You call yourself one of us, yet you still know so little," Angus said evenly. Before Isla could protest, before she could lift her blade to defend herself, he was striding towards her, dagger raised. But he wasn't coming for her—instead, he lunged past her shoulder, burying the blade into the exposed throat of an Admiralty officer.

Angus yanked the knife free to release a gushing stream of blood. His face splattered with more crimson, but it didn't seem to bother him. "Whether I like it or not, you are our aislingeach now," he said, staring at Isla. "You have the dreamwalker pelt."

He scowled as another Admiralty officer approached, swinging his dagger to catch the man under the chin. The officer fell with a wet, bubbling gasp.

"Aye, I followed Eimhir when she took your soulskin from you," Angus continued. "She might have done something unimaginable, something beyond reason, but she was our only hope. Now that it belongs to you again, so does that burden. As long as you intend to keep your promise to our people, I'll help you do what you came here to do."

He nodded towards the quarterdeck, the raised platform seething with bodies. Somewhere amongst them, Cunningham was waiting.

Isla pushed forward as Angus, Darce and Blair followed close at her heels. Every time she landed a blow, her arm grew heavier. Every time a body fell at her feet, the taste of blood in her mouth grew staler. This much violence, this much death...it was impossible not to become numb to it. It was the only way to survive it.

Darce stopped, a grey look falling over his face. "Isla, he's here."

She followed his gaze through the chaos, her heart turning cold. Cunningham was at the *Vanguard's* helm. His fingers were pale and skeletal as he gripped the wheel, his eyes awash with red from burst capillaries. Black veins snaked from his collar to his jaw, crawling under his skin like rancid ink. He belonged to the fathoms. Denying them for this long, corrupting so many blood sacrifices to keep himself from the death he deserved...it had left him as something worse than the monster he was. It had turned him into an abomination.

She glanced at Blair. "No sign of Muir?"

He shook his head, not looking at her. His eyes were fixed on Cunningham.

"You don't have to be here for this," Isla said. "He's still your—"

"No, he's not," Blair said forcefully. "Look at him. Look at what he's done, the oaths he's corrupted. Whatever he is now, he is not my uncle."

"It's not always as simple as that."

Blair met her eyes, holding her in the same steely, blue-grey gaze he shared with Cunningham. But there was nothing there that reminded her of the Grand Admiral. Blair was a different man. A man who loved her brother, who wanted to make something better of what the Admiralty had become.

"I can do this," he said. "I need you to trust me."

Isla glanced at the helm. Cunningham's captains and sentinels closed ranks around him, swords raised, muskets readied. More officers guarded the stairs leading up to the quarterdeck, cutting down any selkie who tried to pass. It was a slaughter. Bodies littered the deck, eyes glazed and pelts soaked with blood. Dark rivers of red trickled across the woodgrain, too persistent for the rain to wash away.

There was no way through. Not without a distraction.

She barely felt Angus's tug on her pelt, barely heard Darce's protests over the wind. Her feet carried her to a section of deck unsoiled by bodies, in full view of the helm. She stopped, then lifted the seal-skull mask.

Cunningham's bloodshot eyes widened as he trailed them down to the fur around her shoulders. A twisted hunger darkened his expression. His thin lips formed the shape of her name. It was like he could see nothing else but her. Like the *Vanguard* had melted away entirely, leaving nothing but the two of them standing opposite one another.

"Daughter," he said, so quietly Isla thought she'd imagined it. Then, he let loose a furious roar. "Bring me my daughter!"

Isla flinched as a dozen cloaked officers turned towards her. Cunningham would stop at nothing to bring her to his side, to bind her to him like he'd bound Mara.

Angus shifted alongside her, a growl rumbling from his throat. "You carry our people's last hope, aislingeach. No matter what has happened between us, I'll not see it lost, not while I can do something about it."

"Wait, Angus, don't—"

He cut her off with a snarl and threw himself on the nearest officer. His dagger glinted as he thrust it into the man's chest, burying it to the hilt. Another officer joined the struggle, and Angus moved swiftly to duck away from a heavy blow aimed at his jaw. He ripped his dagger out of the first officer's chest and drove it into the next one's leg, just above the kneecap.

The second officer howled, but he managed to bring his musket up, levelling it at Angus's head. A faint aura of droplets shimmered around the barrel, keeping the precious powder dry. One of the *Vanguard's* sentinels must have been protecting it from the rain.

Time slowed. The hammer clicked. Then, the air cracked with the echo of the shot.

It happened too fast to make sense of. One moment, Angus was in front of her, breathing down the musket's barrel. Then he was on the deck, buried under a heap of black fur, freckled face splattered with blood that was not his own.

Duncan rolled away and staggered to his feet. A ragged hole tore through his cheek, leaving the skin of his jaw blistered and raw from the burnt powder. He grabbed Angus and hauled him up, then rounded on the officer with the musket.

The officer froze. Duncan's axe flashed. Then there was silence, broken only by the dull thump of a headless body crumpling to the deck.

A furious roar rose from the quarterdeck, and more captains and sentinels spilled down the stairs. Isla turned cold. *Too many.*

She pushed past Duncan and Angus, positioning herself in front of the advancing officers. "Stay back, both of you. They won't hesitate to go through you to get to me. The only way this ends is if I give Cunningham what he wants."

Darce shoved through to reach her. "Isla, no. If you think I'll let him take you—"

"You have to. It's the only way." She squeezed his arm, then drew the pistol from her pelt, pressing it into his palm. "I can give you an opening," she said, lowering her voice. "One of you has to take it. Find another shot. Make it count."

Darce stiffened. "If he hurts you, if he tears that pelt from you..."

A gruff snort came from behind her. "He'll have to go through me first."

Isla turned, her neck prickling. Muir stood in front of her, a wry smile twisting his lips. The veins under his dark skin were an oily blue-green. His eyes were distant and glassy, covered with the same briny film as before. It was like the sea itself had laid claim to him.

Across the waves came a terrible, keening roar, shuddering deep into Isla's bones.

"The Cirein-cròin," she said, reaching her hand to his mottled cheek. "You're still... You have to let it go, uncle. Look what it's doing to you."

"Not sure I can. Not sure I want to, either. The serpent...the *monster*...has always been part of me. If I'm to meet the fathoms, I can think of worse company to keep on the way." He grunted. "Not that I ever intended on going there alone. But if I'm to take Alasdair with me, I need you to get me close."

She stilled, her mouth dry. "Even if it means..."

"I know exactly what it means, and I'm at peace with that." Muir shook his head. "I poisoned my veins with ale, gave up my connection to the tides, lost the respect of my family, all for a chance to make things right. A chance I've waited more than twenty-five years for."

He offered her his hand, and she slipped hers into it, shivering at the icy touch of his skin. "When the time comes, his sentinels will try to bring him back again," he said, voice low. "Only you can stop them. Take him somewhere they cannot follow."

"I don't—"

"Bring her to me, Muir!" Cunningham's roar drowned out the wind. "You will not keep her from me any longer. She is *my* daughter. *My* blood. She belongs to me."

Muir squeezed her hand. "It's time, lass."

She pulled the seal-skull mask over her head and followed him, legs shaking as the Admiralty captains and sentinels parted to let them through. The officers bristled as Muir passed, fingers twitching around their swords and muskets, but none of them dared raise their weapons. Not when Muir's death would mean the death of their Grand Admiral.

When they reached the top of the quarterdeck stairs, Isla looked back. The fighting had ceased. Everyone's eyes were fixed on her. Sentinels stared up at her, their emerald cloaks limp around their shoulders. Selkies she recognised from Caim watched on with wary glances. Duncan was supporting a limping Angus, his umber eyes giving nothing away. Blair stood at their side, curls dripping red, cheeks gaunt and pale as he knelt by the decapitated body of the Admiralty gunman.

Eventually, her eyes fell on Darce. She braced herself for the pain haunting his expression. Instead, she found a resolve that chased the fear from her veins. A look that told her no matter what happened, she had somewhere to return to. Somewhere to belong.

Cunningham yielded the *Vanguard's* wheel to the officer at his side and slowly stalked towards her. His eyes never left her pelt. They carried a glint that turned her cold, a feverish shine that spoke to more than greed, more than hunger. It was obsession. Obsession stretching decades, stained with the blood of everyone who'd ever got in his way.

Muir stopped, shielding her as he drew his cutlass. "It's over, Alasdair. There's only one way this ends, for both of us."

Cunningham's face contorted into something loathsome. "This will end with you rotting in a hole so dark you'll beg me to return you to those canals you crawled out of. That's where you belong. That's where you should have stayed. You have stood between me and my family for the last time."

"Would that I'd done a better job of it all those years ago," Muir said. "I couldn't save Mara from all the ways you broke her. But tides fucking take me if I let you do the same to her daughter."

"*My* daughter," Cunningham hissed. "She is *mine*."

Muir chuckled. "When I look at my niece, I see in her the reflection of those who gave up part of themselves to protect her. Mara, Cat, Cormick. Maybe even me, if she'd forgive me for saying so. But you..." He smiled tightly. "There's not a piece of you that lives in her, Alasdair. That's what I will carry with me to the fathoms: the knowledge that everything you are will die with you."

Cunningham's lips pulled back in an ugly snarl, but Muir was already moving. He lunged with his cutlass, slashing through the sapphire brocade draped across Cunningham's chest. The fabric ripped open, and something wet and black splattered onto the deck.

Blood. Rancid, corrupted blood.

"As if there was any doubt," Muir murmured, half to himself. "Tides take me for ever believing otherwise."

Cunningham pressed a hand to his chest, his expression unyielding as his fingers came away smeared with black. Then he fixed Isla with his dead gaze. "Bring her to me."

His sentinels closed in, but Muir swung his cutlass in a wide arc to drive them back. Isla slipped behind him, hand trembling as she curled it around the hilt of her dirk. There were too many of them. They edged forward slowly, pressing the two of them back against the gunwale. Soon, there would be nowhere else to go.

Only the sea.

Muir's eyes flitted to her, an old glint of mischief in the sobriety of his gaze. He let out a roar and charged through the sentinels, parrying their swinging steel as he thundered towards Cunningham. But the Grand Admiral was quicker to raise his blade, meeting Muir's blow with a deft riposte. A ripping sound tore through the air, and this time, the deck splattered with red, not black.

"No!" Isla lunged for him, but a sentinel grabbed her by the neck, hauling her back. She thrashed against the woman's grip, trying to drive the dirk between her ribs, but the sentinel knocked the dagger loose with a wrench of Isla's wrist, and it clattered to the deck.

A screaming pain shot through Isla's arm, but she ignored it, whipping her other hand to her pelt. Her fingers closed around empty air, and she remembered with a lurch that she'd given her pistol to Darce, its chamber empty.

She lifted her chin. Muir was staggering from the wound Cunningham had scored in his stomach. Blood dripped freely across the deck, leaving a slick red trail at her uncle's feet. Still, he didn't back away. He threw himself at Cunningham again, swinging wildly with his cutlass.

The blow met thin air. Cunningham sidestepped neatly, leaving a deep gouge across Muir's collarbone. The blood flowed heavier, spilling down Muir's chest, soaking his linen shirt a dark, violent red.

Muir gave a weak chuckle. "I came here to kill you, Alasdair. At this rate, you'll do the job for me."

"You always were a fool." A cold sneer spread on Cunningham's lips. "There is no manner of death my sentinels cannot bring me back from. There is nothing you can accomplish here that cannot be undone."

He lifted his blade again, pressing the tip into Muir's shoulder as he backed him up against the gunwale. Blood welled around the steel, dribbling down Muir's coat.

All Muir did was smile. Then, he pulled Cunningham towards him with a vicious tug, driving the blade deeper through his own shoulder.

A scream tore from Isla's throat. Muir let out a wet gasp. The two men grappled against the gunwale, Muir's spine bent over the edge.

Then a shot cracked through the air, and everything stilled.

Isla's mouth was too dry to swallow. A haze clouded her vision, settling over her like a dream. When it lifted, she saw the evidence of what had happened.

A velvet pouch torn open, spilling lead shots across the deck.

The polished gleam of a mahogany barrel smoking in Blair's hand.

The black-blooded stain blooming across Cunningham's back.

Time held its breath. Muir's eyes, filled with the oily wash of the sea, brightened for a fleeting moment. Then his expression slackened, and he tumbled backwards over the edge, his lifeless body falling with the ghost of a smile on his lips.

Isla screamed his name, but she couldn't hear it over the pounding in her ears. Each frantic beat of her heart thumped like a blow. The tides roared, filling her head with their fury.

The firm hand around her shoulder lifted, and out of the corner of her eye, Isla saw the sentinels moving. She could already picture what would happen: their steel searching for the beating hearts of their own captains, plunging through flesh and bone, forging another twisted oath, another corrupted sacrifice.

She couldn't let it happen, not this time.

The wind swirled around her, and she lifted her arms to see the hairs rigid. Glittering frost crept over her skin, sinking its teeth into her flesh. When she breathed, the moisture fell to the deck in icy droplets.

It was the haar. She tasted its rot at the back of her throat.

Muir's voice echoed in her ears. *Take him somewhere they cannot follow.*

She knew what she had to do.

Shouts erupted behind her as she scrambled to her feet, but they were quickly engulfed by the mist. She couldn't look back. There was no time.

She ran, bare feet slipping on the sea-soaked deck. Cunningham's limp body hung over the gunwale, arms draped towards the waves, the black stain between his shoulders blooming across the sapphire fabric.

Her pelt was already spreading across her shoulders when she reached him. The fur rippled over her skin as she buried her hands in his coat and hauled him over the *Vanguard's* edge.

They fell together, two twisting shapes. Then the last of her human form gave way to her soulshape, and the sea swallowed them both.

CHAPTER THIRTY-FIVE

ISLA

Isla pushed the air from her swollen seal lungs, ridding her body of its buoyancy as she plunged after Cunningham's corpse. No matter how much she was breaking inside, the only thing that mattered was reaching him. She couldn't think about leaving Darce behind on the *Vanguard*. She couldn't think about the wry twist of Muir's mouth as he'd fallen into the waves. Her uncle was lost to her, claimed by the fathoms.

But Cunningham, she could still reach.

Icy water closed in, but the cold couldn't penetrate her dense fur and thick layer of blubber. Down here, she *belonged*. She had nothing to fear from the depths. Nothing but...

A bloodcurdling chill burrowed into her bones as the shadows stirred and the Cirein-cròin's huge, monstrous face swam into view.

She pulled out of her dive, stopping level with the serpent's colossal head. She couldn't see the rest of its body. Its long jaws bled from the gloom, its eyes little more than pinpricks.

It moved closer, scales rippling as it bared its teeth. Its maw was so huge that Isla could have easily swum through the gaps between its wicked, curved fangs. This close, she saw how abrasive its teeth were, coated in barnacles and draped with slithering strands of seaweed. Pieces of timber were wedged into its gums, and she realised with a chill she didn't know whether the splinters had come from an Admiralty or Sea Kith ship.

The creature stared at her, its eyes coated in the same film that had bled across Muir's. It snorted out a jet of water from its slitted nostrils, boiling the water until it bubbled.

A sinking dark shape broke her from her trance, and she jolted towards the depths as Cunningham's lifeless body drifted away. She had to get him away from the *Vanguard*. She had to take him somewhere his sentinels' perverted blood oath couldn't reach.

Her teeth sank through the fabric of his coat, finding the flesh around his collarbone. The taste of his blood on her tongue sent a shudder through her. It was sick, *spoiled* somehow. No matter how many times he'd been reclaimed from the fathoms, it wasn't enough to rid his veins of the decay that had begun to take root.

When she whirled around again, the Cirein-cròin was gone, lost behind the mist creeping through the water. The haar was closing in, spreading below the waves as well as above them. She couldn't see the surface anymore. The *Vanguard* was lost to the fog. Even the muffled cannon fire had disappeared, leaving her in an oppressive silence.

Under her skin, she felt Mara's bones call out. The mist swirled, wrapping her in its embrace.

She clamped her jaws around Cunningham's collar and swam.

At once, her throat tightened, its walls thickening with salt. She'd never made the crossing in her selkie form, only as a human. Down here, in her soulshape, the mist's touch sank deeper, percolating her fur and blubber to reach her bones.

She knew what the haar could do to a selkie. She'd seen the hollowed-out stranger it had made of Eimhir.

A fresh wave of anguish washed over her, and she pushed the thoughts away, propelling herself through the misty water. Cunningham's dead weight pulled at her jaws, the depths hungry to claim him for their own. Part of her wanted to surrender him and be done with it, but there would always be a cold trickle of fear that he might return, such was his spite.

There was only one way to end this for good.

After a while, the shifting hues in her greyscale vision flattened, turning opaque. The churning waves and swirling currents dissipated, leaving behind a sea that was too calm, too still. All that remained was the blanket of mist. Then it thinned and faded, leaving her in barren, empty waters.

The soulless realm. A desolate place, cut off from the world of the living. The only place Cunningham's sentinels couldn't reach him.

Isla angled herself towards the surface, bursting through with a puff of water from her nostrils. Overhead, the sky flickered with an eerie glow. There were no storm clouds. Squalls had spirits of their own, and they could not survive in a place such as this. Nothing could.

She spotted a scrap of rock rising from the water and swam towards it, dragging Cunningham behind her. Tendrils of kelp coated one side of the outcropping, their strands faded and hazy. There was a veil here between the living and the dead, a barrier she could only cross because of the haar.

Her pelt shrank back from her face and arms as she climbed out of the water. The damp fur retreated across her pale skin, leaving streaks of seawater behind. She pulled the folds around her chest, closing them over the glistening bone cuirass underneath.

"Thank you, màthair," she murmured, fingers brushing the smooth surface. "For bringing me back."

Cunningham's body lay against the rock, the sea lapping over his unmoving form. It was the first time since the *Vanguard* she'd had the chance to look at him—*truly* look at him. A ghostly pallor had fallen across his face, turning his skin waxen. It made the black veins crawling up his neck more pronounced. His lids were dark and bruised, and even now, even *here*, Isla couldn't help but fear his eyes might spring open again.

These waters belong to me, he'd said, and she'd believed him. Whether he was monster or man, he had turned the sea red. He'd drowned Silveckan's shores in blood. He'd left behind a wound she feared even his death would never heal.

She pressed her fingers to the seal-skull mask, unable to suppress the shiver that came over her. Mara had been here once, on a spit of rock just like this. She'd plucked Cunningham from the sea and breathed life back into his lungs, never realising the moment her lips touched his was the moment she'd sealed her fate.

Isla could only hope that now, she'd sealed his.

She trailed her eyes over his coat. He was gone. All that was left of him was this husk, tainted by corrupted blood and stolen souls. It seemed only right for him to rot in a place as forsaken as he was.

A low, keening wail carried across the water, and she jumped, snapping her head towards the sound.

The Cirein-cròin was here.

She froze, willing her racing heart to steady. Darce had spoken of serpents crossing the haar without any need for bones or ships, but the sight of the monstrous creature still left her dazed.

It reared its long neck, the sea cascading down its hide like waterfalls. The sky's red glow reflected off its glittering scales as it stared at her, eyes so dark it was like looking into one of the trenches down in the depths. It didn't come any closer, just watched her, stooping its lithe neck so low its jaws brushed the water.

Another roar ripped from its gaping throat, making its whole gullet tremble. It was a baleful sound—rasping and melodic all at once. It shuddered into her bones, sending a shooting pain through her skull.

That was when she noticed the gun-anam.

She sprang to her feet, hands scrambling for a weapon she no longer carried. But the wraiths kept their distance, drifting over the water in wisps of mist. A hollow rattle came from their shapeless forms, grating against Isla's ears. It was a bleak cry, a lament that made her soul weary.

One of them crawled closer, souring the air with its brackish stench. Its presence stole the breath from Isla's lungs. She felt salt and ice at the back of her throat. But the gun-anam paid no attention to her. Instead, it floated towards Cunningham's limp, lifeless body.

A chill crept down her spine as another wraith approached. It swirled through the air, rippling with shadows. When it reached Cunningham, it extended a silvery tendril, wrapping it around his pale neck.

The rattling grew louder, and more gun-anam came. They paid her no mind, drifting through her as they swarmed around Cunningham's body. Their mist clung to him like a shroud, obscuring him from her vision. Then, a wail came from inside the shadows. It was an awful sound, thick with years of grief and pain and madness. It sank into her bones, filling her with such despair she wanted to claw at her own ears to make it stop.

She squeezed her eyes shut, trying to block it out, but it was no use. Her teeth chattered, her temples pounded like her skull was ready to burst. It was too much. She couldn't bear it any longer.

As suddenly as it began, the wailing stopped.

Isla cracked open one eye, then another. The mist thinned, slowly dissipating into wisps of silvery spray. Then it cleared entirely.

Cunningham's body was no more. All that remained was a pile of decaying bones.

Isla stared, her mouth dry. He was truly gone. The only trace left of him was these bones, blackened by the haar's rot, dripping with silt and seaweed.

In front of her eyes, the bones crumbled, dissolving into salt. Then that too disappeared, scattered in a non-existent breeze.

It was over. There would be no return for Alasdair Cunningham.

A wretched sob tore from her chest, and she sank to her knees, the rock cool against her skin. So much pain. So much loss. There was nothing she could do to take back all the violence he'd wrought, all the blood he'd spilled. But this...

All I can do is try to close a wound that has been killing my people and yours alike, Eimhir had told her the first time they'd met. *Without that pain, perhaps there is a chance for us to heal.*

This was that chance.

She lifted her chin, blinking away tears as she stared over the horizon. The Cirein-cròin gazed back at her, fathomless and unblinking. For a moment, she thought she might have imagined some glimmer of recognition, a human gleam in its serpentine eyes. Then it disappeared, and the creature lowered its huge head, retreating beneath the surface once more.

No ripples followed it. No waves crested towards her. The serpent was gone, as if it had never existed.

Isla focused on her pelt, waiting for the fur to spread across her body once more and take her back to the water. The Cirein-cròin had returned to whatever place it had come from. It was time for her to do the same.

CHAPTER THIRTY-SIX

DARCE

The haar pushed into Darce's lungs, turning his chest to ice. He couldn't move. He just stared at the empty gunwale where Isla had disappeared, taking Cunningham's lifeless body with her.

"We need to leave this ship." Blair grabbed his arm. "There are still too many sentinels loyal to my uncle here. They'll come for us, especially after..." His fingers clenched around Isla's smoking pistol, the pistol Darce had placed in his hand after he saw Blair stoop to retrieve a pouch of shots from the fallen Admiralty gunman.

The pistol that had put an end to Alasdair Cunningham.

For a moment, he'd thought Blair wouldn't be able to do it. His jaw had trembled, his knuckles turning white as his finger flexed around the trigger. Then, something in his expression had changed, and the shot had rung out, filling the air with the echo of a choice made.

Darce licked his lips, tasting salt. "It's not the sentinels we should be worried about." As he spoke, a deathly chill crawled down his spine. He smelled the salt sharpening, the air sour with a familiar rot.

The gun-anam had begun to emerge from the mist.

They stirred from the shadows, leaving silvery droplets in their wake as they drifted towards a pack of sentinels. A woman with grey hair and a wind-burnt face noticed them first, her weathered cheeks paling in terror. By the time she'd lifted her sword, it was too late. The wraiths fell on her, pouring mist down her throat, smothering her with salt and spray.

When they were done, all that was left was a glassy-eyed corpse with white, waxy skin and seafoam spilling from blue lips.

Blair staggered back. "What do we do?"

The other side of the ship was already shrouded behind a thick veil of fog. Darce couldn't see where Isla had jumped. Even if he could, it wouldn't matter. She wasn't coming back to the *Vanguard*.

"We do what you said," he replied, trying to ignore the ache behind his ribs. "We get off this ship."

The two of them hurried across the deck, stumbling and sliding as the rain-soaked timber underfoot turned to ice. Salt stung Darce's throat. Every gust of wind bit deeper than before. There was no escaping the haar; it seeped into everything, its touch cold and corrupting.

"I'll find the sentinels who turned against my uncle and get them to safety," Blair said. "If I can reach my ship, I can sound a retreat, but no captain in the fleet would dare abandon the fight when the *Vanguard* still sails. If we're to end this, you need to send this ship to the fathoms."

Darce shook his head. "You say that like it's a simple thing. How do you suppose we sink something as—watch out!" He pushed Blair to the side as a wraith emerged from the mist, a shimmering blade in its formless grip. It was like no sword Darce had ever seen, rippling with shadows, an edge so sharp it bled into darkness.

He lifted his rapier, and steel met spray with a watery crash. Seawater splattered across his face, shooting up his nostrils, stinging his eyes. He called on his magic to clear his vision, but the gun-anam was closing on him, reaching for his throat with a silver tendril.

A hulking black shape leapt in front of him, and the gun-anam burst into spray, scattering across the deck. When the water cleared from

Darce's eyes, he saw Duncan standing before him, face grim and axe raised.

"I suggest you sail away from this place while you can," he said in his low, gravelly voice. "We selkies cannot fight with you any longer. The haar's touch is too sickening to endure. I won't lose any more of us to it, not after..."

Eimhir's name hung between them, raw and painful.

"Isla will return," Darce said. "She'll keep the promise she made."

"Perhaps. But by then, it will already be too late for some of us." Duncan shook his head. "Stay and fight, if that is your wish. But you'll do so alone. My people have played their part. I can ask no more of them."

He motioned to Angus, and the two of them leapt over the gunwale. Across the *Vanguard's* deck, Darce saw the other selkies following, slipping into their sealskins as they returned to the water. Soon, only the jewel-toned cloaks of the Admiralty remained.

"We still have the Sea Kith," Blair said. "It's not over."

"Lieutenant!" A shrill voice cut through the air, and Darce whirled around to see a woman waving from the aft deck, her blonde hair giving way to silver at the temples. It was Heather, one of the sentinels who'd turned against Cunningham.

"We have a tender," she called over the wind. "We can get you to the *Midnight Crest*. Come quickly, before—"

She froze, the rest of her words lost to the thin gasp that squeezed from her lungs. At first, Darce couldn't see anything. Then seafoam bubbled from her mouth, and her eyes rolled back until only the whites were visible.

"Heather!" Blair charged towards her, sword raised, but there was nothing for him to attack. The gun-anam had already suffused her body with mist, drowning her from the inside. Its vapour seeped from her pores, abandoning her as she convulsed on the deck.

Blair rolled her onto her back and tried to breathe life back into her, but there was no gasp, no hitch of the sentinel's chest. As Darce reached out with his magic, willing the tides to help him draw the water from her lungs, he knew it was no use. All he could sense in her was rot and salt. She was already gone.

"She's..." Blair trailed off, his eyes dull. "You rescued her son from Baininch Rise. Young Tam, wasn't it? She never got to see him again. She'll never..."

Sorrow rose in Darce's chest, but he fought to smother it. There would be time to grieve later. For now, they had to survive. He put a hand on Blair's shoulder. "We need to reach that tender. It's our best chance of getting clear of the gun-anam."

Blair climbed to his feet. "You're right. It's just...leaving her here..."

Darce glanced across the deck. Everywhere he looked, he found fallen bodies, human and selkie alike. Cloaks bloodied, pelts torn, eyes glassy and distant. The violence here would feed the gun-anam until they were gorged beyond measure.

"Isla was meant to undo this," Blair said, voice thin and strained. "Where *is* she?"

Dread tightened in Darce's chest. The haar stretched across the waves, bleak and unending, showing no sign of lifting. The thread holding his soul to Isla's felt lost, like he could no longer sense the other end of it.

Where is she? Blair had asked.

Grief clutched at his heart. He only wished he could answer.

By the time Darce made it back to the soulship, he could barely breathe. The haar was suffocating him, filling his lungs with fluid.

He couldn't survive this much longer. None of them could.

It only took a few seconds to lose sight of the tender as it sailed back into the mist, ferrying Blair to the *Midnight Crest*. Darce stared after its wake, silently urging the tides to carry the young lieutenant and the surviving sentinels through the swell. The only hope of this ending would come when the *Crest's* sea horn blared through the fog. But Blair couldn't sound the retreat, not as long as the *Vanguard* remained on the waves.

Nishi fixed him with a stony gaze. "You're asking the impossible. The soulship has no weapons. This mist is so thick we've lost our allies. Featherblade hasn't returned from the *Red Gale*."

Darce's stomach twisted. The guidebird always managed to find its way back to him. If it hadn't returned...

"We have to try." Lachlan sat on the deck next to a wounded selkie, a lass of no more than twenty. Her brow was beaded with sweat as Lachlan worked to dress a gouge that had taken half her forearm off.

She moaned as he pulled the bandage tight, and he held her white-knuckled hand, letting her squeeze through the pain before turning his attention to Darce. "Blair is right. The rest of the fleet will never stand down, not as long as the *Vanguard* remains. They won't believe the Grand Admiral is gone. They'll expect him to come back, like he always does." He hesitated. "You said Isla went after him. Do you think she..."

Darce couldn't bring himself to answer. He didn't *know* the answer. If she'd died, he'd have felt it. He'd have followed her to the damned fathoms. But she hadn't come back up from the waves. Wherever she was, it was out of reach.

Nishi let out a sharp breath. "I want to see that abomination of a ship sunk as much as anyone. If you and Jacques believe you can summon enough of a swell to drag it to the fathoms, I'll get you close enough to try."

She returned to the helm, and Darce pushed away the pain clawing at his heart to take his place at the prow. He reached for the tides with all his remaining strength, gasping as their currents surged, singing in their deep, echoing tones. He felt them shifting around the soulship's hull, carrying them where they needed to go. The sea spirits knew what the *Vanguard* was. They mourned the souls stripped away on its bloodstained deck. They wanted it sunk as much as he did.

An abomination, Nishi had called it, and she was right.

The storm raged. Each time the swell spilled across the deck, it felt like the soulship might be swallowed entirely. The endless blanket of the haar had consumed almost everything.

A deep rumble of thunder rattled through Darce's bones, and a flash followed, spearing the sky. It lit up the horizon for only a moment, but that was all Darce needed to realise they'd strayed too close.

The *Vanguard* loomed over them, its hull blocking out the sky. He hadn't been able to see it through the haar until it was too late. Now, it was almost on top of them, close enough to witness the fate that had befallen it.

The gun-anam infested the ship, crawling over every inch of timber Darce could see. A vaporous mass of wraiths crept from the waves, covering the hull in their misty wake. More descended from the clouds, winding around the *Vanguard's* towering masts. They drifted aimlessly, taking their fill from the wretched souls still alive on the ship.

Screams filled his ear, and he shuddered. It was little wonder the gun-anam had come to feed. All the violence the *Vanguard's* deck had seen, all the blood spilled from human and selkie alike... The ship was more than a graveyard. It was a wound, a fissure into the soulless realm itself.

"We need to...go back." He tried to speak, but the air in his lungs turned to ice. "Can't...let them..."

It was too late. The gun-anam had taken notice of the soulship.

They drifted from the *Vanguard's* deck, leaving trails of vapour in their wake as they swept towards them. Their hollow breaths rattled from non-existent mouths. Darce reached for the tides, but the magic slipped from his veins, leaving him numb.

The sea spirits could not save him. The wraiths suffocated everything.

He grabbed the hilt of his rapier, willing his frostbitten fingers to tighten. The handle was like ice in his palm, coated with the haar's frosty breath. Still, he jabbed the blade forward, thrusting it through the nearest gun-anam in the place he might have imagined a heart. The wraith screamed—a terrible, bone-splitting sound—then dissolved into a shower of silvery droplets that scattered across the deck.

Darce staggered away. Already, the droplets were trickling together, finding their way back to the wisping vapour trailing across the deck. It was only a matter of time before another gun-anam was born from the mist. They couldn't be killed. Steel was no match for that kind of pain, that kind of grief.

There was no escaping the haar, not this time.

More of them swarmed him, their salt-thick stench pouring down his throat, their ghostly tendrils leaving frost burns on his skin. His fingers stiffened and the rapier fell, hitting the deck with a dull clatter.

A chill like he'd never felt before wrapped around him, seeping into his bones. The cold permeated every part of him, infecting his veins, eating away at his organs, filling his lungs.

He fell to his knees. Out of the corner of his eye, he saw Jacques and Nishi with their backs pressed together, their cutlasses slow and laboured as the blades grew heavy with ice. Further down the deck, Lachlan was clutching his throat, his cheeks turning blue.

Darce tried to climb to his feet, but his legs wouldn't move. He fell to the deck, vision black at the edges. For a moment, he thought he saw something: a ripple of grey stirring from the depths of the fog.

"Isla..." Her name left his lips in a whisper. If he was to die here, she couldn't die with him. She had a promise to keep, a promise that lived in the pelt she wore. Her soul had always been more than just him.

Darkness crept in, and he blinked it away. The grey shape was more solid now. He could make out the curved outline of shoulders, the shifting folds of fur around two legs.

She was here. Isla was here, standing in front of the gun-anam like he'd breathed her into being when he'd whispered her name.

Her voice was so quiet he barely heard it over the wind.

"No more."

CHAPTER THIRTY-SEVEN

ISLA

At Isla's words, the gun-anam stopped, hovering before her in a cloud of mist and spray. She stared at it through the empty eyes of her seal-skull mask, searching for something buried beneath the agony that had given the wraith its wretched form. This creature was a memory of violence, an echo of pain.

Only she could take it away.

She sank into her pelt, its weight shifting over her skin. The damp fur contained its own memories, its own echoes. She carried them now. They were *hers*, as much as her beating heart. She sifted through them, her mind brushing her ancestors' memories, following the current as it swept her along. Flashes of lives she'd never lived flickered before her: the taste of herring on a woman's tongue, the ache between her legs as she pushed out new life, the chafe of a rope around her neck. They didn't belong to her, but she knew them as intimately as her own.

She was the aislingeach. The dreamwalker.

A low, rattling wail came from the gun-anam, and Isla focused the current towards the creature.

At once, she recoiled. It wasn't just pain; it was deeper than that, more enduring than that. This was a suffering of the soul, an existence so bleak, so fucking *wretched*, that Isla felt she would rather dissolve into the same scattered spray as the wraith than endure another moment of it.

She saw it all. She felt it all. The cold squeeze of dread behind her sternum as a ship's shadow blocked out the sun. The nets coming down around her, digging into her hide the more she thrashed to free herself. The harpoon through her tail, the agony so intense she'd have retched if she'd been human.

It was *her* skin the blade pared away. The crimson blood spilling across the deck belonged to *her*. And when they stripped her pelt, leaving her naked and shivering, it was *her* soul that was lost.

Find them, Mara had urged her. *Take their suffering into your pelt, make their pain part of you. Without it, they'll be able to return to the sea. They'll be able to rest.*

She steeled herself with a breath and opened her soul to the gun-anam.

This was what she was meant to do, no matter how much it hurt. She'd been lost for so long, never understanding why part of her was missing. Now, she gave the wraith what she'd been given—the gift of being found, of being known.

Mist and spray seeped into her pelt, saturating the fur. She drew the gun-anam's memories into her soul—all of its pain, all of its torment. She felt its despair, the itch of its salt-ridden skin. And when it finally surrendered to the fathoms, she drowned with it. Every part of its suffering became hers.

It was over.

She returned to her body with a gasp. The last trails of mist dissipated and fell to the deck in scattered silver droplets. She watched as they trickled along the grooves in the bone, finding their way back to the sea.

This gun-anam would not return. She felt it in the stirring of the wind, the hush of the waves. But the wraith's pain lingered still, seeping into her bones, making her pelt that wee bit heavier around her shoulders.

You will bear it, Mara had told her. And Isla realised it was not a command, but a promise.

"Aye," she whispered. "I will."

Another wraith drifted across the deck, and she sank back into the dream state. The storm and the swell and the bitter wind melted away as she plunged into the memories that lived on in her pelt. She followed the eyes of her ancestors until she found the gun-anam in front of her. Only then could she understand. Only then could she begin to know its pain, and make it her own.

Each wraith took her deeper into the haar, their icy tendrils coiling around her arms, her legs, her throat. But their touch didn't leave the same chill as before. She accepted them into her, clutched their suffering to her chest until it belonged to her. Then, she released them to the sea in a shower of salt and spray, and the sodden folds of her pelt hung heavier.

She didn't know how long it had been when the mists began to thin. The fog retreated, shrinking back across the waves. Thick black clouds clung to the sky, but the torrential rain eased into a light drizzle. All around her, she saw ships of every size: proud galleons, sleek cutters, brigantines boasting the flags of the Admiralty and Sea Kith alike.

And there, rising above the waves like a monster, was the *Vanguard of the Firth*.

"You came back." She spun around to find Darce in front of her. The haar had left its mark on him—his face was drained of all colour and his lips were dry and cracked. Her heart seized as he stooped over, clutching his ribs as he coughed, but when he fixed her with the force of his gaze, she found a need there that burned away whatever chill had laid claim to her skin.

"You came back," he said again, the words rasping. "Isla, I thought..."

He staggered the last few steps towards her, each stride more urgent than the last. Then his hands were on her face, cupping her jaw, pulling her back to everything she wanted. His lips met hers with a desperate hunger, crashing into her with all the wild joy and abandon of the waves themselves. He tasted like salt and iron and *belonging* and...tides, nothing else she'd ever known.

She leaned into him, losing herself in the fierceness of his grasp as his hands trailed to the small of her back. His fingers buried themselves in her pelt, and suddenly she couldn't breathe. She wanted to drown in this moment, drown in *him*, and damn the rest of the tides-forsaken world around them.

"I love you," he said, murmuring the words between her parted lips. He kissed her again, gentler this time, too tender to bear. "I love you, Isla Blackwood. I—"

A rasping cough spilled from his chest, and she pressed her hand against his cheek. "Don't speak. The haar—"

"Is gone," he said. "I'm all right, Isla. I'm safe."

"Only for now." She took a trembling breath. "It will never be gone, not until every gun-anam is given peace. Not until the mists are free from the suffering they carry. They need to heal. We all need to heal."

"Then we heal. We close these wounds, together." His gaze flicked to the *Vanguard*. "And we start with that."

Isla stared at the ship, her neck prickling at the silence coming from its empty deck. No mist clung to its towering masts. No cannons roared from the gun ports. The haar had swept over it, devouring the blood in its path and leaving nothing but bones behind.

A familiar scrape of wood reached her ears, and she found Lachlan alongside her, leaning heavily on his crutch. His golden hair was wet and dishevelled, his cheeks so pale they were almost translucent, but something in his spine straightened as he trailed his eyes over the *Vanguard*.

"All those months I spent on that ship, blind to what I was becoming," he muttered. "Only able to see what had been taken from me, not what I still stood to lose. Isla, I—"

"Don't," she said quickly. "There is nothing you can say that I haven't already forgiven you for, wee brother. Whatever hurt we have caused each other is in the past. Let's leave it there, aye?"

He nodded. "If we're sending the *Vanguard* to the fathoms, let it take all that pain with it."

They made their way to the gunwale together, their hands resting side by side against the rain-soaked bone. For once, the silence didn't echo with unspoken hurt. There were no undercurrents she feared stirring into resentment. For the first time she remembered, she and Lachlan were at peace.

Darce joined them, sombre and unflinching as he stared at the *Vanguard's* towering hull. "It seems unsinkable, even now. I don't know if—"

A low chuckle came from behind them, and Isla turned to find Maggie Grier standing bright-eyed and fervent, her gaze fixed on the *Vanguard's* masts.

"Two-hundred feet above the waterline," she said. "Silvish pine. Bends—"

"Doesn't break," Darce finished gently.

Maggie Grier glanced between them both, her smile widening. "It will this time."

A shiver crept up Isla's spine. Across the deck, the soulship's passengers were drawing near, congregating along the length of the gunwale. Nishi trudged down from the helm, grim satisfaction on her features. Jacques slid an arm around his mother's shoulders, the soft smile on his lips at war with the exhaustion in his eyes. Survivors from Baininch Rise, familiar faces Isla recognised from Eileanan Selch, cloaked Admiralty officers rescued from the waves. They were all watching, all waiting for what was about to happen.

Jacques took his place beside Darce, and the two sentinels exchanged a steady look. Then, the waves stirred.

Isla leaned over, her hands as white as the bone she gripped beneath her fingers. The water was churning in a way she'd never seen, the grey-green swell coiling around on itself like a serpent. Seafoam frothed and spat as the currents swirled, and for a moment, she thought she saw a gaping hole leading down to the depths themselves.

A roar filled her ears, and the sea began to rise.

Part of her couldn't grasp what she was seeing. In her selkie form, she'd ventured to depths no human could survive. She'd felt the currents brush against her whiskers, the riptides pulling her adrift. She knew the sea, or at least, she thought she did. But this...this was something else entirely. When the swell surged, it didn't return to the sea. Instead, it climbed, swirling into a huge funnel that grew taller and wider by the second.

She snapped her head towards Darce, a warning on her lips, but it died the moment she looked at him. He was as steady and certain as she'd ever seen him, his eyes focused and unblinking as he stared at the rising waterspout. The scar around his missing ear twitched as a vein pulsed in his temple. She felt the magic exuding from him, leaping and crashing like the waves themselves.

Higher and higher the waterspout climbed. The funnel spun faster, spitting out seafoam as it writhed. It sucked more of the sea into it with every spiral, growing so large its spray smattered Isla's cheeks.

The huge pillar slowly began to move, filling her ears with the sea's furious roar. As it crept towards the *Vanguard*, the waves whipped up, rocking the soulship violently.

Behind her, someone retched. She tightened her grip on the gunwale, focusing on the swirling funnel. Any second now, it would hit the *Vanguard*.

"Do you think it will be enough?" she whispered, half to herself.

A shrill, ear-splitting shriek tore through the air, and she lifted her head to see Featherblade bursting through the clouds. The gannet circled twice around the soulship's mast, then shot towards the waterspout, flapping furiously as it chased the swirling funnel.

Nishi gave a wry smile. "Aye, it will be enough."

Before she'd finished speaking, another pealing cry tore through the clouds, and a giant sea eagle emerged.

"Swiftclaw," Isla said, heart racing. "That means..."

Over the waves, her eyes found the *Red Gale*. The brigantine carved through the swell, its ruby sails billowing against the sky. Already she heard the wooden clack of the shutters being raised around the gunports. If she squinted, she could pick out the cannons' protruding muzzles, ready to unleash a salvo of iron upon the *Vanguard*.

She searched the deck and found Cam by the gunwale. They tipped the brim of their cavalier hat, giving Isla a resolute nod. Up by the helm, Ruairidh stood by the wheel with one arm raised, his ice-blue eye fixed on the *Vanguard*.

The distance was too great for her to hear his command over the wind. All she saw was the shape of his mouth around a single word as his arm dropped swiftly towards the deck.

Fire.

The cannons roared in a plume of burnt powder and white smoke. Shards of timber flew into the air, sucked into the roiling currents of the waterspout. There was nowhere for the *Vanguard* to go. It was caught between the Sea Kith cannons and the churning pillar rising to the sky. The ship was a husk, abandoned by its crew, holding nothing but remnants of the violence that had spilled across its deck.

A weary groan echoed across the waves as the waterspout reached the *Vanguard's* hull. More timber broke away, whipped into the funnel. The sea devoured the scraps, ripping the wood from the *Vanguard's* carcass like flesh flayed from bone. The ship didn't seem so monstrous anymore. It was pitiful, in a twisted way. Gone were the black sails, the towering masts, the wolven figurehead. Each time the *Red Gale* unleashed another volley, more of the ship crumbled, its entrails sucked up by the swirling tower of water stretching to the sky.

It was difficult to tell how long it took. Isla watched as the ship splintered before her. The hull's timber peeled off, scrap by wretched scrap. The masts snapped, bent at awkward angles. Piece by piece, the waterspout consumed what was left, until all she could see was a drifting portion of deck, the ship's wheel barely visible above the swell.

She felt Nishi stiffen. Lachlan's hand twitched, his fingers finding hers.

Darce let out a long, laboured breath.

The last forlorn scrap of the *Vanguard* bobbed on the waves, then disappeared, swallowed by the fathoms.

The muffled roar of the waterspout filled her ears. Then it faded too, the sea falling back to where it belonged in a grey-green cascade. The swell surged wildly, then settled. Overhead, the clouds parted, letting the faintest crack of sunlight slip through. It bounced off the waves, glittering on their foaming crests.

Isla waited. Every inch of her body was fraught, hardly daring to believe what her eyes were telling her.

Then, she heard it: the low drone of a sea horn bellowing across the waves.

The Admiralty was retreating.

Finally, it was over.

CHAPTER THIRTY-EIGHT

DARCE

Thiel was an old decommissioned port on Silveckan's southwest coast, surrounded by deep bays of grey shingle and greyer water. Darce had never set foot in the harbour—he doubted many had by choice. If Arburgh was dreich, at least it was stark and formidable in its bleakness. Thiel, by contrast, was little more than a scattered collection of ill-kept jetties and wind-battered harbour buildings.

Perhaps that neglect was what had saved it from Eimhir and the haar.

Now, the docks bustled with a purpose they hadn't seen in decades as more Admiralty ships limped in every day. Shutters were pulled from boarded-up buildings, seaweed and rust scraped from iron cleats to make way for new mooring lines. The Admiralty's arrival breathed life into the derelict port, and already, Darce could see the beginnings of something new taking shape. Something rebuilt, something *more* than what the Admiralty had been before.

He found Lachlan and Blair at the end of one of the jetties, heads bowed together as they pored over some kind of manifest. Their foreheads touched, and both men drew back at the same time, something unspoken passing between them.

Lachlan noticed him first, straightening his spine as Darce approached. "Galbraith. I take it this means you're heading out?"

He did his best to mask the disappointment, but Darce knew him too well not to hear it. "You know Isla can't stay here, little laird. And my place is by her side."

"Of course I know that." Lachlan waved a dismissive hand at him. "I just thought we might have more time before, well..." He released a long sigh, shoulders slumping. "But I suppose there's no waiting, not when it concerns those mists. Isla must put an end to them, for all our sakes."

"You could still come with us, you know."

"I...ah..." He glanced at Blair, a flush spreading across his cheeks. "No, I don't think so, Galbraith. I spent so many years worrying about being trapped in my sister's shadow that I forgot I was free to forge my own way. I'd like to find out the kind of person I am standing on my own." His fingers tightened around the handle of his crutch. "I can do some good here. We both can."

Blair looked up, his eyes weary. "It's a mess. We lost more than half the fleet, and the only surviving sentinels are either in the brig or want nothing more to do with the Admiralty. Not that I can blame them after what my uncle"—he winced, a shadow following over his face—"what the Grand Admiral did to them. The way he twisted their oaths, corrupted their bonds to their own captains...I doubt they'll ever trust the Admiralty again."

"Who commands the fleet now?" Darce asked. "Is it you?"

Blair pursed his lips. "I was the one who sounded the retreat. I organised us taking refuge here, out of necessity more than anything else. The other captains...they seem to be listening to me. How long that will last when the storm clears, I don't know." He shook his head. "Before, they'd never have accepted me in command without a sentinel by my side. But now, maybe that will change. I saw how the Grand Admiral used those who served him, how he spat them out when he was through with them. Perhaps this is a chance to make something new out of what he poisoned.

To rebuild the Admiralty with loyalty, with trust, instead of chaining its crews together with blood."

A familiar voice rang out behind them. "That sounds like an Admiralty I could be at peace with."

Darce turned to find Isla walking towards them, a smile on her lips. Her pelt hung loose around her shoulders, dripping water over the jetty from where she'd emerged from the sea. As she approached, the late-afternoon sunlight broke through the clouds and caught the wet fur, bringing out subtle hues of blue and lavender amongst the grey.

His heart swelled with a bittersweet ache. She was a selkie. She was the sea. He couldn't have loved her and kept her from it. That had been Cunningham's mistake. It would never be his.

Isla slowed as she reached Lachlan. Darce saw the tentativeness in her steps, the lingering fear in her expression that if she pushed too hard, her brother might once again slip through her fingers.

Lachlan rolled his eyes and hopped forward on his crutch, pulling her into a one-armed embrace. "Don't worry, I've got rather used to saying goodbye to you. I've learned that sooner or later, you come back."

She choked out a laugh, her face half-buried in the collar of his jacket. "No holding it against me for the next seven years?"

"I'll do my best. You do know I enjoy a grudge."

She drew back, eyes wet and shining. "I'm sorry I couldn't keep my promise to go home together."

A sombre look fell over Lachlan's face. "Blackwood Estate was never your home. Our parents would have wanted you to find a place where you belonged. And I...I want that too." His expression darkened. "Besides, you heard what Quinn said. The conniving bastard bought the deeds to the estate and left orders for it to be torn down in the case of his death. There would be nothing for us to return to."

Blair cleared his throat, running a hand through his mess of curls. "Actually, the wording of his will was quite specific. Aye, he instructed the estate to be torn down. But he also insisted that an Admiralty outpost be built in its place. To do that, he had to bequeath it to my uncle first. Which means…"

"It's yours." Lachlan stared at him, then gave a loud guffaw. "Shite, does that make you my bloody *steward?* Do I have to call you—"

"That won't be necessary," Blair said with a groan. "Please. I've already begun the arrangements to transfer the deed to the rightful Blackwood heir." His eyes flicked to Isla, asking an unspoken question.

She shook her head. "I'm not the rightful heir. I never was. My wee brother is right; those walls were never home for me. But…" She swallowed, turning to Lachlan. "I would like to come back, when this is all over. Say goodbye to our parents properly. Spend some time remembering them, remembering us."

"A round or two in the training yards," Lachlan said, glancing at Darce. "Galbraith grousing at our footwork just like the old days."

Darce snorted.

"I'd like that," Isla said, a pained smile stretching across her lips. "I'd like that a lot."

She turned towards the end of the pier. Two ships were moored there, rocking gently. One stood tall and proud, boasting a ruby hull and sails of scarlet. The other's mast was bone-pale and bare, glistening with a ghostly sheen in the faint sun.

As the murmur of their farewells faded in his ear, Darce glanced back at the jetty. Almost eight years ago, he'd been at Caolaig on the day Isla had left the confines of Blackwood Estate and sailed away from her family. He remembered his hand around Lachlan's shoulder, the dark cloud that had settled across the fifteen-year-old lad's face, the weight of grief and confusion heavy on his brow.

Lachlan looked nothing like that now. Whatever they were leaving behind on this dock, it was not something so easily broken.

Darce gave him one last wave, his heart strangely free for how heavy it felt. Lachlan's mouth twisted into a wry smile, and he forked two fingers back at him.

Cheeky wee prick, Darce thought with a chuckle. *And the tides know I love you for it, little laird.*

Nishi met them at the foot of the gangway, her lip ring glinting in the sun as her mouth split into a wide grin. She clasped Isla's arm warmly, then gave Darce an affable punch on the shoulder, eyes gleaming with amusement.

"Nice of you to stop by," she said. "Was beginning to think you were going to piss off into the mists without saying goodbye."

"You'd only hunt us down," Darce said solemnly. "And I know your mastery at the helm too well to risk such a thing."

"Flattery, Sergeant? After all we've been through?" Something softened in Nishi's face. "Feels odd, doesn't it? To be parting ways just when we've finally fucking won? I know better than to question the will of the tides, but still..." A sombre look darkened her features, and she fixed her gaze on Isla. "Tell me again, Blackwood. Is he truly gone?"

She didn't need to say Cunningham's name. It hung between them like a curse, no quieter for it being unspoken.

Mara. Kerr. Rhona. Sébastien. Muir. So many lost because of one man's obsession, one man's appetite for blood against those who'd wronged him. There was no undoing all the pain he'd caused, the ripples and echoes of what he'd wrought. But there would be no more. That, at least, they could be sure of.

"He's gone," Isla said. "I watched the tides take him. There's no way back."

Nishi released a breath. "Then at least some good has come of all this loss. Kerr would—" She broke off, voice splintering. "I may not have joined him in the fathoms, but I like to think he would be proud. And when we meet again, our crew will be more than it was, thanks to him."

Darce glanced at the *Red Gale's* deck above them. Jacques was leaning over the gunwale, his grey-flecked hair flying in the wind. "Our Îleanach friend is going with you, then?"

A faint tinge coloured Nishi's cheeks, so subtle Darce wondered whether he'd imagined it. "He's not my sentinel," she said, an edge creeping into her voice. Then it softened. "But perhaps he doesn't need to be. If there's anything these past few months have taught me, it's that a bond need not be forged in blood for it to mean something."

Up on deck, Maggie Grier shuffled next to her son. She stared at the towering masts, her lips moving too quickly for Darce to discern what she was mumbling.

Nishi followed his gaze. "Ruairidh agreed to take us to the Karzish Peninsula. There is a place there where trees grow as tall as mountains, their trunks as green as emeralds. Rumour has it the timber can repel water like a shield. Many have tried to build ships from their wood, but nobody has ever succeeded. We're going to change that."

Darce watched as Maggie Grier barked at one of the *Red Gale's* deckhands. The Sea Kith startled, dropping the line he was holding to scurry across to the other side of the deck. The old woman cackled, then moved to the line herself, hauling it over her shoulder between the ragged stumps of her hands.

"Look out for the *Emerald Dew*, Blackwood." Nishi turned to Isla, a smile warming her sharp features. "We'll be looking out for you. The Sea Kith will never be far. You'll find us if you need us." She extended a hand, the sun dancing off her brown skin.

Isla took it, squeezing it tight. "I'm glad the tides brought us together, Captain. These waters wouldn't be the same without you."

Nishi tipped her tricorne hat and trudged up the length of the gangway, whistling a tune as she left. It rang merrily in the hollow of Darce's ear, and somehow he knew it would keep him company on the waves for years to come.

When it was just the two of them once more, alone on the end of the pier, Isla turned to him, her eyes searching his. "You don't need to do this," she said, her voice so delicate he feared it might shatter. "When Mara told me what I must do, I knew what it might cost me. I'd never ask you to—"

He pressed his lips to hers, smothering the rest of her words before she could say anything more. The taste of her was salt and wind and unfettered freedom, and he drank it in like he'd never needed anything else. Every brush of her lips against his, the insistent hunger of her mouth, was enough for him to know he'd never leave her side, no matter what storm might blacken the horizon. He was hers. He was utterly, irrevocably hers.

When they parted, he held her close, sharing the same brackish air with each breath. "I told you once there is no stretch of water vast enough to keep me from you. Wherever you need to go, I'll go with you. Until the ends of the sea itself, if that's what it takes."

The soulship rocked in front of them, its white hull glistening in the waning light. Across the bay, the grey waves danced with colour from the sunset, shimmering in fractals of lilac and orange. For once, the clouds had scattered, leaving the horizon clear. All Darce could see was the open water. All he could feel behind his ribs was a strange new hope.

"It's ours," Isla whispered softly, her palm slipping into his. "All of it."
He felt the pulse of her blood against his, the oath that bound them. There was nothing more he needed.

CHAPTER THIRTY-NINE

ISLA

Loch Mòr's crystalline water glittered under the sun as Isla traversed the floating bridges linking one crannog to the next. Spring had brought a sense of beauty to Caim she'd never seen before. Sea campion and primroses bloomed along the cliffs, peppering the lush swathes of green with purple and white. The gannets and puffins had returned to nest, congregating in such numbers she could barely see the rock under their shuffling wings. There was life here, life that would remain untouched now that the Admiralty had been driven away.

But that didn't mean she'd forgotten what it had cost her, what it had cost them all.

She focused on the wooden slats beneath her bare feet, basking in the cool loch water as it seeped through the gaps. The towering ridge overlooking the loch cast a shadow over her eyes. It was the place she'd last seen Eimhir. The place she took her pelt back and left her cousin for the tides to claim.

Guilt welled in her throat, and she tried to swallow it before she choked. There was nothing else she could have done. Eimhir had left her no choice. But knowing that didn't make it any easier. It was a scar she'd carry until she met the fathoms herself.

The chieftains' enclave was quieter than she remembered it, four of its six chairs bare and empty. Angus and Duncan sat side by side, the burr of their voices fading as she walked into the centre of the room. The weight of their gazes rested heavy on her shoulders. She'd shown them what it was to return a gun-anam to the tides, to draw a sliver of sickness out of the haar's corruption. They knew what it was she carried—the hope, and the burden.

She took a breath. "Any sign of—"

"No." Angus's reply was blunt, but there was no cruelty in his voice. Just the cold truth of what she already knew, but didn't want to accept. "I've searched, Isla. The scouts have been pulling bodies from the seabed for weeks. But you know as well as I do how deep the waters run around Eileanan Selch. There are trenches that sink further than any selkie can dive. You have to accept that your uncle's body may be lost to the depths."

She pressed her lips together. Part of her had been grieving Muir ever since he'd toppled over the *Vanguard's* gunwale. She knew in her heart the only place he could have gone was the fathoms. But that hadn't stopped her wondering if he might have somehow survived the blood oath binding his life to Cunningham's. It was a desperate hope, but the only one she had.

Angus was right. She had to let it go.

She lifted her chin, bracing as she met Duncan's gaze. "What happens next? Will you uphold the truce Blair offered?"

He nodded, dark and solemn. "For now, aye."

"Only for now?"

Duncan curled his lip. "You may believe that we are at peace, but history has taught me such things cannot last. The currency the Admiralty trades with has always been bought with blood."

"And it has left scars on us all," Isla said. "Scars that will take generations to fade. The only hope for our people—for all of us—is to give them the chance to heal."

"Easy words when you're not the one bleeding." Angus countered. "Tell that to Moira, whose wife never returned to Eileanan Selch. Tell it to Fergal's twins, the wee lassies who will grow up without their father. This peace you talk of is too fragile to build a future on. Someday, one of us will find reason to raise our blades again, to draw blood again."

"Perhaps," Isla said evenly.

"That doesn't bother you? The thought of this being for nothing? The thought of what you took from Eimhir being for nothing?"

The words struck deep, but Isla didn't allow herself to flinch. "Maybe you're looking at it the wrong way. If we have managed to carve out some semblance of peace between human and selkie despite all the violence we've suffered, there is hope for those who come after us. We can show them another way. A better way."

Duncan's mouth tightened, though whether it was an attempt to force a smile or hold one back, Isla couldn't be sure. "There is more of Mara in you than you'll ever know," he said. "I used to fear what that might mean for our people. Now..." He looked away, eyes distant with a memory not meant for her. "She would be proud of you, aislingeach."

A hard lump caught in Isla's throat. She raised her hand to touch the bones Mara had given her, forgetting they no longer hung around her ribs. Instead, her fingers found only the fur of her pelt. "Thank you," she said. "For trusting me with this. For trusting me with our people."

She walked towards the enclave's oak doors, but before she pushed through, something stopped her. A sour taste spread on her tongue, a question she didn't want answered, but one she couldn't help but ask.

"Eimhir." Her name left her lips like a wound, tearing a fresh hole in her heart. "Have you seen her? Is she..."

The silence told her all she needed to know.

Duncan let out a heavy sigh. "Nobody has seen her since the night you returned. Without a pelt, there is only one place she could have gone."

Isla's knuckles tightened around the handle of the door. She'd known it the moment Eimhir had told her she'd surrendered her own pelt to force Isla's hand. But knowing didn't ease the guilt pulling at her heart, squeezing so hard she thought she'd burst with the grief of it all.

There were some losses where the pain would never subside. Some losses a person could do nothing about but learn how to live with them.

She didn't return to the sea through the underwater tunnel. Instead, she trudged up the cliffside path through overgrown bracken and blooming gorse until she came out on one of the ridges. Below, the waves dashed against the rock, relentless in their fury. The churn of salt and spray beckoned her home.

Perhaps Eimhir had stood here at the end. Isla only hoped she'd found some peace in it.

"Forgive me, caraid," she whispered. "For all of it."

She filled her lungs with the salty air. Then she leapt, and let the waves swallow her home.

By the time she climbed back aboard the soulship, the sun was slipping below the horizon. It was a clear night, and the sky was streaked with violet and orange. Isla allowed herself a moment to take in the view, wondering that she could still find some kind of beauty in a world that had taken so much from her.

But not everything, she told herself.

Darce crossed the deck to join her, taking his place at her side. He didn't say anything; she didn't need him to. All she needed was this peace, the warmth of his hand against hers, the pulsing of blood through their skin.

"Where is she?" Darce asked.

Isla nodded to the prow. A figurehead jutted from the bow, carved from glistening bone. A woman standing tall, fur spilling over her shoulders, a familiar seal-skull mask over her face.

Mara's bones were where they belonged. She'd been returned to her people, part of the fabric of the soulship that had carried their selkie ancestors across the waves.

"Can you feel her?" Isla asked.

Darce closed his eyes, and the wind stirred around them both, lifting glittering trails of water from the waves. The droplets twisted into spirals above the deck, rippling around the masts until they became sails of silvery spray.

"Aye," he said softly. "I can feel them all."

A chill scuttled over Isla's arms as the haar's breath crawled across the waves towards them. The mists were still thick with rot and corruption, but that would soon change. *She* would change it, like Mara had asked her to.

Soon, the haar would close around them, taking them to the black waters and oily red sky of the soulless realm. But for now, the horizon was clear, cast in the glow of the sun's dying light. Featherblade hovered above the mast, releasing a shrill cry.

In the distance, something answered—a keening lament, a roar from the depths themselves. It was a sound Isla recognised, coiled and serpentine, reverberating with the currents.

She glanced at Darce, but he showed no sign of having heard it. The scar around his missing ear was still stark and jagged, though the wound had healed.

A bittersweet swell rose in her chest. Perhaps some things were only meant for her.

They stood in silence, waiting for the haar to take them where they needed to go. Darce turned to her, a question in his gaze.

"It doesn't have a name," he said. "All these months these bones have carried us, and we still don't have something to call them by."

Isla trailed her eyes over the soulship. Its bones gleamed a pale, ghostly white in the fading light, carrying the selkies who had brought her here.

If she slipped her consciousness into her pelt, she could almost see their memories come to life across the deck. But it wasn't just them—it was Nishi standing tall at the helm, Lachlan leaning against the gunwale, Muir staring out over the prow.

It was Darce, here in front of her, his brown eyes searching hers for the answer she finally knew.

"*Dachaigh*," she said. "Its name is *Dachaigh*."

"What does it mean?"

A fierce gust of wind whipped around Isla's face, and she breathed in deeply, tasting salt at the back of her throat.

"Home," she said, and smiled.

EPILOGUE

There is no making sense of the time that passes. Time doesn't mean anything to a shadow like her. She cannot measure the days or the months or the years. All she knows is the pain she carries, the hollowed-out abyss that is her existence. She is grief. She is loss.

She is gun-anam.

There is little left of who she was before. That part of her has been stripped away. She has no memories, only a rattling echo of the agony she has suffered.

A consuming hunger stirs in her, roiling the currents that make up her shapeless form. There was a time these waters churned with violence, saturating seafoam with blood, but such feasts are scarce to be found now. She trawls the waves in search of pain, desperate to sate herself once more. When she finds it, she'll take her fill, gorging herself on spilled blood.

It is the only time she comes close to feeling alive again.

But there is no violence to be found. Instead, something else brushes the ghost of what was once her mind. A ship carves through the waves, carrying a piece of something lost. It calls to her, reaching a part of her she thought no longer existed.

She turns her wisping tendrils to the surface, drifting towards the ship. Already, she senses what is contained behind the bone hull.

Auld blood.

It stokes something in her deeper than rage. She floods towards the ship with all the fury of the tides, the haar clinging to her wake.

When she emerges, two humans stare up at her, one dark-skinned, the other pale. She floats before them in silence, the wind passing through her like she doesn't exist. But she *does* exist. She is the tides' wrath, the hunger and the horror of all that was done to her. And she'll make these salt-blooded creatures feel that same terror.

But before she can take them, before she can fill them with the sea and drown them in her vengeance, something else stirs, and a voice calls to her over the wind.

"Well, it's about time you found us."

Slowly, she turns towards the voice. A selkie stands by the prow, her pelt slick and damp around her shoulders. The grey fur feels…familiar, somehow. It washes over the selkie's skin like a current, dappled patches of blue-black shifting like inkblots.

The selkie is staring at her, the ghost of a smile on her lips. Her hair is swept up in a loose braid, a few strands of sable still visible amongst the grey. Creases dance around the corners of her sea-green eyes, and in those eyes is a glimmer of recognition.

"Eimhir," the selkie says.

The name touches her in a place she'd thought lost, a place buried so deep even the fathoms themselves could not take it from her. There is such *knowing* in that name, such belonging. It breaks her apart, scattering the hurt holding her together.

But Eimhir does not disappear. She is memory made whole.

Isla, she wants to say. *Caraid*.

There is nowhere for her voice to go. Everything she is, all that grief and pain, seeps into the fur around Isla's shoulders. The rest of her is left behind in a shower of salt and shimmering spray, and she falls back to the waves. She falls *home*.

It isn't like before. There is nothing separating her from the currents now. She is the seafoam on the glittering surface. She is the darkness in the depths, the ripples stirring the ocean floor. She is one with the tides, just as she was meant to be.

Already, the part of her that was once Eimhir is fading. But there is no sorrow for the selkie she was, not this time. She is the sea. She will hold her people in her swells, she will carry ships from shore to shore, she will sigh and yawn and roar with a voice that stretches further than the horizon.

But before she slips away, Eimhir watches. She listens.

Isla collapses onto the deck, her breathing thin and ragged. Her forehead is pearled with sweat, the salty drops trickling down her temples.

"It's time," she says heavily. "Thirty years and more have I searched for her. Longer than I thought my soul could bear. Now she is with the tides, I need carry this weight no longer. It is yours, Cam, if you are willing to accept it."

She turns to the human, and Eimhir realises they aren't human at all. Auld blood flows through their veins, yearning for something they never had.

Cam takes off their weather-worn hat and meets Isla's gaze, solemn and unblinking. "I am."

"You must be certain." Isla coughs as she slowly struggles to her feet, seawater spluttering from her throat. "There is no going back once you take the soulskin. If you ever lose it..."

"I know. I am ready."

"Then I'll tell you what Mara once told me." Isla smiles faintly. "You will bear it, for as long as you are able. And when the time comes that you cannot carry it anymore, someone will take that burden from you. Our people's pain is shared. It is remembered."

Cam hesitates, a crease appearing in the middle of their brow. "Are *you* certain? Without this pelt, without your soul, will you not become one of the wraiths yourself?"

Isla turns to the other human, the auld blood with pale skin and a scar around the place that should have held an ear.

Of course, Eimhir recognises him now. Her sergeant, her sentinel. The wild wind that would follow her anywhere.

"I have been fortunate enough to share both my heart and my soul for all these years," Isla says softly, her hand finding his. "When the tides take us, it will be together. But it will not be today."

When she slides her pelt from her skin, he wraps her in his cloak, pressing his mouth to hers in a kiss he has known a thousand times, and will know a thousand times more. Isla looks up at him, her sea-green eyes shining and bright, and when her pelt falls to the deck, there is nothing missing in the depths of her gaze. This time, it is a choice. *Her* choice.

Isla has all she needs. Eimhir is certain of it.

Cam takes the pelt and slips it around their lean, wiry shoulders as Eimhir waits patiently below. There is a moment of silence, then a sharp intake of breath, and Cam plunges through the surface, taking to their soulshape for the first time.

For a fleeting second, it feels like Cam is looking right at her. Their selkie eyes hold some kind of recognition, some deep knowing. But Eimhir *is* the sea now, and all its swells and currents. She cradles Cam like they are her own, basking in their joy, their belonging, their sense of the world finally being right.

When Cam shoots off through the water, Eimhir doesn't follow. She doesn't need to.

She is never far from her people, here in the sea of souls they share.

AFTERWORD

First of all, thank you for reading! This is the second time I've said goodbye to a trilogy, and I really hope you've enjoyed reading these books as much as I've enjoyed writing them. Before you go, I would greatly appreciate it if you could help other people discover this series by leaving a review or rating on Amazon or Goodreads.

Reviews, particularly on Amazon, are so important for independent authors. Taking just a few minutes out of your day will help more books like this get written, so any kind of feedback, whether it's a written review or a quick star rating, is much appreciated!

Want to see what's in store next? Sign up for my author newsletter at **ncscrimgeour.com** for exclusive updates, sneak peeks and release news!

You can keep up to date with future releases by following me on Facebook, X, Instagram and TikTok at @scrimscribes.

Also by N. C. Scrimgeour

A dying planet. A desperate mission. A crew facing impossible odds. Humanity's last hope lies with them...

Time is running out for the people of New Pallas. Nobody knows that better than Alvera Renata, a tenacious captain determined to scout past the stars with nothing but a handpicked crew and a promise: to find a new home for humanity.

But when a perilous journey across dark space leads to first contact with a galactic civilisation on the brink of war, Alvera soon realises keeping her word might not be as easy as she thought.

Her only hope lies with the secrets of the ancient alien waystations scattered across the galaxy. The mysterious technology could be the key to humanity's survival...or bring unwanted attention from the long forgotten beings who built them...

<u>The Waystations Trilogy</u>
Those Left Behind
Those Once Forgotten
Those Who Resist

www.ingramcontent.com/pod-product-compliance
Lightning Source LLC
Chambersburg PA
CBHW051001210726
48287CB00004B/1331